W9-DGU-992

Kati Woronka

Dreams
in the
Medina

copyright 2013 Kati Woronka

cover image by artist Suhair Sibai

For my dear friends from the Medina, who are too numerous, and indeed too precious, to name here. Each and every one of you made a lasting mark on my life and I love you dearly. I learned a lifetime of lessons about friendship, hospitality, and dreams from you. I miss you so very much and I continue to pray for your safety, for your families and for your spirits during these days of doubt and fear.

AHLAM: DREAMS

The first thing she noticed was the air. The temperature could not have been more perfect. At first, the smell was slightly polluted by an exhaust pipe a little past the door, but then the breeze changed directions and the odor did too. Then, all Leila could smell was the crisp night.

The second thing she noticed was the view, and this was what drew her through the rickety steel doorway onto the rooftop. Beyond the other Soviet-style student residential blocks, a mountain lined with lights rose up over the city. Mount Qasioun. Leila knew well the mountain where it was said that Cain, the second man to ever live, was buried, but she had never seen it so clearly. It loomed at her, dominated her view, and captured her heart. She slipped her scarf onto her head and slowly wandered across the roof to get as close to the mountain as she could, gazing at the row of lights near its peak.

Leila stared at those lights until the other city lights began to draw her attention. The neighborhoods between her and the mountain spread out in front of her like a blanket tossed between two people. To her immediate left and right and all around were the other buildings of the Medina Jamaye'a, the University City, where she had lived for almost two years. Almost two years and she had never known about the roof.

After a few minutes, Leila sensed a presence to her right. She looked over and saw her friend Ghalia standing beside her. "See? The roof is the Medina's best-kept secret," Ghalia said with a grin.

Leila turned and followed her friend to a big concrete block on which Ghalia's sister Mary was already seated. It was only then that she realized there was a fourth person on the roof. Standing behind Mary, fiddling with the batteries in a cassette player, was a girl Leila had never seen before.

Seeing the surprise on Leila's face, Mary said, "Leila, this is our cousin Roxy, visiting for the night."

Leila reached out to shake Roxy's hand and Roxy reciprocated with a very strong, very energetic, handshake.

For the next few minutes, Leila could not keep her eyes off of Roxy as she fussed with the music. Her friends' cousin seemed very grown up, but then again she still had a look of youth. She couldn't be more than 22, Leila thought. She was wearing pajamas, but not of the typical cotton found in the Medina. Roxy's were quite revealing and made out of expensive-looking shiny fabric. Her hair was done in a very stylish do and her makeup had been applied with absolute precision and sizzling flair.

Ever since Leila had befriended Mary and Ghalia, the sisters had been a curiosity to her. Their village was only half an hour away from her own, but they were Druze and she was Sunni Muslim. They spoke Arabic like her, but theirs was a funny-sounding accent, more carefully pronounced and with lots of guttural sounds. Mary and Ghalia walked the streets in tight-fitting trousers with their heads uncovered; Leila had never met women who went out bare-headed before she came to Damascus. She was fascinated at the care with which these girls chose their clothing and applied their makeup each evening, even if only to go to the shop downstairs. Leila would have thought such behavior shameful and promiscuous, but the Druze girls didn't act all that shamefully. Mary and Ghalia did everything together and never went out alone. Plus, their brothers who lived nearby were always stopping by to check up on them, or accompanying them to the *souq* for shopping. Leila sometimes spoke to the boys in her class, and no one ever seemed to think there was anything wrong with that, but the

4

Druze girls only spoke to each other in their corner of the classroom. As far as she could tell, the Druze girls may look like sluts, but they certainly were better behaved than even she herself was.

Mary beckoned Leila to join her on the concrete block. The block stood at chest level and it took a few hops before Leila managed to get herself up. Once on the block, though, her view of the mountain was all the better for having gained a meter's height. Leila settled next to Mary on the fuzzy blanket that the girls had laid out over the rough cement. Mary was holding a handful of sunflower seeds and passed the bag of seeds to Leila, who politely took a small fistful and started cracking them with her mouth.

The batteries finally sprung to life and the music started. Roxy had opted for some very ethereal sounding vocal melody that sounded like it might be the soundtrack to a horror film, thoroughly enhancing the ambiance with its haunting laments. She and Ghalia jumped up and joined the other two on the block.

There was barely enough space for the four girls to sit, but they still found room in the middle to put the bag of sunflower seeds, a pot of hot water, and the matté cup. Matté was a South American tea that all Druze people seemed to drink, but that Leila had never heard of before meeting Druze girls here in Damascus. After a few visits with Mary and Ghalia over the course of the past two years, it still wasn't Leila's favorite, but with sugar it wasn't too bad. So when Mary asked her how she drank her matté, instead of refusing, she replied, "Sweet and with lemon."

The girls teased her a bit about drinking matté with so much sugar she couldn't taste the tea anymore, and she quietly sipped through the metal straw. She knew that they only said it because they felt comfortable around her, but it reminded her of just how different she was from these girls:

5

only a few villages over from where she'd grown up, but a world away. Perhaps her shyness was also because Roxy had joined the teasing with such familiarity.

So Leila worked up the courage to ask Ghalia about Roxy's story. "Is your cousin a student, too?"

But Roxy immediately answered for herself. "I'm studying Arabic literature."

"Really? What year? My cousin just graduated Arabic literature!"

"Second."

"Just like us. So you live here in the Medina?"

"Well, actually," replied Roxy, "it's my third time doing the second year."

Leila recalled being told that if you failed a year twice in a row, you lost your place in the Medina. Of course, most people stayed living here anyway. With seven to twelve girls assigned to each room, no one really noticed when a cousin or friend also moved in. So perhaps Roxy lived with her cousins whenever she was in town – during exams period or to meet with a department administrator, perhaps. But how does one fail a year three times in a row?

But then Roxy added, "And I'm married."

Leila tried, rather pointlessly, to hide her shock. Of course, there were girls as old as forty still living in the Medina, from all different types of backgrounds and even from other countries. But she hadn't ever imagined she would meet a married woman here. Once you were married, you looked out for your husband, cooked for him, kept the house clean and probably had children quickly. You didn't leave him for a night in the student dorms. Leila wanted to ask this woman how it was that her husband let her come stay in the Medina, but eased her way in with pleasantries, asking Roxy how long she'd been married.

Roxy didn't seemed at all perturbed by the curiosity of a

Sunni girl from another village, because she happily kept talking about her unusual arrangement. She told Leila that as far as her parents knew, she was only a student and lived here at the Medina with her cousins. Her marriage of two years was a secret from the entire family, except for these two cousins. And, she explained, her husband was very rich. He owned a house in a nice suburb of Damascus. But he loved her very much, so he wanted her to have fun and was happy to drive her in and out of Damascus whenever she wanted.

"He sounds like a wonderful husband. Why hide it from your family?" Leila asked.

The three cousins exchanged a flurry of glances before Ghalia explained, as if revealing the most shameful tragedy ever, "He is not Druze: he's Sunni."

Buying time by gnawing slowly at a sunflower seed, Leila quickly put the pieces together to form a plausible understanding of who this brazen-looking girl in front of her was. If Roxy's husband was Sunni and rich, maybe he had another wife. Roxy was young and beautiful, and her husband was probably older. Yes, he probably had a family with children and heirs and a good reputation. Roxy must be his "fun" wife. If he was a good Muslim man, though, he would still spend every second night with his first wife and children, giving Roxy the freedom to be a young student during the other half of her time.

Leila had so many questions that she was embarrassed to ask. What would Roxy do when her parents decided it was time for her to marry? Not only was she already married, she was no longer a virgin. Leila didn't know much about the Druze religion, but if her two friends were so well-behaved and avoided all unrelated men so carefully, especially non-Druze men, these things must matter. If Leila did something like that, for all she knew, her older brother or her father might even kill her.

So instead, Leila asked Roxy how she handled times like holidays, when her family would expect her to be back home.

Leila's heart fluttered when Roxy leaned forward, latched her eyes to Leila's, and grinned conspiratorially. "Well, I usually spend half the nights alone, anyway." So she is a second wife, Leila thought as Roxy continued, "And my husband is very supportive. He understands that I don't want to tell my family so he lets me go home for holidays. Eventually, of course, I will tell them. Just not yet. For now, it's fun. I love being married, but I also like being back with the girls."

"Enough talking, Roxy, it's time to dance!" interjected Ghalia. She stopped the otherworldly recording and switched to radio, slowly working the dial until she found some Arabic pop. Then she cranked the volume to its maximum, which was no impressive loudness but was enough for the girls to catch a beat.

Roxy jumped down from the block and Mary tossed her a scarf. Leila had no idea where the scarf came from, but this evening's entire agenda felt like a dream that someone had scripted, so she shrugged to herself and allowed her eyes to gravitate toward Roxy who was tying the scarf low, very low, around her hips.

Roxy started swaying and swirling. Her hips jiggled and throbbed as her hands twisted and tapped. She latched her eyes onto Leila's and smiled. Later, Leila would remember this moment and think that it was likely an older married man might do just about anything to have such energy and charm for himself. She herself would be happy if that moment never ended.

But it did end and all too quickly. In a lull between songs, Roxy turned the music off and said she was heading to bed. She started packing up the cassette player and her cousins decided they, too, were ready to turn in. They gathered up the matté cups and the teapot and the leftover sunflower seeds and the blanket and headed for the door.

"Are you coming?" asked Ghalia, when she realized that Leila was now standing listlessly next to the concrete block, having lost her blanket seat.

"I think I might stay up here for a while," replied Leila. "I can't believe I never knew about the roof before. I may never leave this spot again."

"Suit yourself!" Ghalia answered. "Have a great night."

"Good night!" called out Mary as she headed down the stairs.

But Roxy came over and gave Leila a big hug before rushing down.

Left to her thoughts, Leila allowed herself to consider this woman she had just met. The only things Leila had in common with Roxy and her cousins was that they were village girls and that they were poor, but had excelled in their baccalaureate exams and so been offered a coveted position at the big government-funded university in the city. While the chance to study for a university degree was an honor, Leila considered the highlight of student status to be the opportunity to live in Building 14, which housed about 1000 poor village girls like her and Roxy and Mary and Ghalia, from all corners of Syria. In Building 14, she could meet all sorts of different people. And now, Leila could not get the image of Roxy's long hair or hips, rippling to the rhythm of Egyptian pop music, out of her head.

The sound of footsteps on the stairs jerked Leila out of her reverie. She turned to see a girl pop out of the dark stairwell and walk straight to the opposite end of the roof, immediately starting to pace back and forth as she read and repeated paragraphs from a textbook. What a contrast, she thought, between this girl who was so single-mindedly focused on muttering her lectures to herself, and the Druze girls, who acted so properly whenever family was around but also did some crazy things and managed to fail their courses so casually. Leila dared to wonder if any of them would ever graduate from university: they seemed to have way too much fun cooking and dancing and keeping secrets to study. Leila suspected that the matté was already flowing again and that sleep would evade her Druze friends for some time to come. And she was pretty sure the girls were not talking about English or Arabic literature.

At this thought, Leila was struck with a pang of guilt. She'd spent the entire evening with friends, and now here she was doing nothing on the roof. She was the first woman in her family to go to university. Indeed, only a handful of boys or girls from their entire village had ever pursued higher education. So if she didn't do well, her entire family would think it was a waste of their time and money to let her go live in the big city for four years. She knew that men had approached her parents about marrying her, but her mother had kindly put them off, saying that Leila was to finish university first. If she failed a year, though, or gave her family any reason for concern at all, her mother would be thrilled to start entertaining those offers.

They didn't know this, but Leila had other plans. She loved living in the city and wanted to stay. As an English graduate, she could get a job teaching or translating. If she had to marry when she graduated, she at least asked God for a husband who would love the city and love her.

Leila looked up at the row of lights on Mount Qasioun and imagined the women who were sitting in restaurants on the mountaintop at that very moment, going on midnight. They were the city women. Many of them were still very religious, but they were independent and strong. In Leila's village, women rarely went out at night, and even during the day they only went out to do the shopping or to visit other women in their homes. Leila wanted to be a respectable woman, but she knew that Islam didn't mandate that a respectable woman stay home all the time. She wanted to live her own life, and she wanted to be a graduate in English literature. With that resolve, she wandered back down to her room to grab the novel she was meant to be reading. Then she'd go to the study room on the ground floor. If she studied for two hours before going to sleep, she wouldn't be too tired for class in the morning.

TAKSHEEF: DISCOVERY

Chapter One

A tabouli party was the perfect way to celebrate the end of classes for the year. Leila was without roommates this week – she figured they'd come back when exams started. So last night she had knocked on her best friend Huda's door and suggested that they make a big bowl of tabouli together. Huda, Leila's neighbor from two doors down, was a law student and sometimes it seemed like she was addicted to her books, so Leila often took it upon herself to help Huda put together a social agenda. Fortunately, this time it was not difficult to convince Huda that the last day of classes merited a celebration.

Huda had classes all morning, so when Leila's one lecture was over, she walked straight from her faculty building to the vegetable shop behind the Medina and bought three big bags of parsley, two cucumbers, three tomatoes, an onion, some lemons, loads of lettuce, and a bunch of mint. On her way back to the room, she ran into Mary and Ghalia and invited them to join them for tabouli that afternoon. They not only accepted but also informed Leila that Roxy would be around that evening. Leila was ecstatic.

Then, when Leila got back to her floor, she saw the door across from hers ajar. Leila had met Maha, a first-year psychology student, a few times. A friendly Christian girl, Maha spent most of her time at her aunt's house in a rich neighborhood across town, but Leila had visited with her a few times and enjoyed getting to know someone from a different religion. Leila asked questions about Christians, which Maha gladly answered, and told Maha about the things she loved most about Islam, for which Maha expressed polite appreciation. So Leila knocked on the open door then peeked in. Maha was there along with two other girls, and Leila invited them all to tabouli. She wondered if Huda was inviting anyone – this had a potential to be a big shindig! And right in the middle of exam season.

When she entered her own room, the appointed party venue, Leila's heart sank. Fatima, her roommate, was there, unpacking a bag.

"*Ahlan wa Sahlan*," Leila uttered. "Welcome."

Fatima replied with the Islamic response, "*Aleiki Alsalaam.*"

Leila and Fatima had only really met a few times before, at the beginning of each term, and during last term's exams. Fatima was an Islamic law student, very studious, and very religious. Not likely to condone a tabouli party in her room.

"How are the studies going?" Leila asked.

"They're okay. I have five exams in five days coming up."

"*Ya Allah*! So that's why you came to stay here now?"

"Yes, just to get the exams done."

"How's your family?"

"They're well. They send their greetings. And more food than I can eat: olives, pickled eggplant, canned yogurt. Feel free to eat some."

"Oh, thank you. That's too kind. I just went to the store to get tabouli ingredients. Will you share tabouli with us this afternoon?" *Please don't accept... say no!*

"I have to go to the Faculty this afternoon, and I'll probably be there studying for a while. Thank you."

"Oh, that's alright. My friend Huda is coming over in a little while to help me make it. I hope that won't be a problem?"

"*Ahlan wa Sahlan.*"

Leila was very relieved that Fatima was being friendly. Maybe she wasn't as strict as Leila had remembered from their previous encounters. So Leila dumped all the parsley she'd purchased into her biggest basin and left Fatima unpacking to go wash the leaves in the kitchen, a dank room with an industrial-sized aluminum sink, whose claim to the title of "kitchen" was dubious at best.

While Leila was busy at the sink, Huda came to the door.

"*Ahlain!*" Leila greeted Huda.

"*Ahlan fiki,*" Huda replied.

"Congratulations, you're done!"

Huda sighed. "Now the hard part begins."

"Tomorrow, though. Are you ready for some fun? I've invited some of my neighbors and some other friends of mine – remember those girls I told you about who have the cousin who's married but stays here every other night?"

Huda smiled a sneaky smile. "Oh, the girl who lives a dual life? And who dances really well? And who you said is very exciting?"

Leila was embarrassed as she realized just how much she was looking forward to seeing Roxy. "Well, she does dance well, yes. They're all from the Druze mountain."

"I look forward to meeting her. I haven't really seen anyone today; I came straight here from my lecture. So I didn't invite anyone yet. I'm glad you've got a party going."

Leila finished washing the parsley and the two girls returned to her room. She introduced Huda to Fatima, and thought she caught a hint of scorn when Fatima shook Huda's hand. A girl studying Islamic Law was not likely to approve of someone like Huda, who was an Alawite from the mountains in the northeast of Syria. Huda had no religious education whatsoever and wore skin-tight clothing, even if she always looked tidy and demure dressed in black or gray. Leila worried for a moment that Fatima would tell people in her village about Leila's friend, and that it would get back to her own family, so she hurriedly started setting up the table and showing Huda what she'd bought for the party. Fatima went back to her own chores.

Soon Leila and Huda sat on Leila's bed with the table in front of them piled high with parsley. Huda declared that chopping was the perfect job to distract her mind from the past few sleepless nights of books and lecture notes, so Leila agreed to sort the parsley, picking out the bad spots and forming neat little bunches of parsley leaves, then passing them to Huda one at a time. The only knife they had was a serrated butter knife, but both Leila and Huda had helped their mothers prepare tabouli at home enough times that they were not too challenged. Huda chopped the parsley into little tiny flakes and dumped it into a big bowl. As they worked, the girls chatted.

Huda asked Leila what she had been reading lately.

"Well, right now I'm focusing on studying grammar, which is so so boring!"

"I imagine. Is it hard?"

"Hard? Oh not at all! English grammar is simple. Which almost makes it worse, because at least Arabic grammar is challenging to think through. English grammar really shouldn't even be a university subject, it's so simple. I mean, I think everything we're learning this semester is the same as what we learned last year."

"So the exam should be easy, right?" asked Huda.

"No, because the lecturer is different, so all the questions will be completely different."

"Oh, goodness." Huda sighed in sympathy. "So you haven't been reading any more of that novel *Women in Love*?"

Leila smiled. She was debating whether she should tell Huda about her own love. She hadn't told anyone at all yet – and, to be honest, there was not anything to tell, just a budding hope in Leila's heart that the man from her French class who had smiled at her, might smile at her again someday. Fatima had conveniently just left the room, but still... "I stopped reading it. I got the main points. Anyway, it was just making me think about what I shouldn't think about."

"What do you mean?"

"Oh, it's such an entrancing book. Really strange, I think, but that's what English love is like, I guess."

"You mean like on Hollywood films, like *Titanic*?"

"Well, Titanic is a beautiful story. *Women in Love* is much deeper. Its characters are struggling between their love for each other and for other people. And it even makes me wonder if the two male characters don't even..."

"Don't even what?"

"Well... ummm. Don't tell anyone I told you this, right?"

"Of course not."

"I think they love each other. Maybe even more than they do their wives."

"You don't think that's possible?" challenged Huda. "Of course it happens."

"Oh! That's so awful! It's shameful and forbidden!"

"That may be, but don't you think shameful and forbidden things happen? We're learning about human rights in one of my courses. That's actually my first exam on Tuesday."

"What do human rights have to do with it?"

Huda took on an authoritative tone. "Well, our lecturer explained to us that there are things that are forbidden in Islam but that are allowed in human rights. So like a Christian or a non-religious Muslim might do them. Something like drink alcohol."

"Really?"

"Don't you think even religious Muslims drink alcohol, but in private?"

"Well, I did once accidentally find a bottle in my aunt's house that I didn't recognize. I wondered if that was alcohol but I was too embarrassed to ask."

"See, that's the difference between human rights and Islam, and our culture."

"I'm not sure I understand."

"So when you say it's shameful and forbidden for two men to love each other the way they should love a woman, who says that?"

"God of all the worlds!"

"But see, I didn't grow up with that education. In my family, I wasn't taught the Qur'an or the ways of Islam. So I may not be convinced that it is wrong --"

At this moment Fatima came back in. The two friends kept chopping in silence for a few minutes.

Leila turned to Fatima and asked her, "What time do you have to be at the Faculty?"

"I just have to pray, then eat something, then I'll go. Is that alright?"

"Of course! It's your room!" Leila realized that Fatima felt unwelcome. Well, but why shouldn't she? She was gone all year, and then she moved back in like the room was hers with no warning? Why should Leila all of a sudden change her life because Fatima had just come back?

Huda made a quick save by asking Fatima, "What do you study?"

"Islamic Law, second year."

"Do you like it?"

"It's God's law, what is there not to like?" Fatima said this not unkindly, but matter-of-factly.

"Well, good luck on your exams."

"Thank you," Fatima replied. "And you? What do you study?"

"Oh, I study law," Huda answered, and her eyes lit up.

"What year?"

"Second."

"I knew someone who studied law. She said the second year was the hardest."

Huda grunted. "Well, I hope it is, because this year is hard!"

"Well, good luck to you too."

As they were chatting, Fatima had been putting on her prayer clothes: a loose white skirt and a large white headcovering which came to her waist. She now laid out her rug and began to pray.

Huda turned back to Leila and spoke in a near-whisper. "Islamic law must be hard. I hear that they have to memorize the entire Qur'an and most of the *Hadith*, as well as learn Islamic history and the processes of jurisdiction."

Leila nodded. "They say it is one of the best Islamic law programs in the world."

"I also heard that it's very strict. Women must wear an *abaya* as well as a headscarf, and are separated from the men."

"Well, it's Islamic law, so they need to be sure and follow all the rules carefully. I don't think Fatima goes to lectures often, though. She seems to study very hard from home."

"I guess you need all the time you can get to memorize."

The chopping continued, and as Fatima finished up her prayers, the only sound in the room was the sound of the knife hitting the chopping board. Fatima finished, pulled off her prayer clothes and wrapped them in her rug, then laid the bundle at the foot of her bed. She quietly pulled out some of the bread, olives, eggplant and yogurt that she'd brought, and pulled a chair up to the table where Leila and Huda were working. Huda moved her chopping board over a few inches to clear a corner of space.

"Are you hungry?" Fatima asked.

"*Sahtain* – Bon apetit!" both girls said in unison.

"Thank you," Fatima replied. As she ripped a piece of bread and dipped it in the yogurt, she turned to Huda. "So where are you from?"

"I'm from Latakia."

"The city?"

"No, a village nearby."

"Oh, you must not get to go home very often."

"No. But my course is very hard, so it's better for me to stay here and study anyway."

Leila commented, "It seems like some people study better at home, but others study better here! Whenever I go home, I can't get anything done. I just visit relatives, help my mom, and play with my sisters."

"That's interesting," replied Fatima. "I don't think I could get anything done if I stayed here. I'd spend too much time taking care of myself: cleaning, cooking... At home, my mother does all that for me, and she forces me to study."

"You're very fortunate to have a mother who values your studies," offered Leila. "My mother would prefer I got married."

"Really?" asked Huda. "Your mother doesn't want you studying?"

"Well, as long as I do well, she doesn't mind. But she only studied to the sixth grade, and to her, a good woman is a good mother and wife. She thinks I'm just enjoying my fun years before I graduate and get married and have children."

"But you're not planning on doing that, are you?" asked Huda.

"No! You know I have dreams to work. I'll probably have to get married soon after graduating, but I really hope it's to someone who lets me have my career."

Fatima added, "It's the same for me. My mother makes me study, and she brags to all the other women in our neighborhood that her daughter is studying Islamic law. But I know she is also meeting with potential suitors for me. I want to teach Islam at a school when I'm done, but I think my mother is more interested in my studies because a lot of men want to marry a woman who knows her religion well."

Leila said, "Yes, that's the only reason I think my mother supports me at all – a lot of intelligent, wealthy men want educated women these days."

Huda asked, "So you're just studying to become better market value as wives? That's so different. I mean, my mother wants me to marry someone good, but it's really my choice. And actually, not too many girls from my village get married young. Most are getting married in their late twenties. If I didn't study now, I might just be sitting around the house, helping my mother and drinking *arguile*."

"So the other girls in your village don't work?" asked Fatima.

"Well, maybe they would, but there aren't really jobs for a young woman in the village. What will she do? It's shameful for her to move to the city alone. I can do it because I'm studying and I'm living at the Medina. Some girls have relatives they live with. Most girls just take it easy for a few years until they eventually get married."

"But you won't leave Sham, will you?" Leila clarified.

"I'm sure my family wants me to move home after I graduate – it's hard to be separated. But what will I do if I go home? If I get into graduate school, I can stay here. Or, if I find a good job as soon as I graduate – and somewhere acceptable to live."

Fatima then asked, "They won't expect you to get married?"

"Oh, they will start asking me. But it doesn't sound as strict as your families! If I get a job, that's just fine."

Leila wondered what her family would say if she got a job

as soon as she graduated. Their first question would be where she would live in Damascus once she had to leave the Medina. Their second question would be why she wasn't getting married. Such a plan might work for a year or two if she found a cousin or aunt to live with, but not for long.

Fatima then commented, "My family might let me work, but I think they prefer I get married. It's best for everyone if I quickly marry and have children. Anyway, I want to be a mother and have my own home. It would just be really nice to work also."

"Do you think you can be a mother and work at the same time?" Leila asked.

"If I'm a teacher, I think so, because I'll work for the government and they help with childcare. And then my work hours will be the same hours as my children's. Our generation is different from our parents' – I'll only have two or three children at the most. Not ten like my mother did."

"Well, I hope it works," replied Leila. "You have a very practical attitude. I really don't want to get married if there's not love, and what love will there be in a marriage my parents arrange?"

"Love grows. My mother and father love each other. Anyway, in Islam, marriage is a religious duty, and a good Muslim woman should be a good wife. When we do that, we are blessed with good works and also our husbands are responsible to take care of us. The way of Islam is really the best way," concluded Fatima.

"Yes, I have been taught that and I believe it is true. But can't I have a good Muslim marriage and also be in love with my husband? That is what I want," crooned Leila.

Huda laughed. "Leila, you are such a romantic. God will bring you exactly the right lot in life, just don't dream too much about it. You need to work for it."

Fatima agreed. "Yes, and you know God already has it all

worked out. Just work to be a good Muslim. And now, I must leave you. I'm sorry I will miss your tabouli, but I hope it turns out delicious. I'll see you when I get back this evening. And then we will have to start studying!"

Fatima cleared up her food as the girls continued the chopping. She went to her corner of the room and put on her brown *abaya* and a large cream-colored headscarf. Within a few minutes she was gone.

The pile of parsley was diminishing. They still had a fair bit left to do, but time had passed quickly, thanks to good conversation. Making tabouli on one's own was a terribly boring task.

"So, what were you saying about human rights?" ventured Leila. "I really don't know much about it."

Huda thought for a second. "Well, okay, let's take the example we were just talking about. Can you choose your own husband, or work when you graduate?"

"If my family lets me, I can."

"According to human rights, it's your decision, not theirs. Human rights says everyone can make their own choices. It's not up to Islam, and it's not up to your family; it's up to you. Of course, that doesn't mean you can harm other people in the process, because then you would be abusing their human rights."

"I guess that makes sense. But how is it my choice?"

"Let's say that your family says that you have to marry a man who won't let you work at all."

"That's probably what will happen."

"Do you have a choice?"

"No! If I did, my whole life would be different."

"According to human rights, you do. Your choice is: either you do your family's will and stop working and get married, or you abandon your family and do what you want."

"But my family could deny me if I did that! They'd be so hurt."

"That's your choice. Basically, hurt yourself or hurt your family."

"It's not that simple! I can't do that to my family."

"That's what I mean. You can choose to do that to your family, but you won't. And maybe you shouldn't. But human rights says that you could do that if you wanted to."

"If I did betray them, they might come after me and do something awful to me."

"Well, that they cannot do, because they would be hurting you."

"But who would protect me?"

Huda was silent on this point. Her lecturer had not addressed this question, and she thought she knew why. It should be the government's job to protect a woman such as the hypothetical Leila who left her family. But the truth was that the government would probably support her family and make it look like they were helping Leila, while actually turning a blind eye to whatever the family might do. She knew it and Leila knew it, but neither would say it.

Instead, Huda changed the subject, "So back to your example of the two men. Of course I agree that it's shameful and forbidden, but it is their choice. In Islam they shouldn't. In Syrian society they shouldn't. But as long as they are not hurting other people, it is their right. I have heard that this actually happens in Damascus, although no one really wants to talk about it. But I'm sure some men do it."

"What an awful thought! I'm glad you're learning something in your course. You'll make a great lawyer someday. But let's think about something else."

"Yes, let's. We're almost done with the parsley. Shall I finish chopping while you start the other vegetables?"

Leila nodded. "I told the girls four o'clock or so. We still have an hour. What do you think we should serve to drink?"

They decided that tabouli was best with cola, and Huda offered to go down to the little shop and buy some once the tabouli was ready. Huda started chopping the last bunch of parsley while Leila went to the kitchen to wash the tomatoes, cucumbers and mint. She came back and handed Huda a handful of mint leaves to chop. Leila put a tomato in her hand and used a butter knife to cut deep ridges on the top, then sawed off the ridges creating minuscule pieces of tomato. She repeated the process with the other two tomatoes, the cucumbers, and the onion. In the meantime, Huda finished up with the leafy vegetables and asked Leila where the bulgur wheat was. Leila pointed to a shelf over her bed laden with jars and bags of food. Huda found the bag of bulgur and put a handful of the wheat into a small bowl, boiled some water and poured a bit onto the wheat to soften it. Then she started squeezing lemons onto the mix, grabbed the olive oil and salt off of Leila's shelf, and added some of that. When Leila was done with the other vegetables, Huda added the bulgur wheat and started stirring.

Leila walked over to the table, which was set up as a makeshift dish-drying rack, and grabbed a spoon. She scooped up a tiny bit of the tabouli and tasted it.

"Well?" asked Huda.

"More salt and more olive oil."

So they added a bit of each and stirred again. Then Huda tasted. She put some more on the spoon and handed it to Leila. They agreed it was good as it was.

Leila offered to wash the lettuce that they would use to eat the tabouli in lieu of plates and spoons, and Huda went down to buy two liters of cola and some plastic cups.

She returned fifteen minutes later with two girls Leila didn't know, introducing them as other girls in her course whom she'd run into down at the shop. Leila shook their hands and invited them in. She said everything was almost ready and continued to lay out the nicest, biggest leaves of lettuce on two plates on each side of the tabouli bowl. She did have a few small bowls and spoons, so she set those out for anyone who wanted them.

Soon there was a knock on the door. Leila looked up and saw Maha. She shook Maha's hand and kissed her once on each cheek. Then she shook hands with Maha's two roommates and introductions were made. While Huda was out, Leila had rearranged the beds in the room into a "U" shape to form three make-shift sofas. The table was in the middle. So now Leila ushered her guests to the beds. Huda and her two friends sat on one bed, Maha and her two friends sat on the next bed. Leila felt her heart skipping a beat every now and then as she watched a party starting to take shape in her own room. At home, she hosted guests regularly, but receiving the village women for a Qur'an study, or serving Friday dinner to her aunts, was different – they were older women, and much more strict, and her mother made sure that she did everything with scrupulous propriety. This time it was her party, and these girls were not going to give her a lecture on proper Islamic living. They were just going to have fun and make a memory.

While Leila hovered around the room looking for little ways she could improve the set-up, the other girls made small talk. Then Leila thought of one last thing that was missing: music! She didn't have a radio, but what party doesn't have music?

She recalled hearing music in Maha's room, so she sat down next to Maha and whispered to her, "Do you have a radio we could use?"

Maha hesitated a second, then replied, "Well, it's my friend's. But I don't think she'll mind." She turned to the girl next to her and asked her if it was alright to use her radio.

Maha's roommate smiled and said, "Of course!" She started to stand up, but Maha stopped her and said she would get it herself.

When Maha walked out, Huda looked at Leila. "What do you need?"

"A radio. Maha went to get theirs."

Huda nodded.

Leila wandered to the door and looked down the hall toward Maha's room. She heard movement on the stairs and girls' voices which made her tummy squeeze and twitch. Sure enough, when the voices rounded the bend, there was Roxy with her two cousins.

Leila wanted to run up and give Roxy a hug, but instead she stood in the doorway and smiled at the three. Leila needn't be shy, though, because Roxy shouted, "Leila, *habibti*, my dear!"

Leila replied, "*Ahlan wa Sahlan*," and reached out her hand to shake Roxy's. Then they kissed once on the right cheek, and three times on the left. Leila turned to greet Mary and Ghalia in similar fashion, and invited them in. They all entered the room, including Maha, arms full of a boombox and a pile of cassette tapes.

The three Druze girls sat on the third bed and Maha set up the boombox by a plug near the window. She put in a cassette of Arabic pop music, and Leila began introductions once again. All the girls nodded at each other this time and stayed in their seats. For a moment Leila panicked when she realized that on the sofa to her left sat three Alawite Law students, on the sofa directly in front of her sat three Christian girls who were best friends, and on the sofa to her right sat three Druze cousins. And she, the hostess, was standing alone. She wished Fatima had stayed, then caught herself. Fatima might be from the same village as Leila, but

Fatima was boring and a gossip. These girls with her now were relative strangers, but Leila really enjoyed them.

She caught Huda's attention and the two girls started serving the cola and tabouli. When planning the get-together, Leila hadn't thought about there being too many girls for all to sit around the table, so she ended up piling full three bowls of tabouli and giving them, together with a bunch of lettuce, to each of the three clusters of girls. Huda poured out cola into plastic cups.

Leila pulled a chair up to the table and ate out of the serving bowl, keeping a careful eye on the other girls' bowls to see when they would need refilling. As the girls started eating, each cluster got into its own conversation: the Alawite law student friends chatted about their exams; the Christian roommates about Nancy Ajram, the Lebanese pop star singing in the background; and the Druze cousins about their plans for later that night. Leila sat facing all three clusters and wondered which conversation to join.

Then Roxy looked up and asked Leila how she had been the past few weeks.

Leila blinked and smiled, then replied calmly, "Studying hard, you know. How are you?"

Roxy winked at Leila. "I'm great! I'm still loving being married!"

"Really? Why?"

"My husband has a car and takes me to do all kinds of fun things. Last night we went up onto Mount Qasioun really late. We had dinner at one in the morning, and drank *arguile* for hours! Then we went for a long walk, and watched the sun come up before going home."

"Wow. That sounds so beautiful. I've never done anything like that before," Leila tried to keep the jealousy out of her voice.

Roxy paused for a second, then exclaimed, "I know! We

could all go together. You and me and Mary and Ghalia. We could all go up on the mountain one night. My husband would love that. He'd think it would be so much fun."

Mary and Ghalia looked at her and Ghalia asked Roxy if she meant that.

Roxy replied, "Sure, why not? He's always looking for something different to do."

Leila thought Roxy must be the perfect wife for someone looking for different things to do. She also thought that her family would die of shame if they found out that she had spent an entire night out, on a mountain, with a man they didn't know. So she turned away with the pretense of checking on her other guests. The plate shared by Maha and her friends was emptying, so she left Roxy chattering about an all-nighter on the mountain and filled Maha's plate again. She took advantage of the excuse to join their conversation.

"This is Nancy Ajram?" Leila asked.

"Yes, it's her newest album," replied one of Maha's roommates.

"Ah." Leila nodded. "I didn't think I'd ever heard it before."

"She's coming to Damascus in concert next month. They say it is going to be the biggest show in 2005!" exclaimed Maha.

"Have you been to a concert before?" asked Leila.

"Once," replied Maha. "Last year, when I was visiting my cousins in Lebanon, we went to the 'Amr Diab concert. It was incredible. Great music, and he's sooooo beautiful."

Leila blushed, but she agreed... Whenever an 'Amr Diab videoclip came on TV at home, she turned the music up and stopped to watch because he was very nice to look at. But she was more comfortable talking about his music. "He is a very good singer. It must have been a great concert."

"Yeah, it was one of the most incredible moments of my

life."

Her roommate said, "I've never been to a concert, but hopefully the three of us are going to see Nancy together. They say this tour is her best, and she's becoming world-famous."

"She was number one on Rotana countdown for the last three weeks running," pointed out the other roommate.

Leila excused herself from pop music to check on the tabouli bowls again. The bowls used by Huda and friends, and Roxy and friends, needed refilling, so first she filled the bowl for Roxy and her cousins. Then she refilled Huda's and pulled her co-conspirator aside to ask her how she thought the party was going.

"The tabouli's delicious, isn't it?" whispered Huda.

"*Alhamdulillah* – Praise God," responded Leila. "But do you think people are having fun?"

"They seem to be, don't you think?"

"Yeah, I guess. But shouldn't people be getting to know each other?"

"Oh. Well, little by little. They only just met."

Leila frowned. "Do you think I should do anything to get everyone talking with each other?"

"Like what?" asked Huda.

"I don't know... Can you think of anything?"

"Well, we could play a game. Do you know any games?"

Leila hadn't played any games since she was about ten years old. Neither had Huda, so they gave up on that idea.

"I know!" blurted Huda after a moment. "Didn't you say Roxy is a good dancer?"

"Yeah, she's amazing."

"Well, when we're done eating, ask her to start dancing."

"Do you think that will work?"

"I bet everyone here can dance. I don't mind dancing although I'm not that great. It'll be fun."

"I don't know how to dance," countered Leila.

"You don't? You've never danced?"

"Not really, just playing around with my sisters."

Huda smiled. "That's all dancing really is. It'll be fun." She sat down and grabbed a piece of lettuce, then scooped herself a bit of tabouli.

Leila drifted back to Roxy. She sat down on the bed and asked Roxy about her house. Roxy described a castle: a first-floor flat decorated in marble with brand-new luxury appliances. She said she had a great kitchen, although she never cooked: they always ate out or ordered in. The house had all new furniture, decorated in greens and yellows, Roxy's favorite colors. The more she talked, the more Leila thought this woman lived the dream life. She was with a man she loved who had lots of money and took care of her. Leila would never afford to live in such a beautiful home. And she would never dance like Roxy.

A few minutes into the conversation, duty led Leila to get up once again and offer more tabouli to all the girls. Some accepted, and once Leila was assured that everyone had eaten to heart's content – which was a good thing, because most of the tabouli had disappeared – she asked Maha if she had any good music for dancing. Maha rummaged through her cassettes and put on some traditional Arabic dancing music. Leila pushed the table out of the way and handed Roxy a scarf.

"Why don't you dance for us!" smiled Leila.

Roxy didn't need much more coaxing than that. Mary and Ghalia started clapping their hands, and all the other girls joined in while Roxy took the scarf, tied it around her hips and started dancing.

She looked Leila in the eyes as she twirled the bottom half of her body. Then she spun around and faced Huda and her classmates while stepping in and out. Then the most intense drumming of the music started and she stood still, slowly vibrating from her legs and up through her thighs and to her belly. As the drumming got louder, she vibrated more and more. At the climax, some of the girls made the loud trilling sound, "LaLaLaLaLaLaLaLaLaLaaaaa!"

The music resumed and Roxy returned to normal dance. She turned again to Leila and coaxed her to join her. Leila looked frightened and stepped back. "Not yet. Later. But Huda will dance!"

So Roxy reached her hands out to Huda, who stood up and joined in. Then Huda grabbed one of Maha's roommates. When the song ended, another began, and Huda and Roxy went around the room, encouraging the other girls to join in, and soon everyone but Leila and one of Huda's classmates was dancing. Leila walked to her closet and found another two scarves. She brought those out and gave them to Maha and one of her roommates.

Then she sat next to Huda's classmate. "Why aren't you dancing?"

"I'm too tired today. I didn't sleep last night, studying."

"Oh, well, may you pass and rest well," responded Leila.

"May God strengthen you after planning such a great party. You must have worked all afternoon," said the other girl.

"Yes, well, I think we were all needing a break from books."

They watched in silence for a few minutes, then Maha came over to Leila. "Come on, let's dance!"

"I can't dance!" protested Leila.

"Sure you can. It's easy!"

Leila was very timid and scared to attempt dancing in front of these strangers, but Maha was too persuasive, especially when Huda joined her and each grabbed one hand to pull her up. So she joined in, but felt too nervous to enjoy it. But she jiggled and swayed with the rest of the girls, and soon found herself in a circle with all the other girls standing around her, tapping and clapping. So she closed her eyes and tried to really feel the music. It felt good to let loose and give herself over to the power of the rhythm. After a moment, she opened her eyes and saw all the girls smiling and clapping. She stepped out of the center and joined the circle of girls as they encouraged Ghalia to dance. They continued taking turns until the music stopped.

Maha quickly went to the cassette player and put in some 'Amr Diab. The girls hardly missed a beat.

After nearly an hour of dancing, Leila decided it was time to make the coffee. If the girls wanted to stay later, they were welcome, but she figured some of them needed to get back to their studies. She served half of the coffee in tiny coffee cups and the other half in small glass teacups. The music was turned back down to a normal volume, and the girls sat around together chatting. Leila was still alone on the chair, but as she looked around at her guests drinking bitter Arabic coffee, she was relieved to see that the different groups of friends were all mixed up on the beds. Huda and Maha were bonding, and Roxy and Maha's roommates had plenty to talk about as they discussed music and makeup. Mary sat with the girl who had refused to dance and chatted about... something.

For once, Leila was eager to get back to her studies. By ten o'clock curfew, when the women's building were locked down for the night, the room was cleaned and all the girls had left, except for Fatima who had returned while Huda and Leila were washing up. Leila decided to step up onto the roof for a few minutes of fresh air before going down to the study room.

Before Roxy had left, she had reiterated her invitation to

a night on the mountain with her husband. Leila really wanted to go, but it was out of the question. So she simply told Roxy that it was great to have her over, and that she should visit again next time she stayed in the Medina. If Roxy brought it up again, Leila didn't know how she would respond. She couldn't say no to such a wonderful offer, but she couldn't say yes either. Good girls simply don't do those things.

Leila actually felt very sad. She would have thought that after throwing a successful study break party, she would have felt satisfied. She wondered what it was. Did she offend someone? Did someone offend her?

Then she realized it was probably the feeling of not belonging. There she had sat, on the only chair in the room, looking at three beds cluttered with friends. All the friends were so cool and fun. Leila knew that for the rest of her life she would look back on her Medina years as a highlight because of the amazing people she had met. But these girls actually lived this life. It wasn't just the Medina for them. Roxy took her cousins up on the mountain and on other adventures with her husband. Not because they were at the Medina, but because that's what they did. Maha and her roommates were going to a Nancy Ajram concert, and Maha had been to an 'Amr Diab concert before.

Huda was such a good friend, and Leila once again thought how glad she was to have met her. But even Huda had friends like herself, from her part of the country, who studied hard and shared her dreams. Leila's family didn't understand her and she didn't get along with girls like Fatima. But those were her people, and she did love them. She thought of her conversation with Huda about following her dreams. If it meant abandoning her family... there was no way! Family was the most important thing: family and God.

Chapter Two

There were only ten people left in the room where the final French exam took place. Everyone else had turned in their exams and left. Leila never understood how people finished so fast – she was determined to use every last minute carefully and wisely. She looked up at the clock to see how much time was left. Only five minutes, which was fine. She was almost done anyway. As she looked back down, though, she noticed... him! The man who had smiled at her a few weeks ago. Her hand froze and her heart leaped at the sight of him. So he, too, was a slow exam taker.

The five minutes passed quickly, and at the very last minute, Leila turned in her exam. She had thought carefully through each question and was confident about her answers – even though she suspected that just putting what she thought the professor wanted, directly off the lecture notes, would have ensured her a better mark and saved her lots of time.

She wandered out of the large hall and into the bright sun.

"How did you do?" she heard a man's voice behind her.

Leila turned, expecting to see two people walking out together discussing the exam. Instead, she saw *him*. Looking at her and waiting for an answer.

Say something clever, she thought to herself. Nothing came to mind. So she just said, "I can hope for the best."

"Well, I hope you did well."

"Thank you," she mumbled. After a silence that threatened to end the conversation, Leila finally forced herself to ask, "How did you do?"

"French is easy. Especially because I'm taking the French Cultural Center course. But those questions were phrased in such a complex way that I'm not really sure I knew what they were asking."

"Oh, I know what you mean!" exclaimed Leila. "I also feel like I know the answers, but on the multiple choice, the right answer is never an option. So I have to guess what they're looking for. But that's not just French. I feel like that on every exam."

"You're an English Literature major, right?" *How did he know that?*

"Yes."

"I think exams must be very frustrating for someone who knows English well."

"Well, I don't know that I can say I know English well. But I want to."

Leila just realized that they had started walking side-by-side back toward the Medina. She was walking with *him*! "Do you live in the Medina?" she asked.

"No, no. I'm from Damascus. But I do have lots of friends in the Medina."

"Really? You're originally from Damascus?"

"Yes, my family is a real Damascene family."

"Oh," sighed Leila. He would never want to have anything to do with a village girl like her, she thought.

"And you, where are you from?"

"I'm from Dera'a. Well, actually a little village just outside of Dera'a."

"Oh, that's a lovely region. My mother's from Dera'a region."

"Really?"

"Yes. And during summers, we often went down to spend time with her family."

"That's nice. So you had a home in the city and a home in

the village. What a great life."

"Yes, I guess so. The best of both worlds."

They walked along in silence for a few minutes as they navigated their way through the crowded tunnel under the highway separating the university buildings from the Medina. He walked behind her and helped her to make way when it was too crowded, like a perfect gentleman. When they emerged at the other end, he asked, "So I guess you're leaving soon for the summer?"

"When exams are over. They close the Medina, so I have to go. But I really like living in the city so I'll stay until the last day."

"You like the city? When you have a beautiful village you can stay in?"

"I just stay at home, helping my mother. My family hosts lots of Islamic lectures, so we're always having visitors and setting up the house and cleaning it and preparing sweets and... oh, I'm sorry, you don't want to hear all that!"

"No, to the contrary. It's nice learning about you. I've seen you in class sometimes, and you look like someone who is really interested in the lectures. That fascinated me."

"Really? You could tell that just from being in the lectures together?"

"Sure. Most people don't even show up, or they show up but don't pay attention. You sit right in the middle and take notes."

"I do really want to learn," enthused Leila.

He smiled that smile. "So do I, and it's nice to meet someone else who wants to learn and isn't just here to get a degree."

"What's your major?" Leila thought she knew the answer but didn't want to presume.

"International trade."

Leila wanted to continue the conversation, but they had

arrived at the turn-off for her building. "I'm afraid this is where my building is. Thank you for saying hi. And good luck with your exams."

"Did you say you'll be here for a few more weeks?" He looked straight into her eyes.

Leila felt herself blush as his eyes held hers. "Yes, through the end of exams, until they close the Medina."

"Well, maybe I can see you again. We could meet for coffee in the student center or something."

"I'd like that," Leila found herself saying. This was very wrong. She should have said no, but she was actually very glad she had said yes.

"What's your room number? I'll come by, say, tomorrow?"

"Oh, I have an exam day after tomorrow."

"Day after tomorrow, in the afternoon, then."

"*Insha'allah*. If God wills it. My room number is 105."

"Until then, *Insha'allah*." He smiled that amazing smile as he said goodbye.

"Bye!" Leila ran off and she could feel herself turning redder by the second.

Huda got home a little before ten. She was relieved to find her room empty and hoped she could enjoy a cup of tea and some food for a few minutes before climbing into bed. She'd been studying in the student center library since eight o'clock that morning. Now she was exhausted - she just wanted to eat something and go to sleep.

At ten o'clock, though, there was a knock on the door, and she opened it to a breathless Leila. It looked like she had just run up the stairs.

"*Ahlain*, Leila. Welcome. How are you?"

"Oh, Huda, I have to tell you what happened to me today! The most amazing thing!"

Huda ushered Leila in, shoved the books on her bed over to a corner, and indicated to Leila that she should sit there. "Will you drink tea?"

"That'd be nice. How are you?"

"It's been a very long day," Huda answered, hoping that Leila would get the hint. "I just now got back from a full day of studying."

"Oh. You must be tired."

"Exhausted."

Leila paused. "Should I leave?" she asked.

"No, it's okay, I'm fine."

She looked relieved and smiled. "So let me tell you what happened to me today!"

Huda said quickly, "Let me just grab some water for our tea. I'll be right back." She walked quickly into the kitchen and filled the teapot and hurried back to the room. The quicker she made the tea, the quicker Leila would tell her story and the quicker Huda could go to sleep. She walked back into the room, placed the teapot on a small electric burner, and plugged it in. Then she sat down next to Leila on the bed and asked Leila to tell her story.

"Alright. So... Oh, I need to start at the beginning. No, maybe I'll just tell you about today. Yeah. Let me tell you what happened today, then I can tell you what happened before," Leila was talking very quickly.

"Slowly, slowly," soothed Huda. Talking this way was stressing her out. Leila was a wonderful friend to have around because she seemed to be interested in everything, but right now it felt like too much excitement.

"Ok. Right. Slowly, slowly." Leila took a deep breath and started over. "I had my French exam today, right? Well, when I finished..." and she recounted for Huda everything she could remember about her magical encounter with "him".

Huda listened to the whole story in silence. As she poured

the tea, she said, "He sounds very nice."

"Yeah, I think he is."

"What's his name?"

"His name?"

"Yes, how did he introduce himself?"

"Oh!" Leila gasped. "Why, I don't think he told me his name! Oh no! How is he going to come find me? I never told him my name either! What if he doesn't come find me? I'll never be able to track him down..."

"Calm down," soothed Huda, with a faint smile. "It's not that important. I'm sure he'll come by, and if he doesn't, it can't be too hard to find him. Especially if he lives in the Medina."

"He doesn't live in the Medina. He's Shami."

"Really? Shami as in from Damascus originally?"

"Yes, that's what he said. But his mother's from Dera'a like me!"

"I see. Be careful, I've heard that Damascene people are hyper-conservative, like they don't let their wives go out alone at all and they don't let their daughters complete their studies."

"Really? He seemed so open-minded."

"Well, maybe he's different."

The two girls sat in silence for a moment. Huda was wondering what she could say to comfort her friend and get her to leave at the same time. Leila looked like she was deep in thought, probably imagining a name for this man, wondering if his family was open-minded, and hoping he would call like he'd promised.

Then Leila declared, "I'm just so excited. He has the most amazing smile. That's the part I didn't tell you before, but he talked to me once before, and I've seen him around the Medina a few times before, too. And when he smiled at me, oh...."

Huda smiled when she realized this crush had been plaguing Leila for a while – conservative, chaste, innocent but excitable Leila. Huda had had guy friends before, and a few of them had shown interest in her romantically. For her family, a rendezvous with a man wouldn't be too big of a deal, though her studies had always interested her more than men. So Huda felt like the experienced big sister. "Oh, that's good. I think he really likes you."

"Do you think so? I mean he doesn't really know me at all. But he did say he has noticed me in class."

"What did he notice?"

"He said he noticed the way I took notes in class."

"That's specific. Yes, I think he does like you. Wow, Leila, you have an admirer!"

"And I don't even know his name."

"I bet he already knows your name."

"Really? How?"

"When a man likes a woman, he has a way of finding things out about her."

"Oh, may it be so. *Insha'allah*."

Huda was intrigued, but she was also tired. So she said she was going to eat something and did Leila want more tea and some supper?

"Oh, no," moaned Leila. "I couldn't eat right now. I'm too excited. So how have you been?"

"I've been well. I was studying all day today in the big library."

"How did it go?"

"Little by little..." Huda said despondently. "I have my first two exams back to back, big ones, early next week, so I have a lot to be ready for."

"You work so hard and you're so smart: I'm sure you will do well."

"Thank you, we can only hope for the best."

"Yes," sighed Leila. "We can only hope for the best..." Leila really didn't seem to be herself tonight. The attention of a man did seem to have captivated her imagination.

"Well, do you mind if I have a bite to eat?" asked Huda.

"Oh, I'll leave. I need to go study some anyway. I have another exam day after tomorrow."

"Are you sure you don't want anything?"

"No, thanks. And please, don't tell anyone about this, okay?"

"Of course not. Good luck with him!"

Leila smiled and kissed Huda once on each cheek as she took her leave. Huda shut the door behind her and pulled out some bread, yogurt and olives. As she dipped her bread in the yogurt, she thought about Leila being in love. Somehow it seemed appropriate for a girl like Leila, who always wanted to dream, to have something to dream about. But she also worried for her friend. She was very loyal to her family, and making a male friend in Damascus was risky business.

Then Huda thought about her own life. She thought how nice it would be if she had a guy friend. Someone to treat her to dinner sometimes and to accompany her on outings. But really, a guy would just distract her. A guy would want something from her. At the least he would expect her to spend lots of time with him, but it was very possible he'd expect more. She thought of her older sister's friend who worked in Damascus. Sometimes Huda visited her, and she always had another story of a guy she'd met. This girl was 30 years old, and it was high time she got married, both in her family's opinion and in her own. But every man she met wasn't suitable. One had told her that if he married her she would have to start covering her head. Another man had told her that he just wanted her to bear him many beautiful children, and another man had tried to take her to bed without getting married. They had all expected her to be available to spend time with them whenever they wanted, not when it was good for her.

Huda didn't see how that was fun. Yes, a man's attention feels nice, she thought as she remembered a boy she had been close to in high school. But she didn't want anything to get in the way of becoming a successful law professor. A career would be fulfilling, and she had good friends in the Medina. She was happy with that – as long as she did well in her studies and got into graduate school.

The next morning Huda woke up early as usual and studied in the big central library for a few hours in the morning. She had an appointment that day with her Judicial Process professor and wanted to make sure and get some work done beforehand. She also hoped that he would be able to take the time to help her with her studies, so she wanted to have a long list of questions ready to ask him. Unlike most of her professors, he had always come across as attentive and patient to explain things to his students, and she was desperate for help.

So at 10:45 she packed up her books, abandoned her coveted table in the corner, and walked to the law faculty building.

When she arrived at his office, she found him chatting with another professor, so she waited in the hallway for ten minutes, watching the secretaries and graduate students coming and going. She hoped to be a part of this department for many years to come – completing law as a graduate student, all the way through the PhD, and then as a professor. But now, as she watched all these confident-looking people who seemed to belong and who looked professional and business-like, her heart began to beat faster. She wasn't like them. She was just a poor Alawi village girl. If he hadn't already seen her at the door, she would have been tempted to run back to the comfortable routine of the library.

Just as she was beginning to worry she'd faint, the other man left and her professor poked his head out the door.

"*Ahlan*, Huda. Welcome. Please, come on in."

"Good morning, professor," Huda replied as she walked past him into the room, clutching her books to her heart and staring intently at the floor.

He closed the door behind her and walked around the desk to take his seat, motioning to Huda to sit down across from him. She did so, sitting straight up in her chair and still clutching her books. He leaned back and put his arms behind his head. "So, how is studying coming? Are you ready for your exams?"

"I've been working very hard, sir," she replied.

"I'm sure you have. You're a very good student. I hope you do well."

"Thank you. It's in God's hands."

"Sure, God's hands. You live in the Medina, don't you?"

"Yes, sir."

"How is that? Are you able to concentrate? I know a lot of people say it's too noisy to focus."

"I've gotten used to it." Huda wanted to start discussing the course material and wondered if she should just jump in, but he kept asking her questions, so she kept answering. He inquired about her village, how many siblings she had, he even asked her what year she was born. Huda wondered why in the world her professor cared about her age, and why he didn't just look it up in her student records.

Then he got even more personal. "So, Huda, what are you going to do with a law degree?"

"If I complete my law degree, sir," she replied with appropriate modesty.

"Of course you will!"

"*Insha'allah*."

"So what are you going to do?"

"Well, I want to go on to graduate school, to get my doctorate in law."

"Really? That's excellent. I wish you all the best. Where do you think you'll go?"

Huda was very grateful for this segue into one of the purposes of her visit and lifted her eyes to him for the first time. "Well, sir, that's the thing. My family couldn't afford to send me abroad. I'm not even sure they would want me leaving Syria. And University of Damascus is an excellent school, so I really want to continue here. Is it true that only the top 1% of students are accepted into post-graduate studies here?"

"Oh, Huda," he gazed at her thoughtfully. "That's not my area. You should talk to the postgraduate administrator about that. But yes, I do think it's very competitive."

Huda looked down again. "I was hoping that maybe you could help me figure out what I need to do so that I have my best chances of getting in."

"Well, I am happy to help you study, to help you do as well as you can, on your exams and anything else you need to do to get into the program."

"Really? Thank you! I know I can use all the help I can get!"

"You're very welcome. In fact, I will ask around in the department about the requirements for continuing your studies."

"May God keep you, professor," Huda smiled. "Actually, I also have some questions about my studies now, if you think you'd be able to help me out."

He replied very kindly, offering her all the help she could need. For a passing moment, Huda wondered why he was being so nice to her but she quickly pushed that thought away. She wanted to take advantage of every moment of help she could get. So she pulled out her notebook and opened it to where she had written two full pages of questions she wanted help answering. She pulled her chair up to the desk and sat directly across from him. He leaned forward, so his head was now inches from hers. They pored over her notebook together, and he pointed out pages in her judicial process textbook where she should focus her attention. After an hour studying together, there was a knock at the door. He got up and walked to the door, opened it just a crack, and whispered for a moment with whomever was on the other side. Then he came back and sat down again.

Huda looked at her watch. "I've taken so much of your time. I'm sorry! I guess I should go."

"Was that all?"

"Well, you've already been so helpful."

"More questions? Wow."

"Umm, to be honest, I could use help with all my classes... But I can see that I've taken too much of your time now, so I'll leave you."

He leaned back in his chair again and sat quietly looking at her for a moment. Then he said, "Well, I do have another appointment now, but, hmm..." After a moment's pause, he added, "How about this? Let's meet up for lunch someday. Say tomorrow? We can eat lunch together, and you can ask me all the questions you want."

Lunch? That was a new thought. Could she afford to pay for a lunch at a restaurant where a law professor would eat? And would they really get a lot of studying done while eating? But she agreed.

He gave her the address of a restaurant near the city center and suggested they meet there at three o'clock the next day. Then he said, somewhat conspiratorially, "But don't tell anyone about it, because if word gets out that I'm helping one student more than the others, well, you know..."

Huda nodded and said, "Of course. I so very much appreciate it." Then quickly, because she knew someone else was waiting, she got up, opened the door and left, closing it behind her again.

As she walked away, she heard his door open, and could overhear him greeting another man, probably another professor. She hurried away and back to her dorm room to eat something before returning to the library. That meeting had gone so much better than she ever could have hoped. He may not have had much to offer by way of help getting her into graduate school, but as a second-year student, what she really needed was help passing her classes, and it seemed he was going to offer that. She wondered about his closing the door. She couldn't remember ever being in a meeting at the university where the door was closed. Maybe he'd known they were going to study together and wanted to help create a productive environment. *What a smart professor*, she thought, as she headed down into the tunnel leading to the Medina entrance.

Chapter Three

The next day was a Thursday. Normally Leila would have been going home for the weekend, but she told her family that she needed to stay in Damascus and study. Which was mostly true.

She sat in her room on Thursday afternoon. She had come straight home after a grueling poetry exam. Now she was tired, but she couldn't rest. And she wouldn't leave the room. Not even to go to the bathroom, not even to go to the kitchen to get water for tea. She didn't want to miss the bell.

Fatima was still staying in the room with Leila, but she was out studying all of every day. She would come home around 7:00 in the evening and study in the room for a few hours, then go to sleep. All fanaticism and no fun, that one. So her presence had not had much of an effect on Leila's lifestyle or on the room's atmosphere – except that in the evenings it was now a studious place. None of the other girls had shown up yet, but they would soon.

So now it was 3:00 in the afternoon and Leila sat on her bed filing her nails. She couldn't concentrate on studying, she wasn't hungry and there was no way she could sleep. She didn't know what time *he* would call. She wasn't sure if he was really going to call at all. But they had agreed on "day after tomorrow", after her exam. And that was now.

Praise God, last night she had managed to focus on studying, even though she'd wanted to try on clothes and do her hair. She had even thought about knocking on Maha's door and asking for help styling her hair, despite the fact it would then be covered during the entire rendezvous. But she had caught herself. How would she explain to Maha that she really was a respectable girl, yet here she was styling her hair to meet up with a man who she hardly knew? What kind of a testimony to Islam was that? And more to the point, she had to study. So she'd forced herself to focus.

However, when she finished her exam at noon today, she'd come straight back to the room and gone through her closet. She had chosen an outfit to wear. Again, she felt quite petty, since she would put her overcoat on over her outfit. But she wanted to look nice anyway. Then she'd tried it on and been unhappy with the effect, so she'd changed blouses. Then she'd heard the call to prayer and prayed.

Since then, she had plucked her eyebrows, waxed her arms and filed her nails. She was running out of things to do, and she had no idea when and if he was coming. It might be late in the evening! It was pointless trying to study, but she decided to try anyway. She pulled out a pile of fiction lecture notes. Fiction was her favorite topic and the subject of her next exam. But the first few lectures were about *Pride and Prejudice*, a wildly romantic book which she had thoroughly enjoyed. So she imagined herself to be Lizzy and him, Mr. Darcy. The tall, quiet man who was honorable in almost every way. And she dazzled Him and won His heart with her cleverness.

She stood up and put a scarf on her head, and walked to the window. She opened it up wide and stuck her head out. She couldn't really see the building courtyard from the window, but she could see the pathway leading up to it. It was deserted. It was now half past three, and in June, most people were lunching or napping at this hour. It was probably still early for him to arrive.

The next two hours passed by in similar fashion. Leila would try to study but find her mind wandering, so she'd pace the room and look out the window. Then she'd come up with a manual task to do. At one point she walked into the hall just to see who was around, but it was deserted, and she didn't dare move more than a few feet from the door for fear of missing the sound of the bell. Around 4:15 she panicked when she realized no one had ever rung her bell before. What if it didn't work? Around 4:30 she remembered that once, near the beginning of her time in the Medina, someone had dropped by to deliver something for one of her roommates.

At 5:30 she was half-asleep on her bed when a loud buzzing sound jolted her awake. It was him! He'd come! She jumped out of bed and started to straighten her hair in the tiny mirror on the back of the door. Then she realized that if she didn't go down soon, he might leave. So she quickly threw on her scarf so she could run out to the window and assure him she was on her way down, then finish getting ready calmly.

So she ran out to the hall window with a good view of the courtyard. There he was. But he wasn't looking up, and she didn't dare shout out the window. After waving out the window a bit to no avail, she ran back to her room, quickly put on her overcoat and arranged her scarf properly in the mirror. Then she grabbed her handbag and keys and rushed out the door, stumbling recklessly down five flights of stairs.

Meanwhile, Huda was across town at a very expensive-looking restaurant with her professor. There were no prices to be seen anywhere, so she was worried. She'd brought all the money she had and just hoped it would be enough.

This restaurant was on the second floor of a nondescript building and she'd walked up and down the street three times before seeing the tiny sign in the window. When she entered, there were only two other occupied tables in the room, one with two men and the other with a man and a woman. The room had a total of ten tables and all the curtains were drawn. The carpeting and the curtains were different shades of red, so the whole room had a dark crimson feel. The tables had brown tablecloths with red embroidery, and there was a gold lamp on each table. The walls were decorated with paintings of streets in the Old City of Damascus. There were two waiters, both dressed in bow ties, who came and went, and everyone seemed to be whispering. All in all, the room had a rather sinister feel to it.

Huda had arrived just before 3:00, and was glad she'd come early since it had taken a while to find the place. A waiter had opened the door when she knocked and offered to show her to a seat. When she replied she was waiting for someone, he said she could go ahead and wait at a table. So she sat down next to a window and pulled the curtain aside for a moment to see the street below. It, too, looked deserted: this was clearly a residential area. Huda knew Old City Damascus had some beautiful restaurants – ancient homes with gorgeous mosaicked courtyards that had been converted into eating areas. She had only been to two such places: after all, between studying and her lack of wealth, it wasn't something she could afford to do often. But she did know that there were restaurants with fresh air, fountains and bright sun in Damascus. She wondered what her professor liked about a place like this.

Several minutes later, he walked in, greeted the waiters – apparently he was a regular here – and walked over to her table. "So what do you think of my little place?"

"It's very…" Huda tried to think of something both honest and nice to say and came up with nothing. So she offered a lie: "It's beautiful, and a lovely location."

"Yes, I like it because it's secluded. And the food here is excellent."

"Well, I look forward to trying it then."

The professor called over a waiter and started ordering. He asked for a typical selection of *mezze* appetizers including hummus, eggplant dip, fried potatoes, and a few different salads. Then Huda cringed – he ordered a full meat dish for each. Should she protest, say she wasn't that hungry? She didn't want to cause conflict, so she ignored her anxiety and forced herself to stop mentally counting the money that was stuffed in her purse.

The waiter ran off to get the order started and the professor turned his attention to Huda. "How's your studying coming?"

"Slowly, but I'm working hard and trusting God."

"Your hard work will pay off, I'm sure," replied the professor, and Huda wondered if he was deliberately avoiding all mention of God.

Huda asked him if she should pull out her books for a while before the food came.

He waved at her schoolbag, and said, "The food won't be long. Let's just enjoy lunch first."

Huda shrugged, and sat silently. The professor soon filled the silence by asking her more questions about her family. She couldn't understand why he was so interested in her family, but she methodically answered each of his questions. Her oldest sister stayed at home, never worked and never married after she finished university in Sociology. Her oldest brother was married with two children, and he owned a clothing store. Her next brother also studied law – maybe the professor remembered him? He would have graduated three years ago. No, the professor didn't know him. Her next sister just graduated a year ago in Arabic literature and was now married and teaching secondary school. She had a younger brother and a younger sister, both still in secondary school. Her father was a government employee, but he also owned a store... The questions kept coming, and Huda kept answering even though she was feeling more and more uncomfortable.

Meanwhile, the waiter was placing plates of appetizers on

their table. There was definitely enough food there for five, without any main dishes, Huda thought. Finally, the waiter brought out a bag of bread in a basket, and the professor opened it and handed Huda a piece, then took a piece for himself. He bellowed, "*Tfadali* – dig in!" and started eating with gusto.

While the professor ripped off chunks of bread, alternately scooping dips and using the bread to grab bites of salad, Huda took advantage of the pause in conversation to try to figure out what was going on. It was true that it was illogical to have schoolbooks out while eating, and it made sense that they should make conversation in the meantime. So why did she feel something was wrong about this? Why was he asking her so many personal questions? Come to think of it, how were they going to go over her notes in this dim restaurant setting, even after they ate? Why in the world did she agree to this?

But one thing she was sure about: she respected this man as a leading Syrian lawyer and wanted to learn as much as possible from him. She'd agreed to come to lunch with him because she wanted to learn from him. So she decided she could try to ask him questions from memory.

She finally broke a piece of bread off and dipped it in the eggplant purée. The professor glanced up and smiled. She continued eating in silence for a few moments, then she asked him, "How did you become an expert in judicial process?"

"Hmm," he said, with a full mouth. "I did my Masters in Law and my PhD in Holland, right when they were setting up the International Criminal Court. I was able to intern there and participate in some cases."

"Really? That's amazing!"

He shoved a big spoonful of salad into his mouth.

After a moment, he continued. "The ICC is a great

experience, because it's all about finding the truth. Both sides are researching everything to see all the sides of the issue. In the court itself, though, I discovered that there are loads of rules and procedures to be followed. Here in Syria, those procedures aren't usually followed, because people don't think they're necessary – too Western, too rules-oriented, all that. But what I discovered was, when you follow those rules, that is what makes it possible to find out all the sides of an issue. So that's what I did my PhD on in the end – on developing a set of procedures that would work in Syria."

Huda nodded. She was speechless to be in the presence of such an intelligent and influential person.

The professor continued, "I was on a government scholarship to study abroad, so when I got back, the government wanted me to work with them, and I was able to present my plan. Besides lecturing at the university, I've been a consultant in the courts here, helping them to develop procedures that work in Syria and teaching them how to follow those procedures." Getting no response from Huda, who was looking down and holding her bread in her right hand, he concluded, "And that's how I became the judicial process person." He tore back into his food.

The professor ate on in silence, and after a minute Huda started eating again. She tried to think of an intelligent question. Soon, she blurted, "That's amazing. God keep your work. So, what kinds of innovations have you recommended?"

"You know, you talk about God a lot for a lawyer. Lawyers need to be objective and precise at all times."

"Oh, I'm sorry," Huda said quietly.

"Don't apologize. You need to be strong. Religion is the opiate of the masses, not something that will bring change to society or justice to people. If you want to be an influential lawyer, you can't have religion holding you back."

Huda wondered what justice meant if it wasn't defined as the things that God commanded, but she lacked the audacity to ask.

The waiter brought their plates of grilled meat at that moment, and Huda was glad for the interruption. The professor tore into the plate of meat with salad, bread and chips. She followed his lead and slowly took a few bites off of her plate.

Once they'd eaten a bit in silence, the professor remembered the question Huda had asked him and started talking about reforming the Syrian justice system. Huda tried to pay close attention and not miss a word. Sometimes he said things she didn't understand, so she tried to remember those things to look up later, not having the courage to ask him for clarification.

After they ate, he ordered tea, and as they sipped Huda again reached for her bag. The professor again waved her off, saying they'd get to that later. So she continued to ask him about his work and his experience. After the tea, she started to get nervous about paying the bill. She didn't know what to do when her professor took her to lunch for a study session – should she pay the whole thing? But they hadn't actually studied at all. Might he pay? She decided to wait and see if he did anything. If he didn't, she'd have to ask.

She was getting a little concerned about the purpose of this tryst, though. Weren't they supposed to be studying?

Back in the Medina, Leila was settling into the student café with Ahmed, for she now knew that that was his name. When she'd arrived down in the courtyard, he'd been chatting with another man. She'd stood at the gate for a moment, wondering if she should interrupt, then he'd looked up and smiled his big smile. He'd quickly taken leave of his friend and come to meet her, shaking her hand.

"*Ahlan*," he said broadly.

"*Ahlan fik*," Leila replied.

"How was your exam?"

"Praise God, that's all I can say!"

"I'm sure you did wonderfully."

"*Insha'allah* If God wills." Leila had said with a sigh. Then she had remembered to ask her big question. "I realized I never found out your name."

"Oh, no, I guess you didn't! It's Ahmed. I'm very honored to meet you."

"I'm Leila, it is good to meet you too."

"Well, Leila, shall we go have some coffee?" He briefly made a gesture like putting his arm around her shoulder to lead her to the café, but his arm never actually touched her.

They walked side-by-side toward the student center. Leila tried to think of something brilliant to say to break the silence, but she was too nervous. She glanced over at Ahmed, who was confidently walking, with his hands in his pockets. He was wearing the latest fashion in jeans, loose with pockets by the knees and little rips all over. His shirt was a white button-down, which made his dark features all the more striking. He glanced at her, but she looked down before their eyes could meet.

This dance of the eyes repeated itself a few times before they arrived at the student center. When they entered the café, Ahmed chose a table near a window, but not too far from the door. Leila was glad he didn't choose a table in a secluded corner, considering she was already feeling rebellious by meeting up with him at all. After helping Leila into her seat, Ahmed sat down across from her and motioned to a waiter. He ordered a cappuccino for himself and asked her what she wanted. She said cappuccino was good.

Now they were settled in their seats and Leila figured it was high time they start to chat. She started by asking him more about his language studies. "French lessons at the French Cultural Center must be quite different from lessons at the university, huh?"

"Oh, yes," Ahmed replied enthusiastically. "I learn so much. Our teacher is a real French woman and she tells us all about life in France, even explains to us how to cook some French foods. And we do lots of conversation practice."

"Wow, you must be so advanced in French," Leila stared at the table.

"Well, I have been studying for years. Plus, I have relatives who live in Africa and I went to visit them once. There we always spoke French."

"Really?" exclaimed Leila. "You've travelled to Africa?"

"About five years ago. My brother and I went for our summer holidays one year."

"What's it like? It must be so very different."

"Yes, it's very different from here. For one thing, everyone there is black!"

"Everyone?"

"Well, not everyone. There are also some white people. Like my family, who have lived there for more than 50 years."

"Did you go on a safari? Like they show on television?" Leila asked.

Ahmed smiled. "No, I wasn't in that part of Africa. I was in West Africa, where it's part-dry, part-beach, and part farmland. I didn't see any elephants or lions the whole time I was there."

"Oh, that's too bad. I think a safari must be beautiful."

"Do you like animals, then?" asked Ahmed.

"Well, kind of. I don't want to spend lots of time with them. But I think it's incredible that God made so many different types of creatures, and each one looks different, and acts different, from the others. To see so many different animals living in the same place..." Her words drifted into a deep sigh.

"Someday, if God wills, you will be able to go on a safari, then."

Leila smiled and stared out the window. She was captivated by the idea of traveling, of seeing a place so different from Syria.

Their cappuccinos arrived, and they each put two spoons of sugar in their cups and stirred.

Ahmed then asked her, "If you could travel anywhere in the world, is that where you'd go?"

Leila looked back at him. She thought for a moment, then said, "I don't know. That's a hard question. I'd like to go everywhere but hope to go nowhere. You know, my family is very conservative. I don't think they'd ever let me go!"

"That could change someday, couldn't it?" offered Ahmed. "I mean, if you married someone who travelled a lot, maybe you would go with him."

"Such a thing would be the greatest gift..." Leila stopped herself. She was talking with a beautiful young man about marriage. An image of her brother sitting with her mother at the next table over flashed in her mind, so she quickly changed the subject. "Anyway, I don't know where I'd like to travel, but probably I'd want to go somewhere where they speak English so I could practice. I love British novels."

"Britain is beautiful," agreed Ahmed as he smiled and gazed at her.

"Really? Have you been there too?"

"No, not yet anyway. I would also like to go there."

"Is that your first choice for where you'd travel?" asked Leila.

"Hmm... I don't know. I asked you, but I don't have an answer myself!" He laughed, a lovely, quiet and happy laugh.

Leila laughed, too, and teased him on. "Well, so where

would you go?"

He leaned back and grinned while he thought. After a moment, he declared, "Brazil."

"Brazil? Why Brazil?"

"Well, for one, I love coffee. And the best coffee comes from Brazil. Also, I love football, and the best footballers come from Brazil. And I like the beach, and Brazil has lots of beaches."

Leila had also heard great things about Brazil and imagined it would be a fun place to visit. But she also had heard that Brazil had many naked women on the beaches and couldn't help but wonder if that was what Ahmed was really thinking of.

But Ahmed continued, "I also have relatives who live in Brazil, on my mother's side. I don't really know them at all, but when my mother talks about her uncle who went to Brazil, she talks about him being a fun person and says that he is very successful there. I'd like to meet him."

Leila thought that was was very considerate. "So you love your family a lot?"

"Of course. Don't we all?"

"I guess I do, too. But my whole family lives in Dera'a. All my aunts, uncles, cousins. Well, I have a few cousins working in Lebanon, but they still come back to Syria on the weekends. They're just there to work. So I guess I'll never get to travel."

"You're very fortunate to have family close by. Sometimes I feel like my family has lost its soul because we're all spread out."

Leila was impressed by his sensitivity. Her cappuccino cup was almost empty, and there was something she needed to know about him before she could continue being his friend – that was, if he wanted to be her friend.

So she said, slowly, "Family is very important in Islam.

The Prophet, peace be upon him, loved his family and said that man is fulfilled through his family."

"Yes, I know. Because of that, when I pray, I always ask God to give me a good family, a wife who truly worships God and who is both good and faithful."

"That's a good prayer. I'm sure God will accept it."

"*Insha'allah.*"

Leila continued, "But don't you think that a faithful Muslim woman is most likely to care only about Islam and her family... maybe she wouldn't care about anything else in life, like studying or working?"

Ahmed thought about that question for a moment. "I see your point. But that's a very conservative, old-fashioned understanding of Islam. I read about my religion and I read that women are equal to men. It is man's duty to provide for and protect his wife and children, and it is woman's duty to serve her family well. But that doesn't mean only cooking and cleaning the house and teaching her children how to pray. That also means being a person who cares about life. For example, what kind of children would such a traditional woman raise? Not children who are prepared to be productive members of society, always trying to do good. No, I think her children would not be good Muslims, because all they would know is how to pray. They wouldn't understand what their religion is about. I don't know. That's a hard question, but no, I think probably the most dedicated of Muslim women, just like the most dedicated of Muslim men, is someone who wants to learn and understand the world, and to question her faith to always make it stronger. Not someone who just sits around the house, you know?"

Leila nodded. "Yes, the Prophet, peace be upon him, loved his wives and consulted with them. His first wife, Khadija, was a leader in the community and even supported him financially."

"Exactly." Ahmed smiled again and nodded.

They chatted a bit more about Islam, which then turned into a discussion of education and their career goals. Leila told Ahmed how much she wanted to stay in Damascus and work when she graduated, and he seemed to think that was a great idea. He himself didn't know what he would do, but expected that his father would want him working in the family business.

Leila was enjoying herself very much until she saw that it was getting dark. She shouldn't be out with a man after dark, she thought, although maybe it didn't matter whether it was dark or light if you were out alone with a man. But she said, "I think I should go. It's getting late."

"By God, it's still early!" protested Ahmed.

But Leila insisted, "I really should go back and study. But I've enjoyed myself, for sure!"

"Really? You did?"

"Oh, very much!"

Ahmed smiled. "Well, then, let's do it again! Do you have a phone?"

Leila looked down. "No, I don't."

"OK. Well, let me give you my phone number and you call me when you have some free time." He wrote it down on a napkin and gave it to her.

She took the napkin, folded her hands and frowned. "Or... Well, feel free to stop by my building. I'm usually home studying in the afternoons these days." Starting today.

"Very good. I'll do that!" And he smiled that beautiful smile again.

Leila pulled out her wallet to pay, but Ahmed pushed it away. "No, don't even think about it."

Ahmed called over the waiter, asked how much it was, gave him the money, then stood up and accompanied Leila back to her building. They said a quick goodbye, shook hands, then Leila walked into Building 14, leaving Ahmed behind in the courtyard.

Huda was back in the Medina by now. Her lunch with the professor had ended in a rather unusual way. When they'd finished the tea, he had said that there was a room in the back where they would be in peace to study. She had gathered her belongings and followed him, eager to get to the learning part of their appointment. The professor had stopped to chat briefly with a waiter, who handed him a key. Then he had led her past the entrance to the dining room and back into the building corridor. He'd walked to the back of the building and used the key to unlock the door, then pushed it open and gestured for Huda to enter first.

She had stepped into the room and looked for a light switch, since it was completely dark even though it was still light outside. When she'd found it and flipped on the light, she saw a window with closed blinds and a thick curtain pulled shut, a table with two chairs and a lamp in one corner, and... a bed. She had turned around to see the professor pushing the door shut behind him and gesturing for her to sit at the table. Huda had all of a sudden felt very uncomfortable and suspected she was doing something patently wrong. But she had gone ahead and sat down and pulled out her books. The professor had sat in the other chair and started looking through her notes and answering her questions, but all of a sudden he seemed to be in such a rush. He wasn't explaining things well at all, not like he had that other day.

Huda had had trouble concentrating, trying to figure out what she was doing in a closed, darkened room with a bed, alone with her professor. She wasn't really even learning anything in this study session.

So she'd thanked him for his time, stood up and walked out of the room. He had protested, saying they had only just started and he still had plenty of time, but she had said she was getting sleepy after that nice meal – in retrospect not the wisest thing to say – and opened the door. She again had thanked him for telling her about the Syrian judicial system and for suggesting such good food (she couldn't really remember afterwards whether it really was good or not, but she suspected it had not been). Then she'd walked down the hall and started down the stairs, when she remembered she hadn't paid for her meal.

Without looking towards the door to the bedroom, she had marched back up the stairs and into the dining room and asked the waiter how much she owed. He'd looked very surprised and asked her what she meant. For the lunch, she'd said. He'd replied not to worry about it, the professor was a regular and had a tab with them. She had said that she wanted to pay her own way, and he'd said that there was no need. Huda's priority was to get out of there as quickly as possible, so she'd stopped arguing, thanked him and walked out of the building.

She'd come straight back to the Medina, marched up to her room and locked herself in it, reliving the afternoon and making herself sick as she began to piece together what had happened. First she acknowledged that there was a possibility he was really just helping her study in a secluded room. But she scolded herself: if this were really about studying, there were a million more appropriate ways he could have done it. She thought of how he'd asked her all those questions about her dreams and her family and started to feel sick. For the first time she thought of the professor as a man, not just a brain.

Her stomach churned as she thought of the greedy way he'd eaten his food, and he was already so fat. He must be at least fifty years old. Then she thought about the waiter's surprise when she'd gone back to pay and, when she realized what the waiter must have thought was happening in the room, she ran out to the toilet to vomit.

How could she have been so stupid? What would she do? Huda was miserable as she went back to her room and sat down on the bed, shaking. She sat there for an hour with her head in her hands. Then there was a knock at the door. She thought of ignoring it, but then remembered that today had been a big day for Leila. Maybe hearing Leila's tale would help her get her mind back in order, because it was the beginning of exam time and she couldn't let herself be distracted.

Chapter Four

At ten o'clock curfew that night, Leila and Huda were up on the roof. Leila had gone straight to Huda's room after her date with Ahmed and told Huda every last detail, but once she'd finished talking she realized that Huda was in a bad mood. So Leila had invited her friend up to her new favorite spot on the roof, and now they leaned on the ledge on the side that looked up to Mount Qasioun. For half an hour they sat there without talking.

Leila was looking up at the mountain and dreaming of freedom. This time it wasn't just a distant dream, because she could imagine a way she could get there. Ahmed was the first person she'd met since she started university who seemed to understand her. His mother was from her region, so she knew he understood where she came from. He didn't seem to agree with the values of village life, but he did know Islam. He had quoted *Hadith* to her and talked about his perspective on doctrines. He seemed like the kind of guy who prayed five times a day and fasted during Ramadan but who didn't force his friends to do so or abandon his friends because he had to pray at exactly the right time. A reasonable Muslim. When he talked about his idea of the ideal Muslim woman, she had felt flutters in her heart. He loved traveling and languages and learning. He could be someone who understood her.

She thought about his travels to Africa. He had family there... and in Brazil. He must be very rich, she thought. His family would not likely accept a simple village girl like her. Still, his father had married a Dera'awi woman. Ahmed was so sophisticated. So intelligent. And so very handsome. He could have any girl in Damascus, she thought. She wondered if he *did* have any and every girl in Damascus. Still, he understood her. And she understood him. Well, she thought she did, although she realized that he hadn't shared as much about his thoughts and dreams as she had shared about her own.

So she dreamed him into her future. She could marry him, stay in Damascus, get a job as a translator or working at a multinational firm for a few years before she had children. He would take her with him on trips – maybe each year they would holiday with different relatives of his. Maybe sometimes she could accompany him on his business trips for his father's business. She would become sophisticated as she worked with professionals and lived among Damascenes. Together they would present to the world an image of Islam that was progressive, committed, and full of meaning. And she could be one of those women sitting late at night with her family up on the Mountain, seeing and being seen.

While Leila looked out from the roof and fantasized a life of freedom, Huda looked down from the roof grateful for the immense amount of space, and the locked gate, that separated her from the rest of the world. Here she was safe. No one could get to her. She was with women who were either her friends or were harmless. She wouldn't get herself in trouble as long as she was in or on Building 14.

As she sat there, fear began to settle into her gut: a tight knot grabbed at her when she thought of leaving the building. She looked down on the walkways through the Medina grounds, where a few clusters of men still wandered alone. Those men were all students, young, and enthusiastic. Over in the distance, she saw a group of guys sitting around a friend playing the guitar. He was singing a ballad, and she could see the little orange tips of cigarettes lighting up as the guys around him smoked and listened. They seemed so full of life, and so tender-hearted. But for the first time she wondered if that was just an image they portrayed. She wondered what they dreamed about and what they did behind closed doors. Huda glanced at Leila, staring at the mountain with a faint smile on her lips. What about this Ahmed guy? What did he really want with Leila?

Huda still didn't know what her professor wanted with her, but to think of her afternoon at the restaurant made that knot of fear tighten its grip. She wondered if other girls had been there before, if they had gone the distance to see what it was he really wanted, and what he offered in return. If they had given it to him. If they had regretted it afterwards. She wondered if these women around her were really as trustworthy as she thought they were.

But they couldn't do anything to her. Those men maybe could. She looked down at the gate and feared ever walking out of it again.

"Why are you crying?" Leila interrupted her thoughts when she noticed tears on her friend's face.

"What? Oh... Oh, it's nothing." Huda wiped her face with the back of her hand.

"Are you sure?"

"Yeah, yeah. It was just a hard day, that's all."

"Were you studying all day?"

"Well, in the morning. Then I had --" Huda gasped.

"What? What is it?" Leila asked, wondering what terrible thing had happened.

Huda stood up. "I just realized I left my books in the big library. I left there for lunch thinking I'd come back, and I never did. Oh, I hope they'll still be there in the morning."

"I'm sure they will. Who would mess with them?"

"Well, I hope you're right..."

"*Insha'allah*. If God wills, they'll still be there."

Huda sat down and felt tears welling up in her eyes again. "But what if God doesn't will?"

"What do you mean?" asked Leila. "Everything is *nasiib*, God's allotment to us."

"Do you really believe that? I mean, does God really want bad things to happen to us? If my books aren't there in the morning, then I won't be able to study, and I could fail my exams. Then what? That was God's will?"

"Wow, Huda. What's going on?"

"It just seems like at a time like this I should do something, not just hope for God to do the right thing."

"God, the Lord of all the worlds, is all-powerful. Do you really think you can change what he has already written for you?"

"Well, maybe he hasn't. Maybe bad things really do happen, and it's our job to change them!"

"Wow, you're really stressed," observed Leila. "I think you probably need to take the day off tomorrow. I'll ask God for you, but I'm sure if you're living a righteous life and worshiping him, he won't make bad things happen to you."

"Oh, maybe. Maybe I am just a bad person." At this, Huda burst out in tears again and Leila sat next to her, awkwardly. She reached out her arm and put it on Huda's shoulder, which made Huda cry even harder. So Leila pulled closer to Huda and hugged her. Huda leaned her head on Leila's shoulder and had a good long cry.

After a few minutes, Huda stood up and walked around in a circle, wiping her face and her eyes with her sleeve. She really needed a tissue, but neither girl had one and neither one suggested that they return to their floor. She sniffled and tried to re-gain her composure.

Huda then asked Leila, "Do you think I'm a bad person?"

"No, why would I think that?"

"Well, I'm not really all that religious. I mean, I believe in

God and all, but I don't have a faith like you do. Maybe I need to do more to help the poor, and study less."

"No, I think you're a good person. You do care about others and you are studying, but only so you can help people more later."

Huda knew that Leila was saying that just to make her feel better – they both knew that Huda's main motivation in life was her own career, not helping other people. But it did somehow make her feel better.

Then Leila said, "Don't worry about your books. I'm sure they'll still be there in the morning. Anyway, it's too late to do anything about it now – it's not like anyone is going to need your table overnight."

"I hope you're right."

"You know what you need? A day off. I think a day not thinking about studying and not worrying about anything might be just the best thing to get you back to normal. And tomorrow's Friday, so we really shouldn't study on a Friday anyway."

"Why not?"

"Well, Friday, you know, it's the day off. It's the day to go to the mosque and be with family – but we don't go to the mosque and our families aren't here. So we can pray together in the morning and do something special in the afternoon – we'll be each other's family!"

Huda thought about what had happened to her earlier that day. She looked down at the building gate and thought that she really didn't want to leave the building tomorrow. She'd have to go out to get her books, but the last thing she wanted to do was to be outside, to be around any men, really. The last thing in the world she wanted was to see that professor again.

But she was too ashamed to explain any of this to Leila, who was beaming about her idea and making plans. "We can cook ourselves something nice for lunch, maybe stuffed squash, and then we can go to the *souq* and shop, and then we can go for a walk... Who knows, maybe we can call Ahmed and he can take us out..."

They started the walk back downstairs, Huda thinking that she would explain to Leila in the morning and Leila chattering about fun things they could do. When they got to their floor, Leila saw a note on her door.

"I wonder who that's from!" she walked quickly over to it.

Huda silently unlocked the door to her own room as Leila read the note.

"It's from Roxy!" exclaimed Leila. "She's here tonight and came by to see me, and she said she has a question – she wants me to come by."

"Tell her I said hi," offered Huda.

"Do you want to come with me?"

"No. I'm really tired. I think I'll go to sleep."

Leila didn't push when she noticed Huda's eyes were still red. "Alright. Rest well. What time should I come by in the morning to start our day off?"

"Oh, anytime. I have to go out first thing to get my books." Huda really wished Leila would offer to go with her. She dreaded going out there by herself.

No luck. "Ok. I'll be by around ten or so, then. See you then!"

"Yeah. See you then. Good night."

"Good night. Sleep well."

The next morning, Leila knocked on Huda's door at half past ten. Huda, feeling much better but still a little shaken up from her trip to the student center at 8:00 that morning (she'd felt a strange increase in her heartbeat every time she passed a man – fortunately there hadn't been that many of them out early on a Friday morning), opened the door and

Leila rushed in.

"You'll never guess what. This is perfect!" Leila squealed as soon as the door was open, without even greeting Huda with a good morning or a kiss on the cheeks.

"What?"

"So last night, I went over to Mary and Ghalia's room, and they were there with Roxy. Roxy was there spending the night – I guess it was her night 'off'," Leila winked as she sat down on the bed. "So remember the note that said she had a question? Well, she wanted to invite me – and you, of course – up to spend tonight up on the mountain with her and her husband and Mary and Ghalia. Well, I tried to explain to them that I couldn't – I don't know if they really understood that I just can't go out and spend all night out with no *mahram* chaperone. But anyway, I did tell them that I couldn't spend the night out, so Roxy said that maybe we could do it earlier in the day. I said that it's still a bit *haram*, and that I'd promised to spend the day with you, and she said that that was perfect, because you and I and the three of them and her husband could all go up on the mountain in the afternoon together, and she promised to have us back for curfew!" Leila stopped to take a breath, and Huda sat down waiting for her to finish. "So anyway, Roxy said that her husband would really like to invite us, her friends, out, and he's a real gentleman that way. So she pulled out her phone – she has a mobile phone, can you believe it - and called him, and he said that that'd be fine. We could go up around 5:00 and be back well in time for when they close the building gates. So, what do you think?"

Huda took a gulp of air and tried to figure out what to say. She couldn't think of a worse way to spend the afternoon. She had thought she'd be able to convince Leila to just stay in the Medina with her that afternoon, but not with all these other people involved.

"Doesn't it sound like fun? I have been dreaming of going up on the mountain for so long!" Leila enthused.

"Actually," started Huda. "Well, actually, I don't think I should go. Maybe I should stay in and study..."

"Study?" exclaimed Leila. "Today's the day off, remember?"

"Yes, I know. But you know me. I'll take the morning and the afternoon, but maybe at 5:00 you go with them and I'll stay here."

"Do you not like Roxy?"

"No, it's not that. It's just not a good day for me to go out, that's all."

"Huda, did something happen yesterday that you're not telling me? Were your books there when you got to the library, by the way?"

"Yes, my books were there. And no, nothing happened. It's just that--" she couldn't think of what to say, so left it at that.

Leila conceded, "OK. We'll leave it for now, but let's see how you're feeling come 5:00. Agreed?"

Huda agreed to leave the decision for later, and Leila asked her if she was ready for Friday prayers. Huda had never done Friday prayers before so didn't really know. Leila explained that they would wash for prayer together, then pray, then read the Qur'an. Nothing too unusual.

So they went together to Leila's room, which was empty since Fatima had left for the weekend, and for the next hour they did all these things together. Leila was surprised at how little Huda knew about her religion – Leila had to teach her how to wash correctly, then they couldn't pray at the same time because Huda didn't have a prayer rug. So first Leila prayed and then Huda, but only after careful instructions from Leila. Leila told her exactly how it had to be, step by step, but Huda still did her own version of the rituals. Leila shrugged and waited patiently on her bed for Huda to finish. Then Leila asked Huda to keep her scarf on, and she herself covered her head and pulled out the Qur'an. First she recited the *Fatiha*, the opening chapter of the Qur'an, then she started reading from her favorite chapter, the one about Mary. Huda listened as Leila chanted, only glancing at the pages as she recited the verses from heart. Leila asked Huda if she wanted a turn, but Huda knew Leila would be offended by her butchering of the Qur'anic poetry. So that was the end of their prayer time.

It was just about noon when they finished. The girls took stock of what food they had between the two of them and concluded that stuffed koussa was the best thing to make: they just needed the squash to stuff, some parsley and a tub of yogurt. The stores would just be beginning to open, so they took their time getting dressed before going to the store.

It really was a lovely afternoon. The girls sat and chatted about faith and religion and living a good life while they gutted the squash, made the filling of rice and parsley and tomatoes and spices, then stuffed the squash. Around 3:00 p.m. they put the stuffed koussa into a pot in the deserted hallway to start cooking. An hour later they were digging into their Friday lunch. They had made enough for three meals, but they didn't have a refrigerator, and it seemed there was no one else on the floor to share their lunch with, so they put the lid on the pot and put it in a cool shady corner of the room for later.

The girls were sitting on Leila's bed cross-legged, sipping strong sweet tea, when the bell rang. Huda looked at Leila as if to ask whether she was expecting someone. No, Leila assured her, she hadn't been expecting anyone – maybe it was Roxy with some updated plans for the evening.

Leila grabbed a scarf and walked over to the hallway that

had the window onto the courtyard. To her amazement, Ahmed sat on a ledge, cross-legged, smoking a cigarette. Leila's heart skipped a beat and she ran back to her room.

"It's Ahmed! He's downstairs!" exclaimed Leila as she rushed into the room.

Huda raised her eyebrows. "He just came by, on a Friday afternoon?"

"Yes, I guess so. I only just saw him yesterday!"

"He must really like you," commented Huda.

"Oh, what should I do?"

"Calm down, throw on something decent, go down there and find out what he wants."

"Right, right." nodded Leila. "What should I wear?"

Huda smiled. "Don't worry about it. Just put a nice scarf on with something. Then tell him that you can't stay long. For now, just find out what he's doing here."

"Right." Leila walked to her closet, found her brown overcoat, put it on over her pajamas, and slipped a black scarf on her head. "Wish me luck!" she yelled over her shoulder as she ran out the door, leaving Huda sitting there wondering about this guy who was back after less than a day, pondering whether there was anything to be concerned about.

When Leila got downstairs, she came out to the gate and saw Ahmed sitting alone on a ledge, fiddling on his mobile. All of a sudden it occurred to her that maybe he wasn't here for her. Maybe someone else had rung her bell. She quickly looked around the courtyard and didn't recognize anyone. So she walked up to him. "*Ahlan*. Hello," she said.

Ahmed looked up and his face quickly broke into a big grin. "Well, Good afternoon, Miss Leila!" he said.

"How are you doing?"

"I'm well, thank you. And have you had a good Friday?"

"Yes, thank you. My friend Huda and I are taking a day

off. No studying."

"Congratulations. I'm sure you deserve it."

"Hopefully it's good. I didn't expect to see you so soon!"

"You didn't?" He seemed genuinely surprised.

Leila wondered if there was something she had missed yesterday. Had he said he was stopping by and she'd forgotten? "Well, no."

"I really wanted to see you again. I had such a wonderful time yesterday and didn't want to wait. And you said I could come by sometime, didn't you?"

"Yes, I suppose I did!"

"Are you happy to see me?"

Leila felt shy all of a sudden. She nodded her head yes, then quickly looked down.

"So!" He motioned for her to sit down. "Can you go out now?"

"Oh... I promised Huda that I'd spend the whole day with her. And we're going out with some friends later. So I don't think I can talk long, actually."

"That's too bad. What are you going to do?"

"I'm so excited!" Leila's face brightened as she thought of the mountain. "My friend's husband has a car, and he's going to take her, her cousins, and me up on Mount Qasioun. I've never been up there and have wanted to go for so long."

"Really? It's not that special." Ahmed smiled, and Leila thought he was probably teasing her. "Come with me. I'll show you some truly amazing things in Damascus!"

"Oh, that's so shameful! Don't even say such a thing!" Even if it was a joke, it might be going a bit too far.

"I'm sorry. You're right."

"And anyway, I really want to see the mountain. It's a dream of mine."

"OK," Ahmed consented. "So can I go?"

"What?" Leila was shocked.

"Why don't I go with you to the mountain?"

"I don't know. How would I explain it to my friends?" Leila was sure he must know how awkward such a situation would be.

Ahmed didn't answer for a moment. He pulled out a cigarette. Leila was relieved that he didn't offer her one – good girls didn't smoke. He lit it and took a few breaths. Then he turned to Leila and suggested, "What if my sister came with us?"

"Your sister? But I've never met her." Leila thought that was a great idea – that meant that he wasn't embarrassed about her to tell his family, and it made the whole thing much more respectable. But it must be a big deal to tell his sister and bring her.

Ahmed seemed to brighten as he considered this idea. "I'll go home now and invite her to go with us. I already told her about you, and she said she'd like to meet you – I think the two of you would get along great."

"Alright," conceded Leila. "That'd be nice. But, I don't think he has room in his car for two more. I don't really know my friend's husband, but there's already six of us."

"Well, then, does your friend have a phone?"

"Yes, she does!"

"Do you know her number?"

"No."

"Well, you have my number, right? Why don't you call us when you know where you'll be on the mountain, and we'll come to meet you there."

Leila was surprised at this whole plan. It all sounded too good to resist, and it seemed like there wasn't any reason to do so. So she said she'd call him. She had a feeling Roxy would find the whole thing exciting and would be happy to make it happen.

Leila stood up, and Ahmed stood up with her, stomping

out his cigarette. He shook Leila's hand, smiled and winked at her, Leila's heart melted, and they said goodbye, but only until the evening.

When it came time to go find Mary and Ghalia, Leila was alone. There was no way she could convince Huda to join her. She didn't understand why, but Huda absolutely refused to go out with them. At this point Leila was too committed to cancel her plans, and really, she was very excited about the whole thing. So she left Huda in her room, hoping that everything was okay, and went to Mary and Ghalia's room to walk together to the front entrance of the Medina, where they were to meet the happy couple.

The three girls were standing outside the Medina gate when a big grey Dodge sedan pulled up, and Roxy jumped out of the passenger side of the car. She ran around the car and gave each girl a loud kiss on each cheek.

"Wow, what an outfit!" she exclaimed when she saw Leila in her nicest chocolate brown overcoat and two scarves on her head, white on the bottom and pink on top.

"Really? You like it?" Leila was surprised but flattered.

"I've never seen you dressed up to go out before!" Roxy explained.

"Oh. You mean..." Leila's heart sunk. She must look like a real rag in her big overcoat compared to these three fashionable women.

"No! No! It suits you," Roxy beamed. "Come meet my husband."

Roxy ran back around to the passenger seat, Mary opened the door to the backseat and gestured for Leila to get in first. As she inched over to the far end of the wide bench seat, Roxy said, "Bassel, meet my friend Leila who I was telling you about."

Bassel turned and reached out his hand to shake Leila's,

then he shook hands with each of the cousins. He was much older than Leila had imagined: he had to be at least in his 40's. He looked rich and had a jovial face. He wasn't ugly, but Leila didn't find him attractive either. He had gray hair, was not thin but not fat, had sun-worn skin and gave Leila the overall impression that he was someone who would be fun to have as a father.

Once they were all settled in the car and had greeted all around, Roxy turned to Leila and asked if her friend was coming soon.

"She's not coming. I'm sorry. She said she couldn't come."

"That's too bad." Roxy didn't seem to mind either way.

"Yes, she told me to say hi to you all," said Leila.

They all smiled and nodded. Bassel pulled onto the highway and started driving. Roxy leaned on the back of her chair facing Leila. "So? How's it going? Anything interesting besides schoolwork?"

Leila cringed. "Yes, schoolwork. That's not going so much. I don't want to think about it!"

"Good." smiled Roxy. "Neither do I."

"Actually," said Leila. "There is something else going on and I need to ask for your help." She looked around the car. Bassel was intent on driving very fast and swerving around cars. Mary and Ghalia were staring at her, waiting to hear the request. Leila hesitated.

"What is it? Is it scandalous?" asked Roxy. "I love good stories!"

"Well..." Maybe she wouldn't tell. She'd call Ahmed later and explain to him that it hadn't been appropriate to call him. Hopefully he'd understand. He had to.

Ghalia put her hand on Leila's arm. "We won't tell. We'll keep it our secret."

"You promise you won't tell?" Leila looked at all three girls, and they smiled.

"Go on," smiled Mary.

Roxy grabbed both of Leila's hands and asked, "Is it a boy?" At which Leila felt her face turn bright red and the other girls burst out laughing.

"Enough! I'll tell you," Leila sighed. "Well, I have a friend who would like to come along. He came by this afternoon and when I told him what we were doing, he asked if he could join us up on the mountain, him and his sister."

"'So there is a boy!" smiled Roxy.

"Well, he's a classmate, a friend from class, that's all."

"Yeah, right," said Roxy. "I thought you looked different, and it wasn't just the outfit. You have that I-met-a-boy look."

"There's an I-met-a-boy-look?" asked Leila.

"Well, there must be, because you have it!" retorted Roxy.

"I *do* rather like him. But that was it. He said he and his sister would like to go up to the mountain tonight, and maybe they could meet us. Since you have a phone, I thought maybe..."

"You want me to call him and tell him where we'll be! That's alright, Bassel *habibi*, isn't it? If Leila's friends join us on the mountain?"

"They are very welcome."

"Do you know where we'll be?" Roxy asked him.

"Not yet. But you can call and tell him that we'll meet him near a restaurant called The View. It's pretty well known."

"Here you go," said Roxy cheerfully, handing Leila the phone.

Leila looked at the phone. She hadn't thought that it would involve her calling him. She had imagined loud and confident Roxy would call. "Can't you?"

"Why? I don't know him. It's fine. I have plenty of credit on my phone."

So, with a trembling hand, Leila pulled the napkin on which he'd written his number out of her purse and dialed the number on Roxy's phone. Her heart was pounding as it rang, but the conversation actually went quite smoothly. Ahmed answered immediately and she recognized his voice. She told him that they were on their way to The View restaurant and they'd meet him there. This was her friend Roxy's number, and maybe they could just call her when they got to the mountain. Ahmed said they'd be there within an hour. He'd told his sister already, and they were looking forward to it. And that was it.

Leila gave the phone back to a beaming Roxy and looked out the window. They were now on a winding road, already headed up the side of the mountain. It looked quiet and desolate, and Leila wondered that a place that looked so glorious from below could be so barren from close up. The air was getting fresher and cooler, she noticed, and already they were passing a few families picnicking on the side of the road. For about ten minutes they drove back and forth, passing the exit for a suburb which Roxy told her was where she lived, and the tomb of the unknown soldier, and more picnickers. Then they pulled onto a straight and flat street. Leila gasped.

Out her window, the right window, was all of Damascus. The whole city lay out below her like a big gray rug. There were hundreds of houses, lining hundreds of streets, little pockets of green here and there, little figures moving around like ants, which Leila assumed were cars. It went on as far as she could see, until it blended into the smog near the horizon. It was the most breathtaking sight she had ever seen.

Mary and Ghalia were chatting about something, occasionally looking over Leila's shoulder at the city. Roxy and Bassel were discussing where they'd go first and where they should park. And Leila just stared.

Soon, Bassel parked and they all got out. Bassel tossed a

few Syrian Lira to a young man who offered to look after the car for them, and Roxy suggested maybe they should walk along the pathway on the mountain ridge for a while before going into a restaurant. The three girls all agreed. Mary and Ghalia started off arm in arm, and Roxy grabbed Leila's arm to walk behind them. Bassel brought up the rear. Leila was silent as they walked, taking in the spectacular scene. After a few minutes, Roxy started telling her about the last time she and Bassel had come, where they'd walked, what they'd eaten, how crowded it was. Leila half-listened, nodding occasionally. From behind, Bassel would occasionally point out landmarks: the Old City and the Omayad mosque, the university and the Medina, the central bus station. Leila followed his eyes and her wonder increased as she began to actually recognize places.

After a bit they stopped and sat on a ledge where they had a commanding view of Damascus. They continued to look and point as they identified familiar landmarks. Then Bassel explained to them how, just a few years before, there hadn't been any restaurants on the lookout road. They'd been shut down several years earlier, for security reasons, he thought. But it was now three years since they had re-opened access to restaurants, and very few spots remained like this one, where they could sit and enjoy the view without dealing with waiters and restaurant windows and the like.

Mary and Ghalia seemed reasonably impressed, but Leila knew that she would never in her life forget this night. She almost forgot about Ahmed, but Roxy came up to her as they were all deep in their own thoughts and asked, "The View is about a ten minute walk that way. Do you want to go meet them, or should we wait for them to call?"

"Oh!" exclaimed Leila. "We're not going to eat at The View?"

"Well, Bassel thinks this other place just this way is

better, and it doesn't require a reservation. Often you don't get a seat at The View without a reservation."

"I see. I don't know. Can you tell him to go to the other restaurant?"

"Why don't you go to meet him?" Roxy asked with a twinkle in her eyes.

"Oh, no, I couldn't do that. Well, I guess if you came with me... Can you come with me to meet him?"

"Are you sure you want me to?"

"Yes, please, Roxy! Don't leave me alone."

So Roxy told Bassel that she and Leila would go over to wait for Ahmed, and he and the cousins could go on into the restaurant. Roxy took Leila's arm again, and they headed down the road to find Ahmed and his sister.

"So," said Roxy once they were walking alone. "Tell me about this Ahmed."

"There's not much to tell," replied Leila meekly. "He's in my French class."

"French! So romantic!"

"Oh, please, don't say that. No one can even know that we're friends. Can you imagine if my family found out?"

"That'd be bad?"

Leila almost asked Roxy how she'd feel if her family found out about her marriage, but caught herself and said, "In our family we don't do those kinds of things."

"Alright, then. I promise to keep it a secret. But tell me about him. Is he good-looking? Is he kind?"

Leila started telling Roxy all about him. She started with the practical things, like that he was a good student, studying Business, from Damascus. But Roxy was being such a good listener and Leila was basking in the attention, so soon she found herself explaining to Roxy how her heart melted every time he smiled, and that it seemed they had so many common interests.

Roxy listened in silence. They arrived at the restaurant, and Roxy pulled her phone out of her bag to make sure she'd see if it rang. Then she asked Leila if she'd met the sister.

"No, never. I never really even talked to him before this week."

"Well, I hope she's nice."

"What do you mean?" asked Leila, surprised at the tone in Roxy's voice.

"Well," said Roxy, "His sister has a lot of control, doesn't she? If you want to win him, you need to win her, because she's the door into his family."

"I hadn't really thought of it that way before. He just suggested today that he bring her, because I said I couldn't meet him alone."

"He's a clever guy. He seems to know what he wants and how to get it. I can't wait to meet him."

At that moment, Roxy's phone rang. She answered it, then with her phone to her ear stood up and looked down the pathway in one direction, and then in the other direction. She told Leila to wait there and went to ask something of the man standing at the entrance to The View. She then talked a bit more on the phone and hung up.

"What is it?" asked Leila.

"He didn't know which direction we were, so he went to a different restaurant. But he'll be here in a moment."

Leila's heart started beating more rapidly. He was here, on the mountain. She wondered if it would be awkward, their second scheduled meeting. She wondered what it would be like with her friends and his sister with them. She felt her whole body tense up as she nervously considered the situation she was getting herself into.

And then he was there, with a young teenage girl who was wearing a multicolored headscarf and a very stylish bright pink tunic over rather tight jeans. She had makeup on and was just a tad heavyset.

Ahmed greeted Leila, then introduced his sister Nisreen. Roxy introduced herself to Ahmed and Nisreen. She then led them back in the direction of Bassel and the girls.

Nisreen grabbed Leila and pulled back, leaving Ahmed walking ahead with Roxy. She oozed, "I'm so glad to finally meet you! Ahmed has talked a lot about you."

"Really?" Leila hadn't known Ahmed all that long, and was it really normal for a brother to talk to his sister about such things?

"Oh yes. He tells me everything. He's my favorite brother."

"How many do you have?"

"Oh, just Ahmed," Nisreen said matter-of-factly. "But he has been telling me for more than a month about a girl in his French class – you. And I'm finally getting to meet you!"

"A month?" asked Leila. That very first meeting in the tunnel store was a month ago. He had noticed her then?

"Yes! Anyway, he's told me all about you, that you're smart, that you're from near our mother's village, that you have the same interests as he has." Nisreen kept rattling off things that her brother had said about his new friend, making Leila more and more embarrassed. But then Nisreen changed subjects. "He told me you're an English literature major and you read lots of English novels. I want to be an English literature major when I finish my baccalaureate."

"Really?" asked Leila. "Why?"

"Why not? Don't you like it?"

"Yes, I love it! I love learning English, and I love reading things that were written in English. And I love reading stories written in England and America."

"I love reading, too." Nisreen looked up at Leila with a big grin.

"What do you read?" Leila asked.

"Oh, everything. I read novels in Arabic and novels in English and things from other languages that have been translated. Like Paulo Coelho. Have you read *The Alchemist*?"

Leila frowned. "No. Who is he?"

"He's a Brazilian author who writes about spiritual things, but in novels."

"Really?"

"Yes. I've read a couple of his books. He uses things from all the big religions and from other types of spirituality also."

Leila was a bit surprised that this young Damascene girl would be allowed to read things that drew from many religions. It seemed like it might not be a good idea for a good Muslim girl.

Nisreen went on. "*The Alchemist* is my favorite. Maybe it's his most famous book. It's about a man who travels from Spain down to Morocco and all the way across Africa to Egypt to find someone who can make gold. And on the way he has lots of adventures and learns things about himself and about ultimate reality and all."

At this point, Leila couldn't resist asking, "But isn't that against Islam?"

"Oh, I'm too young to know everything about religion. Ask Ahmed. But he told me it's good to know a lot about a lot of things, to be a better Muslim than if we don't know much about anything. Does that make sense?"

"Yes," murmured Leila. "He did say something like that to me also."

"Well, don't you agree?" asked Nisreen.

"I'm young, too, I guess. It sounds good, but I also think it's important to be faithful. The most important thing is to be a good Muslim: pray, fast, be a good daughter, please your family."

"Well, I can do all those things!"

"I guess you can," smiled Leila. "So you want to be an English major?" She was already feeling a big-sisterly affection toward this enthusiastic and confident, but also innocent and impressionable, girl.

Nisreen told Leila that she studied English at the American Language Center as well as for her baccalaureate, that she watched films in English and tried to listen without using the subtitles, that she wanted to travel to Britain someday, that she had already read a few books in English and hadn't understood everything, but she did understand some and really liked it, and didn't Leila think that it was so romantic to get a degree for reading English novels?

Leila barely got another word in before they arrived at the restaurant where Bassel, Mary and Ghalia were sitting. They already had drinks but hadn't ordered any food yet. Roxy was very thoughtful in introducing Ahmed and Nisreen as "Leila's friend Nisreen, and her brother Ahmed." She sat down next to Bassel, had Nisreen sit next to her, and then Ahmed. Leila sat on the other side of the table next to Ghalia, which placed her directly across from Nisreen and facing Ahmed. Then Bassel said that Leila should get to sit closer to the window, since this was her first time on the mountain, so he offered to trade places with Leila. Roxy was having way too much fun with Leila's little romance to lose her moment, so she told everyone to stand up and then instructed them where they should sit: Leila by the window, next to Nisreen, then Ahmed, then Bassel. Across from them were Mary, Ghalia and Roxy. This put Roxy right across from Ahmed, in a place where she could carefully keep directing his attention toward the window, and Leila.

She needn't have worried, though, as once they had ordered, Ahmed looked over Nisreen's shoulder and chatted with Leila. He asked her what she thought of the mountain, and Leila assured him nowhere else could have been so beautiful, so he promised to try to impress her more the next time. As the meal went on, he chatted with Bassel and with Roxy, Leila and Nisreen continued to get to know each other, sometimes everyone talked together, and sometimes Leila just enjoyed the view. But every few minutes Ahmed would look over and make sure his girls were doing alright, and whenever he smiled at Leila, she felt a flutter in her tummy.

It was a glorious meal. Bassel ordered all different types of *mezze* dishes: hummous, muttabel, tabouli, kibbe na'em, kashke, fried potatoes, fattoush, buraq, stuffed grape leaves, and some things that Leila had never tried before that evening. There was normal flatbread, and fresh naan bread, and even some sweetbread. Then there was an assortment of grilled meats, spicy and not spicy, served with loads of parsley and some cut up vegetables. There were two arguile pipes. Roxy, Mary and Ghalia shared one, and Bassel and Ahmed shared the other after Leila and Nisreen politely refused. There was tea and cappuccino and big baskets of fruit at the end. Bassel tried to convince them to order cakes and ice cream, but Leila was sure no more food would fit, and it seemed everyone else was quite filled up as well. Ahmed and Bassel got into a bit of an argument over who would pay, but Bassel won in the end. After all, this whole party had been his idea.

It was nine o'clock at this point, and when Leila caught a glimpse of Ahmed's watch, she gasped.

"Roxy!" Leila hissed, trying to get her attention from across the table. "Roxy!"

Roxy looked over and raised her eyebrows.

Leila pointed to her wrist. Roxy looked at the clock on her phone and smiled. Leila understood her to be saying, "We have plenty of time!" But Leila never got home this late and didn't want the other Dera'a girls asking what she was doing out so late.

It turned out Mary and Ghalia were planning on spending the night at Roxy's that night, so it was only Leila who needed to rush down the mountain. Leila was beginning to worry she would end up at Roxy's house as well, but she felt she needed to get back to the Medina. When Ahmed caught on to all the hissing and gesturing among the girls, he looked at his watch and said, "Oh, it's time to be going, isn't it?"

"No, it's still early," pronounced Bassel.

"Please," pleaded Leila. "I actually do need to go."

It seemed the others were in no rush to leave, and Leila wondered if she should catch a taxi, although going alone on that isolated road seemed like a bad idea. Then Ahmed offered to take her.

"I need to be going myself. Nisreen needs to be at school tomorrow, and I should get her home."

And that settled it. Ahmed and Nisreen would take Leila back to the Medina in a taxi, and the others could stay up on the mountain as long as they wished. Leila was sorry to leave them, thinking how much fun they might have as the night went on. But leaving wasn't very painful at all if Ahmed was taking her. She got up and exchanged kisses with Mary and Ghalia and Roxy.

When she said goodbye to Roxy, Roxy whispered in her ear, "He's a great guy. Enjoy it! I love you, *habibti*." Then she gave Leila a big hug.

Chapter Five

Huda's first exam was a few days later. She hadn't left the building except to buy the most basic of supplies at the store right outside her building. She missed her morning walks, but she'd gone up early a few mornings to walk around the roof a few times. Her new study corner was in the building library, where no men dared tread.

She had seen Leila a few times in the hallway, but had tried to avoid her as much as possible. Leila seemed so happy these days, talking about her new friend Ahmed, her adventure on the mountain, and not much at all about her exams. Huda hadn't told Leila anything about her eery lunch date, but Leila seemed to know that something was wrong because she too didn't make much effort to talk with Huda. As long as Huda didn't volunteer any information, Leila seemed happy to ignore it. It seemed she didn't want to allow sadness to invade her kind of joy.

So Wednesday morning, Huda awoke early as usual and went up to the roof to walk a bit before getting ready for the day. Her exam was at 10:00, and she knew that, as much as she didn't want to go to the Law building, she would not give up her life because of one bad memory. So her plan was to be all ready, study in the Building 14 library until 9:45, then walk into the exam room just in time to take the exam.

This she did. She arrived in the exam hall just before ten, and at ten o'clock sharp the doors were closed and the exam began. When she started reading the questions, she began to calm down. She knew this stuff. She'd memorized every lecture and planned for every possible essay question. She was ready. So the exam became therapeutic as she went through the questions almost by rote. When she finished, she read over her answers and felt surprisingly confident and calm as she read question after question and felt sure that she had put the correct answer the first time.

When she finished reading it over, only a few people had already turned in their exams. She picked up her purse, walked to the front, turned the papers over to the invigilator, and walked out of the room. She'd planned on stopping to pick up some food and walking straight back to her room, but she was feeling so much better now, that the thought of some fresh air was becoming irresistible. Maybe she would go for a walk up the highway, just a little walk before going to her room. Maybe buy some juice at her favorite juice stand to celebrate.

As she walked out of the building, though, fate had the professor pass right in front of her! She felt a bit of nausea as she saw the short gray-haired, potbellied figure walking her way. He was on his way into the building, chatting with a colleague. When he noticed her, he quickly took leave of his friend and came over to intercept Huda on her way out. Huda tried pretending she hadn't seen him, but he planted himself right in her path, and there was no escape. So she figured she should act like all was normal.

"Hello, Professor."

"Hello, Huda. How are you?"

"I'm okay. Just took my constitutional law exam."

"You did well, I hope?"

"I think so, thank you." Huda nodded and was about to walk away, but he didn't seem ready to let her.

"What happened the other day, *habibti*? Why did you leave so quickly?"

Huda froze. Did he just call her *habibti* – his dear one? What should she say? She took a deep breath, then stuttered, "It was getting late. I didn't want to take too much of your time. Actually, I'm late for an appointment now. I should really get going."

The professor seemed a bit irritated. And Huda was working very hard to avoid looking in his eyes, because she had a feeling that that sight might give her nightmares. So she took her leave.

As she walked toward the steps, the professor called out to her, "Huda, I really need to talk to you. Why don't you come by my office tomorrow? It's important."

"Really important?" Huda asked him.

"Yes, it's about your scores."

That caught Huda's attention. What could he possibly know about her scores on the first day of exams? But the way he said it, it sounded like he really did know something, and she couldn't take any risks on failing. So she agreed to come find him after her exam the following day. Then she ran straight back to her room.

When she finished her second exam the next morning, Huda dutifully went to her professor's room. The night before, she had knocked on the doors of some of her course mates in the hopes that one of them would go with her to her meeting. No one was home, except for one girl who had another appointment. She'd said she would cancel if it was important, but Huda hadn't wanted to explain why she was desperate for company, so told her friend it was no big deal. She'd thought of Leila, but knew that Leila would want to know everything, and Huda wasn't ready for that.

So here she was in the law building, all by herself, heart beating wildly, once again in her professor's office with the door closed.

"Huda, I really need to talk to you about your scores," began the professor.

Huda sat bolt upright in the chair across from his desk.

She'd brought her books, though she was sure she wouldn't be getting any more tutoring from him.

"Why?" she asked with what she hoped sounded like the most natural type of alarm. "Is something the matter?"

"Not necessarily. That depends on you."

"I'm studying very hard! Is there something I'm forgetting to do?"

"Not yet. But there could be."

Huda wondered if he could see how nervous she was. Probably. Nonetheless, she was grateful that he still cared about her scores, even after the unsettling lunch encounter. "Thank you, sir. It's very important to me to do well. I'm working as hard as I can."

"I know you are, Huda."

"I'll do whatever I need to do to succeed!"

"Whatever you need?"

"Yes! Just tell me what's missing, and I'll work to do it."

"I'm glad to hear of that kind of commitment, Huda."

"Sir, I very much want to be a successful lawyer and help Syria."

Then he seemed to change the subject. "Huda, you ran off on Thursday with no explanation."

"I told you, sir, that it was late. I didn't realize it was getting so late."

"Are you sure that's it?"

"Yes, sir. Why?"

"Well, see, I love my students and am happy to help them. But it's not really that simple."

Huda wanted to ask him exactly what he meant, but she was scared to hear the answer.

He continued, "You see, academic success is not just about studying for the exams."

"I really try to learn about law, not just pass the exams," Huda assured him.

"I know you do. But there's still more."

"An internship? It would be such a privilege to work as a law intern."

"No, that doesn't usually happen at this stage. You're still too young for that."

"Oh."

"No, what I'm saying is... Well, if you want my help, you need to really be committed."

"But I am, sir."

"Running away in the middle of a study session is not commitment."

"Sir, with all due respect, were you all that interested in studying? I felt that you were tired."

"Yes, I was. You're right. But studying, well, studying is about more than just the content. You should have stayed with me when I was tired."

"But I let you rest."

"You could have rested with me."

At this, Huda could take the façade no more. "Sir, I don't know what you think of me, but I am a respectable girl from a respectable family. I realized afterwards that it was inappropriate for me to go to lunch alone with a professor, and I shouldn't even be sitting here alone in a closed room with you now. I admire you very much. I am eternally grateful for the help I've received from one of Syria's most influential and important lawyers, but I can no longer accept tutoring from you."

She stood up and turned to leave.

"Sit down, Huda." The tone in his voice was not so kind anymore.

"Why?"

"Sit down."

She sat down.

After a moment's silence, he stated, "You don't

understand. You don't have a choice. We will study together. Today is Thursday. You don't have any exams on Saturday, do you?"

"No."

"Saturday, 3:00. Same restaurant. We will study together." There was no mistaking the threat in his voice. Then, after another pause, his tone was back to that of the jovial, helpful professor. "I really just want the best for you. You are a good student, Huda. I'll see you on Saturday!"

Huda arrived back on her floor in a daze. She felt like she should be shaking and weeping, but she felt nothing. She unlocked the door, threw her bags on her bed, changed into her slippers, went to the toilet, then went straight back to her room and sat rigidly on her bed, both feet on the ground and both arms at her sides.

A minute later – or was it an hour later? - Maha poked her head in.

"Happy Thursday!" said Maha cheerfully.

Huda looked up and stared at Maha.

Maha's smile disappeared and she walked into the room. "What's the matter?"

Huda looked down, so Maha silently sat beside her. After a moment, she said, "Huda?"

Huda looked up again. This time she answered, "Hello, Maha."

"What's with you?"

Huda managed a small smile. "It's been a very long day. I think maybe I've been studying too hard. I don't know what I'm going to do."

Maha looked relieved. "Oh, that's alright. We all have days like that. You just need a good rest. When's the last time you took an afternoon nap?"

"A nap... yes, it's been a long time."

"Well, here," Maha stood up and fluffed Huda's pillow. She moved the books onto a nearby chair. Then, as she helped Huda to lift her feet onto the bed and rest her head, she soothed, "Yes, there, just make yourself comfortable. What you need is a good nap. I know, I'll come back in a few hours and let's get sandwiches together. How about that? And I'll find Leila. That will be a nice way to spend a Thursday afternoon. Then tomorrow you'll be all ready to go again!"

Huda obeyed Maha and lay down. She didn't close her eyes, but she made herself comfortable and began to stare blankly at the wall. Maha opened Huda's window so there would be a breeze as she slept. Then she let herself out, pulling the door shut behind her.

Maha walked straight to Leila's room and knocked on the door. After a few seconds she knocked again. Then again. After the third knock, she could hear rustling in the room. Soon the door opened, and Maha was looking into the sleepy face of a girl she had never met.

"Who are you?" asked Maha.

"I live here. Who are you?" asked the new girl.

"I'm looking for Leila. I'm a friend of hers, and I have to talk to her."

"Leila's not here."

"Do you know when she'll be back?"

"I don't know. Maybe tomorrow? Maybe Saturday? She went home for the weekend."

"Oh," said Maha. Before she could utter more pleasantries, the door was shut in her face.

Three hours later, Maha approached Huda's door, feeling obligated to look after her friend's friend but wishing desperately that Leila were with her. She pushed open the door and found Huda on the bed exactly where she'd left her.

Huda was still staring at the wall. Maha wondered if she'd moved at all, or slept at all. So this is what studying too hard can do to a person!

"Huda! Huda!" Maha shook Huda on the shoulder. "Wake up!"

Huda blinked a few times, looked at Maha, and sat up. "Did I sleep?"

"Well, I don't know."

"I don't either," Huda mumbled as she looked around the room and settled her eyes on her watch. She picked it up and looked at the clock. Four-thirty in the afternoon. "I don't know whether I slept, but I don't think I was awake either."

"You didn't act too awake when I came by earlier."

"Thanks for getting me to lie down. I do feel a bit better now."

"Yes? I guess you really needed the rest!" Maha sighed happily. With Huda sorted, Maha could go join her aunt who doubtless was doing something fun this evening.

"You're right. I am so tired." Huda breathed, and Maha noticed a tear coming out of each eye.

"Huda?" Maha put her hand on Huda's shoulder and sat down next to her. "Huda? Are you okay? Did something happen?"

Huda put her hand up to her face and noticed it was wet. She looked at Maha. Then she put her face in her hands and started sobbing. Maha just sat there for a few minutes with her hand resting awkwardly on Huda's shoulder.

After several minutes, Huda looked up. She asked, "Why are you here? I hardly know you. You don't owe me anything."

"I don't know," Maha mumbled. "I just came in when I saw your door open to say a quick hi, and..."

"You don't have to stay. I can take care of myself."

"Let me ask you something, Huda," Maha ventured. "Do

you have anyone? I know you have your family but they're hours away, aren't they? If I hadn't come in, what would you have done?"

Huda wiped her face and looked curiously at Maha. "I... I... I don't know. I'd probably wake up and go on with life."

"Even Leila's out of town today," Maha pointed out.

"She is?"

"Yes, one of her roommates just told me she's gone for the weekend."

"Oh."

To Maha's surprise, Huda didn't seem too disappointed. She wondered if she should leave or if she should try to get Huda to tell her what was wrong. She didn't really want to know, but she couldn't just leave Huda either. So for the next few minutes the two girls sat silently side-by-side, Huda deep in whatever thoughts she was having, and Maha feeling more and more awkward.

Finally, Maha suggested, "You like walking, don't you? I've seen you coming back from a walk sometimes in the morning. The weather is cooling off a bit now. What do you say to a walk?"

Huda hesitated a second but soon agreed, "Okay. Yes, a walk would be good."

They walked on the pavement by the highway in silence for a few minutes. Maha led the way as Huda obediently followed. Eventually, it was Huda who broke the silence.

"Where are you from, Maha?"

"I'm from Sednaya."

"Sednaya is beautiful. I've been there once. To the church on the mountain."

"Really? What were you doing there?"

"I love churches. It's like I can feel God there," Huda said in a faraway voice.

"Is that so?" asked a surprised Maha. "But, umm, don't you go to mosque?"

"Mosque... Yes, I've been to mosque before, the big famous ones in Damascus. But tell me about your church."

"Well, I guess, if you want. I've actually only been to the church on the mountain twice myself. We have a smaller church in Sednaya town. It's Protestant."

"Protestant?" asked Huda.

"Yes, like Injili," Maha tried to clarify. Seeing Huda's blank expression, she tried, "Evangelical?"

"I've never heard of it."

"It's very small. I don't know too much about it religiously, but we have a *shebab* youth meeting every Sunday afternoon for the young people, so whenever I'm home on a Sunday, I go to that. It's a lot of fun."

"Is that church? Do you have *bakhour* incense and the eucharist?"

"Oh, no. I don't think we ever have incense in the Protestant church. Why incense?"

"Every church I've been to has had incense."

"That's interesting. My church never uses incense. It's very small. I guess it's not really much like the big churches in Damascus, or the tourist churches. It's simple. We don't have any fancy decorations or icons or painted windows or statues or, well, you know, it's just kind of plain. But I guess it's still church. I don't really go that often. The *shebab* meeting meets in the basement, not the main room where the adult services happen."

"So it's not really church?"

"Well, it's led by the church leaders. And we do have a singing time and a prayer time and a Bible teaching time and an offering time."

"An offering time?"

"You know, when you give your gift of money to the

church."

"You have to pay the church to go?"

"I never thought of it that way before." Maha frowned. "I wonder if that's what it's for. I don't always give anything. Sometimes I put my hand in the bag empty and no one ever checks. Usually I just put a little bit of change."

"That's odd," declared Huda.

"Every church meeting I've ever been to has an offering."

"When I visited the church in Sednaya and the churches in Bab Touma, I never saw that."

"Really? See, I can learn something about my own religion from you!"

"I guess. Alawites like to know about everything."

"That's good. I'll ask my parents or maybe the leader of the *shebab* group about offerings next time I go."

"So are your cousins also... what's it called, Prostetant?"

"Protestant. Yes. My whole family is. But I don't think it matters all that much, you know? I mean, all my neighbors were Orthodox or Catholic, even a few Muslims. And I went to school with all different kinds of people. That's just the church my family belongs to."

The girls continued walking in silence a few minutes. When they reached a good turning point, Maha suggested they turn around and Huda obediently followed.

She then asked Maha, "Did you have somewhere you need to be today? It's a Thursday night."

Maha hesitated, then answered, "No, nothing planned."

"Are you studying hard for exams?"

"Well, I'm trying. I don't seem to get a lot of studying done in the Medina."

"So what do you do?"

"I have an aunt who lives in Bab Touma. She lets me study at her house."

"It must be a very nice house!" Huda imagined a house

like those restaurants with big courtyards.

"It is, actually. It has ten rooms and a nice courtyard. It's been in the family for years."

"Wow!"

"My aunt is actually very fortunate, because her husband is too sick to work and she has three daughters. But she rents out four rooms to foreigners, mostly Arabic students. They pay a lot for rent, to live in an Arabic house."

"If I had a house like that, I'd never leave."

"It is very nice in the summer. We can stay up late in the cool evening breeze. Sometimes they turn the fountain on in the courtyard and we drink coffee and eat fruits and do arguile, and sometimes one of her other nephews will play music for us. And the house has lots of rooms and corners, so it's not too hard to find a quiet place to study."

"Do you study hard?" asked Huda.

"Well, my course isn't as difficult as yours. But, thanks to God, I did pass most of my classes in the first exams."

"What are you going to do when you graduate?"

"Oh, I don't know!" Maha laughed. "That's years away. I have relatives in Lebanon, so maybe look for a job there? I have an uncle in Canada, so maybe go there. I might work here, but there aren't really any jobs here."

"What are you studying again?"

"Psychology."

"Is your family happy with that?"

Maha frowned. "My family doesn't really say all that much."

"Really? So what do they want for you?"

After a pause, Maha answered, "Well, I need to help out and make sure everyone's well. They want me to be happy, find a good husband. A Christian, of course. They want me to be well-off so I guess I have to work hard."

"It sounds like they love you very much."

"I suppose. That's what family is, isn't it?"

"Yes, you're right. We'd be nowhere without family."

Then Maha asked Huda, "Do you have any family around Damascus?"

"No. They're all back in the village or in Latakia."

"Why Latakia?"

"Well, I guess because that's the closest city to my village."

"Do you think you'll go there when you graduate?"

Huda frowned. "Well, there aren't really many jobs there. I think I'll find the best thing if I stay here in Damascus."

"Won't you miss your family too much?"

"Oh, I miss them so very much! But that's what it takes to get ahead. If I want to have a job and build a career, I can't be with my family. Don't take me wrong, I love them very much!"

"I wouldn't doubt it for a second. I can't imagine being so far from family as this," affirmed Maha. "Hey, here's a shawarma stand that makes amazing sandwiches! Are you hungry enough to eat? I'm inviting!"

"No, no, it's fine," protested Huda.

"You have to eat something. You don't want to get yourself sick!"

Huda actually was very hungry and felt quite relieved that her body was beginning to act a little bit normal again, so she agreed to eat with Maha.

They both ordered large chicken shawarma sandwiches, which were served up to perfection with loads of thinly sliced chicken, a heap of garlic mayonnaise, and even some pickles and tomatoes, then toasted with some chicken grease to take on a crunchy toasty flavor. Huda lightly protested but allowed Maha to pay for the sandwiches and a cola for each, and they sat down on little stools outside the shawarma stand.

The girls chomped away hungrily. The weather was pleasant now, and cooling down quickly as the sun set behind the mountain. The movement on the streets was picking up with men walking by to go to local cafes, women scurrying off to do shopping, and the car traffic growing as evening business hours began.

After a bit, Maha ventured to ask, "When I came by this afternoon, you really didn't seem well."

Huda looked down and said, "I'm sorry to have bothered you. I guess you could be at your aunt's house today."

"No, that's fine. It's been good to get to know you a bit. I only really knew you through Leila."

"Leila's like that. She has all kinds of different friends and involves us all."

"Yeah, she's a lot of fun. You guys are pretty good friends, huh?"

"Well, I've only known her for a few months."

"But still," Maha pushed. "It must be nice having a kindred spirit here in Damascus when you're far away from your family."

"I don't know. I really envy you. You live with your cousins."

"Maybe it's best when we have a little bit of both." Taking a deep breath, Maha finally blurted out, "Is something the matter?"

Huda didn't answer for a minute. She was the strong one, the one in her family who was going to make it, the fighter. She had done well for herself since she came to Damascus – until now. Who was this Christian girl, almost a stranger? Of course she wouldn't understand, and anyway, Huda was not about to tell her about her own shame. But Maha had been so nice to her today, and Huda was disarmed by the thoughtful tone in which she'd asked the question.

So the words started pouring out. She told Maha

everything, starting with what happened that day, but then realized that the story wouldn't make sense without background. So she told Maha about how much she looked up to her professor and how helpful he was, about their study session last week, then about the whole odd experience at the restaurant.

As she described the back room, Maha nodded and said, "You don't have to tell me everything. I don't want to push you."

But Huda asked, "Can I trust you? Do you promise not to tell anyone? Now that I've started, I might as well tell you the whole thing."

Maha put her hand on Huda's arm, looked her in the eyes, and nodded.

So Huda kept going with her story and told every little detail. She swore to Maha that she never did anything wrong and begged Maha to believe her. She wasn't sure whether Maha believed her or not but she went on to describe what had happened yesterday and today.

When she finished, Huda concluded, "And I don't know what happened after I left his room. I know I told him I'm a respectable girl and he had no right to imply anything, and I think he threatened me. The next thing I remember is you telling me to lie down."

Maha just sat there, stunned. She'd heard stories of this happening. She suspected it had happened to one of her own cousins, but no one had ever actually come out and told her about it. The first thing that came to mind was that she needed to be careful around her own professors.

Huda looked at her and said, "Well? Say something! Do you hate me now?"

Maha replied, "Hate you? Oh. I can't even imagine being in your situation. But it's not your fault!" She did wonder, though, what it was that Huda might have done to lead her professor to think that she was that kind of a girl. But who was she to judge? She herself wasn't a complete stranger to men and flirtation.

At Maha's reassuring words, Huda started crying. Not a dramatic weeping, but a quiet sobbing. They were still sitting out in public, on the stools outside the shawarma stand, so Maha helped her to stand up and led her back to the Medina.

When they arrived back on the floor, Maha intended to go straight back to her own room, then maybe head over to Bab Touma, but Huda asked her not to go.

"Please, now that you know everything, can you help me?"

"Help you with what?" Maha asked her.

"What do I do?" Huda's voice reminded her of a preschool child on her first day of school, unsure of how to talk to the other children.

"Oh," said Maha slowly. "Why don't you come over to my room and I'll make us some coffee."

Huda followed Maha obediently and sat down on the cushion against the wall in Maha's room. She watched Maha in silence as she prepared the coffee, bringing the pot up and down, up and down, keeping the pot from ever quite boiling over.

Maha put a plate on the coffeepot and brought it and two little cups over to the rug. She sat down on the rug facing Huda.

"So," asked Maha. "What do you need?"

"What do I need?"

"You said you needed help deciding what to do?"

"Oh... yes." Huda let out a deep sigh. "He threatened me. He said I had to go."

"You had to go or what?"

"Well," thought Huda. "Well, I don't know, come to think

of it."

"But he threatened you?"

"Yes, I'm sure it was a threat."

Maha pondered this a moment, then commented, "I have heard of this happening before, actually. You're not the first person."

"Really?" Huda brightened up for the first time that day. "Who? What happened?"

"Well, I don't actually know anyone *personally*. But I think... the stories were usually that the professor could threaten to fail them and used that against them. I wonder..." She was going to say that maybe the professor took advantage of Huda's obvious desperation to do well, but stopped herself.

Huda didn't say it either. She just said, in that tiny voice, "I can't fail."

Chapter Six

The big Pullman coach pulled into the bus depot in Baramkeh. Traffic on a Friday evening was heavy, and the last fifteen minutes of the trip had been spent sitting more than moving as the bus navigated the last three blocks to the depot. Most of the other passengers had already alighted and gone in search of taxis, but Leila stayed put in her front seat. She wanted to get off the bus in the exact spot where it was due to arrive, in case Ahmed really would be there to greet her.

Her heart was about to burst after a full day with her sisters. She had wanted to tell them so many times about Ahmed but had held her tongue. It had been pure torture, and she just wanted to talk to someone. If he wasn't there, she'd go straight back to the Medina and find Huda, but she really really wanted him to be there.

The bus pulled into its lane and the driver set the parking brake while his assistant lifted his seat away from the door and turned to the few remaining passengers, "*Yalla!* Let's go, guys! Everyone off."

Leila picked up her bag and stood up nervously. She took her time getting off, allowing several passengers to go in front of her. Then she took the plunge into the aisle, stepped down the stairs and... locked eyes with Ahmed.

He was there. And Leila felt loved. He broke into his amazing grin and she smiled back briefly before looking down. When she got off the bus, he shook her hand, took her bag, and asked if she had any luggage. When she said no, he led the way to the street and a taxi.

Neither one said any more than the essential until they

were settled in the little yellow car, Ahmed in front by the driver, and Leila in the rear with her bag. At the rate traffic was moving, the trip to the Medina would take an hour.

Then Ahmed asked, "Did you have a good trip?"

"Fine, thank you," Leila replied. Then she said, "You came."

"Why wouldn't I? I said I would, and anyway, I missed you."

"You missed me? I was only gone for a day."

Ahmed looked hurt and said, "Of course I missed you! Shouldn't I?"

Leila was taken aback, until she remembered that she had been thinking of him every moment that she was gone. "I guess I missed you also."

"That's better," smiled Ahmed. "So what did you do at home? Tell me, how is Dera'a?"

"The same as always, boring, I guess. I wish I didn't have to go."

"Did something bad happen?"

"No. I just really love Damascus. Whenever I go home I feel like I have taken three big steps back. Back to childhood, back to tradition, away from myself... Oh, I'm not making any sense. I'm sorry. You don't want to talk about that."

"To the contrary! I'm very interested. I know how you feel, too. I love visiting Dera'a, but my family there is so different from how I think."

"Well, home is the only place where I really belong. I mean, I think I belong. I don't know if it will ever be the same again after living in Sham. But going home is going home. I fall into the routine, sit with my sisters, help my mother, I know where things go. But is it possible that life can really be nothing but Qur'an studies, cleaning the house, cooking, and occasionally going on walks with my sisters? Because that's all I do at home."

The couple fell into silence after that, Leila wondering how she could open up so much more to a complete stranger than she ever did to her own sister or mother. Ahmed chatted for a few minutes with the driver.

Then Ahmed turned back again and commented, "You know, since traveling I have never been able to get used to life in Sham again. I wonder if it's the same thing. Once our eyes have been opened to how big the world can be, it's hard to live in a small world again."

"That's so poetic! See, no one at home thinks that. But it makes sense. Yes, I think you're right. That's exactly how I feel. I love Damascus, but my family expects me to go back home when I graduate. Maybe it would be better if I'd never come."

"Don't say that. Hey, if you never came to Damascus, I'd never have met you. What a tragedy!"

"Really?"

"Yes, I believe everything happens for a reason, and I'm so glad I met you."

Leila felt her face getting hot and said nothing.

Ahmed continued, "I don't want to just drop you off at the Medina. What do you say to going out to dinner first?"

Leila had already broken so many rules with Ahmed, and while she loved every moment, did he have no limits? "It's late. The girls will wonder. No, I really need to get back home."

"I understand. Then how about just some ice cream?"

Leila paused, then gave in. "Well, if it's on the way, I guess it can't hurt."

Ahmed gave the driver his new instructions, then turned and grinned at Leila. "It's so close that it won't take but a second!"

The driver took the next possible u-turn into slow-moving traffic moving the other direction. A few blocks down he turned onto a side road and zipped down the street, but soon met more gridlock there. As they inched their way to the next intersection, Leila glanced at her watch. Eight o'clock. She tensed up with the thought that she'd get to the Medina only a few minutes before curfew. Could she change her mind again now? Then she realized that if her bus had arrived this late, Ahmed had been waiting at the bus depot for more than an hour. She looked at the back of his head and his gelled-up black hair and decided just to be grateful for ice cream.

Sure enough, it was half past nine by the time Leila got back to the Medina. She felt like she was floating as she rushed into Building 14, hoping no one noticed but not really worried. The evening with Ahmed had been worth it.

The elevator appeared to be broken again, so she started up the stairs to her room. The hallways were bustling with girls cooking, washing clothes, drying hair, or just pacing back and forth memorizing books. Upon arriving at her floor, she intended to go straight to knock on Huda's door rather than return to her room. This weekend, she expected her room to be full and she didn't want the Dera'a girls knowing she was back so late. But she noticed Maha's door was opened, so decided to say hi to Maha first. Surely Maha wouldn't mind that she was returning to the Medina late.

Leila poked her head in and saw Maha alone, sitting on the mattress on the floor. Maha looked up and exclaimed, "*Ahlain*, Leila! You're back!"

"*Kifek*? How are you?" replied Leila.

"Oh, I'm fine. We missed you this weekend. How was home?"

"The same as always. Lots of work around the house and no studying!"

"Did you just get back now?" asked Maha.

"Uh, yes. Just now."

"It's a good thing you made it before curfew!"

"For sure."

"Hey, come on in. I was just needing a cup of coffee. Will you drink some?"

Leila hesitated just enough to be polite.

"No, really." Maha quickly insisted. "Actually, I was hoping to get to talk to you."

So Leila removed her shoes and stepped onto the rug to join Maha on the mattress. "You didn't go to Bab Touma to study this weekend?"

"No," said Maha soberly.

"Have you been able to get work done here?"

"Well, actually, that's what I need to talk to you about. But first, let's have some coffee."

Maha stood up and walked out to the kitchen to fill her coffee pot. When she returned, she closed the door behind her and locked it. Leila watched and waited in silence as Maha prepared the coffee.

Maha made the coffee and, without saying a word, brought it over and sat on the rug. Finally, it was Leila who broke the silence.

"What's going on?"

"Well, it's not my place to say. No, I really shouldn't say anything..." stuttered Maha.

Leila stared at her. "What do you mean? Should I be worried?"

"Well... ummm... She'd be so mad if she knew I said something, so you need to act like you don't know. It's for her to tell, anyway. But I just wanted to warn you."

"Warn me?"

"Yes. It's Huda. You're her closest friend and we all kind of figure you two look out for each other. But she told me she hadn't said anything to you. I just wanted to tell you to be careful, to be sensitive right now. I don't know how I got wrapped up in it, maybe I was just here at the right time, but yesterday afternoon I found her in a daze in her room, so I just took her for a walk. She obviously wasn't well. She doesn't seem to be much better today."

"It must be all that studying," declared Leila. "She studies too hard. I'm always trying to tell her that."

"No. I think it's more than that."

"Like what?"

"I've already said too much," Maha declared with her brows tightly furrowed. "I just thought you should know so you wouldn't be shocked when you saw her."

Leila was beginning to be worried. She needed to go see her friend... but did she really want to know what the problem was? Maha seemed so concerned, and she hardly knew Huda.

"Well, um... thanks, I guess," muttered Leila. "I guess I should go."

"Just be easy on her, I think she's had a difficult few days."

Leila quickly drank a few sips of her coffee and put the cup down. She stood to leave. Maha's eyes followed her as she put her shoes back on and picked up her purse.

"Thank you for the coffee, Maha."

"Good luck," said Maha with a faint smile. She didn't stand up, she just watched as Leila unlocked the door and let herself out.

Left alone again, Maha wondered if she'd done the right thing. She didn't know what to do with Huda. Today hadn't been much better than yesterday, so Maha had made her lunch and practically force-fed her. She'd almost convinced Huda to go with her to her aunt's house in Bab Touma, thinking that being in a real home might be a good change. But Huda seemed to have been overtaken by fear of leaving the building. So Maha tried to get Huda to lie down for a nap and sat with her until it seemed Huda was asleep. Then she'd gone alone to Bab Touma, but only stayed an hour, long enough to get some food and do some shopping with her cousins before returning to Building 14. She had checked in on Huda and found her sitting on her bed with the table piled high with open books in front of her. But it didn't look like she was actually studying, just staring blankly at the pages. At a loss, Maha had made some tea and drunk a cup while watching Huda's cup get cold. Then she'd brought her own books over and tried to study with Huda. When Huda's roommates had started arriving, Maha figured she was no longer needed since Huda wasn't alone in the room anymore. By then it was too late to go back to Bab Touma, so she'd settled in to study in her own room, and that's where Leila had found her.

Maha felt completely incapable of doing anything to help Huda and couldn't quite figure out how she'd landed in the position of helping a girl she hardly knew, particularly when she should be studying for her first-year exams. So she wanted Leila to know what was going on. Leila and Huda were friends so maybe she could help somehow. But Huda had confided in Maha, and not just because she was in the right place at the right time, she knew. Maha suspected that Huda didn't yet trust Leila, that they didn't have that type of friendship. As a stranger, Maha must have been safer. But what was she supposed to do with this knowledge? All she could think of was to keep making Huda tea.

Leila stood in the hallway. To her right was her own door. To the left was Huda's door. She looked back and forth, relieved that at that moment the hallway was empty. In Huda's room lay a big mystery, a dear friend, and possibly a lot of hassle. And probably not an opportunity to tell Huda about her evening with Ahmed. To the right she would be met by schoolbooks and suspicious gossips from Dera'a.

A sense of duty won, and Leila went to knock on Huda's door. One of her roommates opened the door. Leila said, "Good evening!"

"Good evening back."

"How are you?"

"Hamdulillah."

After a moment's silence, Leila asked, "Is Huda there?"

Without another word, the girl opened the door wider and ushered Leila in to where Huda sat silently on her bed. The table was set up with open books on it, but Huda seemed to be staring into space.

Leila went over to Huda, put her arm on her shoulder and said, as cheerfully as she could, "*Ahlain*, Huda!"

When Huda looked at her, Leila kissed her on both cheeks as if nothing could possibly be amiss, and sat herself down on the bed.

Huda made room for Leila and smiled at her. Then she looked down at her hands in her lap.

Leila tried asking, "How are you, Huda?"

This got no response, so Leila tried again. "Did you have a good weekend?"

Huda looked up, smiled and shrugged. Then returned to staring at her hands.

Leila wasn't sure what to do, so she glanced around. There were four other girls in the room. They were all pretending to study but each caught Leila's eyes ever-so-briefly and shrugged as if to say, "She's been like this since I got here. I don't know what's going on!"

So Leila decided that what Huda needed was the roof. The roof was medicine for any problem. So as cheerily as possible she told Huda to get ready. She was going to drop her bag in her room and come right back to escort Huda up to the roof.

For half an hour, the girls sat on a blanket Leila had placed on a big concrete block. For half an hour, neither one uttered a word. For the first time she could remember, Leila did not want to be there. But she felt she couldn't leave. Huda stared at the Faculty of Literature buildings in silence.

Finally, though, Huda started talking, and Leila listened.

"I'm going to fail. All these years I have had only one dream, and I worked so hard to achieve it. I have never been so naïve as to think that God would just hand me my dream, I knew I had to work for it. But I thought that God would help me. I thought that if I just did my job and dedicated myself, then that would be rewarded..."

She wiped a tear from her eye and looked back up at the literature buildings. She let out a laugh, "University of Damascus is supposed to be one of the best in the Arab world. A beacon of education, of knowledge, of progress. Whenever I'd tell people back home I went here, they were so impressed. They thought that meant I was a real scholar. I thought that meant I was a real scholar.

"To think I actually wanted to work here! Why would I spend any more time in this place than absolutely necessary? This isn't a place of learning, it's not a beacon of knowledge! It's no different than the rest of this country. Just as antiquated, just as traditional, just as patriarchal. I was such an idiot. I'm going to fail and I don't even care anymore."

She got off the block and walked over to the edge. She looked over the ledge and spit. Then she marched back up to the block and looked Leila straight in the face, "You are a dreamer. You love to learn. But do you know where it'll get you? Nowhere. Believe me, I know that now. Syria isn't for women. That's just something they tell us so we'll feel better. Or maybe so that we'll make more disciplined wives. But they don't care about us. You know what you're going to do? You're going to end up married, with ten kids, hosting Qur'an studies in your house – but don't worry, you won't actually attend, you'll be too busy cleaning, making tea and putting together trays of sweets. Do you hear me? Give up!"

Huda shuddered and leaned against the block, her elbows resting on the blanket and her face in her hands. Leila was frightened by her friend's performance. Huda needed someone else, not her. What could Leila possibly say? She didn't stop to actually consider the truth of what Huda was saying. Instead, she wondered what had set Huda to thinking that way, so irrationally, so different from the Huda she knew.

Huda climbed back onto the block. She sat across from Leila and took Leila's hand. Then she continued, "Do you hear me? What are we trying to do here? It's pointless. It will never get us anywhere. On our own talent, that is. You have to be rich, or well-connected, or... in the end it's hopeless. I should just go home."

At this, a reply made its way out of Leila's mouth. "I don't know where all this is coming from, but I do know that you're not the Huda I know. Nothing so significant can happen in two days to change who you are, and you are a person who loves the law. You love it because it conveys rights, because there's process, because it's fair. What happened to all that?"

Huda didn't answer. She just looked back up at the Faculty buildings, smiled for a second, and then resumed her blank stare.

After a while, Leila said, "It's a lovely night. I think I'm going to go get my books and study up here for a while. What do you say? Do you want to study together?"

Huda looked at Leila curiously and murmured, "I don't think I'm going to study tonight. But you're right it's nice out here. I'll keep you company for a while."

"Well, alright. If you're sure. Do you want anything from downstairs?"

Huda shook her head and lay down on her back. So Leila climbed down off the concrete block and rushed down to her room. She quickly grabbed a pile of lecture notes and returned to the roof, where Huda was looking up at where the stars would be if they had been visible through the smog. Leila set the pile of notes on the blanket and chose one booklet. She glanced over at Huda, couldn't think of anything useful to say, so started working her way through the ream of papers, pacing back and forth on the roof as she memorized her notes on meter and rhythm in poetry.

Every so often Leila went over to check on Huda, who never seemed to move. Her eyes were open and she was breathing, but she was just staring at the sky. Leila wondered if this wasn't just a stress response. No one should live to study the way Huda was doing lately. Maybe a few hours of fresh air, open sky, and no law was just what the doctor ordered. Leila, on the other hand, didn't study enough, so she made herself keep memorizing.

It was after 1:00 a.m. when Leila decided to stop. She walked over to Huda and waved her hand over her eyes to try to catch her attention. Huda looked over at Leila and sat up.

Leila asked her, "Do you feel better? Ready to sleep?"

"You know, you're right. I shouldn't just take defeat. I do believe in justice. I do believe in opportunity. I can't just give up."

"Good! I'm glad. So tomorrow you can go back to studying."

"Hmmm. Yes, maybe."

"Come on! I know you can ace all your courses. You're going to be the best law professor Damascus has ever seen!"

"Tomorrow I'll worry about it."

"Yes, tomorrow. Tonight, let's just get a good night's

sleep."

Huda got down and helped Leila fold the blanket. The two girls headed down the stairs back into the building. They bid each other a good night and went to bed. Leila slept well, proud of herself for being a friend to Huda and glad she'd made some progress on her studying. Huda, on the other hand, lay in bed for a while longer, fretting and wondering what the next day would hold. She still had no idea what she would do. But exhaustion took over and she soon drifted off to sleep as well.

Chapter Seven

The next week was full of studying, exams and Ahmed, so Leila didn't really see Huda. She figured that was a good sign. It probably meant that Huda was nestled back at her corner desk in the big library. Leila didn't really have time to check, though, as she had three exams during the week, and between exams there was studying and numerous visits with Ahmed. So she didn't really have time to check in at the student center.

Leila and Ahmed were developing a routine. Every evening between 6:00 and 7:00, her bell rang. She was getting better at being prepared. Now she had a scarf all ready and an overcoat picked out, and she was getting skilled at quickly putting them on properly. When the bell rang, she'd quickly dress, grab her handbag and head down the stairs. Ahmed would be sitting on the ledge halfway down on the right, and every evening she could count on him looking up just when she walked out of the building. He'd smile that amazing smile, she'd return a shy smile, and then they'd shake hands. She would then sit down beside him and quickly pinch herself to be sure this was not just a dream.

They talked about everything: about what she was reading, what he was studying, and how their exams were going; about her brother's business and her father's job, and his family history; about places they'd been and places they dreamed of seeing; about their religion, especially about what a modern understanding of Islam meant; and more than anything else, they talked about their dreams for the future. Leila was constantly amazed by how well he understood her. She had never felt such a personal connection to anyone in her life.

Each evening, after chatting for about an hour, Ahmed invited her somewhere: to dinner, to eat ice cream, to the coffee shop. Each evening, Leila found the strength to refuse. She was growing increasingly anxious that one of her Dera'a roommates – there were six girls besides herself, all from her village or nearby, staying in the room now – would begin to take note and word would get back to her family. So every evening, she refused Ahmed's invitation because it was too late. She needed to be home early to avoid critique. Surely he understood.

After a few days, she suggested that instead of sitting outside her building, they walk around the Medina grounds. He eagerly agreed. So after that, when Leila came down after her bell rang, they would no longer sit in front of her building's entrance. Instead, they walked.

On their third walk, while they were passing through a dark and secluded stretch of garden, Ahmed took her hand in his, but after the initial surprise passed, Leila pulled her hand away.

The next evening, he did it again, and this time she didn't have the courage to resist. His hand was warm and strong, and she could smell his powerful cologne as she drew closer to him. It felt good... and it wasn't like anyone could see them there. When they came back out in the open, she quickly pulled away again.

It was now Thursday evening. Leila was completely enraptured, but she was also becoming a nervous wreck. She was always looking over her shoulder, always nervous someone from her village would notice her with Ahmed. If her family found out, that would ruin it, even if he was from a good family – wealthy, Muslim, and mother from Dera'a. But when she wasn't with him, she was even more frazzled by a desire to see him again.

After their walk Thursday night, they lingered a bit outside her building. She looked up into his eyes and he looked down into hers, and it seemed that he was zeroing in on her soul. Just when he started to say something, Leila caught a glimpse of a girl who had recently moved in to her room.

Quickly, Leila took a step back and declared, "I need to go. I'm sorry, I need to go now."

Ahmed was still looking at her. "Wait a second! Tomorrow's Friday. What are you doing?"

"I can't talk right now. Sorry. I need to go."

"Well, can I --"

"Sure, come by, I should be around," Leila said quietly as she walked away toward the building entrance. Hopefully if her new roommate saw her, she wouldn't notice that she'd been talking to that man.

As she neared the entrance, a girl's voice called out, "Good evening, Leila!"

Leila turned and feigned surprise at her roommate approaching. "Oh, hello! How are you?"

"You know, studying a lot. How are you?"

"I'm fine. Also studying a lot. I had three exams this week, you know."

"Yes, you told me," her roommate said. "Next week's my big week!"

"Really? How's the preparation?"

The girls started climbing the stairs together.

Her roommate replied, "Slowly. It's coming along."

"Well, *muwafa'a* – may God help."

"Thanks. You too," On the next landing, the girl stopped and turned to Leila. "Leila, who was that man you were talking to?"

"Who? Oh, him. He's just a distant cousin who studies here. I had to give him something for his mother." This was

DREAMS IN THE MEDINA

the story she had rehearsed to herself over and over during the past week for such a moment as this.

"He's handsome! Don't you think?"

"Handsome? Well, I guess so. I hadn't really noticed."

"You hadn't noticed? I'm so sure. He's gorgeous! Surely, you..."

"I need to get up to the room. Sorry." Leila interrupted her and continued the trek up the stairs.

"Okay then." As she followed Leila, she said, "Well, if it ever works to introduce me, do!"

"Sure, if he ever comes by again, sure," Leila muttered. This wasn't the reaction she had been prepared for, and she certainly didn't want to share Ahmed. She walked resolutely the rest of the way up the stairs until she came to the room. She walked in, with the other girl following her, and without saying anything, went to her bookshelf, put her purse down, grabbed some books, and marched out of her room and up to the roof.

Sharing a room with conservative Muslim girls from Dera'a is a very different experience from living on a floor with Christians, Alawites, Druze and Kurds. Half of Leila's roommates were Shar'ia students, which just made the experience more... well, more Muslim. For the past month and a half Leila had only gone home on alternate weekends, so on the Fridays when she was in Damascus, she had grown accustomed to sleeping in on her day off. Even though she was in Damascus to study, she figured that a leisurely Friday morning was reasonable. She didn't want to have a panic attack like Huda. So her Friday mornings in Damascus became a treasured routine. A good night's sleep was followed by a proper breakfast of yogurt, olives, eggs, tomato, cucumber and even once some falafel from the stand downstairs, all rinsed down by some good sweet Dera'a tea.

Then, as mid-day approached, she did her morning and noontime prayers - since she'd slept in she needed to do a double set - and since it was Friday, she took advantage of having washed and prayed to read the Qur'an a bit. One Friday she had walked over to the big mosque down the highway, planning on listening to the sermon from the women's section, but she had stopped in at the imports supermarket on the way and been distracted by the different types of soap and cereal, such that when she noticed the time, the sermon would have been half over already. After she felt sufficiently spiritual and faithful for a Friday morning, she might have lunch if she was hungry, rest a bit more... and then pull out her books and decide whether she would study in her room, the little library, or the big library. By then it was usually 5:00 in the afternoon. Of course, there was the week when she met up with Roxy and her family at 5:00. Then there was the Friday when she decided to make stuffed squash and by the time she was done it was almost time for the building to close. And there were always neighbors to be visiting.

But she was happy with her Friday routine and still felt like she got more studying done than if she went home.

This week, though, she had six roommates, all from Dera'a, all religious, three of whom were Islamic Law students, and it seemed the other three wished they were studying Islamic law. At 4:00 in the morning – Leila had been asleep for about two hours – the lights to the room came on. *What is this, Ramadan? Is there an emergency?* Leila groggily wondered. She opened her eyes and saw her six roommates in the process of getting out of bed and putting on slippers to go wash for prayers. Fatima came over and nudged her, "Leila, are you awake? It's prayer time."

Leila couldn't believe this was happening. Did she really have no choice? She thought about just rolling over and going back to sleep. Sharing a room with three sisters at home, she had perfected the art of sleeping with noise around her. But she couldn't do that today. She had to pray with her roommates. Curse final exams and roommates who come to study during June!

So she got up and sat on the side of her bed for a few minutes. One girl had just started to pray and another was putting a large scarf and baggy skirt on over her pajamas. A third walked in the door with partially wet hair and her pant legs rolled up, water dripping off of her calves. They all looked so focused. They didn't seem inconvenienced, but neither did they look excited. They just did it. Because that's what one does, especially on a Friday morning. Then Leila thought that this was what the brotherhood of Islam was all about. Or in this case, the sisterhood. In the presence of her sisters in the religion, she was inspired to try harder, to be faithful, even when she'd only had two hours of sleep and felt like she didn't care. It would pay off.

So Leila stood up, unfastened her hair clip and re-rolled her hair into a tighter bun, reached under her bed for her slippers, and stood up to go to the kitchen to wash.

She was the last girl up, so the last girl to pray, as they were all sharing the same prayer rug. By the time she started, two girls were already asleep again, and a few others looked like they were headed back to their beds. But Fatima was puttering around the dishes, heating water for tea. It seemed Fatima wanted to send the message that she was the only true Muslim in the room, the only one strong enough to wake up with prayers and not just get them over with and go back to sleep.

But Leila decided that if she was awake to pray, she'd better do it right, so she looked away from Fatima, closed her eyes, and tried to focus. Then she stood straight on the rug and began the ritual motions. As she kneeled and prostrated herself, she felt a peace come over her. There was something that calmed her spirit in these centuries-old rituals that she had repeated countless times since she'd started as a nine-year-old girl. They helped her to focus, helped her to see life more clearly. She shut out all thoughts of Ahmed, of when he held her hand and how that felt, of Huda and the fact she hadn't seen her for so long, of her exams, of *Women in Love*, of her family in her house in the village... she pushed all those thoughts aside and focused on reciting the *Fatiha*, the opening of the Qur'an.

"*In the name of God, the Most Gracious, the Most Merciful: Praise be to God, the Lord of the Universe. The Most Gracious, the Most Merciful...*"

... she thought about God and how he was so big and powerful and mighty, how she was as nothing compared to him...

"*King of the Day of Judgment. You alone we worship...*"

... she tried to imagine what it would be like to stand in the presence of the Prophet, God's chosen envoy. He must have radiated such knowledge and wisdom, glory and kindness...

"*...and You alone we ask for help. Guide us to the straight way...*"

... she recalled how the right path, the life she lived, reflected that she was born into the Final Religion. It was not only a duty, it was a source of honor and pride...

"*...The way of those whom you have blessed, not of those who have deserved anger, nor of those who stray.*"

... Leila ended her ritual prayers and then concluded with a set of her own requests of God. Even though she was still half-asleep, plenty came to mind...

She whispered, "Oh, God, the Gracious, the Merciful... thank you for Ahmed. I'm so happy to know him. Please make him love me and care for me. If it's to be my lot, please,

I'd really like to marry him. Oh, but God, please help me pass and graduate! Please God, I know you are Lord of all the worlds, but more than anything, I want to graduate, to get a job, to speak and read English well, to discover the world, to meet people from other countries, to explore, to learn... Oh, Lord of the Worlds, I want to learn! Thank you for letting me come to Sham, to live in the Medina. And, I pray also for Huda. Hmmm. Help her to relax, and if it's your will, I just know how much she wants to pass. And if something else is bothering her, be with her for that, too, and may she come to walk the straight path also. Yes, Lord, be with Huda. Oh and be with Ahmed and his sister and the rest of his family. I don't know, bless them, and help them to like me whenever they meet me. Well, I guess that means they should meet me. When can that happen, oh God? I guess also please care for my dear mother and my good father, and my sisters, and my brothers, and... and... God, I figure if you are Lord of all the Worlds, you know all this. So can I go back to sleep now? Is that allowed? Please help me to study and to pass. Oh, anyway..."

And with that Leila drew her prayers to a close, stood up, stepped off the prayer rug, put on her slippers, folded the rug and draped it over the chair in the middle of the room. She walked straight to her bed, crawled under a sheet, rolled over, and went back to sleep.

It was almost noon when Leila awoke again, feeling warm. She opened one eye and discovered that the sun was shining brightly into the room. She opened her other eye and looked over at the bed directly across from her. Empty. Then she propped herself up on her elbow and looked around the room at the other beds. All empty. She looked behind her to where the table sat and saw one girl, whose name she wasn't remembering at that exact moment, studying.

"Sabah al-Kheir! Good morning!" greeted the girl, glancing up from her book when she saw Leila moving.

"Sabah al-Noor," Leila mumbled sleepily. She sat up and turned to face the girl. "What time is it?"

"It's mid-day already! You slept the day away," smiled the girl... *Aisha*! Yes, that was her name.

Leila rolled over onto her back and stared at the ceiling with a faint smile on her face. She was feeling strangely happy this morning – err, afternoon. It was amazing what a good night's sleep could do. Amazing what waking up in the middle of the night can do. For the first time in weeks she had a sense that things were going to work out. Why? Had she been worried before? She didn't think she'd been worried. The last several weeks were really quite fun, especially considering it was exam season. Was she worried about passing? No, she really wanted to succeed, but worried... no. Ever since she'd met Huda, whatever concern she'd felt about succeeding at university seemed to have melted away – anything was better than true worry! No, it wasn't that. Was it her family? It's true she was rather dreading going home for the summer, but there was nothing to fear there. She was dreading it for the sheer boredom. Being home meant three months of blah. Nothing to fear, nothing to anticipate, just... yeah. Not that. Was it Ahmed? No, it couldn't be! He was, without a doubt, the most beautiful thing that had ever happened in her life. Someday she would tell her grandchildren about her great romance, maybe when she had teenage granddaughters. She'd tell them about how he had spoken to her, visited her and rung her bell, just as she had dreamed would happen. She'd tell them about how he smiled the most amazing smile that made her heart melt, about how they could talk for hours and--

Her reverie was broken by the sound of the bell. It must be Ahmed... The yucky feeling was suddenly back. The peace and happiness had fled as if the bell was a message to her heart.

"Are you expecting anyone?" Aisha asked.

Leila turned to her side again and looked at her roommate, who was already standing up and settling a scarf on her head. Leila knew exactly who it was. He was impressively predictable, which made her feel all the more loved, and all the more uncomfortable.

"No, not that I know of," Leila replied, hoping to buy time to settle her nerves. "Are you expecting someone?"

"No. But maybe it's my cousin. He's in town these weeks and maybe he's checking in on me."

"Oh, that's nice!" exclaimed Leila, relieved. "I guess you might as well go check, then!" Maybe it really was Aisha's cousin after all.

As Aisha left the room, Leila sat up straight on the side of her bed, with her arms to her side. She looked down at her slippers. Alright, maybe the problem was Ahmed. No fair. How could the most wonderful thing in her life be the reason she didn't seem to know how to be happy anymore? She was so glad Aisha had gone to the window to see who it was. She had no desire to talk to him today, and wasn't so sure she ever wanted to see him again – her daydream about telling her grandchildren about him was never going to happen. She may never tell her family, not even when she was a grandmother, about how she had been so open with a man during her Medina days. Not even if, by some incredible miracle, she someday married him and her grandchildren were his grandchildren. She wanted nothing more in life, but her stomach seemed to be tying up in knots with the idea. How would that ever happen? Oh, she had never wanted something so much. One week had been all it took to transform her heart.

Leila was still sitting there when Aisha rushed back into

the room.

"Quick! Leila! There's a guy downstairs. He kept looking up at the window but I didn't recognize him. I didn't see my cousin either. Leila, he shouted up at me and asked for you. A guy actually shouted at me from all the way down in the courtyard. He wants you!" From the way Aisha said this, Leila could see she was clearly impressed by Ahmed, probably by his good looks and his willingness to make a fool of himself to find Leila.

"You didn't tell him I was here, did you?" asked Leila, with a tone of shock in her voice.

"Are you kidding? A guy like that? OF COURSE I told him you were here and that you were coming right down!"

"No! You have to go back and say that you were mistaken, you thought he meant someone else. That I left while you were at the window. Anything."

"Leila! There is a handsome, friendly, confident young man downstairs wanting you, and you want me to make him go away?"

Leila looked down and was silent for a moment. She didn't even know this girl. Who was Aisha to be telling her what to do and who to talk to? She didn't know anything, and anyway, what good Dera'awi village girl would be encouraging her to talk to a guy? Maybe Aisha thought he was her brother or something. No, it was too late for her to still think that. Leila's reaction had given that away. So she said the only thing she could think of. "'*Aieb*. Shame." And she kept her eyes on her slippers.

Aisha sat down next to Leila. For a few moments neither girl said a thing. Leila wondered if Aisha was imagining what might have transpired between Leila and Ahmed for Leila to be acting so ashamed. Maybe Leila should have just gone down: the gossip might have been less.

But she kept trying to convince Aisha. "*Habibti*, dear. I

hardly know you, but I know your family. You are from a good family and so am I. I was raised to be a good girl, and I don't guess a good girl would go down to talk to this man." She could only hope that Aisha didn't know that Leila had been going down to talk to this man almost daily for the past few weeks. She knew Aisha wanted to know more: how Leila knew him, who he was, and where he was from, but hopefully she would be polite enough not to ask.

Aisha stood up and looked at Leila. She smiled and there was kindness there. "I understand. You're right. I shouldn't encourage you to do something wrong. Now shame on me, huh? Maybe he'll just go away."

"No, I don't think he will," muttered Leila.

"What if the two of us go down together to send him away?"

"No, if he knows I'm here I will have to go with him."

"Why? Why can't you just say no?"

Leila had no answer.

Aisha got the point and moved on. "Alright. I'll go back to the window and look out. Eventually he'll look up and see me. As eager as he seemed, it shouldn't be long. Then I'll tell him that I was mistaken, that you're not here at all."

Leila hoped her gratitude showed in her smile as she looked at Aisha walking back out the door.

Ten minutes later, Aisha walked back in and announced, "Well, he left. He sure seemed disappointed. I think he really likes you! But he said he'd be back in a few hours."

"You didn't tell him not to bother? That I wouldn't be coming back?"

"How could I say that if I told him I didn't know where you were?"

"Right. I guess I will just have to not be here in a few hours." The two girls sat in the room in silence for a moment.

Then Leila said, "I've inconvenienced you. You have lots of studying to do."

"Malish. It's not a problem," replied Aisha. "I was needing a break anyway."

"Well, can I make you some tea?"

"Lovely idea. Thank you." She went back to her books and began to straighten them while Leila went out to the kitchen to fill the pot with water.

While she was filling the pot, Leila thought about Aisha. She was so nice! It would have been lovely to have known her earlier. Maybe then she wouldn't have felt so alone among the girls in the room. When she returned, Aisha looked up from her books, smiled and said, "*Shukran*. Thank you."

Leila asked, "Why don't you come here during the school year? It'd be nice to have you around more often!"

"I need to be home with my family most of the time," she answered.

"Really? They don't distract you from studying?"

"Well, yes, they do, I guess." Aisha put her pen down. "But what can I do? My mother passed away two years ago."

"Oh! May God have mercy on her!"

"Thank you. I'm the oldest daughter, so I usually have to be around to do the housework."

"How many brothers and sisters do you have?" Leila asked as she spooned some sugar into the pot and placed it on the electric burner.

"Five: two brothers and three sisters. The oldest sister is eighteen, and she's not married yet, so she is looking after the house right now. She's engaged, though, so I don't know how that will work after she gets married."

"Oh! I didn't realize that at all."

"It's just life."

"Why are you doing university?" asked Leila. "Do you think you'll ever get to graduate and get a job?"

"I don't know. But I love learning. Even though I have to do all the cleaning and cooking at home, I love it when the work is done for the day and I can sit in my corner with my books. I love studying, reading, learning. So I'll keep doing university as long as I can."

"What's your major?"

"Sociology."

"Is it interesting?"

"I love it," declared Aisha. "It's all about learning about people and how they interact, and culture and community."

"That does sound interesting! Well, may you pass, and I hope that you can keep studying."

"My father talks about taking another wife. None of us want him to replace my mother, but he is so lonely. There are a few older women in our family. I have a distant cousin who never married and another aunt who is divorced. My father's siblings are encouraging him to consider them."

"Does he?"

"He and my mother lived a true romance. They were first cousins and grew up playing together, but when they got married, they truly loved each other. Everyone was happy: their families because it was a good marriage, and them because they always seemed so content together. He treated her like a queen, and when she got sick we worried that he might die himself, he was so broken up about it."

"What did she die of?"

"Cancer."

"Oh, that must have been so hard!" Leila had heard many other stories of women her mother's age dying of cancer, and the stories were all terrible.

"It was hard for all of us, but more than anyone my father, for sure!"

"That's a beautiful story, though, how much he loved her. It gives me hope."

Aisha smiled and winked. "You sure you don't want to be here in a few hours?"

Leila's heart stopped. Fortunately, just that moment the water boiled over. She unplugged the burner, pulled the pot off, and reached up to her shelf for her stash of tea.

As she scooped some tea leaves into the pot, she observed, "Your parents were cousins from the same village. They were the lucky ones."

Leila grabbed two small glasses off the dish rack and carried them with the tea to the table where Aisha's books were piled up. She then excused herself and walked out into the corridor. Tears were welling up and she needed to regain her composure. Half an hour ago she was on top of the world, and all of a sudden... What was this? She paced up and down the hall a few times, thinking but trying to force herself not to think. On her third pass by the kitchen she heard a door open. She thought it was Maha's door, but she pretended not to notice and ducked back into her room.

Aisha was sitting by the window, flipping the pen around in her hand and gazing down at the highway. Leila went over to her bed and carefully folded the blanket and placed the pillow on top of it, then smoothed the sheet down. Aisha didn't move, and Leila imagined she was thinking of her mother.

When she was done making her bed, Leila pulled the chair over to the table and poured a tiny bit of tea into one of the cups. It looked dark enough, so she went ahead and poured out both cups. Aisha pulled herself away from the window and sat to face Leila who handed her a glass. She accepted her tea with a quiet *"Shukran."*

"You miss your mother, don't you?" said Leila matter of factly. "I can't even imagine what that's like."

"She's my mother, isn't she? I will never stop missing her."

Both girls stared at the tea so intently that one would have thought they were going to find the solution to the world's problems there.

Soon Leila blurted out, "Is it better to have loved and have lost, or not to have loved at all?" She had read in a text for her poetry class that it was better to have loved and lost, and had found it a rather exotic statement at the time. Now it seemed more profound, but she still wasn't so sure she believed it. Her Arabic translation wasn't quite as poetic, but the meaning still seemed to be there.

Aisha repeated the question, "Is it better to have loved and lost, or not to have loved at all? That's an interesting question."

"The poets say it is better to have loved and lost, but I was never sure. I don't really know anyone who has loved and lost, only people who have never loved. And I guess the rare person who loved and didn't lose. I mean the statement isn't, I don't think, exactly about your father, it's more about the person who pursued a forbidden love – at least I think that's what it's saying. But in some ways, I think it's about your father also – for he wouldn't have lost so much if he hadn't loved your mother. You say he lost his true love, not just the mother of his children."

"You mean, if he'd known he was going to lose her so soon, would he have tried not to love her so much?"

"Yeah. I guess that's what what I mean."

Aisha pondered this a minute, took another sip of tea, then said, "Some nights, my father doesn't get home from the café until late at night. I can't help but wonder if... Well, you know. On those nights it seems that he is trying to dull his pain. Other nights, he stays home, and we have this little reception room where he can receive guests, but on those nights, when he has guests, he asks me to bring the coffee when they've only just barely arrived. So they leave and he just wants to be alone. When I walk by, I think I hear him crying."

Leila watched Aisha closely as she said this. Aisha was speaking slowly, and Leila felt a bit guilty for bringing it up, but she was soaking in every word.

Aisha continued, "But I can't go in there and comfort him. He makes it clear he doesn't want company. Well, sometimes my little brother, who is ten, goes in there and the two of them sit together. It seems they just sit there in silence, but that does seem to provide some comfort. The rest of us have just learned to let our father mourn in his own way. I probably shouldn't be telling you all this. I'm sorry."

"No, no! You will never know how much it means to me to hear you share. To know that there are people who truly embrace their emotions. Please, please don't stop! I promise not to tell another living soul."

"I guess our family always was a bit different. And you're right, I loved my mother. She always showed nothing but love to me, and that made it harder to lose her." Aisha looked like she was about to cry herself, but she swallowed quickly and went on. "Anyway, is my father happy? No, not at all. But you know what? I think he may be content. I think that on the nights he stays home, he is mourning what he's lost, but he enjoys mourning it because as long as he feels her loss, she is still somehow with him. I think he is content. He is always reliving all the happy memories and making himself miserable, but there's something else, this deeper version of happiness, that he seems to feel at the same time. Does that make sense?

"I can imagine only."

"Anyway, so it's on the nights that he acts happy, that he goes out with the other village men, that he does God knows what, those are the nights that I think he's actually the most miserable. Back to your question, I think on those nights he seems to think maybe it really is better to not have loved at all, so he tries to forget. But he doesn't. Well, maybe he does, but I don't think so. It's just not him."

"Wow, your father is a true romantic. There are so few of those in the world anymore."

"I guess so. And my mother was glamorous, like a movie star. Well, I don't know that she was really all that beautiful, but in our house she was, because she was confident, full of love, and she knew she was loved."

"Oh, that is so beautiful!" exclaimed Leila. She now had tears running down her cheeks, even as Aisha had spoken with perfect calm.

"Maybe that's why I'm sitting here talking about it. My family was always different somehow."

"How can I not be jealous of you? If Ahmed had been here to see you instead of me, you would have gone down in full confidence!" Leila exclaimed.

"Ahmed! So you do know him. And I can see in your eyes... Yes, I think I would," smiled Aisha. But then the smile faded, her eyes narrowed, and she tilted her head. "No, I can't answer this question. I don't know Ahmed."

"What does it matter? He is a romantic like your father."

"Are you sure about that?"

"What do you mean?"

"Nothing," Aisha said quietly, picking up a book and starting to rummage her papers on the table again.

"What?" Leila couldn't end the conversation here! She had to know. Her heart had been pulled in too many different directions in too little time.

"No, really, I don't know. How can I know? Just be careful is all I'm saying. Remember, my mother was my father's cousin. He was allowed to love and lose and she was allowed to love back. Is that true about Ahmed?"

Leila poured out another cup of tea for Aisha and then

quickly stood up. "I'm sorry to take your time. You are too kind to me, but I should let you study. You're a good roommate. God keep you and your studies." She picked up the teapot and her cup and went out to the kitchen to wash them out.

Half an hour later, Leila came down from the roof and started dressing to go out. The roof always did its job. She may not be feeling that peace she felt when she woke up, but she now knew what she would do. She wasn't worried. She was a bit nervous about running into Ahmed on the street, so if she had to spend the day in the building library to avoid him, that's what she would do. Ideally, though, she was hoping that they'd be home and have a great idea.

Ghalia opened the door at Leila's knock. "Leila, *Ahlan wa Sahlan*! It's been a while!"

"I am so glad to see you, *habibti* Ghalia!" They shook hands and exchanged kisses as Leila walked in. Mary was sitting cross-legged on the bed sipping matte. Leila walked up to her, shook her hand, and kissed her once on each cheek. Mary gestured to the other end of the bed and Leila took a seat.

"So, how are you doing? How are your studies?" asked Mary.

"*Shway Shway*, they're moving along. It's not easy. But I think I'll pass."

"*Muafa'a*, may God agree!" smiled Ghalia. With a gleam in her eye, she then asked, "And Ahmed? How is he doing?"

Leila felt her face turn red. She hadn't really thought she'd pull this visit off without that coming up, had she? But she just said, "Let's not talk about Ahmed right now, okay? I want to know about you, how you're doing! How are your studies?"

Mary shrugged. Ghalia sighed. Then they both smiled.

"Fine, I get it," nodded Leila, knowing neither girl was likely to have so much as held a book in the past week. "No worries. But then what is new with you?"

"Not much, we went home for a few days last week."

"Oh yeah? How was that? What'd you do?"

"Well, a cousin got married, so we went to her bride's party, which was wonderful. We danced til three in the morning!" enthused Mary.

Ghalia continued, "And of course there was the hair, the makeup, the nails, the dresses."

"Did you get new dresses?" asked Leila.

"We had them made before, actually. We made photos with them this time, though. Do you want to see?"

"They're ready already? That's fast!"

"The professional ones are still coming, but at least we got a few made for now."

"I'd love to see your photos!"

Ghalia reached over to the lowest shelf and pulled a little envelope off from the top of the pile of books. She sat down in the small space between Leila and the foot of the bed, so Leila scooted over a bit to be sandwiched by the two girls.

Ghalia pulled the photos out and handed them to Leila. For the next fifteen minutes, Leila appropriately oohed and aahed at each photo of Mary and Ghalia in highly ornamented bright-colored dresses. They were tasteful and quite beautiful, but perhaps just a tad over the top. But Leila kept that thought to herself as she expressed amazement at the beauty, not only of the dresses, but of the elaborate hairdos held together by sequined pins, full bottles of hairspray and wads of gel. Their makeup was equally astounding. Leila thought they both looked like supermodels, and she told them so. She also thought they looked like they were trying too hard, and did not bother to tell them that.

There were about thirty photos, some of just Mary, some of just Ghalia, some of the two of them striking poses to better show off their bodily contours or their hairdo's. Some were family photos, with brothers, cousins and parents. And there were a few photos with the bride, whose white dress was even more elaborate, sequined, detailed, creative and gaudy... and whose hair was piled even higher with tighter curls and brighter pins. Even under all the makeup and sequins, though, Leila saw that she was a beautiful bride and a happy woman on the occasion of her wedding.

When they were finished reviewing the photos, Ghalia gently placed them back in the envelope and returned them to their spot on the shelf. Mary filled the matté cup with fresh hot water and handed it to Leila, who slowly sipped at the bitter herb tea.

"How's Roxy?" Leila finally asked.

"Roxy?" asked Mary. "She's good, I think! She didn't make it to the wedding, so we haven't seen her for a while."

"Oh? She hasn't been coming by here?"

"No, something with her husband's family this week, I don't know exactly what. But she's been with him all week."

Leila nodded, disappointed.

"But we're going to have dinner with her this afternoon!" offered Ghalia.

"Really?" Leila's eyebrows lifted.

"She's coming by in an hour or so to pick us up, and we're going to Old Damascus to an Arabic house that's now a restaurant and supposed to be really great."

"That sounds nice. Is her husband taking you?"

"Yup. You know, he really liked you. He thought you were a well-behaved girl, if that's a good thing to say."

After all, Leila thought, Bassel was old enough to be her father.

Mary then said, "Hey, you should come!"

Yes! Yes! "Oh, I don't know."

"Yes, come – it will be fun!" added Ghalia.

"Have you ever had dinner at an Arabic house restaurant?" asked Mary.

"Well, uh, no, I haven't."

"Then you have to come! You can't live in Damascus and never go to an Arabic house for dinner."

Oh the shame. If only her family could see her now. But really, what was worse, going in mixed company of people who weren't even of her own religion to a restaurant, or spending time alone with a young man? Well, looking at it that way, there was only one other problem. "Will I be back before curfew?"

"Oh, sure, plenty of time. Anyway, Roxy said she's staying with us tonight, so I think we have to," said Ghalia.

But then, Mary ruined her excitement. "Hey, I have an idea!" she exclaimed. "We could invite Ahmed! It could be like a repeat of last time! That would be so fun!"

"I don't think that's such a great idea," said Leila.

"Why not? I'm sure I still have his phone number written down somewhere from last time. Well, if not, Roxy will have it, I'm sure she saved it in her phone memory."

"No, I think he's busy today," Leila said.

"We could try to call him anyway," offered Mary. "Make sure he knows he's welcome."

"I don't think that will work. Anyway, he might feel obliged, and you know how that goes..."

"Did something happen between the two of you?" asked Ghalia, suddenly sobering.

"No, nothing happened. I just don't think he should come. Especially because his sister is really busy studying for exams, and I don't know how that would look."

"Oh, I don't get you, Leila," sighed Mary. "I'm sure Roxy will ask, though, so you might want a better story."

"Thanks," muttered Leila.

Mary got up off of the bed for the first time since Leila's arrival and walked over to her closet. She pulled down a small cosmetic case and grabbed a small bottle, then walked back to the bed. Ghalia rummaged around the stuff on the table and rearranged some rumpled papers, an ash tray, and the matté tray. But when Mary sat down, she pushed it all over to the corner closest to Ghalia and placed the cosmetic case on the table. Leila then saw that the bottle was nail polish remover, and Mary pulled some cotton out of the cosmetic case. Ghalia asked Leila if she wanted more matté, and when Leila declined, she picked up the matté tray and went out the door. Leila let her slippers slide off her feet and sat back on the bed. She watched Mary wipe off the thick red nail polish left over from the wedding. Once again, Leila had that slightly uncomfortable feeling of being exotic, or perhaps too plain, among her friends.

Mary scrubbed and scrubbed, dirtying four separate wads of cotton. Leila just watched and pondered. Pondered her choice of friends, Ahmed, her family... all the usual things. Then she pondered the fact that she was hardly studying and it was finals season. She pondered the look in Mary's eyes as she picked the last bits of red nail polish out from the little cracks. Mary seemed so content, so solemn... Solemnity wasn't always content, though, was it? The more Leila watched, she began to wonder at this solemnity. It was almost as if... no, she didn't want to think it. But no, there really was something there in Mary's eyes – or the lack of something – that made her think Mary looked almost... dead. Yes, it was like there was no life. She was so intent on doing her nails, but was there any life beyond that? This got Leila to thinking about Huda, dear Huda. How might she be doing these days? It had been a while since she'd seen her friend. But Leila had no doubt there was life in Huda's eyes. Those dreams, that ruinous degree of motivation: if nothing else, it was life. Living for nail polish and hair is not living for much at all.

What are we supposed to live for?, wondered Leila. *Huda has life, but do I want that kind of life? Mary doesn't really have life, just emptiness and shallowness, but at least she has fun. What do I have? Ahmed. But, do I really have Ahmed?*

Ghalia interrupted Leila's thoughts when she came back and sat in the chair, across from the table. She grabbed a piece of cotton, soaked it with polish remover, and started rubbing at the gold-colored paint on her own nails. Then she looked up at Leila, "So, how are the studies?"

Leila just sighed loudly.

"I know how you feel! I'm going to repeat this year, I'm sure."

"Why do you know? You may do really well! Don't lose hope." Leila forgot for a moment that Ghalia wasn't particularly concerned about passing.

"Well, I've already missed two exams. If I fail a third, well, you know."

"You *missed* two exams?"

"The first exam I just wasn't ready for, so what was the point? I had absolutely no idea."

"Which one was that?"

"Grammar. I know nothing of English grammar."

"Oh, I'm sorry to hear that. I think I did alright on that one, so if you want help for the re-take, let me know!" Leila offered.

"Thank you," Ghalia smiled and reached for a second piece of cotton.

"What about you, Mary? Did you do grammar?"

"No. Same thing."

"Funny, I didn't even notice you weren't in the exam."

"Well," observed Ghalia with a wink and a laugh, "you haven't been noticing much of anything the last few weeks."

"Oh well, *malish.*" Leila tried to steer the conversation away from Ahmed. "Why did you miss the second one?"

"It was the same day as the wedding, and there was no way we were going to miss the wedding!"

"I'm so sorry! You really must be feeling the pressure."

"Pressure? No. Actually, I think it's good, because next year we can really focus and learn everything well – it will be easier for us, because it will be our second time."

"Well, I guess there is that," said Leila, unconvinced.

"But I hope that you do well!" said Ghalia.

"Thank you. And if I can help you..."

"Well, thank you." Ghalia went back to rubbing her fingernails. Mary was now busily filing her nails into carefully rounded figures.

Leila watched the two girls for a few more moments, then Ghalia blurted, "Hey, Leila, I almost forgot!"

"What?"

Ghalia stood up and pulled a couple of books off of the shelf above her bed. She handed them to Leila, who took them and studied the cover of each. They were both in English. The top one looked like a collection of sayings and poems. That could be interesting. The other one was more mysterious. Its cover said, *Holy Bible.* Holy she knew, but what did Bible mean? She opened it up to the table of contents and read a list of about 60 chapters. It was a biggish book, hard-bound. As she read the chapter titles, she recognized the names of prophets, like Joshua, Isaiah, Daniel... Holy meant it was a holy book, maybe even one of the heavenly books translated into English? Fascinating!

"What are these?" she asked Ghalia, who had sat down again and was watching Leila study the books.

"We have a neighbor who is a fourth year, so she's

graduating. She's an English literature major also, and I guess she had these books for studying. She's going back home and didn't want to take all her books back with her. I don't know, I guess that's why she came over and gave them to us. She said that since we were also learning English literature we might want some stuff to read in English and gave us these three books. But you know, I don't read much, neither does Mary. We pretty much study by the lectures. So we thought of you. You like to read. Maybe you'd like to have some extra books to practice your English."

"Yes, I do like to read. Mostly novels. These don't look like novels, but they might be interesting anyway."

"See, I thought you'd say that!" smiled Ghalia.

"But this one here," Leila held up the big hard-bound book. "It says it's a holy book. Do you know what that means? Do you know what it is? Is it a heavenly book? Or just a book about religion?"

"I have no idea. Why, is that a problem?"

"Well, if it's a heavenly book, I should treat it as a heavenly book. I shouldn't really read it if I'm not *wudu'*, if I haven't done ablutions. And I guess I should treat it well. I don't want to do something that's forbidden."

"But are there heavenly books in English? I thought that was kind of a modern, casual language."

"Maybe. I guess I should ask a *sheikh* about that," said Leila. The *sheikh* who came to her family's house on Thursday nights would know, but maybe she'd just ask Ahmed. He was pretty smart. Oh, yeah, Ahmed.

After a moment's silence, Mary looked up from her nail painting. "Hey, Leila, you should do your nails!"

"Me? No way!"

"You and your modesty! It will look great. Have you ever done your nails before?" She had already grabbed one of Leila's hands and was examining it. "Your cuticles look so soft and gentle. And so neglected!"

"I did a manicure once, about a year ago when my cousin got married. But I had to wear gloves when I went out."

"Oh, no one cares," insisted Mary.

"*Ya rait!* I could never..." Leila leaned her head back against the wall.

"Come on, I'll do it now. I love doing people's nails. And then if you don't like it, you can wipe it off! That'll be great fun!"

"Do we have time? I thought you said Roxy was coming soon." Nails would be fun but bad, beautiful but *haram*, forbidden.

"There's plenty of time!" Mary picked up a nail file and started shaping Leila's fingernails. As she worked on Leila's nails, she kept commenting on Leila's soft hands and untouched nails, how they were beautiful but really needed to be cared for regularly. Mary had read in a magazine that nails should be filed and cuticles cleaned out at least once every two weeks, and she passed that indispensable advice on to Leila, along with various tips about how to shape her nails with the file and how to choose a color that was complementary, seductive, or whatever other effect might be desired.

When Roxy finally phoned, Ghalia picked up the mobile and took it out to the corridor since the music was now blaring from the radio. When she came back, she announced that it was time to go and went into the little alcove with the wardrobes to get dressed. Mary started packing up the manicure kit.

"Wait!" said Leila. "I need to take the paint off."

"You what?"

"I can't go out like this!"

"What do you mean? You look great, so much more alive,

with painted nails," soothed Mary.

Leila blushed slightly but continued to protest while Mary put the nail polish remover into the bag. Leila looked down at her hands and had to admit that they did have a certain vibrance to them that was usually lacking. Mary had done them in a rather demure soft rose color which complemented her beige overcoat nicely.

Mary stood up and started to take the cosmetic bag to the closet. Leila looked at her then back down at her nails. Maybe it would be a nice treat to go out with decorated nails tonight. After all, they were among friends. And then, as soon as she got home, she could take it off. Home – her room. She didn't want those girls to see that she'd gone out with painted nails. And come to think of it, she didn't have any nail polish remover in her room...

"Wait a second, Mary," she insisted, and stood up and walked to the closet where Ghalia was already dressed and folding up her pajamas. "I need to take it off now. I really do."

Mary looked at Leila and grinned. "*Malish*, it looks good!"

"It does look nice. I love it," Leila stated as she reached to take the case from Mary. "But you must listen to me when I say I have to take it off."

This time Mary handed Leila the bag. "Too bad, you could use some life in the way you dress from time to time."

Chapter Eight

That night the girls were back at five minutes before ten. The night guard was banging on the gates with his keys, making a horrid rattling sound. He leaned languidly by the gate as he slowly and very deliberately pulled it shut. Every minute he drew it another few inches toward him, and with each tug a few more girls tore themselves away from their male friends and sprinted in. Who had the courage to hold out til the last minute? Leila certainly didn't. When Ahmed had visited her she had insisted on being safely tucked away in the women's-only (except for that lucky, cocky night guard) building by 9:00, or perhaps 9:30 at the latest.

But tonight Roxy's husband dropped the girls off on the highway, at the far end of the Medina, at ten minutes before ten. Leila was not a runner, but her instinct was to start sprinting toward Building 14. Roxy didn't share that instinct. Once Leila and Mary and Ghalia were out of the car, she lingered, chatting with her husband. Annoyed at this untimely display of love, Leila started walking toward the gate, but when no one followed, she turned back and saw Roxy step out of the car, shout something at Bassel, and slam the door shut before stomping with her cousins toward the gate. She walked slowly and resolutely, almost as if in a military march, and clearly there was no point trying to talk to her, much less rush her to make curfew. So Leila joined the parade and followed the girls into the gate, one slow, determined step at a time.

Once through the gate, Roxy reached back and grabbed Leila's arm, then the two walked silently with arms linked. Mary and Ghalia followed, also arm-in-arm.

Leila's heart was pounding as they walked past three other women's buildings, and emanating from each she could hear the distinctive bang of keys on gates. Each time a key hit metal, she'd pick up the pace for a second, but Roxy would slow her down again. Leila glanced over at Roxy and saw that she was frowning and gazing straight ahead. Sensing her friend's tension, Leila just submitted to fate.

As they approached Building 14, Roxy turned to the girls and asked if they needed anything at the shop. Leila wanted to scream, and started to protest that there was no time, but Ghalia mercifully answered that they had everything they needed.

Leila was sure they'd speed up at the end, at the very least to give that snobby guard the impression that they were trying. But no, Roxy slowed down. At least it felt that way to Leila. There were fewer than a dozen girls left challenging the number of inches through which they could slip. Leila started rehearsing humble apologies in her mind, arguments and tears that might eventually get them through the gate.

By the time they had strolled through the courtyard, they were the last girls outside the gate. There were now fewer than 20 inches of space remaining. They approached the guard.

"You're late, girls," he sneered.

"*Lissa*," replied Roxy. "Not quite yet."

"Ten o'clock. You know the rules!"

"There's still two whole minutes." Roxy gazed straight into his eyes.

And just like that, the guard swung the door open and the four girls walked through.

So that was how it worked. Fair is fair. It wasn't ten o'clock yet, so they were in. Roxy had just stood her ground, said she knew, and the guard hadn't even given them a hard time. He'd even opened the door for them. Was he intimidated? Leila sure was.

Ironically, as they started up the stairs, Leila heard some other girls' voices. It turned out they weren't the last ones in that night, but this last batch of girls was shouting and running, making quite a spectacle of themselves. They got in too, but Leila noted that they were the Turkish girls, foreigners, and everyone knew the rules didn't apply quite the same for foreigners.

As they were walking up the stairs, Leila told the other girls that she'd like to take a detour to the roof. Roxy quickly volunteered her company, while Ghalia and Mary said they would head back to their room. So Leila and Roxy dropped the sisters off on their floor and kept going up the stairs to the top.

"I do love it up here; don't you?" Leila exclaimed the moment they stepped out into the open.

Roxy just nodded slightly and walked off a bit to the right. The way she walked gave Leila the impression that Roxy wanted to be alone. Roxy, the outgoing leader, the one who loved friends and husband and family and managed to make them all think she loved them equally, even while screwing with them behind their backs? Leila watched Roxy's wanderings for a few minutes then decided to sit on the big concrete block for a while.

She pulled out the books Ghalia had given her. For some reason she had lugged them around with her as they'd wandered around the old city of Damascus this evening, and her shoulder was feeling the strain. But now that she had a few minutes to herself, she found herself studying them again. The book of poems and sayings was beautiful. It was just a little paperback, but she flipped through it for a few minutes and her heart fluttered with each quote she read.

She had no idea what the other book was, but she found herself captivated. As she held it, she almost felt some kind of force emanating from it. It was heavy and sombre looking, a big brown hardback. And it was long – more than 1000 pages long. She wondered if it was a heavenly book, if it would be against religion to read a bit. So she uttered a quick prayer, "I take refuge from Satan... in the name of God the gracious and merciful", figuring that protected her enough in case she was doing something wrong, then opened it up. She turned to the first page of the second, shorter, section and started reading.

Leila was seriously disappointed. It was a list of names. So and so was the father of so and so, who was the father of so and so, who was the father of so and so. As she read through the names, she recognized the names of famous prophets, like Abraham and David, and she saw the Christ mentioned. She knew that the Christ was the second-to-last prophet, and possibly the second-most-important.

After a few more moments, Leila slammed the book shut. It was horridly boring. Or so she told herself. But she also had to admit that she was trembling a little bit. Something about that list of prophets scared her. Maybe it was God warning her that she had to be prepared to read a "holy" book, not just pick it up on the roof. She put the books back into the plastic bag and set it on the concrete block. Then she hopped off and walked over to Roxy.

As she got close, Leila thought she heard Roxy crying. Leila hadn't imagined that someone as strong as Roxy might ever cry and was unsure how to try to comfort her. Instead, she made a bit of noise to warn Roxy she was there, then looked out in the other direction. A minute later, Roxy turned to Leila. Her eyes were red.

"Is everything alright?" asked Leila.

"Fine."

"Are you sure?"

"Of course! I couldn't be happier," Roxy said a little too cheerily. And before Leila had a chance to press, Roxy asked,

"So, what's with you?"

"With me? Nothing, I'm doing great!"

"Ghalia warned me not to mention Ahmed. So I didn't. But Bassel wanted to invite him and I couldn't think of a good excuse not to."

"I'm sorry! Did I cause any trouble?"

"No, no. No problem. But, I do love a good scandal, so spill all!"

"It's not important, I just didn't want to see him today, that's all."

"Are you still..."

"He visited yesterday, if that's what you're asking."

"Ah, good." Roxy seemed very relieved. "He seems so great. So smart, so handsome, so right for you."

"*Insha'allah* – if God wills it."

"Sure."

Each girl then fell into her own thoughts, leaning on the ledge and looking out at the lights of Damascus and at the mountain beyond. After a few minutes, Roxy stood up and said it was time to leave. She invited Leila to come chat and drink matté, but Leila declined, saying she thought she'd stay a few more minutes then go down to study – after all, she had been neglecting her studies lately. She expressed again her thanks to Roxy for another fun evening out, and the girls exchanged kisses.

Leila really did mean to go down to her room but as she was gathering up her books from the concrete block, Maha came up the stairs.

"Good evening, Leila!" Maha said cheerily.

"You seem happy tonight," replied Leila.

"I am happy tonight!" Maha acknowledged as she gave Leila a kiss on each cheek.

"May God make every day happy for you," Leila said as she put the books into the bag.

Maha smiled but said nothing.

So Leila asked, "Well, are you going to tell me?"

"Oh, it's nothing. I just had a great time at my aunt's house. Normal but just good family time. Somehow a night with family warms the heart."

"That's very profound."

"Yes, I guess it is, isn't it?" Maha smiled. "So, what about you? How are you?"

"I'm well." Leila tried to feign happiness equal to Maha's. The last thing she wanted was to avoid another round of questions about Ahmed.

But Maha wasn't suspicious. She just asked, "What did you do today?"

Relieved, Leila recounted her activities of the day, starting with her arrival at Mary and Ghalia's room. She told of her harrowing return to the Medina right at 10:00 and of how she came to be on the roof. Then it occurred to her that Maha might be able to help solve the mystery of the big brown book.

So she said, "When I was over in the girls' room this afternoon, they gave me some books in English that were left behind by someone they know who is graduating. They thought I'd like them – I guess I have a reputation for liking to read English stuff. Plus, they don't really study at all, so they'd never bother with them. I don't know if they've ever read a book except what they needed to get into university... So they gave the books to me, and they look interesting, especially this one," and she reached into the plastic bag to hand the big brown book to Maha. "...but I don't know what it is. It looks like something religious. I thought maybe it's Christian?"

Maha took the book in her hands, opened it up, paged through the first few pages, then leafed quickly through the tome. She opened it to a page at random and pondered. "I think this is a copy of the Holy Book. I don't know so much English, but see how at the top of the page is a title, then there are big numbers and little numbers. In the Injil that's how it's laid out: chapters are the big numbers and verses are the little numbers. Yeah, look, see? This says Isaiah, and that sounds like Isha'ia, one of the books in the Old Testament."

"Old Testament?"

"Yeah, the older half. You've never heard of an Old Testament?"

"No, and what is 'the Holy Book'?"

"You know, our book, the Christian book."

"You mean the Injil?"

"Oh, the Injil is the New Testament. Everything about Jesus and after."

"So your Old Testament: is that the Taurath, the Torah?"

"Yeah, maybe. Something like that."

"So this is your book."

"Yeah, I think so. I've never seen it in English, and my English isn't so great, but yeah."

Leila was glad she hadn't kept reading, since this was in fact likely a heavenly book. But she was confused about something.

"So, is this a translation of the Injil?"

"What do you mean?"

"You said you'd never seen it in English before. What language do you read it in?"

"Huh?" Maha didn't seem to understand the question.

"I mean, what is the language of the Injil? It's not English?"

"English? Why would the Injil belong to English people? God's not American!"

Both girls were silent. Leila thought this was an obvious statement, but it had not occurred to her before that if she thought God spoke English, that might mean that God was

American. Of course, all good Muslims know that the Qur'an is God's holiest book, and it's in Arabic – does that mean God is an Arab?

After a minute, Leila said, "I guess I'm glad you don't think God is American, although I didn't really think you thought that... but I'm confused, because I want to know if this is a heavenly book. If it's not what God sent down, then it's just a translation, isn't it?"

Maha thought for a moment. "I'm trying to remember what I learned in Religion class. I think the Bible was written in a bunch of different languages. Of course there's Aramaic, the language they still speak in Ma'alula – I have family members who speak it, and they're proud that they speak the language Jesus spoke. But the really old books came down to the Jews. So they were in Hebrew. Plus, I think some of it was written in Greek... Yeah, I'm pretty sure each book was first written in a specific language, whatever language its writer knew."

"So which is the right version?"

"Well, I don't think it matters, does it? Each translation is done by professionals, people who are trained in the original languages and in translation. In my church we always read it in Arabic, and some people have it in very old Arabic, but others have a translation that is a little bit more modern."

"That is so strange."

"Why?"

"Well... the Qur'an is only really the Qur'an if it's in Arabic. Because that's the language it came down in. Any other translations are just translations."

"Oh. Well, I don't know."

"Yeah, I don't know." Leila put the book back in the bag and decided that to be on the safe side, if she were to ever read the book, she'd do ablutions first. Then she said to Maha, "So, enough of that. How are you? What's new with you?"

"With me? Not much. Study study study. It's that time of year."

"Why did you come back tonight? Why didn't you stay at your aunt's?"

"Since there is family over I didn't think I'd get much studying done there. And, I have study group early tomorrow morning."

"Really?"

"For my exam on Sunday."

"May God help you pass."

"Thank you," Maha replied. Then she asked, "Have you seen Huda lately?"

"Huda? No. I've been so busy, and I figure she's been busy studying..."

"Studying? I don't think so."

"What do you mean?" asked Leila, a little bit alarmed.

Maha stared at Leila for a brief minute. Then she asked, "When is the last time you talked to Huda?"

Leila thought for a minute. It must have been a week ago. "I think it was right after I talked to you that time."

"Really? It's been that long?"

"Why?"

"I wonder, has anyone been checking up on her?"

"I think her mood passed. I figure she went back to studying the next day."

Maha was silent for a moment, then continued, quietly. "You never found out what happened, did you?"

"She had a panic attack from studying too much. She just needed to take some time off to rest up and balance her life a bit," pronounced Leila.

Maha walked over to the ledge, leaving Leila standing near the door with bag in hand, wondering if she should say goodbye, follow Maha, or just leave. She decided to go over to the ledge. When she came up to Maha, she asked if anything was wrong.

"No, no. Nothing's wrong. I'm just worried about Huda, that's all."

"Worried? I didn't realize you two were so close."

"It's just that when she was having her attack she came to me, and I wasn't sure what I should do."

"Oh, I'm sure you were good to her. May God bless you for your efforts."

Maha laughed and said, "Thanks, but that's not what I'm worried about. I'm thinking I'd better go check on her. I haven't seen her all week either."

"I'm sure everything's fine," Leila said. "But I'd like to see her, too. It's been a while. I'll go down with you."

Maha seemed relieved and started for the door. Leila followed her, puzzled. She had never known Maha and Huda to be good friends, but Maha seemed really involved. As far as Leila knew, Huda and Maha had only met that one time at the tabouli party. But maybe they'd visited when she was at home or with Ahmed or... Yeah, she had been quite involved in other things the last few weeks. She shrugged and started down the stairs.

When they got to the room, they knocked on Huda's door. Some girl who neither Leila nor Maha recognized answered and said she hadn't seen Huda all week, and that she thought Huda had gone home to the village. Then she closed the door, leaving the two friends in the hallway.

Leila was stupefied. "The village? In the climax of finals? That's not like her."

"Do you have a phone number for her?"

"No! I figured I'd ask her for it before we left for the summer. I hope nothing's happened!"

"Me too," said Maha. She sounded doubtful.

"What aren't you telling me?"

"Oh it's nothing. It's up to Huda." Maha bid Leila good night, leaving Leila alone in the hallway wondering if she should be feeling guilty.

Chapter Nine

After a very poor night's sleep, Leila woke up around 11:00 Saturday morning. Her first thought was that she really needed to start studying for her last few exams. Her second thought was that she had had very odd dreams. Ahmed was definitely there, and so was Huda. Ahmed with Huda? No, that would be too strange. Roxy was there, sobbing, but it also seemed she was planning some really big party. No, she was pressuring Leila to plan a party and for some reason Leila couldn't... Or was Roxy planning to arrange a marriage and asking Leila to arrange a meeting at a restaurant in Old Damascus, where Ahmed would meet some girl's mother?

She walked out into the hallway and went to the kitchen to wash for prayer. Just as she was finishing, she heard someone unlocking what sounded like Huda's door. She peeked her head out of the kitchen door and, sure enough, it was Huda. Leila called out to her:

"Huda! You're here! I was so-o-o-o worried about you!"

"Hi, Leila," Huda said in a tired voice.

"*Alhamdulillah A-salama*! Praise God you're back safely!" Leila walked up to her and starting pumping kisses on Huda's cheeks, first right, then left, then back to right, then left, then left again, then left one last time.

"*Allah aselmek*. Thank you. Yes, I'm back." Huda smiled weakly.

"You went to the village?"

"Yes." Huda finished unlocking her door and walked in.

Leila helped her carry some plastic bags into the room and put them on the floor near Huda's bed. "Why?" she asked. "Why in the world..." Her voice trailed off but the question was obvious.

"I had to go."

"Why? What happened? Is it true you've been gone all week? Does that mean you won't pass this year?"

"Hopefully it will all work out," said Huda. "What time is it?"

"It's just after eleven o'clock. Do you have something?"

"This afternoon only."

"Good. We can chat. Or are you going to jump right back into studying?"

"No, let's chat," determined Huda. "I brought some good flower tea back from the village. Do you want some?"

Leila nodded and sat down on Huda's bed. She reminded herself to be quiet and listen, then said, "OK. I'm ready to listen. I promise."

And Huda told Leila the story of her last week, leaving out some details that were hopefully inconsequential.

"When did I last see you... last Friday, right? I was in bad shape. I don't remember those days very clearly, actually. Did I tell you anything? No? I didn't think so. I don't think I was in any shape to talk, was I? Thanks for coming by and I'm sorry I couldn't accept your hospitality. I wasn't just panicking because I was studying too hard. I was studying too hard, that's for sure. You know, it has always been my dream to have a big career as a lawyer. I had it all planned out: after university I was going to go on to post-graduate studies, then my Masters, then do a qualification and specialization abroad, in France preferably. Then come back and do my doctorate – or maybe I would have done that in Europe also.

"But to do any of that I needed perfect scores. My family doesn't have money, nor do we have *wasta*, connections. I think I already explained to you that it's even harder for me, because I'm from just a few villages over from where the president is from, so everyone thinks we must have really good *wasta* and so they need to punish me, or at least – as they say – make it clear that *they* are not going to give me any special privileges because of who I am. As if I'm anyone important!

"And that's why I studied so hard, and I guess I did some stupid things, because I started to get desperate. So when a professor called me into his office last week and threatened me, I couldn't handle it. Oh, do you want sugar in your tea?"

Leila took the sugar bowl that Huda offered her, but she didn't start spooning sugar into her cup until Huda started talking again.

"I really don't know what he was threatening me with or why he picked on me, but I do know that it was me who first contacted him for help. If I'd just stayed anonymous, attending and memorizing lectures like the rest of the students, none of this would have happened. But I thought I needed to start building my *wasta*. No, that's not really why I went to him. I was stupid and thought maybe a professor would actually help me to understand the material. I don't know what grudge he has against me: if he thought I was pretentious, or if he dislikes my family – I can't see how he knows my family though! Or if he just wants to see girls fail. But last Thursday when he called me to his office, I thought it was all over. I felt like he was telling me that my dreams were over, just like that.

"That's when I lost it. I think Maha told you she saw me and that's why you came over, isn't it? Oh yeah, you have a new boyfriend, don't you? I forgot! How's that going? I'm so sorry to worry you; you should be focusing on your own life.

Leila smiled, but she held her tongue and waited.

Soon enough, Huda continued, "I guess I can finish my story first. One thing at a time, right? Everything in my life had been focused on my one dream, my big dream. And I knew that one little thing could ruin it: nothing less than perfection would make it happen, and that's why I was studying so hard. But I learned that even perfection may not be enough. Something else can ruin a dream. When that happened, I lost my ability to focus. That's when I collapsed. I couldn't think, couldn't study, couldn't talk, couldn't sleep. Maha took me out that one night, and that was good because she made me eat. When you saw me I think I was in a daze, too much of a daze to think. But the thing is that I panicked at some point, and when you saw me, the thought of leaving the building was too much for me. That's why I didn't go with you. I was scared of the outdoors.

"The next day, though, something changed, and I was able to control myself enough to realize that if I was going to be useless, at least I could go be useless with my family nearby. If I was going to fail, there was no point staying in Sham, so I might as well go home anyway. Plus, I longed to be near the beautiful mountains and flowers and fresh air of home: it's so beautiful this time of year. So I left. I got out of bed, got dressed, and went to the bus station. Four hours later I was in Latakia and took a van up to the village.

"When I got to the village, though, it wasn't what I expected. At first it was: everyone was so glad to see me, and they started preparing a great meal and word spread around the village, and my old friends came around to visit. That first day I felt so loved, so embraced, so glad to be home...

"Then as we were getting ready for bed that night, my sister asked me what I was doing there. Had I really finished exams already? When I told her no, then everything changed. She suddenly stopped talking and went to sleep. So I slept also and had the first good night's sleep I've had in months – well, at least since a few weeks before exams started. I slept like an angel, until noon the next day!

"When I woke up, half of me felt wonderful. I was home. I could hear birds chirping and smell the scent of the vegetables in the garden and of the orange trees drifting my way. But the other half of me felt like trash because I knew I had not returned home under good circumstances.

"I went into the family room and everyone was sitting there. My sisters, my mother and my father. I asked my dad if he was back from work already and there was that silence. Just like my sister the night before – they just kind of ignored me. Anyway, to make a long story short, eventually I found out that my father had been laid off from his government job, one year before he was eligible for retirement. All of a sudden our family was without income, which meant that my glorious future was the only hope for our family. Except that by the time I achieved my glorious future we might have died of poverty, but I guess they were willing to take that risk. Out of love? Out of desperation to have something to be proud of? I don't know. But apparently while I was killing myself studying for a stupid academic dream, my family was..." Huda's voice broke off and she took a deep breath of air.

"They're eating nothing but bread and the occasional egg. And whatever is growing in the garden – thank God for the garden. My sister is working now at the shop. It's a terrible job. My father is looking, but at his age no one is going to give him a job.

"After I found out, I felt terrible. I'd been spending their money even though they didn't actually have any, and then I was wasting their investment by giving up on my studies. It was like I'd abused them and was now betraying them. It was an awful week. They kept asking me why I was back if exams weren't over yet, and I kept avoiding the question. There was nothing I could say that they'd believe. Leila, I tell you, family is everything, and I love my family. I don't think anything ever hurt me quite so much as keeping a secret like this from them.

"In myself I was trying to decide what to do. Should I try to take my exams or just give up? Is there any way at all I could recover? And now here I am. In the end, I couldn't tell them that I'd failed, so it seems I have to come back. I missed two exams last week, but if I was going to fail them anyway... what can I say? I just need to work things out with the professor. I don't know what's going to happen, but I'm going to go see him this afternoon. I wish I could ask you to come with me, but I feel I have to go alone. I can't let my family down."

That afternoon, Leila sat on her bed and pondered Huda's story. There was obviously more to it than she had let on, who knows, maybe even Huda didn't even know the whole story. But this situation with the professor sounded scary and very strange. Leila should have been there for her friend, but how? She didn't know what was going on. She was surprised and a tad jealous that Maha had all of a sudden become Huda's confidante. It should have been Leila. But as she thought more she decided that maybe it was better that it was Maha.

The bell rang, pulling Leila out of her thoughts. It just so happened that Aisha was alone with Leila in the room again. Aisha was quietly studying, giving Leila space for her own thoughts, but when the bell rang, she asked Leila if she was expecting someone. Leila smiled ever so slightly.

"Same story, huh?" Aisha raised an eyebrow with a smile and started to get up.

"No! No! Don't go. Just pretend no one's there!" urged Leila anxiously.

"But why? He seems so nice; it could be love waiting for you."

"Don't say that."

"I'm sorry. You're right. I'll just go tell him no one's home."

"It's better if he just thinks there isn't anyone here at all," protested Leila.

By this time Aisha had thrown on a scarf and put on her sandals, but she sat down again. "Okay. Well, I'm not expecting anyone, so if that's what you want, fine."

"Thank you, *habibti*." Leila was sure it was Ahmed, but she wasn't sure what to say or how to deal with him. And now all of a sudden she felt like everything that had gone wrong in Huda's life was somehow her fault, punishment for her relationship with Ahmed.

Meanwhile, Huda kept her appointment – one week late. She showed up at the restaurant, that dastardly, dingy, disgraceful and yet decorous place. She thought about covering her head for the first time as she entered the neighborhood which housed both society's most elite, and women with no shame, in the same buildings. But somehow doing so seemed false to her so she simply kept her head down, avoiding eye contact or even crossing paths with any of the men on the street. She walked slowly. She felt she was marching to her doom. Though the appointment was clearly for last Saturday, something in her gut told her that one week's delay was insignificant.

She entered the building and walked up the flight of stairs. Everything was eerily quiet, and she caught sight of the door at the end of the hallway, just barely ajar. She imagined herself going in there right now and trashing the furniture, especially the mattress, and tossing the chair out the window. Then her doom would be averted, or at least postponed.

But she found she barely had the strength to knock on the

door of the restaurant.

A mustachioed waiter opened the door. She didn't recognize him from her previous visit. Huda stated that she had an appointment with the professor and was ushered quickly in. There he was at the same table, framed by the dim light of the sun shining through thick red curtains. His table was covered with food, and he was scarfing it down with his hands. He sat alone.

When he saw Huda, he stood up. "Huda! You're late."

"I'm sorry, sir."

"You're very late."

"I'm here now, sir."

"You're here now. Excuse me for not greeting you properly," he held out his hands to illustrate that they were coated with food, then gestured to the seat across from him. "*Tfadali*. Have a seat."

Huda sat down nervously, clutching her bag tightly. She didn't look at him. Instead she studied the vast assortment of food that this man had ordered.

The professor gestured to a waiter, who quickly came over. "Get the young lady a plate and silverware, and –" he turned to Huda. "What do you want to drink?"

Huda glanced up at the waiter standing at the ready, then quickly glanced back down. Focusing her eyes on the small spots of red tablecloth peeking out from the numerous plates of food, she raised her eyebrows to say no. Out of the corner of her eye, she saw the professor wave the waiter off.

For the next half hour, Huda squirmed in her seat while the professor ate. He didn't say much and she said even less. Actually, she didn't say anything. She just kept staring at a little hole in the tablecloth she found, apparently from a cigarette burn. The professor ate hommous, tabouli, fattoush, muttabel, and skewers of meat. He ate as if he hadn't had a proper meal for years. His hands just got messier and, though Huda didn't dare look, she was sure his face was covered with smears of pasty foods as well. Every so often he would comment on what made this tabouli so good, or how the hommous didn't have enough garlic.

As he was slowing down, he finally asked her about her studies. Huda felt her heart pounding out of her stomach and her arms shaking. She started the little speech she had prepared:

"Actually, I have a little problem that I needed to ask you about. I hate to bother you, I really do, but, well, family problems have come up. My family called me last weekend and told me to come back to the village immediately. That's why I didn't come last week. I didn't even have time to tell anyone I was leaving. I thought my mother had died or something like that, but when I got there it wasn't that. Anyway, it's not important. *Alhamdulillah*, Praise God, everyone is alive, but there was a big problem when I got there. And I couldn't come back until this morning. I'm telling you this because, well, I missed two exams this week. You know how hard I study; I didn't miss them out of laziness or anything like that. It was a family emergency. You understand, don't you?"

The professor tugged a few tissues out of the small kleenex box at the far end of the table and started to wipe his hands off. It appeared that he had no intention of washing them, even after such a display of full-body eating. He waved the dirty tissues at Huda and grunted.

Huda took that as a cue to continue. "Anyway, what I'm wondering is... can I take those exams? Can I take them late? Should I go talk to the professors, or is there some procedure?"

The professor finally responded, "Well, if you miss an exam, you miss the exam... Normally, there are no exceptions."

Huda took great heart in his use of the word "normally."

He put down the kleenex and gestured to the waiter, then waved his hand over the table. The waiter understood and started clearing the plates, and the professor continued, "But I'll see what I can do. Did you bring your books?"

Books! So he really did want to help her study?

"Yes, sir, I did! I have so much to catch up on, especially after this week with my family!"

"OK, then, come along."

And Huda followed him out the door, down the hall, and into her room of doom. This time she did not register shock, she did not protest, and she did not leave until he indicated she was done. Over the course of the next two hours, a series of things happened which she'd never even imagined could happen. Her clothes were all removed and he touched her in places no human being had touched her since her mother had stopped bathing her around the age of 3. At first he touched her gently and she even felt a faint pleasure, something slightly familiar which made her even want a bit more, a sensation she had not at all expected to feel.

But then, he stopped being so gentle and started rubbing her body with more than just his hands. At this point Huda closed her eyes and refused to open them again. The professor didn't seem to notice. He kept touching her and rubbing and pushing and slobbering. She clenched her eyes shut even harder and tried to think of the flowers in her garden in the village, or other distant and happy things. At the very least she wanted to envision the graduate law diploma that would be her prize for this suffering. The pain and the fear dominated her and she was able to mentally transport herself to a scene of her village, seen from above as if she were a bird. His grunting and groaning noises floated back at her, but as if from a great distance.

When the light in the room eventually flipped back on,

Huda moaned and rolled over in the bed, slowly daring to open her eyes. She looked up just in time to see the professor grab his wallet and keys off the table and let himself out of the room, closing the door behind him without even looking in her direction. Huda slowly pulled herself up and tested her various limbs then checked her watch and saw that nearly two hours had passed. As quickly as the bruised muscles in her arms, legs, chest and face would allow, she dressed herself, tidied the bed to make it look like nothing had happened, found some makeup in her purse and did her best to hide a bit of purple on her cheek, and left. She stumbled all the way back to the Medina, an hour's walk, forcing herself to move quickly as if her march could serve as some kind of penance for what she had just done, for the innocence and purity which she feared she had left in that room and the shame she had surely brought to her family. As she walked, the tears flowed and she couldn't shake the dull pain, both physical and emotional, that coated her. But she also felt hope: hope that she would succeed, and hope that her family would not be disappointed.

On Sunday, the bell rang once again in the Dera'a girls' room, this time in the early evening. This time, Leila was alone in the room. All the girls were in the library or at the university, presumably finishing exams for the day. For five minutes after the bell rang, she sat on the edge of her bed, trying to decide what to do. Her heart was lunging for the door, trying to drag her body off the bed so that her eyes could at least catch a glimpse of her *habib*, her dear one. Her body was paralyzed, though, as if it couldn't determine whether to follow heart or mind. Mind was telling her to stay put, listing several dozen reasons why it was better to stay on the safe side, not to give love, much less forbidden love, a stronghold over her life.

But it was Heart that won the tug-of-war for her body, and Leila put on a scarf and headed into the hallway to look out the window. She tried to peek out so no one would see her, but then she could only spot the trees and some empty benches. So she took a gulp of air and stuck her head out the window. The courtyard was empty except for a very handsome man with a winsome smile staring up at her window, his sister at his side. Nisreen waved cheerfully as soon as she saw Leila. Leila waved back and ran back to her room to quickly put on a better scarf and an overcoat.

TAJREEBA: EXPERIENCE

Chapter One

I want to be like a pearl, hidden in an oyster, unopened, waiting to be discovered... If I could live in Saudi, where I wouldn't even be allowed to show my face, that would be so ideal.

I want to be strong. I never cry, and I never let people see when things go wrong. In fact, it's better to tell them a different story. I need them to think I'm strong.

I want to have influence, I want to have power, I can make a difference! ...but some things are too big for me to change.

I want to be special, I want everyone to notice me... I can be beautiful, tantalizing, exotic, alluring. I'm a good girl, though, not like those girls who have no shame, who only attract attention. They ruin it for the rest of us.

I want to travel, I want to do amazing things, the world is MY oyster. I mean, I've seen it on TV and on the Internet: it really is amazing. Oh, but my home, my bed, my mother's food... is so comforting and so comfortable. Why would I leave that?

I want to be free, but I want to be safe. I'm nothing without family, without my parents and then my husband, and it's better that way. They look after me, we look after each other.

I want friends, I want that personal connection and relationship. I can't even imagine what it would be like to have someone to whom I could tell everything. What would it be like to be able to share my heart?

Two years later, Leila was once again seated on her

favorite concrete bench, gazing out at Mount Qasioun and at the city lights. It was a beautiful, warm summer night. Actually, this had been a rather cold year, and tonight was the first night that she felt comfortable sitting up here for an extended period of time. It was also exactly one month before her last exam. Her one month pre-anniversary of the rest of her life.

As soon as she'd returned home from her evening walk with Ahmed, she'd changed quickly into her pajamas, replaced her headscarf with a simpler, warmer one, grabbed an old blanket she'd found in an abandoned dorm room last year, and slipped up the stairs. She'd also brought some pumpkin seeds and biscuits. Tonight was a roof night. If she could stay up all night on her concrete block, she would.

As she gazed at the mountain, she thought back to the first time she'd been up there, with Ahmed. And Roxy and Roxy's husband and Ahmed's sister, and the girls. How fascinated she'd been to see the world from above, to breathe the fresh night air above the Damascus pollution. Back then she'd believed that she needed to take advantage of every single second. Since then, she'd been back up the mountain a few times with Ahmed, and she'd seen much of the rest of Sham. The city had grown normal to her, simply the place she lived. But nonetheless, it still had a magical quality, and the thrill of stepping out onto the rooftop or of wandering down a narrow alley in the old city had yet to disappear.

She hoped it never would. Even if she lived in Damascus for the rest of her life, she wanted everything to feel special. She wanted to never lose the magic. She wondered if the building where she and Ahmed were going to live would have a roof. Not that a respectable Shami woman would spend time alone up on her building's roof. On this roof she had learned to avoid the spots with sewage fumes wafting from the pipes, but most of Damascus's roofs were also filled with obstacles such as satellite dishes and diesel tanks.

But when that day came, Ahmed would be with her. A chill went up her spine. On that day, she may never want to leave the house again. Or they could enjoy the roof together. Her mind wandered off to the home that she had constructed in her mind, with a cute honeymoon room and another room that would be used for storage for a while until they had their first baby. She had planned the colors for the salon in a dozen different combinations, allowing herself to include details like traditional Damascene woodwork mosaics with pieces of marble, and silk curtains... after all, she was marrying someone from a good family with excellent career prospects.

Just then she heard the sound of tires screeching down on the Autostrad. For a moment she weighed the potential of witnessing something interesting, unlikely though it may be considering the buildings and trees between her and the highway. As always, she obeyed her curious character. She got off her concrete perch and walked over to the far end of the roof. She didn't get far: there wasn't actually a way to access the landing closest to the Autostrad. Every time she came up to the roof, some noise attracted her interest and she went to check it out. And every time it was a futile effort because she couldn't get to that side of the roof. Would she ever learn?

She wandered back to her blanket. There was a section worn through that she'd carefully folded over. The fold had released, so she tucked the corner of the blanket under the hole again and sat on it. She once again marveled at how she was alone up here. Alone. Why did the other girls not come up on an enchanting spring night like this? It was even more deserted than usual, maybe because many of the girls were home during the lull between courses and exams. But there was something more than that, she pondered. When the girls came, they never came alone. While for her the Medina was the epitome of freedom – she could sit up here alone on the roof by herself and not worry about anyone – it seemed the Medina was actually frightening to other girls for the exact same reason.

In the village, Leila barely had a second to her own thoughts between her mother telling her what to do around the house and talking about potential husbands (comments Leila endured in silence, secure in her knowledge that soon all would be known), and her sisters talking about everything from makeup and dresses to the latest videoclip on TV, to their own studies. But, it wasn't just because it was home. Did she even know what alone meant when she came to Sham four years ago?

This thought stopped her in her thoughts. Alone. No, Leila didn't want to be alone. She was looking forward to a lifetime of companionship with her true love. She was looking forward to bearing his children and spending time with them. She was thrilled that she had found a true friend in his sister. No, alone is a bad thing. And yet the roof. Alone was what she loved so much about it. Never mind that sometimes she came up here with friends, and when she did it seemed like their conversation was that much better for having been held on the roof... what she truly loved about the roof was that here she could be alone.

Alone in her thoughts, no one watching, no one caring... just for a little bit. Or tonight, with the magical weather on a momentous day, for a few hours anyway.

How ironic it felt when, just a second later, she heard voices in the stairwell. It sounded like two, no three, girls, and the sound of their footsteps reverberated as they drew closer. She shifted in her position right in the middle of her concrete block, not wanting anyone to get any ideas – unless of course it was Maha... or maybe Huda, someone she wouldn't mind seeing right now.

But it was in fact three girls, looking very young. They wore bright-colored pajamas, one in orange with white stripes on the top, one in red with a pink teddy bear patched onto the jacket, and the other in a plain sky blue hooded outfit. They didn't have anything on their heads, and judging from their accents, it sounded like they were from near Tartous. Or maybe from near Huda's village. In unison all three glanced in her direction and then carried on over to the furthest corner, not surprisingly to the corner that looked out towards the men's buildings. One of the girls pointed at a male dorm and the other three strained their heads in that direction, like they were trying to identify something in a window several hundred meters away. They all giggled and stood on their tiptoes for a few minutes. Leila smiled at their childishness. She was sure they must be first-years, possibly even only just arrived in Damascus a few weeks before exams.

But then she remembered her first year and how she'd started to explore Damascus with the girls in her room. Back when they didn't know each other and thought they enjoyed each other's company. Back when spending time with anyone was better than spending time with no one. Back before the others had all become so exasperatingly traditional. Yes, back then she could have done exactly the same thing. This sparked a memory of a room in the closest male dorm in which some guy had danced for hours on end each night. About a year ago, as she recalled, she had casually glanced in that direction, and different men had been sitting in the room. That had been the end of her dancing man. But she had watched him, and not too long ago either! After a few minutes, the girls gave up and walked past her, still giggling, without even so much as a glance in her direction, and disappeared back down into the darkness of the stairs.

Leila all of a sudden felt a strong urge to lie down. Yes,

she was safe, in fact the guard had just started banging on the gates signaling the impending ten o'clock curfew. Yes, this was the one place in the world where she was completely out in the open and exposed to the elements, but was nonetheless safe from questioning or wandering eyes. But she could never be sure. She wasn't sure what there was to be concerned about. It wasn't like those girls were going to tarnish her reputation in any way. Still, it didn't feel right to let loose and lie down. Just like once she'd tried to dance up here but had quickly stopped. She had been too nervous about who might pop up the stairs.

But tonight was a special night. Her last first perfect night of the year. Her one-month countdown until it all changed. She glanced furtively around her and assured herself that no one could see her, much less care, and she lay down. One more month. She couldn't wait to graduate, to grow up, to get a job and, most of all, to be with Ahmed. But would anywhere be quite so much fun, quite such a home, as this? Swaying back and forth between these two thoughts, she drifted off to sleep.

Huda marched impatiently up the stairs to her room. The elevator was out again, but she wouldn't have expected it to be working today anyway – it only worked when she *wanted* the exercise. No, today was not her day. In fact, she was beginning to wonder if her day even existed. She was out of breath when she got to her door and quickly unlocked it. She slipped in and one of her roommates, who she barely knew, was sitting in bed studying. Huda said a quick hello and proceeded to take off her jeans, polo shirt and shoes, changing into her pajamas and slippers. She wasn't sure whether to sit down and pout or to keep moving. Would the answer just come to her if she did one of these two things?

She grabbed the teapot and walked out to the kitchen to

get some water. She walked quickly toward the kitchen, refusing to glance in the direction of Leila's door. It hardly seemed like talking was the way to solve her problems. She stuck the teapot under the tap and turned the spout on full-blast, but instead of filling the pot quickly, the water splashed right out of the pot all over her clothes and the floor. She issued a quick *YA ALLAH* and turned the water off. She put the pot down on the counter and tried to brush the water droplets off herself as best she could. Then she shook her hands and wiped them on her trousers. She tried again, this time turning the tap on very gently.

As she was walking back to the room, Leila stepped out of the bathroom.

"*Ahlain, habibti!*" hailed Leila, in her newly-acquired typical Shami greeting. She was learning to speak Shami in anticipation of becoming a true Damascene.

Huda forced a smile and replied with, "*Kifek?*"

Leila replied quickly that all was well and said she would come by to chat just as soon as she'd washed her hands. The bathroom was way too nasty for one to hope to come out with clean hands, so Leila had developed the habit of washing her hands in the kitchen.

Huda wandered back into her room and rummaged around the shelf over her bed for the *bakhour*. She put the coal-like substance in an incense burner and quickly lit it. As she placed it gently on the table next to her bed, she stood over the rising smoke and breathed deeply. A calm came over her as she let her mind wander to the visit she'd made to the Armenian church last year. A friend had taken her to celebrate Easter, and she and two Armenian friends had sat shoulder-to-shoulder in the crowded cathedral right off of Bab Sharqi in the Old City. A rich smoky smell had overtaken her and, not knowing where the scent came from, she had enjoyed it deeply. The spiritual beauty of the elaborately ornamented building, the deep pervading scent, and the beautifully repetitive chants had been a balm to her soul. The next day she'd asked those Armenian girls - now safely back in Armenia, Huda presumed, as she hadn't seen them all year - where she could get some *bakhour* for herself, and a few days later they'd brought her some as a gift. Huda used it sparingly, but today was definitely one of those days when she just wanted to calm down, to feel more lovely. The tension in her limbs began to slowly loosen as the *bakhour* spread throughout the room. She glanced over to her roommate and was glad to see that she didn't seem to care one way or the other what the room smelled like.

After a moment, she felt ready to think. She quickly rehearsed what she would say to Leila. Leila was going to ask how her interview went, and then Huda would have to tell her that things weren't going well, and so on and so forth. Leila knew, but then again she just didn't seem to get it. Leila knew that Huda was never going to have a successful political career and a PhD after her name, but she didn't seem to get why Huda was disappointed. Leila knew that Huda was scrambling for internships, but didn't seem to see why it was so important to get one. Leila knew that Huda's family was in a tough situation, but didn't seem to imagine how tough. So while it was fun to be able to travel from time to time to a distant world through Leila's novels and imagination, it was painful to keep going through the details of her job search with her friend.

Huda put the teapot on the electric burner and rummaged around her shelf for some biscuits she had tucked away. Money had been tight, but her family worked hard to make sure Huda could stay at the Medina. She knew they sent her more than they could afford, but the only way she knew to make it up to them was to help them out as much as possible once she graduated. And she could only do that if she got a good job.

Leila walked into the room with a smile on her face. "Isn't the weather beautiful these days?" she exclaimed. Then she quickly added, "What is that smell?"

"You don't know *bakhour*? It was a gift from the Armenians last year."

"Oh, I thought it smelled familiar. It's what they burn in churches, isn't it?"

"Yes, isn't it soothing?"

"Whatever. Seems a bit strange to me. But why fill your room with smoke when it's a glorious day out?"

"Yes, I suppose it is nice out," replied Huda. She walked over to the window and slid it wide open, while Leila said a quick "*Ahlain*" to the roommate still studying on her bed. Sure enough, the weather was warm but not hot, dry but not restrictive. A perfect late spring day. "Yes, it is a nice day. Thanks for reminding me... we have to enjoy the breeze, huh?"

"What do you say to a walk? Are you busy now?"

"No, I just got back from my interview."

"Your interview! How was it? I hope everything is well, God willing."

"Al-Hamdulillah," Huda said in what she hoped was a voice confident enough to express hope but doubtful enough to be honest.

"Tell me. No, better, you don't have anything now, do you?"

"No, not right now."

"Then tell me while we walk. Let's go up the street to that juice stand."

Juice in Damascus was expensive these days, thought Huda. She said, "Well, maybe. Or we could just walk up the Autostrad."

"Oh, I'm in the mood for some juice. Let's go. I invite

you."

"Well…"

"Come on, turn off the water. Stop that thing burning. You can drink tea later," and Leila pulled the plug for the electric burner out of the wall and stared at the incense burner, looking for a wick to blow out, until Huda came and put it out for her. "Let's go, get dressed. I'll be back in five minutes, *insha'allah*."

And like a tornado, Leila disappeared again. Huda was a bit bewildered, but she had to admit that the day was already a bit brighter. She looked at the window. The view wasn't great – just rooms on the other side of the building – but the air was fresh, not quite like the village, but as close as Damascus ever got. A walk would be good.

As they walked, they chatted about useless things, just chatter. They talked a bit more about the weather, about the way the greenery in the Medina was already less green than it had been when the rains ended, about how much had changed around them, such as the new park that sat where several dozen houses used to stand just across the street from the Medina.

When they arrived at the juice stand with so many different types of fruits hanging in nets from the ceiling and in baskets along the bar that you could hardly see the juiceman standing by his blenders, Leila took charge. She asked Huda what she wanted, and Huda politely refused anything. Leila insisted, and Huda got on her tiptoes and started peering at the menu behind the bar. Leila ordered a banana and milk and strawberry shake for herself. Then she asked Huda, who was still hesitating. Leila suggested that she also drink a banana and milk and strawberry shake, but Huda said a cocktail without milk might be better. So Leila ordered for her a fruit cocktail with honey. Huda's mouth began to water as she watched the juiceman cut up fruits and drop them in his blenders.

Just a minute later, two enormous glass mugs were passed over the bar. Leila's was a pale pink color, kind of like cotton candy, and Huda's a bright red like the shade of a raspberry. Huda reached for her purse, but Leila pushed her away. When Huda first met Leila, she had been a simple village girl with simple village tastes. Now she acted like a city girl, and Huda imagined that guy Ahmed must somehow be involved in Leila's new little extravagances.

They sat down together on plastic stools and sipped their juices quietly for a minute.

Finally, Leila asked Huda the question. "So, what happened at your interview today?"

"Malish. It's not important," muttered Huda as she stirred her cocktail with her straw. "But I'm not going to get it."

"Why do you say that? You are so smart and so motivated. You can't really have any competition."

"*Kul Shi Bida Wasta*. Everything Needs Connections."

"Well, yes, but you're so intelligent and have so much to offer. They'll notice that. Anyway, what you need the connections for is to get into the interview. Once you're there, then they can see your wonderfulness for what it is. And you got the interview."

"You weren't there. Don't worry about it, really."

"Did something happen?" Leila asked, suddenly wondering if she should be concerned. She never found out what exactly had happened to her friend two years ago, but she knew that Huda had come back from the summer break a changed person. She no longer talked about graduate school, she still studied hard but didn't get herself sick over it, and that shine in her eyes when she talked about lawyer stuff had faded to almost nothing. Leila had always wondered before whether Huda was strong or just acted that way, but since then it seemed that Huda was as fragile as a crystal teacup. Anything could get her down, but Huda still tried to act independent. Leila tried to forget the fact that whatever happened, happened the same week as all her dreams came true, but the fact was that she still felt somehow responsible. When she fell in love with Ahmed, something had dashed Huda's dreams to pieces.

So even though Huda seemed to be avoiding specifics, Leila pushed. "Come on, *habibti*, dear, you can tell me."

"You know," replied Huda after a few stirs of her cocktail, "You're right. Maybe it did go alright. Yeah, it's just that feeling you get after something stressful."

"Are you sure?" asked Leila, brightening up. "Well, I really do hope you are successful. Nobody deserves it more than you!"

"Thank you." Huda forced a smile and took another sip of her cocktail. "Thanks for the juice, anyway. Going for a walk on a beautiful day and drinking juice is the best way to celebrate. Out here, anything is possible!"

"Really? You think so?"

In response, Huda lifted her head to the bright, deep blue sky. She tilted back as far as she could and closed her eyes. After a few seconds, she looked back at Leila and smiled, and Leila seemed convinced.

Leila took another sip of her drink, and Huda asked her, "So, what is the last novel you read this year?"

"Well, I'm not finished reading it, but I should have read it months ago. It's called *Lord of the Flies*. Lord of the Flies, how do I translate that to Arabic? It sounds kind of funny, doesn't it? It's a book about boys who get stranded on an island and how they become awfully mean to each other. One of them takes over and forces the other boys to obey, and some of them even die."

"That's not a fun romance!"

"No, I guess it's not. But it is interesting."

"Interesting? But it's all about people dying and stuff. I didn't think you liked that kind of thing."

"True. But this one's different. It's not like any other book we've read. Plus, it's the last one I'm reading. I only started reading it because there's nothing left to read." Leila took another sip of her shake and set her glass down on the stool between her and Huda.

"But you said it's interesting."

"Yes, now that I've read it, it's one of the best I've read in my whole four years at University!"

"Why?"

"It's about the nature of people. What is the natural, the basic way that people are? It gives the idea that people really are, at the center, at the root, selfish, living just for their own success or pleasure. In the book you see these boys who are young, not educated yet, and you see what happens when there are no parents, no teachers, no rules, just survival."

"What happens?"

"The strongest win and the weakest lose. The winners abuse their power and start acting like even more than they are."

"That sounds about right." Huda nodded her head somewhat bitterly. "People are just concerned about themselves."

"Is that really how you think? I always thought otherwise."

"What do you mean?"

"I can't say that I ever thought about what would happen if I were stranded on an island with boys, but I guess I always expected that when we most need each other, that's when we kind of step up to the challenge and do something good."

"I wish I agreed with you. But that kind of thinking hasn't

gotten me anywhere. It's best to just fight for myself and my family, you know? Be strong."

"But that doesn't mean that people won't ever help you!" protested Leila. "Or that you can't ever help them."

"I wouldn't expect it. Everywhere I look, people are just looking out for themselves. Look at our country. Fine, I haven't traveled to compare, but I think Syrians are a very hospitable, generous people – to outsiders. But what do we do to our own? What do you do for the guy who rides through your neighborhood on his bike picking trash? What have we ever done for the old women who clean our building every day?" Huda stopped as she thought of the two old women, probably gypsies, though she'd never bothered to look at them carefully, much less talk to them, so she really didn't know. But every morning they were there, washing down the steps of the building. All they had was water, so it didn't do much good. But they did it, every day. And she'd heard that when girls left clothing in the stairways or had anything to give away, those old women with tattoos all over their faces, and with greasy bright red hair sticking out of colorful scarves, they took those bags of clothes and didn't let anything go to waste.

"Really," continued Huda. "I have never even stopped to talk to those women."

"Well, neither have I," admitted Leila. "But they're not... well, why would we talk to them?"

"Oh, I don't know... But it seems like if I really cared about others, I'd do it. Honestly, I'll tell you the truth. All I want is a good job, enough to support my family, and maybe a family of my own someday. I'm happy putting food on the table and having a warm room to rest in at night."

"You're not going to go invite the cleaning women for tea tomorrow morning?" Leila asked this with a glint in her eyes and hoped that Huda caught the joke.

"No, I don't think I will," admitted Huda. If she thought it was funny, she didn't lead on. She took the last sip from her cocktail and set her glass down on the stool. "And you, aren't you pretty much only concerned with your own situation, your own comfort?"

Leila raised her eyebrows. Then she picked her cup up again and stared into it.

After a few seconds that felt like an hour, Huda quickly filled the awkwardness she'd caused. "Anyway, I don't know. Whatever. It's no big deal. Maybe I should try harder to care, that's all. I'm just so tired of this world, where it seems like life is about nothing more than getting ahead, or enjoying what one already has."

"Yes, I guess so. It's like when I think about after I graduate. Here in the Medina, we've been studying, improving ourselves for ourselves and for our families. We've been friends, we've helped each other out. When we graduate, we'll each go to our own little place and just live life. Doesn't that scare you?"

"Scare? Yeah, maybe a little. But I don't think it's leaving the Medina that scares me. It's the responsibility. when I graduate I'll have my family closer, but they will expect things of me. They've never expected anything of me before."

That comment got Leila thinking about her own family and how they still didn't seem to expect anything of her, but she wished they did. They really didn't know who she was becoming. She'd experienced so much and her life was headed in a direction that they didn't imagine.

Leila cut her thoughts off and took the last sip of her shake. "Are you done?"

"Yes. Thank you so much. This has been a beautiful outing." The girls stood up and started back toward the Medina.

"Hey, do you remember that tabouli party? That was

almost exactly two years ago, remember? It was the last day of classes of our second year."

"Yes, that was so fun, and Maha came, and that crazy friend of yours... what's her name?"

"Roxy?"

"Yes, Roxy, crazy Roxy. And they danced, and you even danced a bit!"

"And we all ate so much, yes, and we danced, and talked... it was so much fun."

"Maybe we should do another one before we graduate," suggested Huda, though she sounded a bit tired and hardly enthusiastic.

"Can you believe that in a month we'll be moving out of the Medina forever?" exclaimed Leila.

"Not really, no."

"I'm going to miss it so much."

"Me too."

They walked in silence back past the new park, the construction site, and the city hospital that may be the one thing that hadn't changed a bit. As they neared the back gate, where guards for some reason decided today was a good day to check the ID's of the residents as they entered the complex, Leila mused, "Another tabouli party, huh? It'd be like a step back to the past."

Chapter Two

Nisreen was dressed as stylishly as always. She did follow all the rules, with her hair, neck and ears carefully covered, but she wore her black scarf in the latest style imported from the Gulf: loose and tall at the back. Her arms and legs were covered, and her contours disguised by a tunic that was just loose enough to be modest, but shapely enough to catch people's eyes. She was waiting at a table near the back when Leila arrived at the In-House Coffee in Shaalan. Nisreen stood up to wave Leila over to her table, and Leila walked up and greeted her with a handshake and a kiss on each cheek. Then both sat down.

"*Kifek*? How are you?" asked Nisreen.

"*Alhamdulillah*, everything is fine," replied Leila.

"How are your exams?"

"Well, we'll see. So far I'm just studying. They start next week."

"*Mu'afaqa* – may God help you pass."

"Thank you. And you? *Kifek*?"

"Yes, all is well, thank the Lord." With this, Nisreen stood up. "What's your order?"

Leila stood up, too. "No, today's my turn. Let me treat you."

Nisreen grabbed her purse and declared, "Next time."

"You always say next time."

"OK, really next time. But for today, what do you want?"

Leila stood there awkwardly for a moment, unsure what she should do in this strange new-style coffee shop where they went to the counter to order instead of waiters coming to serve them. And of course, In-House Coffee was one of the more expensive places in Damascus. It obviously had to be Nisreen's turn every time they came here, as embarrassed as Leila was by it... So she said, "Oh, anything is fine."

"Come on. I know you really like the Snicker's Latte, or the Chocolate Milkshake, or what else?"

"You know, a Mocha Latte sounds good today."

"Great. I'll be right back." And Nisreen marched up to the counter, leaving Leila free to take her seat and observe the people around her. Other than Nisreen and herself, there wasn't a single woman wearing *hijab* in the shop. Her overcoat was really out of place. At the table right across, a girl who had so many blonde highlights in her hair that at first Leila thought she was a blonde, sporting thick eyeliner and dark mascara and bright pink lipstick and a frilly white blouse, and whose jeans were about two sizes too small and lined with silver sequins down each side, sat trying very hard to look aloof as she stared at the table between her and a very, very good looking guy. Perhaps even more handsome than Ahmed, Leila thought. Though seated, it was clear that he was tall. His hair was just long enough for waves to be visible. He had a five o'clock shadow, and his clothes looked like they'd come straight from a Benetton catalogue. He, in turn, was smiling and talking and laughing, alternately looking the girl straight in the eyes and then leaning back and staring at the ceiling, as if he didn't have a care in the world. Even with her aloof demeanor, the girl laughed and smiled and encouraged the guy's overt flirtations. There was a big mug in front of each, though Leila couldn't make out what was in them.

Sprawled on the easy chairs to her right were three guys, each smoking and, judging from the number of cigarettes in the ashtray, they'd been there for quite a while doing little but smoking. Each had a small half-empty espresso cup, and they all looked thoroughly relaxed as they puffed and chatted, actually, laughing more than chatting.

At the table just beyond the flirting couple and the chillin' *shebab*, there was a rather academic-looking young man with a laptop computer. He wore eyeglasses, last year's style if Leila remembered correctly, but definitely not this year's. His clothes were also stylish but a bit out of date, and in need of ironing. His drink of choice was some kind of a fruit shake. Even so, he couldn't have been much older than Leila, and was quite attractive, in a nerdy sort of a way.

Right past the diligent student, two men with graying hair sat doing the older-generation version of the *shebab* to Leila's right. They too had espresso cups and seemed to be chain smoking, though it seemed their conversation topic was much more consequential as they leaned in towards each other over crossed legs and waved their arms, apparently on the verge of an argument.

In the easy chairs to the left of that table was a group of girls, all dressed in different versions of the first girl's ensemble. They all had cold drinks, each one a different color: orange, dark pink, chocolate brown, coffee brown. At first glance they seemed to be having the time of their lives, but as Leila waited for Nisreen to come back, she kept looking back in their direction, and it began to appear to her that they were nervous, then fake, then just plain bored, informing any observers that they were there in this posh coffee shop drinking fancy drinks, all dressed up, because that's what girls of status do, and nothing more.

Nisreen came back soon, with two big mugs filled to the top with foamed milk. Leila shifted in her chair and moved the ashtray out of the middle of the table, trying to make herself useful. Nisreen put the two mugs down on the table and sat down herself.

"So, what did you get?" Leila asked.

"The same as you. It sounded like a good idea."

Leila smiled and put her hands around the mug. The air conditioning was giving her a bit of a chill.

The girls sat in silence for a moment, each in her thoughts and sipping at her mocha.

Soon, Leila asked Nisreen, "So? How are you feeling about exams?"

Nisreen reached over to her bag which sat on the chair next to her. She pulled out a book, then a notebook, then a workbook, then another notebook, and put them on the table.

"What's this?" asked Leila.

Nisreen giggled. "Malish? Do you mind?"

"Do I mind what?"

"Well, I thought maybe you could help me." Nisreen's eyes twinkled, and it was clear she wasn't nervous at all about her first year English literature exams.

Leila thought back to her own first year exams. She had known approximately no English at all back then. That year she had passed because of her memorization skills and nothing else. But with graduation now in view... it had worked! A warm feeling came over her. "Of course I'll help you," she smiled with a hint of a patronizing tilt to her head. "I'm sure you'll do fine, though the first year is pretty hard!"

"Yeah, I just thought it'd be good to go over a few things to confirm them."

So Leila and Nisreen pored over Nisreen's books. It was obvious that Nisreen knew what she was doing. After all, she had been studying English at one of the best language centers in the country for several years already. And she was an avid reader. Really, Nisreen knew at least as much English as Leila knew, if not more. But what Nisreen did not know was how to pass a university exam, and that was something that Leila had mastered.

After about half an hour, they got to fiction, Leila's

favorite subject. Nisreen pulled out her notes on *To Kill a Mockingbird*, a book that Leila remembered clearly by virtue of not having understood it at all.

Nisreen asked her, "What did you think about it? Did you like it?"

Leila tried to remember the study notes she had used in order to pass the examination on that book. She remembered it was something about a death and a lawyer, and some children. "Well, it's kind of a tragic book, isn't it? Not really all that romantic."

"Well," Nisreen raised her eyebrows with a knowing look – she knew her friend was a sucker for romance. "I don't think it's supposed to be romantic."

"Well, maybe not. But still." Leila could think of nothing of substance to say about the book. "Then, what did you think of it?"

"I loved it! Absolutely thought it was one of the most interesting things I have ever read!"

"Really? Why?"

"It was so thought-provoking. And if you just changed the names, the scenery and the details of the story, it could have been about here."

"What do you mean?" asked Leila, hoping that as Nisreen talked, the plot would come back to her.

"Isn't it obvious?"

Leila paused a moment. Should she say yes? Would it betray the fact that her first year literature was completely lost on her if she said otherwise? But she couldn't resist a provocative statement like that. "I've never heard that before, so why would you say it applies to Syria?"

"First, you have these kids who play around. Two boys and a girl. But the girl is presented as a rebel, because she plays outside."

"A rebel? I thought the girl was the hero?"

"Well, yes, but don't you think the author maybe glorifies the hero?"

"Hmm. Go on."

Nisreen did. "So we have the girl who is supposed to be meek and quiet but isn't. But as she gets older, it seems she starts to follow the rules more. I mean, that is *exactly* the story of most of my friends! When I was younger we had so much fun, but now most of them are engaged to be married — and I'm only 18 years old."

"That's true about my friends, too. But we were all pretty quiet girls when we were little as well."

"Your luck in friends," Nisreen winked.

"OK," conceded Leila. "Maybe you have a point. But don't you think that's a common theme in Western stuff? It seems like most films in Hollywood are about rebellious girls who do well for being rebellious."

"Perhaps," Nisreen replied. "But I'm just starting." And after a pause and a nod from Leila, she continued. "The real story is about the girl's dad, don't you think?"

Leila nodded her head down in agreement.

"This guy is accused of something awful, and the dad is assigned to defend him. Like a formality. It's like we have elections here. We totally do. But it doesn't seem that anyone really takes it seriously..."

Was Nisreen really talking about politics? Here? No, she must mean something else.

"...So here comes a guy and says, you know what? This man is innocent, and I'm going to prove it! At first no one really believes him. The book makes it seem like it's just the most ridiculous thing in the world to think that a white lawyer would actually try to help a black man — and a black man who supposedly attacked a white woman! Here in Syria, it's like a Kurd is accused of stealing from a Shami, and everyone's toting him off to the justice, and another Shami guy comes in and says that that's wrong, because it's obvious that the Kurdish guy didn't do it. Honestly, can you EVER imagine that happening?"

What could Leila say? Kurds, politics... So she just nodded her head again in a "go on" gesture.

Nisreen gladly did continue. "In the end the Shami proves that the Kurd is innocent, but they take the Kurd to the justice anyway. And he runs away and someone kills him and no one bothers to take *that* guy to the justice. See? Just change the names and scenery and you have Syria."

Finally Leila found her voice. "That's difficult stuff you're talking about!"

Nisreen's eyes twinkled. "I love English literature, don't you?"

"You know I do, but I don't really think about it that way. I like nice love stories and all that."

"Yes, I know you do. But I love the controversy. I love that we can talk about things in English that we can't talk about in Arabic. I love that they have us reading books like this. Do you imagine that when *To Kill a Mockingbird* first came out in America, that it wasn't just as scandalous as if it were a book about Arabs, but arguing that Kurds are innocent victims?"

"I really never thought about it that way. And, may God forgive us, I'm not sure you should think about it that way either!" protested Leila.

"Oh, don't worry," said Nisreen. "It's no big deal. It's fun to think about, but don't worry, I'm not standing up in class declaring my opinions. You're practically my sister and you like philosophy, so it's different."

Leila just sat there quietly. A family that talked about this kind of thing was inspiring to her, but she was feeling a bit frozen, panicked.

Before Leila had to figure out how to defend Atticus Finch

or else continue the conversation on a lighter note, she looked up and saw her favorite sight in the whole world: Ahmed.

It had been a week since she'd last seen him but, considering her shock and thrill at the moment, she wondered that it hadn't been a month or a year. As soon as she caught a glimpse of him, her heart started beating just as hard as it had on that first day when he'd talked to her after their French final. And she knew that the guy at the table across the way had nothing on him. Yes, Ahmed was certainly the winner of Leila's mental beauty pageant. He walked up to their table and first greeted his sister with a kiss on each cheek, then shook Leila's hand warmly. He took a seat next to Leila and immediately slouched in his chair, much like those guys to her right had been slouching. They had left shortly after Leila arrived, replaced by some other guys who had taken their seats. But then they had also left, and now a girl in *hijab* but very Western clothing sat chatting with two university-looking guys.

"*Shloankom*? How are you?" Ahmed said, leaning back with one leg crossed over the other. He twiddled his fingers against each other and gazed over his hands, back and forth between his sister and girlfriend.

"We're fine!" replied Leila with a smile. "We're discussing my favorite topic."

"English novels!" chimed in Nisreen.

"Good, good. I'm glad it's fun for you!" he said in a voice that made it clear he was thinking it was about time they changed subjects.

"Yes," Nisreen chimed in. "We're discussing the meaning of life based on a book written in America."

"America, eh? So they really do have the best culture after all!"

"No, silly." said Nisreen giving her brother a look that

only a sister can give. "But you have to admit that Americans are good at philosophy and criticizing life and stuff."

"Some of the best philosophy has been written in America," Leila pointed out.

"Really? Why do you say that?" asked Ahmed.

"Well, that's what they told us in Poetry. And it makes sense. In a country so big with so many problems, you'd think that they would have a lot of people trying to think about things."

Ahmed grunted. "America seems to me like a place where people do things without thinking about them. You know? They just do stuff without thinking of the consequences. Like they're too confident to think."

"Now you're talking politics," countered Leila. "But I'm talking about the normal Americans. I mean, do you really think that all Americans are like their foreign policy?"

"Of course not. But it's not just politics, it's what we see in films. And the fact that the American people haven't stopped their government from doing such awful things. If they were really all about thinking and analyzing, don't you think they'd change something?"

"Well, I don't know." Leila tried to think, but all she could come up with was the thrilling realization that Ahmed was sitting next to her.

Nisreen had an answer, though. "America is a big country. Did you know that the population of America is more than 10 times the population of Syria? It's actually about the same as the population of all the Arab countries combined. Do you really think that all those people think the same?"

"Of course not; that'd be silly. Even in Syria we have a lot of diversity."

"Well, there you go. And maybe among all those millions of people, there are just enough to challenge each other and to think. I mean maybe they have 18 million people – as many people as there are in our whole country – who always challenge ideas and philosophize and even present counterarguments to the government. But those are only 18 million people. In America that's like, what, 10%? No, more like 5% of the population. Who's going to listen to them? And would you be surprised that they don't make films about them? It's so few, and probably much more boring a group of people than what we watch."

"Well, yeah, but---"

Nisreen wasn't done. "You know how our father only ever puts the TV on MBC Action and on any other channel showing horror films or else violence. Hey, even you! When do you want to watch a deep, philosophical film? You always choose a TV show like Friends, or a film on MBC2."

"That's not true!" protested Ahmed. "I like a variety."

"Oh yes, I'm sorry. You also watch Al-Jazeera news." Nisreen's voice had risen and taken on a sarcastic tone.

Leila now sat silently fingering her mug. She would never in a million years talk to her older brother like that, and she was feeling a bit ashamed for Nisreen. But when she glanced up at Ahmed, he was smiling! This man was full of mysteries. Was it possible that he was actually enjoying his sister's verbal attack? Nisreen was still talking, and Ahmed continued to lean back in his chair. Maybe Leila should withdraw herself. She decided to offer to get another round of drinks.

As soon as Nisreen stopped to take a breath, and before Ahmed could jump in with a retort, she interjected. "Can I get anyone anything else to drink?"

Ahmed and Nisreen stopped and turned to Leila. For a moment they didn't say anything, just stared. After two years she still felt like a complete outsider, but her mind and soul were aroused by them still.

After a few seconds, Ahmed came to. "No, no. Relax, of course. What do you want, girls?"

Nisreen asked him for a small tea, and Leila asked for an orange juice, and he headed up to the counter.

As had become their tradition, Ahmed and Leila walked the 45 minutes back to the Medina. Leila treasured these walks, the rare opportunity to use her limbs and not feel threatened by the stares of guards and shopkeepers as she walked. Not to mention the matchless companionship. This time, Ahmed had helped Nisreen find a taxi home, and then he and Leila had set off down the road that passed by the Kuwaiti embassy and the National Library. Today's walk was in a particularly quiet neighborhood with nice sidewalks, and they walked side-by-side for the first fifteen minutes without talking. Silence wasn't the norm between them, but Leila determined to just enjoy it. And she told herself not to notice the fact that he hadn't taken her hand this time as usual.

Finally, Ahmed spoke. "So, how's your studying?"

"Well, I haven't really started yet. You know, I try to keep up with things. This weekend I go down to visit my family, then I'll come back and really focus."

"Wow, you are so relaxed about it. I so admire that about you! So dedicated and confident, but relaxed."

"Ha! But you're the smart one!" retorted Leila.

"No. You dazzle me."

"Whatever."

"How about we agree that we're both smart."

"That's better." Leila stole a glance at him and smiled as they caught each other's eyes, before looking back at the street. Was it her, or was there something different, some kind of reserve? "Why do you like me?" she asked all of a sudden, without having even formulated the question in her mind.

"What?"

"I mean, your sister. I love her like my own life. She's my baby, the light of my eyes. And I know you love her. But..." she hesitated. What exactly was she saying?

"But she's a very outspoken spoiled girl."

"No! Not at all!"

"She is."

"Well, if she is, then--" Leila stopped. She was about to ask him why he let her be that way.

He understood. "She's clever, too, though, isn't she?"

"Very clever!"

"Too much so, perhaps."

"May God have mercy! No, I wish all the best for her."

"Yes," said Ahmed absent-mindedly. "I do love her."

They had diverged far from her original question. Leila was debating whether to ask it again when he added, "But that doesn't answer your question." This was why she loved him.

"No," she said quietly. "It doesn't."

"Well, here's the thing." And he stopped.

And she waited.

Just then they arrived at the Omayad Roundabout, which entailed crossing five streets to get to the side headed for the Medina. They crossed busy street after busy street in silence.

Leila was getting the impression that Ahmed was trying to say something... and that it wasn't a declaration of his love for her. A chill came over her. Where just an hour or two ago, she had been sure of nothing but her future with him, she was now worried. Before she let the thought overcome her, she asked again, "So, what is it?"

"Leila, I do like you. Very much," he began. "You have lit up the past three years for me."

Leila held her tongue and avoided saying something stupid.

After a moment, he said, "I love my sister, but I don't want my sister. You're amazing. Not only are you beautiful, but you fear God. And you're smart, in an adorably innocent way. You have hope. I need hope, and you give it to me." He paused a moment. "And that's what makes it so hard for me."

"What... what's hard for you?"

"Well, this is our last year of university, you know?"

"Yes, can you believe it?" said Leila as cheerfully as she could.

"I need to graduate with good marks to get the scholarship to do graduate studies abroad. And, you know, to do well..."

"What can I do?"

"Well, that's the thing," he said slowly. "I think what you can do is stay away from me."

"What do you mean?"

"I need to concentrate. I can't have you keeping after me."

"Keeping after you?" Where she'd felt a bit scared a moment before, Leila felt her blood temperature rising. "Is that what I am? A bother?"

"Didn't I just say you're the best thing that's happened to me?" responded Ahmed in a raised voice. Was he mad?

"But--" Leila crossed her arms tightly and stared hard. They were now standing facing each other, noisy traffic swirling around them.

"I just need to not see you for a while," he finished lamely.

Leila was feeling quite disturbed. She couldn't put her finger on what was disturbing her, but it was definitely there. They started walking again.

Somehow, after they passed under the bridge, and once the tall buildings of the Medina came into view, again it seemed like the right question came to her without her actually thinking of it. "Then what?"

Though she was staring straight at the pavement ahead of her, she felt his eyes on her.

"Then what?" Ahmed repeated the question.

"Yes."

No answer. He didn't understand. She let him wonder for a minute, then went on.

"This is also my fourth year," Leila reminded him. "And I have passed every exam so far in my four years. So that means that, if God wants it, I'm also graduating in a month."

"Yes, I wish you the best on your exams."

"Don't you get it?" Leila all of a sudden wanted to pummel him with her purse. Instead she settled on some strange combination of shouting and weeping. "Isn't your mother from Dera'a? Don't you know what it's like for us girls? Don't you care?"

Ahmed seemed rather hopelessly confused and for the moment Leila was satisfied to see him uncomfortable. She knew his family was just as conservative as hers, and his ability as a man to ignore reality grated on her.

Leila continued. "My mother has received calls from several women in the village and from nearby villages. She keeps reminding me that this is the summer I should get married. She's been trying to set up appointments for this weekend, but I keep telling her I need to focus on my studies. I can't keep doing that. My family will not let me wait. Maybe a few months, but by this time next year... What can I do?"

They were now nearing the main entrance to the Medina. He would walk her all the way up to her building's door. Surely by then he would get it.

But when they walked through the gate, he stopped. Leila thought she had grown skilled at reading his eyes, but she had no idea what she saw there right now. "Here you are," his lips said. "I hope you have a good weekend with your family. I'll miss you. Good luck on your exams."

And he walked back out the Medina gate, no kiss on the cheek, not even a handshake, leaving Leila feeling a bit dizzy and, for once, at a loss for a coherent thought.

Chapter Three

Roxy stumbled into the living room and opened the little cupboard that sat behind the dining table. On the bottom shelf, at the end closest to the wall, there was a dusty pile of papers. Second year Arabic literature lecture notes. She grabbed a handful off the pile and wandered over to the sofa.

She sat down and opened the first booklet, but her eyes wouldn't focus. Her cheek was throbbing and her arms ached. Every bit of her body longed to lie flat, but she forced herself to stay sitting. She couldn't make out the words on the page, but she made her good eye follow the print at the average speed of reading. When it reached the bottom, she turned the page and kept going.

After half an hour, now on a second lecture, the pain in her right arm became too great to bear. The booklet dropped out of her hand and she fell back against the sofa. Immediately the images that she'd been pushing away by focusing on her lecture notes came back to her. An arm swinging. Her hand held up to her face, covered in blood. A large, imposing figure standing over. Her beloved Bassel's voice booming out in anger. Her own face covered with the nasty muck that develops from crying very, very hard.

But this time, no tears came. Just images. And pain. Lots of pain.

A floorboard creaked near the door, and Roxy's entire body froze up in fear. No, she told herself, today's not my day. Today I'm safe. And sure enough, no one entered the apartment.

She slowly stood up and walked into the kitchen, her beautiful kitchen with granite surfaces and top-of-the-line appliances, with wood cabinets to her exact specifications. The kitchen which she had perhaps used twice in her married life, since she and Bassel had eaten out or ordered in almost every meal, and when he wasn't with her she either ate leftovers or stayed at the Medina.

As she opened the stainless steel dual-compartment refrigerator, the phrase "sold her soul to the devil" crossed her mind. She shut it out as she held the ice pack, re-chilled for the fourth time today, up to her cheek.

Roxy wandered back to the sofa and this time tried the television. She found a soap opera set in the Old City of Damascus. It was a comedy, and she almost laughed a few times - would have laughed if it didn't hurt so much - but as she watched the plot unfold between a young man and a young woman who met through friends at a coffee shop in an old Arabic house, she was reminded of how she first met Bassel.

It was the end of her first semester at university. She had always been a bit different than her sisters and cousins in that her number one goal was always to meet as many different people as possible. At school she was the one who had hung out with the three Christian girls in her class and who chatted with strangers. They all laughed at her, but she loved meeting new people, not for any specific reason except that variety somehow seemed more exciting. So coming to the Medina had been wonderful! In her room all the girls were from Sweida just like her – she didn't know them from before, but she quickly found them boring – but her neighbors were from all over Syria. She even had some neighbors from Jordan, the first non-Syrians she had met. She hung out with her exotic neighbors and, whenever she could, dragged them with her to experience Damascus. It had been so fun to do things she'd never done before with people she'd never met before.

So before they all went home for the break at the end of January, she'd convinced half a dozen of her neighbors to visit a cafe she'd heard of in Bab Touma. When they'd arrived, she'd been pleased to find that the cafe was as trendy and hip as she had hoped. She and her friends had all ordered tea and Nescafé off the menu. Oh, for the innocence of the Medina, where poverty was the rule... but somehow they hadn't felt poor back then!

They sat at a corner table, giggling, throwing sugar at each other, taking bets as to who could get which guy to look at her, ooing and awwing at the clothes of the upscale women at nearby tables, and just about convincing themselves that they belonged in this dark, recently renovated cafe decorated with Arabic antiques and wood that was carefully carved to appear rustic.

And just as she was finishing her flower tea, he walked up.

One of her companions was a girl she hardly knew. This girl didn't actually even live in the Medina: she was supposed to be living with her brother and his wife. She was from Aleppo, and apparently had become friends with some of the girls in her course who were from near Aleppo, and she stayed in the Medina with them sometimes.

He came up to greet this girl. Roxy's heart melted. Something about the air of confidence and the sly look in his eyes grabbed her, even though he was clearly twice her age. She couldn't stop staring. Well, she couldn't stop trying not to stare, which meant that she kept glancing up at him, then staring at her glass as she twiddled with it. Each time she glanced up she became bolder, especially as she realized that he too was looking at her, even while chatting with the girl who Roxy later learned was his niece.

That was all it took. He invited himself to join the group, since his friends had just left. He ordered them several *saj* sandwiches: cheese, zaatar (thyme) and labne (yogurt). He also ordered two salads and a plate of fries. And a round of sodas for the girls. They were all quite flattered by his attentions, and the volume of giggling kept increasing. But he had managed to seat himself by Roxy and was teasing her in little innocent ways: asking why she didn't eat and pushing a plate of *saj* toward her, stealing her soda and pretending to drink it. And he got bolder as the evening went on. Soon he was playing with her hair and leaning over her, always in a playful way.

Roxy loved the attention. She always wanted a new experience. Boys at the high school across from hers had flirted with her. She was a pretty girl with a sense of style, so she'd come to expect boys to stare and joke and provoke. But this was the first real man to be interested.

By the end of the evening, her heart had melted. Bassel paid the bill in a rather grandiose manner, counting out the money in front of all the girls. When it came time to leave, they all walked out together and he offered them a ride back to the Medina. Some of the girls were horrified, but Roxy was the leader and she led. A twenty minute walk later they found themselves crowded into Bassel's car. His niece shared the front seat with Roxy. Five girls squeezed into the back seat. Roxy realized now that she couldn't remember who any of the other girls had been.

He took them the long way, the very long way, back to the Medina. Roxy loved it as they wound all the way up the mountain and slowly drove along the row of restaurants. They were showing off for who knows whom, but she felt safe. Not only was he fun, but he knew how to look out for them. A real man, Roxy remembered thinking.

Finally, the girl from Aleppo, spoilsport, convinced him to take them back to the Medina. It was only 8:30, and Roxy didn't see why they couldn't keep seeing Damascus from the vantage point of a private car. It was new and marvelous.

They'd all piled out, and she must admit a bit of soreness from sharing a tiny bucket seat for an hour, but once the girl from Aleppo – what was her name? Her niece now, come to think of it, but she'd never seen her again. Anyway, once she had gotten out, Roxy couldn't resist turning back to Bassel to say goodbye. She'd said the first slightly clever thing that came to her mind, "That's the best you can do? Learn how to drive, man! *Yalla*, it was good to meet you."

But just as she was turning away to join her friends walking through the gate, he had grabbed her arm. She turned back and saw him reaching across the front seat and through the window, looking up at her. She'd protested, but he didn't let go until he'd said what he wanted to say, what she wanted him to say: "If you want a good time, come here tomorrow at 6:00."

Then he'd let go, put the car into gear and driven off. And Roxy, refusing to be shaken, had quickly run to catch up with her friends. No one seemed to notice, not even the girl from ... her niece.

Things had progressed quickly. She hadn't really considered not going to meet him. Adventure was all that had mattered back then, she thought ruefully. Looking back, Roxy supposed she should be grateful he had treated her well back then. He didn't try to take advantage of her in any way, although he was wonderfully flirtatious and playful, and even to an innocent 20-year-old it was obvious that there were sparks flying. After a few rendezvous, he'd told her he was married, but also well-off. And he'd proposed. Just like that. He'd told Roxy to think about it and get back to him, and he gave her a number to call.

She had thought about it, for a long time in 20-year-old Roxy time: a whole two days. A few months later, once she'd worked out the details with studies that no longer seemed important and a family that could never know she was married, much less to someone who was not a Druze, she had moved into this flat, still under construction at the time.

This beautiful flat with nice hardwood floors and rich Persian rugs. With the nicest kitchen she'd ever seen and an enormous fluffy bed. She tried to focus on the good. She was well-off, of course. She didn't have to cook or clean, and she had experienced more fun and excitement in the past four years than most women experience in a lifetime. Her family still loved her.

That thought, though, made her nose twitch, and a moment later she was sobbing. Her family loved her because they didn't know. To make things worse, she was practically imprisoned in this house that was almost an hour outside of Damascus, and Bassel never took her to meet his friends. Except for Mary and Ghalia in the Medina, and their friends there, she had no one in the world.

The ice pack was losing its chill and the pain was again throbbing in her cheek. She checked to see if it was too soon to take another dose of pain killers. It was. She curled up into a fetal position on the sofa and let the tears flow as she decided that, in fact, the only thing she could truly be grateful for was the fact that Bassel had never wanted her to have children. What a world would she have brought them into?

Around the same time as Roxy drifted off into a fitful sleep with soap operas floating through the room and tears moistening the cushion, Leila's bus pulled into the Dera'a coach station. Her last trip home before graduating. This felt like a momentous trip. Next time she came home it would be for good. Or for as long as it took for Ahmed to find a way in with her family and for her to move out again. She knew he was not in a rush, wanting to work a bit and get established first, so it would be a long engagement, maybe as much as a year.

As she alighted, her ears were filled with the familiar sound of hawkers calling out in her native accent. She quickly grabbed her small bag from the stow and walked past the taxi drivers and boys selling socks, to the bus stop where she would catch a *service* van for the short ride home. This was a routine she'd mastered over the years, and clearly others had grown accustomed to her as well, since they no longer tried to ply their wares and services on her.

It wasn't hard to find a *service* at this time of the day, and fifteen minutes later she was dropped off just twenty meters from her front door. She nodded to a second cousin, who was manning the supermarket on the corner, and smiled as she passed a dozen kids, mostly cousins, who were playing in the street. She walked quickly around a Mercedes Benz that was parked right in the middle of her street and ducked into the door of her building, walking swiftly up two flights of stairs.

Just seconds after she knocked on the door, her 17-year-old sister whisked her in and whispered urgently, "Hurry! Come here!"

Leila quickly removed her shoes and followed her sister into their bedroom. "What's going on?"

"You're late!" whispered Nuha.

"Late? It's only afternoon! I usually get here later in the evening."

"Well, we've all been waiting for you. For more than half an hour. Didn't you say you were coming early?"

"This is how long it took," retorted Leila.

"Anyway, you have guests. There are some women here to see you."

"To see me?" cried out Leila.

"Shhhhhh!" Nuha looked like she was about to clamp a hand over Leila's mouth, but she mercifully restrained the urge. "Be quiet! Yes, they are here to see you."

Leila put her bags down on the floor. She looked Nuha straight in the eye, and asked, "When did my mother plan this meeting?"

"I don't know. But they had an appointment."

Leila now restrained her own urge to shake her sister. She took a deep breath and calmly said, "Go call my mother."

Nuha shuffled out quickly and Leila began to unbutton her overcoat. She could feel her blood boiling – until this moment she had never known what that English phrase meant. But she felt hot from the inside out and was trembling ever so slightly. She threw her overcoat onto a pile of blankets in the corner and shook her arms wildly. She had to contain herself before her mother entered---

--The door to her room swung quickly open and shut. Leila's mother was not a slender, nor a graceful, woman, but she was moving with a smooth stealthiness as she sidled up to Leila and kissed her once on the left cheek and five times on the right.

Leila held her mother's hand up to her forehead and kissed it. Then she let herself speak. "Nuha said there are women here to see me?"

"Yes, where have you been! You're late."

"The road took that long."

"Well, you're here now. They were about to leave, but I was able to stall them. Oh... this is awful that you are only just getting here after a long journey and there's no time for a bath, but the only day they had time this weekend was today."

"Who are they?"

"Oh, my daughter, my dear, they are from the family of the mayor himself. Their son is set to inherit one of the biggest businesses in our town – some kind of oil-producing business, what do I know about those things? But they are rich and respectable."

Leila weighed her options as her mother rummaged around in the closet, picking out an outfit for Leila to wear. She decided all she could do at the moment was go along. Her mother may have made a meeting behind her back, but she wouldn't be so... so... tyrannical as to make an engagement without her permission. There would be due time to discuss this in the days to come. But for now, she said, "Let me go wash up."

"Yes, go. I'll put some things out for you. Quickly, though! Look your best, of course, but you don't want them to think that you're this slow for everything. They already think that, I'm sure, but..." she kept muttering on about these two women, but Leila was already half-way to the bathroom. She quickly washed her hands and her feet and decided she needed to wash her hair. She flipped her head over and quickly moistened, shampooed, massaged and rinsed. The water was hot since the water tank sat on the top of their building, and today was a particularly hot day, so Leila was soon in a sweat. This wasn't the calm last-visit-with-her-family-as-a-student that she'd been expecting. She fumed as she patted her head madly with a towel.

As she walked back to her room with the towel wrapped around her head, she heard the television on in her older brother's room. She peeked in and saw her father, two brothers, sister's fiance, and two little boys who were neighbors and sons of a cousin, all crowded on the single bed and on the floor. They waved at her, each sporting a knowing smile, then went back to watching some kung-fu film.

Lucky guys, she thought, as she quickly walked back to the room. Then she wondered where this young man might be, this chap on whose behalf the women had come. Was he lounging around watching a film somewhere? Was he working hard making olive oil? Or was he – and Leila gasped to herself – was he the guy sitting in that car she'd stepped around as she'd walked into the building? She tried to remind herself who was sitting in the car. She could barely make out the figure of a young, dark man, but she wasn't sure. And she didn't want to be sure, she told herself, because this was not going to happen.

Nuha was back in the room and mother was back with the guests. Leila kept towel-drying her hair while Nuha asked which makeup she should pull out. It took about fifteen minutes to get her hair dry enough to look nice and to apply her makeup. It only took a moment to put on the outfit that her mother had chosen for her. It wasn't what Leila would have chosen if she were trying to impress a man, but-- oh wait, she wasn't supposed to know anything about that, was she?

And so it was that after fifteen minutes, Leila walked into the salon of her house and greeted two complete strangers with a handshake and a kiss on each cheek, as if they were family friends she'd seen only just last week. As she smiled and exchanged pleasantries, she took these two women in. Both were short and plump, without makeup or visible jewelery except for enormous gold rings on their hands. The older woman was quite old indeed, and wore a black *abaya*, the style women in Damascus wore, and a black scarf with a silver floral imprint. The younger woman was wearing a finely tailored blue *abaya* and a striped scarf in various shades of brown. Leila's best guess at her age put her in her mid-thirties. They exuded an aura of a comfortable life in comfortable homes with fattening foods. The wizened and aged demeanor of the woman who she knew to be the groom's mother, plus a quick glance at their weathered hands, told Leila they were still hard workers. They were surely expected to personally maintain their families' households in perfect condition. And their attire was that of women from a very devout family.

She took a seat by her mother and made small talk about her studies, about her desire to be a teacher and a mother, about her opinions on modesty. She knew that a young bride was supposed to be demure, humble and kind, so she played the part by simply answering their questions. She didn't try to turn them away, although she was tempted to "accidentally" trip on her way in, then to make some joke about the purple décor on the older woman's (her potential mother-in-law's) purse, then to answer their question about her studies of English Literature by only speaking to them in English. But she just sat there and answered the questions and smiled, but not too much.

After a few minutes her mother gave her a look which Leila understood to mean, "Go make coffee for your guests." Leila gratefully stood up and asked them whether they liked their coffee sweet or bitter or so-so. They protested that they didn't want anything, Leila insisted, they insisted, she insisted... and eventually it was agreed that they'd take it so-so. She escaped to the kitchen, where Nuha was setting out plates on their nicest tray with the biscuits that her father had been tasked with purchasing from a well-known sweets shop.

"So?" asked Nuha eagerly.

"I don't know. What do you think?" retorted Leila.

"They're rich! You can tell by their clothes."

"Yeah, sure, they're rich." Leila tried to convey in her tone that wealth was not what mattered to her and that she was not interested. Still, they were nice enough, so she told Nuha, "But I guess they seemed like good people."

"Yes, did you see the way the younger woman smiled at you!" Apparently Nuha had been peeking.

"They did seem kind and concerned."

"That's the most important thing, you know."

"Is it?" Leila whispered and furrowed her eyebrows. They

were still only one room away from the salon.

Nuha glanced at the door and went on in a whisper, "Don't you want to marry into a family that will look after you? A mother-in-law who will treat you well is everything."

"Ok. It's important..." Leila hesitated. Nuha was her closest sister and should be her closest friend, but they had never talked about this.

"What? Tell me."

"Well, it's just, what about love?"

"What about it? I can dream of it and hope for it, but can you really know you have love until after you're married? Long after you're married..." Nuha's whisper drifted into nothingness.

Leila didn't say anything. She finished making the coffee and poured it into three of their nicest china demitasse cups. She placed the cups on the smaller of their fancy trays, then filled a glass with drinking water and placed that on the tray. "Anything else?" she asked her sister.

"Go, go!"

So Leila carried the tray somewhat gracefully into the salon. She served the potential mother-in-law first, then the potential sister-in-law, then her own mother. She placed the glass of water in between the two potential in-laws and then put the tray on a side table.

She resumed her seat next to her mother and listened as the two older women chatted. Nuha entered just a bit later and repeated the ritual with the plates of biscuits: one for mother-in-law, one for sister-in-law, then one for mother. Tray to the side.

After a few more minutes, the potential mother-in-law turned to Leila and asked her some direct questions:

"Do you want to work after you're married?"

Leila knew that this was her chance to diffuse any interest, but she didn't want to incur her mother's wrath. So she answered that she would either work or not work, depending on what her husband thought was best.

"How many children do you want to have?"

She donned her most coquettish smile and declared, "*Allah Kareem*. God is generous."

"Would you be willing to travel to the Gulf? Our son has a job opportunity there that he is considering."

It wasn't hard at all for her to reply favorably to this one.

Then the mother of the boy turned to Leila's mother and said, "I'm glad it was possible for this visit to happen. I know the timing was difficult, but I'm pleased we could meet your daughter. We can't stay too long, but I would like, if you are willing, for our son to meet her. He's downstairs."

So that was him in the car. Leila still couldn't remember what he looked like, though.

Leila's mother replied, with the pathetic coyness of a woman who is past her prime, "Would you like me to send someone down to call him?"

But his sister quickly jumped in and offered. Leila's mother told Leila to show the sister-in-law to the door then go back to her room to put on *hijab*.

The sister went down and Leila left the door slightly ajar then walked into her room. Not surprisingly, Nuha came out of the salon at that moment and joined Leila.

"He's coming!" Nuha giggled.

Leila wanted to say, "If you're so excited about this, why don't you marry him?" But she didn't.

Nuha fawned over Leila as she put on her scarf. She gave her feedback on whether it was straight and how to make it straighter. Maybe another pin here. No, not that pin, this one. Maybe an extra gathering there, you know, to make it look like a flower. When Leila was done, Nuha quickly threw a scarf over her own head and they went to visit the men in banishment. The girls found the men in the same position they'd been half an hour ago, watching another action film. Leila and Nuha stood by the door for a brief moment watching, then Leila caught herself. She was on assignment. "Nuha, go check with mother what I should do! Go! I'll just stay here til one of you comes and gets me."

Nuha disappeared into the salon, and Leila forced herself to relax and watch the film, reminding herself that this was not a serious event in her life.

Soon, she heard the front door opening and looked into the corridor in time to see a figure fly out of the salon and run into the smaller salon, the one that they only ever used when it was very cold and they didn't want to heat the whole house. Leila smiled as she realized that Nuha was cleverly sneaking into the only room that had a window into the main salon. Nuha would probably spend the next half hour standing at the crack in the curtains covering the window that separated the two salons.

Leila quickly pulled the door to her brother's room shut. The man in question couldn't see her yet.

Standing by the door, she could make out a man's voice and a woman's voice echoing through the central hall. Then she heard the salon door opening. As the voices faded away, she peeked out and saw that the coast was clear, so she snuck over to the smaller salon. Sure enough, Nuha was glued to the crack in the curtains. Leila came up to her and hissed, "Well?"

"See for yourself!" and Nuha stepped out of the way.

"No, no. I'll see soon enough. But what do you think?"

"Oh, no, I'm not telling you until you see him yourself. I don't want to mess up your opinion!"

"Alright, then," Leila shrugged and sat down. Nuha resumed her post and, after sitting a bit on the divan wondering what to do, Leila walked back to catch a few more scenes of the action film.

Those scenes seemed like the longest she'd ever watched. While her eyes were on the screen, she kept repeating to herself, "Ahmed, Ahmed loves me, this is not real, Ahmed", so she would remember to think of this day as practice and nothing to be nervous about. After eternity and a day, the salon door opened and her mother nodded at her.

Mother and daughter walked together back toward the salon. Leila's mother whispered, "When you go in, don't shake his hand. Just smile and go sit right next to his mother."

"What?"

"*Yalla.* Come on." And they walked into the room.

He stood up as they entered, and Leila looked him straight in the eyes – dark brown – and smiled. Then she walked purposefully to his mother's side, who took her hand and said, "Leila, this is my son Mohammed."

It took all the energy Leila had during those first moments to not look in the direction of the window into the other salon.

But this was a momentous occasion to the rest of them, so she decided she'd might as well check this guy out. She took advantage of the fact that her mother was chatting with Mohammad to take a look at him as he answered her questions. He was good-looking enough, but he still had a definite village look about him. Though he was sitting, she could tell he was shorter than Ahmed. His hair was dark and spiky: it was entirely possible that he had put quite a bit of effort into it, but the effort hadn't paid off. Ahmad's wavy swept-back look was much more becoming. Mohammad's clothes were stylish, but five-years-ago stylish. In a rating system she'd developed with Roxy and Mary and Ghalia, she gave him about a 5 out of 10.

Meanwhile, her mother was asking him all the questions that she should want answered: about his studies and job, especially the opportunity in the Gulf. He had studied engineering at University of Damascus and graduated five years ago, which meant that he wasn't all that old. Now there was a call for engineers in his specialty – electrical engineering – in Qatar. He didn't own a house, but he had money saved up so that they could buy a house if he didn't go to Qatar, or else for when they got back. He was the second brother in a family of five siblings, very responsible, the first in his family to get married.

Altogether, not all that bad, Leila was thinking when all of a sudden she realized that all eyes were on her and she had no idea why. So she queried, as politely as she could muster, "What?"

Mohammad looked in her direction, but not directly at her, as he repeated his question: "I hear you're an English major. Why English?"

Trying not to roll her eyes at the banality of his first direct question directed at her, Leila tried to explain, without too much fervor: "I love literature, especially novels, and I very much like to learn about other languages and ways of thinking."

He continued, "What do you do with an English major?"

Besides read and make babies? she thought. Instead she answered, "I'd like to work as a translator. Either that or teach English. But I think translation would be interesting, and it has the added benefit that I can do it at home." Bonus points for working without leaving the house.

He nodded. The bonus points registered.

His mother then broke in, and the spotlight was off of Leila for a few more moments.

She tried to follow the rest of the conversation and laugh when appropriate. They talked about general things, the construction site slowing down all traffic in downtown Dera'a, identifying common friends, the potential for this year's olive crop, background on the men in Leila's family. Mohammad was on his best behavior and, Leila figured, she was too. She only looked at him when he was talking, but she noticed that he wasn't looking at her all that often either. Or, he was trying very hard to avoid her noticing him looking at her. Wasn't that the point? Afterward, Nuha would tell Leila that he kept creaking his neck and stretching his back and shaking his shoulders at a disturbing rate: every time his head moved he stole a glance at Leila.

Finally, the visit was ending. At his mother's cue, Mohammad stood up, nodded to all the women with his right hand on his chest, and walked out. Then there was kissing all around among the women, including Nuha who came out of hiding as soon as Mohammad left, and then, just like that, they were gone.

"Well? Well?" nudged Nuha. "What'd you think?"

Leila produced a faint smile and shrugged. "What did you think?"

"They certainly liked you! The women were so nice to you. And did you see the way he kept trying to look at you without looking at you?" She imitated his neck and shoulder gestures. "It was adorable!"

Mother pitched in, "They are such a good family, so kind of them to come by."

Leila started unpinning her headscarf. She said, "Yes, they were nice." and allowed her voice to fade off as she walked into the room to change into her pajamas.

Her mother plodded in after her and sidled up next to her oldest daughter.

Leila kept folding her clothes, staring at them.

With her arms bunched at her side and her eyes on some unidentified spot in the distance, Mother finally said, slowly and solemnly, "Well?"

Leila kept folding her clothes, staring at them hard.

After a few moments of silence, Mother went on. "They are such a good family. And by all counts, very religious. Even if he hadn't graduated from university, he could have his own house and car and a business."

Leila kept folding her clothes, staring at them as hard as she could.

"But he is well-educated! An engineer. And he might travel; I know how you've always wanted to travel. And so respectful."

Leila was running out of clothes to fold, so she straightened the pile of clothes, which required her utmost attention.

"And, you know," and here it came. The lecture. "You're about to graduate. You're already getting old, I don't know what you want to do with all that education. It's time for you to grow up, stabilize, settle down. You don't want to wait until you're too old and no man will have you. Men want to be sure you're young and healthy and can bear their children. And as a good Muslim girl, you should want to complete a family. Plus, my dear, it's time for you to start living your life and do something worthwhile with yourself."

Leila patiently finished straightening the pile of clothes, then slowly looked up. She saw a nervous woman, one who loved her and wanted the best for her and was honestly scared that Leila had ruined her chances at a happy life by going to university. Mother was staring, Leila saw, apparently at nothing, and twiddling with an invisible thread on her robe.

Finally, Leila answered, "I'm sorry, Mama. I know they are a good family. But it's still too early for me."

"Still too early? You're graduating in a month!"

"I need to study for exams. I can't start thinking about an engagement now."

"They'll wait, I'm sure!" Mother's protest was desperate,

weak.

"Well, it's not just that..."

"What then?"

"Mother, I just can't see it. I know, it takes time. But I can't commit to something I'm not sure about, not the way I should. Not now. Please, Mama, let me finish my exams first."

Mother turned around and plodded out. And that was that. No Mohammad. No marrying into the top family in town. No connections with local big business. No peace or security for her daughter. What she didn't know, thought Leila as she gazed at her mother's slow-moving back, was that things would soon get better.

The rest of the weekend passed uneventfully. That first evening was a Thursday, and the *Imam* was coming to speak. The house had already been clean for their matrimonial guests, but there was another quick sweeping to be done, as well as work in the kitchen. Leila and her sisters did that, then helped prepare the vegetables for the next day's Friday family dinner. They sat on stoops in the kitchen and picked leaves off of parsley, peeled garlic and chopped onions. By the oven, mother sat on her own stoop, rolling up balls of dough then flattening them and tossing them up and down to make large flatbreads. She then placed them in the oven and by the time the next ball was ready, the previous one was done.

For the hour that they sat in the kitchen, all the women in the family together, Leila was the topic of conversation. The two younger sisters had been at school earlier, so Nuha told them everything. She described their vast wealth then declared that he wasn't all that good-looking, but one could look past that. If one wanted to.

"I don't know. I think it's important for there to be a

connection," Leila finally stated.

"Yes," said Nuha. "But look at what a great situation he's in!"

"Perhaps. I don't know." She saw her mother glance up at her with sadness in her eyes.

The girls went on to debate the virtues of love and attraction in relation to the ultimate trio: job, house, and car. Leila let her younger sisters chat away, only throwing in a controversial comment when they started to agree on the supremacy of the ultimate trio. What was it with these girls? Her own flesh and blood, and teenage girls who were free to dream. But they insisted on being pragmatic, even heartless. And these were her sisters. Roxy, Maha, they got it. Huda, well, she may choose the boring route in the end, but at least she'd had a taste of pursuing a dream. At least she knew, not just with her mind, but with her whole body, the concept of passion.

Every so often, her mother glanced at her with that sad look in her eyes. And the next day, as they made lunch together and drank tea together and entertained relatives who came to visit, it was the same. Leila's visitors were the main theme of conversation, everyone trying to decide whether Leila should accept if an offer came. Leila didn't tell them she'd already decided, and neither did her mother. But her mother was subdued all weekend and hardly talked to her eldest daughter: she just gazed at her with sadness.

Chapter Four

When Leila returned to the Medina late Saturday afternoon, there was a note with her name on it, taped to her door. She took it off and wondered where her roommates were: she'd expected a busy room during final year exams. But when she unlocked the door, three girls were in fact sitting on their beds with books open in front of them.

Leila tried to hold back her irritation that they'd just left her note on the door for anyone to read, for who knows how long.

"*Masa al-kheir!*" she said, as friendly as she could muster.

"*Masa al-noor,*" replied the nosy one who had pestered her about Ahmed two years before.

"*Kifek, habibti,*" replied Aisha, the kind one.

Leila didn't recognize the third girl. A first year, perhaps? Maybe replacing Fatima, who'd been recently married to someone living in Damascus, which meant that she was finishing her Shari'a training as a married woman.

Leila put her purse on the bed, and the bag of food stores on the floor. She sat down and opened the note. When started to read it, her face boiled. How long had it been posted on her door?

When she'd finished, she read it again. Then a third time. By the third reading, she'd decided what she needed to do. She stood up and walked out of the room, went down the five flights of stairs, across the open entry area connecting the two sides of the building, then up three flights of stairs to Mary and Ghalia's room.

The moment Ghalia opened the door, Leila asked,

"Where is she? I need to see her!"

"What do you mean?"

"Roxy! I need to talk to her."

"I don't know. I haven't seen her for almost a week."

"Yeah," chimed in Mary from her bed, where she was waxing her legs. "She's been home all week. Why?"

Leila stared from one to the other, trying to figure out if they were lying. She took a slow step into the room.

Ghalia opened the door wide. "*Tfadali.*"

Leila looked around the room and saw no one. "No... um... thank you..."

She wandered slowly out of the room with her head spinning.

"What is it?" asked Ghalia, now ever so slightly concerned.

"Oh..." Leila glanced back. "Nothing. Sorry I can't stay. I really should, um, get back to studying."

"But is everything okay with Roxy?"

"Why wouldn't it be? I don't know. You said you haven't seen her, so she must be busy. If you see her, let her know I came by, okay? I just had a little question for her."

And Leila walked slowly back to her room.

The roommates were exactly where she'd left them, absorbed in their books. Leila sat down on the bed and unfolded the piece of paper that she'd been gripping tightly. She read it a fourth time:

"*Leila, habibti, dear, my heart. How are you? I miss you. Please come to me. I need to see you, I just need some help. With 1000 kisses, R.*" No date or time, Leila couldn't even be sure it was Roxy, but for the handwriting and the dramatic flair.

What truly alarmed Leila wasn't the content: Roxy always communicated with a bang and so if anything, this sounded quite unimportant. But the words were smudged in three places by what seemed like tears. Tears?

Leila had no idea how to find Roxy, and it the sun was quickly disappearing, so she decided to study tonight and look in the morning. She unpacked the bread and labne and vegetables and yogurt, and organized them on her shelf. Then she pulled out her Translation notes to start studying for her first exam.

After perhaps half an hour, in which her eyes learned a bit but her brain absorbed nothing, she put her book down. Something was gnawing at her and not letting her study. She looked at a clock: six o'clock. Leila had been to Roxy's home once before, when Bassel had taken her and Mary and Ghalia to spend a night with Roxy. He'd ordered in a feast for them and they'd stayed up late doing each other's nails and eating sweets. That was more than a year ago, but Leila might recognize the house. It would take probably an hour to get there, but Leila was pretty sure a *service* van in that direction passed right outside the Medina gate. She decided she had to try.

Leila didn't take much with her, just her purse and a few sets of lecture notes in case she found herself with some down time. She pinned her scarf, pulled on her coat, grabbed her room key, and walked out without saying anything to her roommates.

At the highway, the sun was still bright enough for her to read the route descriptions on the top of each van. Nothing said it went to Zabadani, the town where Roxy lived. She kept straining her eyes to read, and several *service* vans slowed down for her, but none of them seemed like what she needed. Finally she walked back to the gate and asked the guard sitting in the gatehouse what *service* would go to Zabadani. She felt suspicion in his gaze as he looked at his watch and asked her, "You want to go to Zabadani? Today?"

She said nothing.

Finally, he smiled and said, "OK. Well, what you want to do is..." and he proceeded to give her more complicated instructions than she'd expected. All she captured of his soliloquy was the name of the *service* she had to catch right now.

She did so and asked the driver to help her get to Zabadani. She took a seat in the front row, directly behind the driver, and every time she looked up at the windscreen, she saw his eyes in the mirror, gazing at her questioningly.

No Medina girl should be so stupid as to go alone to a town an hour outside of Damascus when the sun is about to set, unless one is going home. Since she obviously wasn't going home, she hoped no one got the wrong impression. She rummaged in her purse and found her prayer beads. She started praying *"Subhan Allah*, Glory to God" and moved one bead over each time she said it. When she'd said that 100 times, she ran out of beads. She started again, *"Istaghfar Allah*, May God Forgive." Then *"Alhamdulilah*, Praise God," then she decided to start reciting the 99 Names, one for each bead. She forgot a few, but this took all her concentration, and soon she had shut out the questioning eyes of her driver and the stupidity of what she was doing.

After an hour, somehow Leila found herself in the center of Zabadani. The sun was now low in the sky, and as hard as it would be to find Roxy's house in daylight, it'd be pointless at night. It was going on half past seven and she needed to be on a *service* back to Sham by 8:30 to make curfew. So she quickly walked around the central square, hoping something would look familiar. As she looked at the buildings around her, she muttered under her breath, *"Ya Allah, Ya Allah, Ya Allah."*

Then, there it was. Not just something familiar, but she could swear it was Bassel's car! She walked toward the car and peered in. If this was his car, then that meant that his house was here. But which house was his? More specifically, which of his houses was Roxy's, and which one was her husband currently occupying? Leila felt her face turn red with the very thought of walking in on his other wife with his children, while looking for Roxy.

But as she looked inside the car, she saw bright red and tan beads on the driver's and passenger seats, and a back seat that looked all torn up. This was not like Bassel's car at all. Rather than beads, Bassel had a pair of red stuffed hearts hanging from his mirror, and his car was better-maintained. Back to nothing. She looked at her watch: 7:45.

She started to walk back to the square, but there was something familiar about that tree a hundred meters up the hill. She decided to check it out. As she neared the tree, things started to look familiar. She looked up and saw that the next two buildings on her left were still under construction. Roxy's house was in a complex of buildings that were still being built, wasn't it? Leila walked past those two buildings and saw a small side street off to her right. Now she was sure: that was Roxy's street!

Leila picked up her pace. There were only three buildings on the street: one on the right, one on the left and one dead ahead. The sun was now going down and the buildings on each side were dark, like no one lived in them yet. But the one at the end, that one looked just right. She walked in.

Then she stopped. What if Bassel was there? How would she explain her sudden arrival? Even worse, what if Bassel was there and not Roxy? For that matter, what if she'd come all this way and Roxy wasn't home? And why had she come here – what was the matter with Roxy? What was she going to discover inside that house?

She never considered turning back, because she couldn't think that she might have wasted this trip. But she did stand rooted in the entry way for a good five minutes.

Finally, Leila took a deep breath and recited the Shahada, "There is no God but God and Muhammad is the Prophet of God." Now for figuring out which flat was Roxy's.

She walked the half-flight of stairs up to the landing and read the labels on each of the two doors. Neither had a name she recognized. Then she walked up to the next floor and read the label on the right. No. Then the label on the left. The name looked vaguely familiar: "Abu Ibrahim Massoud." She couldn't be sure, but she thought Bassel's son's name was Ibrahim and the surname looked familiar. She decided to knock.

No answer. Leila knocked again, harder.

Finally, what felt like ages later, she heard shuffling toward the door and what sounded like someone opening the peephole cover. Then the deadbolt being loosened, the chain being removed, the lock turning, and finally, the door slowly opening.

Nothing had begun to prepare Leila for what she saw. She'd been so concerned about finding Roxy that she'd not taken very much time to think about why Roxy had been crying. The fleeting suspicions that had passed through her mind were nothing compared to the reality now before her.

Roxy was a beautiful girl. Her hair was jet black and came to the middle of her back, and it was always perfectly styled. She had the classic oriental eyes: enormous ovals around brown irises with a hint of green around the edges. She usually made her amazing eyes more amazing by using dark eyeliner to distinguish their contours. Her skin was pale and absolutely free of blemishes. Her body was shapely and round in all the right places, and Roxy was skilled at using that to her benefit as she swaggered while walking, and swayed when dancing. Her physical beauty and her conspiratorial energy had created an enchantment that, to Leila, had always bordered on the erotic.

Today, a different girl opened the door. The first thing Leila noticed was her multicolored face. Her left cheek was an especially frightening combination of purple, blue and brown. Her right cheek was streaked with red scratches. Then Leila noticed her hair which had apparently not been combed in days.

Leila stood in shock in the doorway. Finally, she asked, "Roxy? Is that you?"

In response, Roxy pulled the door open and gestured for Leila to quickly enter. Then she closed the door and quickly re-did all the bolts.

Now the two girls stood face-to-face in the foyer. Roxy was hunched over and her eyes were swollen. From crying or from punches?

Leila continued to stand there, mute, unable to process the thought of a Roxy who had lost her luster.

Roxy also stood facing Leila, but she looked like she was about to keel over.

Finally, Leila took control and said, "Let's sit down." She then led Roxy – without touching her, Leila was too scared she'd fall and break into pieces – to the sofa.

They sat, Roxy on the sofa and Leila on an armchair to the side. Leila's mind was racing. How long had this been going on? How had Roxy come to the Medina? Who else knew about this? What, of all things, was Leila, a village girl from Dera'a, doing here? Then she thought back to her own childhood. She could remember occasionally hearing her father shouting and the sound of blows. She could remember seeing her mother huddled up in a corner after those altercations. Leila had hated those days and had always gone to hide in a corner of her own. But those days were not very common, and always by the next morning, everything had been back to normal.

This was the next morning – at least – and things were

clearly not back to normal.

It felt to Leila like an hour that they sat in the lounge without speaking. Leila pushed all thoughts of the ten o'clock curfew out of her head. She'd sleep on the street before getting up and walking away from this. So she just sat, feeling like she was defining awkwardness.

It was Roxy who finally broke the silence, who knows how many minutes later, with the most awkward of all awkward questions. "Would you like tea or coffee?"

"Me? Tea or coffee? Huh?" Finally Leila snapped to herself. "No, stay there. I'll just get us some water."

She stood up and walked over to the kitchen with its granite surfaces, stainless steel appliances and big island in the middle. She found two glasses, filled them with water from the filter and walked back over to the sitting area. She placed a glass on the table nearest Roxy and took a sip from her own.

Then she made herself talk. "What happ-- no, where is he--, wait, no, what I really want to know is, How long?"

Roxy reached forward and took a sip of her water, then continued to clutch the glass as she leaned back in her seat. "I don't know. At first it was nothing, it was just playing around, you know? I don't know. But it's my fault, really, this time."

"Your fault?"

"Well, he wanted to go out and I wanted to stay home, and I insisted. It was so silly, I was just tired. And then the next time I saw him, I couldn't stop crying. I should control myself better."

How does one answer that? "Oh." Then a few seconds later, Leila asked, "And the time before that?"

"I don't remember. Something similar, I guess."

"When?" Leila asked.

"I don't know! I just don't know!"

"How can you--" Leila stopped herself. Of course Roxy knew, but that didn't mean she wanted to remember. Then she said, cautiously, "I don't understand you, Roxy. You break all the rules, that's just what you do. But still, shouldn't you try to be a good wife?"

"Oh, I do," and the tears started falling. "Of course I do. Well, I try, but I don't know what to do."

Leila thought back to the wisdom her mother had been pounding in over the last decade or so about how to be a good wife. Did Roxy feed her husband when he was hungry? No, Leila knew that. But she did do the honors of serving the tea and the like. Did Roxy keep her husband content in bed? Leila didn't even know what that phrase meant, but it sounded like the kind of thing Roxy would do well. Did Roxy keep a clean house? Not so much – the maid came twice a week to make sure that was done. Did Roxy bear her husband children for him to show his family that she was a good choice of wife? Well, his family didn't even know she existed, but that point aside, no, she'd had no children in more than three years of marriage.

But from the first time she'd met Roxy, Leila had been in awe. Roxy was like no one she'd ever met, and if Ahmed hadn't entered her life at the same time, she may have been completely obsessed with this sensual, confident woman who didn't follow any rules. Roxy wasn't made to cook and clean and make babies, and nor did it seem that that was what Bassel expected of her. But maybe that was the problem.

"You know, *habibti*," Leila ventured. "Maybe you need to be just a bit more conventional. You know, be a bit more of a normal wife."

"May the Great God forgive you for saying that," spat Roxy.

"Why?"

Roxy didn't answer. She just broke down in tears again.

Leila had never seen someone cry like this before. "Roxy, please stop crying. If you keep crying, I may get upset."

But Roxy didn't seem to hear her.

So after a few moments, Leila stood up and wandered around the flat. She discovered things very much out of order, piles of papers on this little table, unwashed cups in the sink and on the dining table, an unmade bed, a broken vase near the television. There was no sign of food in the flat.

"Roxy?" she called from the kitchen.

A muffled "hmmmm" came in reply.

"When's the last time you've eaten?"

Roxy now looked up and blew her nose. She stared at Leila standing in the kitchen. "I don't know. I haven't eaten today."

"Yesterday?"

"Mmm. I don't think so."

"OK," and Leila pulled open the refrigerator door. Eeeww. That beautiful almost-new stainless-steel exterior was absolutely rancid on the inside. Moldy yogurt on the top shelf, next to some shriveled slices of green pepper. The second shelf was empty except for some kind of growth on the rack. The third shelf had some closed takeaway containers, but the overall smell in the refrigerator assured Leila that she didn't really want to check what was inside them. A 2-litre bottle of cola with maybe an inch remaining at the bottom, and two half-lemons that had been partially squeezed sat in the door. After this quick survey, Leila slammed the refrigerator door shut, waving her arms wildly to diffuse the odor. Apparently the refrigerator did not come under the purview of the cleaning lady.

Then she looked around for the bread and for conserved food. She found a jar of za'atar, thyme spices, and half a piece of crusty bread.

She then checked for tea and coffee and sugar, and finally

enjoyed some success when she discovered a healthy stock of each of those items. She filled the *dowleh* with water, no sugar, and set it on the stove to make some coffee. While the water boiled she started washing the cups in the sink. Then she prepared the coffee, placed two small cups and the *dowleh* on a tray and walked over to Roxy, who was now sitting with her feet up on the sofa and watching Leila. She had stopped crying. Finally.

"You don't have any food in the house," declared Leila matter-of-factly.

"Oh? Are you hungry? I'm sorry. I can go out and get something."

"Don't be silly. I'm going to go find us some supper after we drink our coffee."

"No, no, you're my guest. Drink coffee. I'll go get food." Roxy started to stand up.

"I really don't mind," protested Leila. "I'll do it. But before anything, drink your coffee." And she poured out the two cups of very bitter coffee.

Leila's mind was racing. She didn't have the slightest idea what to say to Roxy. But she was determined to try. "Roxy, *habibti*, I don't know what to say. I've never seen you in this state before. You're completely broken. What did you do?"

"I already said, I'm trying... I don't know."

"Well, maybe tell me the story from the beginning."

"There's really not too much to tell," said Roxy. "It kind of just happened. Well..."

"What?"

"There is one thing."

"Tell me."

"Bassel drinks. I don't think you knew that. He drinks. A lot. Mostly wine and Araq, but sometimes other stuff, too.

"Oh, God, have mercy on us!"

"Yes, but see, I knew all this before we were married. And

he knew all this. I was young, and I've been thinking about just how young and naïve I was. But I knew everything I had to know. Do you see what I mean?"

"How, do you mean?"

"I knew he drank, I knew he has a strong personality, that he's very passionate. By God, that's what I liked so much about him! I just didn't stop to think about what that might mean."

"What else?" Leila probed.

"I knew about his wife and his children. I knew that my family would never approve. But he was fun, and I liked that. And look at the house he gave me!"

"Money isn't everything, you know."

"I know," conceded Roxy. "But these three years have been a blast. Who can deny that? I don't know. I don't think I have any regret."

"It was your lot in life."

"No," Roxy said firmly. "It was my choice."

"Well, yeah."

"No, really. It was my choice, and now I'm here. That's all."

"Oh Lord, may God keep you!"

"Yes, and hope for the best."

Leila took one more sip of her coffee, then decided to flip her cup for Roxy to read her fortune. She swished the remaining grinds in the bottom of the cup, then quickly flipped it over and placed it a little lopsided on the saucer. She gently placed it on the tray and watched as Roxy did the same.

"Is he coming today?" Leila finally asked.

"No. I hope not," replied Roxy. "He shouldn't, I'm not expecting him."

"Alright."

The girls waited for the grinds to dry in silence. Leila

looked at her watch. Nine o'clock: too late to return to Sham. Her fate was in the hands of this home now.

Eventually, Roxy checked Leila's cup and decided it was ready. She held it close to her face and peered in, twisting it so she could see from different angles. Finally, she started reciting, "The greatest and most tragic things in your life are about to happen. This is a special year for you. I see a broken heart and a door opening. I see happiness mixed with bitterness. Someone is thinking of you today but it's not the person you want or expect."

Leila pondered these words. She wondered what the greatest thing and the greatest tragedy might be. Marrying Ahmed and failing her exams... or graduating and losing Ahmed? A broken heart? Please, no! If not Ahmed, who would be thinking of her today? Surely not that stranger Mohammad? But then who?

Then she realized Roxy was peering into her own cup. Leila waited until Roxy placed the cup back on the saucer, then asked, "Well? What about you?"

"Oh, the same as always. Fun and laughs and tears and pain." Leila couldn't coax any more detail out of Roxy than that. At least she had thought of a bit of a diversion from sitting, crying and talking.

Leila stood up and straightened her overcoat, which she'd not yet taken off. She carried the tray back to the kitchen and placed it on the counter.

Then she walked back to the sofa and asked Roxy whether she should take a key with her.

"Wait just a minute," replied Roxy. "Let me go with you."

"No, no, it's fine, really!" Leila protested.

"I'd really like to get out and get some fresh air."

Leila thought for a moment. "That makes sense, but I don't know that now's the time."

"Well, when is the time? Except for when I went to the

Medina to look for you two days ago, I haven't been out of the house in... oh I don't know how long."

A bit of color – the healthy kind – was beginning to return to Roxy's face. "But... ummm..." How to put this delicately? "Do you want people to see you?"

"I'm with you, aren't I? No one will notice if I cover up!"

"Do you mean, you want to wear *hijab*?"

"Why not?"

"Well, I guess. But what about..."

"My face? I don't know. I'll wear a black scarf and look like I'm from the Gulf."

"Do you own a galabeya?"

"Me? Of course not!" exclaimed a Roxy whose eyes all of a sudden had that glint of mischief in them.

"I don't get it. What are you going to do?"

"*Yalla*. Come with me." And Roxy led Leila into the bedroom with the unmade bed and clothes strewn about.

For the next fifteen minutes Leila watched as Roxy improvised a nice traditional outfit for herself, black skirt, black blouse, black scarf. But when she finished, it was still not conservative-looking enough to warrant covering her face. So Roxy decided to try powder. For the next fifteen minutes, Roxy worked on her face in the mirror, powdering it until it was so white she was unrecognizable. But on the upswing, so were her bruises. Then Roxy asked Leila to help her pin the scarf properly, so Leila tried to be gentle as she helped tie Roxy's matted hair into one big bun at the top of her neck, then wrapped the scarf so her ears, hair and neck were all securely concealed. Leila couldn't find a pin among Roxy's things, but she was wearing two, so she took one and used it to pin Roxy's scarf securely under the neck. She spotted some sunglasses on the nightstand and gently tucked the earpieces under the scarf and straightened them on Roxy's face.

Finally, at about ten o'clock, the girls stepped out into the fresh air. Roxy was not completely stable on her feet and she clung to Leila's arm. But Leila could feel her enthusiasm as she breathed in the fresh night air. Leila tried to hold on to Roxy in a way that was gentle enough to not hurt her but strong enough to reassure her.

The next morning, Leila opened her eyes to unfamiliar surroundings. She soon recognized it as Roxy's flat. She lay on the sofa where Roxy had spent the last several days. A ray of light hit her on the arm, and there was some sunlight peeking out through the blinds in the dining area and from under the front door. Otherwise, the spacious salon was still dark. Leila slowly pulled her arm out from under the blanket that she'd discovered in the closet and rubbed her eyes until she could see more clearly. Then she sat up to a chorus of sore muscles complaining about having spent the night on a sofa made for looks and not comfort. Leila's eyes wandered around the room, looking for a clock. The space was filled with an aura of calm and peacefulness. It gave Leila the impression that if no one else had, at least the house had enjoyed a good night's sleep. There was no sound at all inside the flat, but there was a distant echo of car horns and people moving around on the street outside.

No sign of a clock, though, so Leila stood up and walked into the kitchen. The fancy-shmancy microwave had a clock, didn't it? No. There was no sign of anything that kept time. Leila wandered around all the different piles of disorientation in the lounge. She peeked into the hallway and saw that Roxy's door was only slightly ajar. She walked up as quietly as she could and caught a glimpse of a lump under the covers which she figured must be a sleeping Roxy. Leila pulled the door as far closed as she could without risking any noisy clicks and resumed her hunt for a clock.

The television caught her eye, and she decided to turn it on - somehow it would tell her what time it was, or at least it could remind her that there was a world out there. As she fumbled for the remote, she came across her purse, and remembered her own watch. Now almost fully awake, she fumed at her own silliness and rummaged in the purse until she found the watch. Ten o'clock! What time had they gone to sleep? It must have been early, no later than midnight. She had slept so long.

Leila turned the television on anyway, then folded the blanket she'd slept under. She sat down on the sofa and stared at the images flashing across the screen while she let her thoughts wander back to the events of the previous evening. She still couldn't figure out why, of all people, she was the person sitting here in Roxy's living room. She didn't know why Roxy had come to her for help, and since Roxy's answer to everything the night before had been "I don't know," she figured Roxy was keeping more secrets. But then again, who was Leila to expect Roxy to give an answer to everything? *If my head had been banged up in as many ways*, thought Leila, *I probably wouldn't know why anything was happening - much less know why I did the things I did!* Leila decided to just accept that something internal had guided Roxy to her door, to writing a note. And that all this was in fact God's will, somehow or other.

Leila knew that you didn't always have to be able to explain everything - certainly she'd never asked the question "why" before she went to the Medina. With images of her weekend in Dera'a still fresh in her mind - yet somehow it also felt like that must have been years ago - she once again confronted the realization that the Medina had changed her. The Dera'a Leila would not even talk to Roxy. The Medina Leila had been drawn to Roxy from the beginning. The Dera'a Leila, if summoned to this situation, would have not asked why - she would have simply told Roxy to be a better Muslim and a better wife. The Medina Leila couldn't hold back the questions. The Medina Leila found herself suspecting that this wasn't Roxy's fault. The Dera'a Leila wasn't going down without a fight, as that Leila kept thinking of reprimands and simple suggestions to pass on to Roxy. The Medina Leila, though, was growing louder, asking questions like: Why does this happen? Why Roxy? She doesn't deserve to suffer like this! How can I help her?

Leila was surprised at the sympathy she was feeling for her friend. Maybe she needed to focus on religion, on what God and the Prophet had to say. God was not against men marrying multiple wives, as long as they could care for all wives equally. Roxy certainly seemed to be well cared for, here in her beautiful house and with her life of adventure. Leila wondered how the other woman lived, and remembered that Roxy had pointed out the other woman's house from across the street the day of the sleepover. Bassel was quite careful about alternating his nights between the two wives. He sometimes doubled up, but generally made up for it later. This all seemed to fit the requirements of the religion. So why did it feel wrong?

All of a sudden, Leila wished Huda were here with her right now. Between her sharp thinking and her legal knowledge, she always seemed to have an answer for this type of question.

An answer came to her, as clear as if Huda were sitting on the easy chair right across from her: *Because it is unfair. I don't know what God intended - I don't get God! But if God is good, then he didn't intend this. And if God isn't good...*

Leila started to protest the thought, but it kept coming.

Anyway, many legal scholars have pointed out - ask your shari'a *law friends - that the injunction of treating all wives equally was meant as a statement of impossibility.*

Bassel may be trying to be fair and treat the two equally, but it's impossible! How could he come up with a fair formula for giving his wife enough to care for her children without cutting Roxy short, or provide fully for Roxy without the other wife thinking he needs to give her more? And time? Sometimes he gets home at lunchtime, other nights at dinner time, other days only in time for bed - how is he going to calculate all of that? Really, fairness isn't fair, so Islam doesn't really allow multiple marriages. It just illustrated that it's not possible!

Leila had heard all this before, of course.

But Huda's voice kept going. *Of course, there is the issue of the Prophet himself, who had 12 wives. That is a bit hard to explain.*

Leila cut the voice off. Huda didn't have any problem with criticizing the Prophet, peace be upon him, but Leila had been telling her for years that this was forbidden territory. Huda never really conceded, so Leila knew exactly what Huda thought, but surely this time Leila could keep control of the conversation. She decided to quickly think of something else. Ponder a different question. After all, what did number of wives have to do with all this in the first place? Bassel's sin wasn't taking a second wife. Roxy knew that she was a second wife, and she was in the wrong here for having married without her family's permission.

Huda's legal expertise rang in Leila's mind. *Legally, she only needed a male representative to marry him: any man from her family could give permission.*

Leila made a mental note to ask Huda about that legal question one of these days. But none of this mattered. The real question, the only thing that Leila needed to understand, was, *Whose fault is this?*

Whose fault? Huda asked. *You ask whose fault? Look around you. Roxy sold her life into slavery. Now in*

European law a woman has control over her body, but here in Syria that's not true. Of course, Syria has signed the United Nations documents about the rights of women, but well, we never worked out these issues. So for now, a woman is a part of her family. Yes, she has her rights, to make her own decisions and choose her own life, but at the same time, she is giving up the protection of family if she leaves them - and there's no other good form of protection in place here except for family. So, morally, this is not Roxy's fault! She's not the one whose arms did the damage, she's not the one with the temper! Anyone who says otherwise is lying! Maybe she's a terrible wife, and maybe she's skilled at making her husband angry at her, but she is not the one who beat herself up. It is Bassel's fault. The only thing she did was wrong was allow herself to be vulnerable. Now, she can go to the court and get a divorce on the basis of his violence, but she'll get nothing. And she has given up her family's support. The court would send her back home, but they wouldn't want her. Do you see what I'm saying? This is not Roxy's fault, but it is her doing that she is in a place where, today, there is nothing she can do about it.

Leila knew that this was what Huda would say. She also knew that it was true. And yet it went against everything she had ever been taught. She had always been taught that it was her responsibility to keep peace in the home, to make a good home for her family, to be a good wife. But she also had been thought that family was always there for her. She'd never doubted that, and even though she herself was in a secret relationship, she knew her limits. She'd never follow Ahmed to the end unless her family supported it. Or would she? Well, of course she'd be with Ahmed forever, and of course her family would accept it. Marriage to Ahmed wouldn't be slavery; it would be freeing, wouldn't it? Leila started feeling a bit cold in the dark airy flat. She unfolded the blanket and draped it over her shoulders and forced her thoughts back to Roxy.

No more coherent thoughts would come, though. Leila felt stuck in a circle of questions about blame, Islamic law, Syrian law, family, and a mixture of hatred and acceptance toward Bassel. She stared blankly at the TV screen for a few minutes, until she heard a key in the door. Her heart skipped two beats, then picked back up so hard and fast she could feel it in her arms and ears.

She had not until that moment remembered that this was Bassel's home and as such he could be back at any time. She hadn't thought of bolting the door last night, and certainly hadn't considered what it would mean for Roxy if Bassel saw Leila sitting in his living room. She looked around for a place to hide, but there was no way for her to move more than a few feet before the door would swing open. So she quickly took the blanket off her shoulders and swung it up over her head, producing a very heavy and bulky makeshift *hijab*.

But it wasn't Bassel who walked in. It was Roxy. Leila blinked very hard. Wasn't Roxy sleeping in her room? But no, here was Roxy, dressed up in the same costume as she'd worn on their dinner outing the night before.

"I thought you were asleep." Leila accused.

"And a good morning to you!" replied Roxy.

"Oh, excuse me." Leila spotted some bags in Roxy's hand and dropped the blanket onto the sofa, jumping up to help Roxy with the bags. "Good morning. What time did you get up?"

"I haven't really slept in days," replied Roxy, matter-of-factly. "But your visit has brightened my week! I feel so much better. So I decided to get some food for you."

Leila peered into the bag she was holding and saw some fresh bread and... clothespins? She put the bread on the counter and laid the clothespins aside. She took the other bag from Roxy and found some teabags - flower tea - and stringy cheese and a bag of pickles. A rather strange breakfast, thought Leila, but she quickly decided to make the best of it. She took charge of the kitchen, and neither of them said a word. Roxy sat on the sofa and started flipping channels. The mystery of when and why and how she'd gotten herself out that morning remained unsolved.

Leila put the cheese and pickles on plates, and then remembered the za'atar she'd seen the night before. She put it all on a tray and placed it on the coffee table. She boiled water and made tea using the Lipton she'd found before, and brought that over with a bowl of sugar and some cups and spoons.

They ate silently, Roxy still in her escapist universe and Leila trying to think about a plan of action.

"Roxy?" she ventured after a bit.

"Hmm?"

"Is Bassel coming tonight?"

"What day is today? Yes. I think so." Roxy said this without enthusiasm and without fear. She just said it.

"How can you say that so calmly?"

"Oh? I don't know. I just do."

"But, but..."

"I'm used to it, Leila," she replied simply.

They kept eating in silence. Leila was glad to see that Roxy was in fact eating, not just picking at her food.

Finally, though, she said, "Roxy, I don't understand any of this, but I know you need to get out of here. At least for a few days while you heal."

"It's okay, really."

"Look at yourself, Roxy. No, it's not."

"Please, don't say that. This is my life!"

"We'll talk about that later. For now, I'm saying, I'm saying... Your face needs to heal. You need time to rest. You need a good night's sleep."

Roxy looked at her friend. Leila couldn't interpret her expression, but it was somewhere between exhaustion, excitement, and terror. Leila could easily imagine that she would be scared if her husband might come at her hitting her as soon as he walked in the door. But Leila thought there was something else. "What is it?"

Roxy closed her eyes, put down her bread, and sat back. She took a deep breath. After a moment, she opened her eyes and sat up. "No, everything's fine. But maybe it would be good to be out of the house for a bit. But I'll have to tell Bassel something, give him some kind of an excuse."

The two girls plotted and schemed over how to get Roxy to safety. They needed to figure out what to say to Bassel that would let him know Roxy wouldn't be around, but without it being glaringly obvious that Roxy was leaving to escape him: she wouldn't be just visiting friends or family looking the way she did, but he would see right through a family emergency type of excuse. They were both at a loss as to where she could go. She wasn't ready to tell family, which meant Mary and Ghalia. Leila's roommates would never be sympathetic to their plight, and all their other friends in the Medina also had roommates. After almost an hour of discussion, during which Leila kept the teacups filled and happily observed Roxy drinking and eating almost normally, they came up with a plan. Roxy would tell Bassel that she'd had a time of soul-searching and decided that she was going to take her exams this year. She needed to "find herself", she'd tell him, and furthering herself academically seemed like the best way to do it. She'd call him on her mobile once she was safely inside a woman's building at the Medina, so he wouldn't have a chance to stop her. He'd probably be angry but eventually accept it. Leila would call Maha. Maha's room was empty half the time. Plus, she was a relative stranger and her roommates were both related to her. Maha seemed like the kind of person who might like to know she was helping someone.

By the time they'd made their plan, it was almost noon. Roxy looked at her mobile and saw the time, emitting a little gasp. "*Yalla*! It's almost lunchtime! He may come home for lunch. Let's go."

Leila dressed quickly, and Roxy re-did her conservative outfit. They put the food away but didn't bother to clean up in the kitchen. Roxy filled an overnight bag with a random assortment of items: pajamas, socks, a hairbrush, nail polish, toothpaste, eyeliner and a wad of lecture notes. Leila was feeling rushed, so she didn't point out that toothpaste without a toothbrush wasn't very useful, or that Roxy might be away long enough to warrant a change of clothes or at least a change of personal attire.

With an air of intrigue, Leila finally opened the door and stepped out. Roxy furtively followed and locked the door, then put the sunglasses back on her face. The two girls stood silently on the landing and, hearing nothing, quickly walked down the stairs, into the open and over to the far side of the street, where they walked quickly to the *service* stop on the main square. Only once they were safely on a van and had looked around to be sure they didn't know any of their fellow passengers did they lean back. Five minutes later, Roxy was asleep with her head on Leila's shoulder.

After a good bit of back and forthing and detective work and running around town while Roxy sat on Leila's concrete block on the roof with Leila's roof blanket, it was finally all sorted out. Roxy was settled into Maha's room and would have the room all to herself for at least two days. Leila was relieved that neither Maha nor her roommates were at the Medina this week, and she hadn't had to tell them anything beyond the most basic of details. The only challenge had been to track Maha down at her aunt's house in Bab Touma.

With Roxy safe, Leila finally unpacked the food that her mother had sent and put her own schoolbooks in order. She'd head back over to spend the evening and night with Roxy, but for the moment she was surprised at the feeling of relief and of accomplishment which came over her as she sorted through her things and changed out of the clothes she'd worn all day and all night. She felt really good, come to think of it, really good. As soon as she had that thought, though, the good feeling disappeared, and she was hit by a pang of guilt for enjoying her friend's pain.

She thought of Ahmed, and wondered what he was doing right now. Was he thinking of her? Perhaps he'd been right to ask for some time apart - this weekend she wouldn't have had time for him anyway. But she found herself recounting the whole story of Roxy to him in her mind, wishing she could say it to his face. He'd have an answer to her questions, just like Huda. But she'd trust his answers more. Then again, she couldn't break Roxy's trust - it was better to not be able to tell him than to have to keep it a secret.

Then her thoughts turned to Huda. Leila hadn't talked to her for almost a week. Last they'd talked they'd been considering another tabouli party. Tabouli parties seemed like a universe away.

What about Mary and Ghalia? Roxy didn't want to tell them, Leila knew, but if she saw them, Leila wasn't sure she'd be able to keep the secret.

In short, within fifteen minutes, Leila had concluded that she needed to just stay near Roxy, looking out for her and helping nurse her back to health. And she had to avoid all her other friends. But hopefully she would fit in some time for studying.

Chapter Five

The next morning, while Leila was out for supplies, she ran into Huda at the store. For a brief second she considered hiding from her friend and returning to her place at Roxy's side, but Huda caught her eye and left Leila no other option.

They greeted each other warmly, with several kisses on each cheek.

"So? How was your time at home?" asked Huda.

"Home?"

"Didn't you go to the village over the weekend?"

"Oh, I did!" exclaimed Leila. "That seems like so long ago."

"Really? Why?"

"Oh," Leila replied quickly. "Just life, you know?" And she started picking out some tomatoes.

But Huda prompted, "So?"

"So what?" asked a distracted-sounding Leila.

"Was it a good weekend?"

"Oh... Well... Um..."

"What?"

Leila realized she hadn't yet told any of her friends about her guests and inadvertently let out a giggle. Roxy seemed to be doing alright at home alone, maybe even wanting some alone time, so she asked Huda if she wanted to go to the cafeteria, and Huda agreed.

As they walked, Leila prefaced her story by commenting, "Between you and me, I was so mad at my mother. You can't believe what was waiting for me when I got home!"

"What?"

"Who, you mean. Women! The mother and sister of a

groom."

"No!" Huda was genuinely shocked. They didn't do things that way in her village.

"*Wa Haiat Allah*. By God's life."

"Tell me everything!"

The girls walked into the cafeteria and sat at a table near the wall. A waiter quickly came up and both ordered plain black tea.

Leila then promptly recounted the whole tale from beginning to end. She told about how she had struggled to act respectfully towards her mother. She told Huda about Nuha peeking through the curtain, and about the little bits of mischief she'd imagined up to mess with the women's minds. She told how this was the first time she could remember being jealous of her brothers and dad watching a kung-fu film.

"But, this wasn't your first time, was it?" queried Huda.

"No, no, of course not. But it was my first time since I started university. When I came to Sham I convinced my parents to wait until I graduate."

"So four years."

"Yes."

"Well, at least you knew what you were doing. I wouldn't have had a clue!"

"Oh, believe me, everything has changed in four years. I knew the actions, the routine, but I'm a different person today than I was four years ago. *Wallah*, by God, I am completely different."

"How so?"

"Well, I've been thinking a lot about this lately. University, Sham, the Medina... it's all changed me. Don't you feel different?"

"Well, yes, absolutely, but..."

"But what?"

"Oh, Leila," sighed Huda. "I don't think anyone has been changed by the Medina the way I have."

"What do you mean?"

"Don't you know? Did you never figure it out?"

Leila was silent as she realized their conversation had all of a sudden become very serious. What was with this week, she thought, was there no rest? First Roxy, now Huda. But also, Ahmed, and her mother. Couldn't things ever be normal again, simple and happy?

"Huda, what has happened to our innocence?" she asked, instead of answering Huda's question.

"My innocence is gone, gone..."

Leila hesitated before speaking it: "Two years ago?"

"Almost to the day."

"Tell me."

"You really never knew?"

"I knew something, that you had trouble with a professor and that your family was in a tough spot. We all knew that much. But I never knew what happened."

"My life ended that day. I thought it was beginning, but it ended."

Leila had not imagined that this was the direction their conversation would take. Had she known, she would have run back to Roxy and her already-familiar problems. She would have ignored this girl who she called her best friend. Worse, she would have pretended she didn't know her, she would have made up some excuse, anything to avoid this. What did the Medina do to her? It taught her to talk about real things. It showed her what it was like to feel, to really feel.

She thought back to a conversation she'd had with Maha earlier that year. Leila remembered sitting in Maha's room, in a haze of cigarette smoke, drinking countless strong cups of Arabic coffee. Maha's books and reams of lecture notes were strewn across the large carpet. She'd been poring over them when Leila arrived and hadn't bothered to clear the space out just because she had company. Instead, the girls sat on the mattress and drank coffee off a tray set unceremoniously on top of the papers. The conversation had grown more and more theoretical with each cup of coffee and with each cigarette that Maha lit and with each one that Leila declined. Around the third round of coffee, they'd begun to discuss some of the more unusual personalities they'd come across since moving to Damascus.

When Leila asked Maha if her Psychology course was helping her understand why some people were different, Maha had grinned as if she'd just been waiting to be asked. She rummaged through her piles of schoolwork, adding to the chaos, until she triumphantly held up a small blue and white textbook. Then she explained to Leila that she was taking an abnormal psychology class and started reciting all the different ailments to Leila, referring to the list in the book's table of contents to refresh her memory. A lot of the concepts were taught in French or English, because apparently they didn't even exist in Arabic. In Arabic, everyone was just expected to be alright. There was no mental illness in Arabic, and therefore in Syria.

So they had pondered whether their country really was a healthier place, or whether there was some fear in considering that things just might not be perfect. In Leila's family, everyone knew there were problems but no one discussed them: the odd day of her father's abusiveness towards her mother, the four-month stretch that her sister wouldn't get out of bed, the year that her brother had gone missing – her parents had said he was making money in the Gulf, but the whole family had known that they actually had no idea where he was. And Leila considered her family to be quite stable and supportive, especially as she got to know different girls at the Medina.

Maha's lecture notes gave no Syrian examples. All the examples were from Europe or America, quite often from films or books. But Maha had lowered her voice to a whisper and told Leila that she suspected the professor was trying to convince the students that, while they had to understand the problems to pass they exam, they would never encounter them in real life. She didn't believe him, though.

Then Maha had admitted that one disease had particularly intrigued her, so she and Leila had pored over its description together. They thought of half a dozen girls in the Medina who they suspected had this ailment, and one of them was Roxy. In English, it was called manic-depressive, or bipolar. Maha had recited from memory the list of symptoms given by her professor. Leila didn't remember all of them, but some had stuck in her memory. Sometimes this person would demonstrate unrealistic expectations, reckless behavior, less sleep needed, easily distracted, dramatic... Then, at another point in time, this person would be extremely sad, cry a lot, neglect themselves, sleep too much, withdraw from friends.

As they'd read about this phenomenon together, Leila had timidly suggested to Maha that this might apply to more than just individuals. Maha had quickly agreed that, in fact, she believed that this was their culture. Sometimes Syrian culture was manic: grandiose, reckless, passionate. And sometimes life in Syria was depressive: weeping, bitter, withdrawn.

But the most common treatment for this disease was a drug which kind of took out the extreme emotions. People with this disease often didn't like taking the medication because they would stop feeling. Life became a bit less wonderful and a bit less miserable. It was just lived.

And so, they'd decided, Syria was a bipolar country on

lithium.

So as she sat facing Huda and prepared to hear yet another story of a life that was lived more fully than had been expected, with more pain than had been dreaded, Leila remembered that conversation with Maha and her own personal conclusion: Moving to the Medina - leaving the shelter of her family's home - had knocked Leila off the medication. She was now experiencing reality, sometimes in all its multicolored glory and, at other times in all its dark shades of misery. She'd known love and passion and parties and adventure - but she'd also experienced and shared in her friends' experiences of the most acute types of pain imaginable.

Realizing she was about to be thrown into Huda's story, Leila longed for a big burst of that lithium. Did all the marvel of the last four years make the pain of the last four days worth it? But she was past the point of no return, so she asked Huda to tell her story.

"I sold myself out. I was so desperate to succeed that when I learned the price, I paid it. I don't know how much you knew about what I was doing two years ago."

"I saw you studying, killing yourself in the library. And then you disappeared. And I am so sorry, my dear friend, because I was not there for you."

"It's not your problem. It was all my choice and would have been," Huda smiled ever so slightly. "I don't want to relive all the details today. It's too painful to think about. But there was someone in my department who I trusted, to whom I entrusted my fate, and he took advantage of that. He took my heart in his hands and ripped it in two, then tied it in knots, then tossed it around. He ruined me. But that wasn't enough. He asked for more. At first I refused: I was too scared. I was scared of failing, but I was terrified of him. So I ran home. That's when I disappeared."

"This was right in the middle of finals, wasn't it? We all thought you were crazy for leaving."

"But that's what I'm trying to say. It was too hard, I couldn't eat, couldn't sleep, couldn't dress, could barely walk. I was petrified with fear. For days I didn't leave my room, until I finally got up the courage to go to the bus station and go home. I knew my family had high expectations of me, but I have always been completely sure that they love me. And that's what I learned: we always go back to family when we're really truly in need."

"That's true."

"And my family was wonderful, but they hadn't expected me to come home. They had been keeping a secret from me and were no longer able to when I was there. They hadn't wanted to distract me from my studies, but I showed up at home right in the middle of finals. I think they were mad at me, but they never said so. They were always wonderful."

"What was the secret? I forgot."

"My dad had lost his job and we had no money. Well, my older sister was working and my older brother, too, but they couldn't spare enough money to keep us all alive. My parents didn't want me to quit my studies. They believed in my dream. They believed so much in my dream that I didn't have the heart to tell them I was fleeing my greatest fear and was considering dropping out. Also, I realized they were investing in me. If I got the job I dreamed of, I could help them.

"So I had no choice. I had to come back. I couldn't disappoint my family. Seeing my family's love and their sacrifice, and how wonderful they were, gave me the strength to face my own fear."

"What was your fear?"

"Of this professor. He did offer to help, but there were conditions."

"What kind of conditions?"

DREAMS IN THE MEDINA

"*Ya* Leila, do you truly not know?"

Leila looked at Huda dumbfounded. She had a feeling she should know, and deep down she realized she did know, but she wouldn't let her mind think it. She would torture Huda by making her spell it out before acknowledging that she could think of something so dirty on her own. No, she didn't know. She had a sense it was awful, that it involved sex and maybe worse, but, no, she just stared at Huda.

Huda leaned in and spoke in a very, very low voice. She'd been practically whispering before, but now Leila had to lip-read to keep up. "He never explained it to me, either. But he made it clear that if I did not 'study' with him at this clandestine, nasty place, in a private room with a bed in it... that there would be consequences. This was what I knew before I left for Latakia. When I came back, I went. And it was everything I had feared. He didn't care about the books - what I don't get is how, before that, he had seemed to care about my potential as a lawyer, but that didn't seem to matter anymore to him. All he cared about was me as a girl. I didn't know what to do, and I needed his help, so I just let him do to me what he was going to do."

Leila was staring at Huda's lips, determined to catch every word. It was one thing to make her say it, another to make her repeat it. She didn't catch everything, but she understood enough to be sorry she'd asked.

But Huda continued, back in her normal quiet voice. "I sold myself for my family's sake. And, I suppose, for my own. Because, as you know, my dream was my own, not just my family's. If that was what it took to become the big-name lawyer in politics and lecturing at the university, I think deep down I was willing to pay the price."

Leila nodded.

"But, Leila, *habibti*, the thing is..." and for the very first time - ever - Leila caught ever so slight a glint of wetness in

255

her friend's eyes. "The thing is, I gave him everything, and he just played with it and threw it out. He's a very important person, and so even though I studied like mad for my exams, I expected I would pass with top scores, because he would make sure I did. I thought I had guaranteed my success, not the way I'd wanted to – I'd wanted to succeed by my own skill – but I'd paid a high price for success nonetheless and expected to receive the award. I will never trust a man again, which is maybe good since now I can't get married, for what he did to me. When I received my marks after exams ended, I had passed, but barely. I was the last student in my class among those who passed.

"Since then, I had to give up on the dream, but I am still worth more to my family as an unimportant local lawyer than with no career at all. They don't know what happened to me, so they've suggested I consider marrying, but they haven't pushed it. They love me so much. They are sacrificing, living on very little, sharing what they can, expecting me to eventually graduate and get a job and help out.

"Now I study, and am applying for internships, but I'll do everything on my own. I don't ask for help, and I don't study with groups, and I won't look for any favors. I avoid my department as much as possible. I've only seen him a few times since, and have managed to walk the other way or avoid his glance - I don't think he wants to see me either, or else he would come find me. But anyway, that's why I haven't gotten any internship yet, I'm sure, no *wasta*, no connections, just the disdain of a powerful professor. But I have to keep trying.

"So, yes, the Medina, or better, the university, Damascus, has destroyed my innocence. But I don't think - I hope not! - in the same way as yours."

Leila could say nothing. The only thing that came to her mind was a stupid joke. And more questions. How had this happened? What was Huda going to do if she didn't get something? How was her family getting by? Surely there was some other way! She worried for her friend, that she had carried this secret all these years, and obviously she had not moved on. The pain was still very real, though Leila imagined that two years ago Huda wouldn't have been able to talk about it at all. Anyway, Leila was a bit embarrassed by her own complicit ignorance.

So, feeling there was not any appropriate way to continue this conversation, she stood up and suggested, "Well, let's get back to work?"

Huda seemed to agree that it was time to move on, because she nodded as if they'd just been discussing the weather, and they headed back toward Building 14, discussing the weather as they walked.

When they arrived at their floor, Leila stopped. She thought for a moment, then said, "Come to my room. There's something I want to give you."

"What is it?"

"Come here."

Huda followed Leila to her room. Leila asked her if she wanted any tea or coffee, and Huda assured her that the tea at the cafeteria had been sufficient. She stood in the doorway and watched as Leila traipsed over to her bed, dropped her shopping bags on the floor, removed her shoes and stood on the bed. She started rummaging through the books on her shelf, making a mess as she shuffled papers and threw some piles of books onto the mattress. Glancing over, she saw Huda still standing at the door, so she gestured for her friend to come in and take a seat. Huda walked in and shut the door behind her but stayed standing up, far from the line of fire of the books Leila was tossing onto her bed.

Almost five minutes elapsed, during which Huda attempted to make small talk with Leila's roommates, who seemed quite content to stare but didn't see much point in chatting. Finally Leila pulled a little booklet out from under some lecture notes and waved it triumphantly.

"Here! I found it!" She smiled as she stepped off her mattress and back into her shoes. She handed it to Huda without a word.

Huda took it from Leila and stared at the cover. "*Hadith lil'Nisa*" Sayings for Women.

She looked up at Leila questioningly.

Leila smiled. Then she took it back and pointed to the cover. "See? It's a book of *Hadith* - you know, sayings of the Prophet, peace be upon him - that are specific to women! I just thought... I don't know. I can't imagine..." she looked around the room and, though none of the girls seemed interested in her or Huda's existence, she lowered her voice. "Well, I don't know what life is like for you, but I thought you might find these encouraging."

"Encouraging?" asked Huda, with a barely-contained laugh. "The *Hadith*?"

"Be careful, *habibti*. These are the words of the Prophet."

"But why would they be encouraging?"

"To remember how special you are as a woman. That God has a place for you."

Huda took the book from Leila and thanked her with a dim smile.

"So," said Leila. "Are you going to study now?"

"I need to. You?"

"I wish. But I have some things I have to finish first."

"Alright. It was good chatting. Thank you for being a friend," Huda said quietly and with a smile as she walked out to the hall and headed for her own room.

Leila looked at her watch, saw it was still early in the afternoon, and headed for the roof.

Huda was relieved to find the room empty. She put the tissues she'd just bought on the table and placed the sugar and lentils on the shelf with her food stores. Then she plopped down on her bed and kicked her shoes off onto the floor. She rolled over onto her tummy and looked at the cover of the book Leila had just given her. "Sayings for Women..." Leila said that this book would help reassure her of her specialness as a woman. What a strange thought: special, as a woman. Wasn't she a woman and that was what she'd been born to be? *Nasiib*, she thought, it was her lot in life. Whatever may be written in the book, God had chosen to make Huda a woman, and because she was a woman she was judged based on that and not on her skills as a lawyer. Because she was a woman, she'd been ruined. Her brothers were never so motivated or as hard-working as she was, but they had many more opportunities and options. Special, yes. But a woman nonetheless.

She opened up to the first page. The first *Hadith* was beautiful: "The whole world is a provision, and the best object of benefit of the world is the pious woman." What did that mean, she wondered? She read it out loud to herself a few times. Lovely words. Too bad it didn't apply to her, because she could hardly be considered pious!

Nasiib, her lot in life. No one could be pious who had done what she'd done. But she had truly not had a choice. She didn't know how to be pious: she'd been raised by a family that told her not to worry about religion, to leave that to the men. Her job was to live her life. *Nasiib*, her lot in life. She'd make the best of it.

She turned the page and read, "Act kindly towards woman, for woman is created from a rib, and the most crooked part of the rib is its top. If you attempt to straighten it, you would break it, and if you leave it, its crookedness will remain there. So act kindly towards women." Huda recalled learning in religion class in school something about woman and Adam and a rib. It seemed that this *Hadith*, then, was saying that woman is crooked because she is rib, and since a rib can't be straightened neither can a woman. Crooked is bad, Huda surmised. Somehow this was meant to encourage her. After all, the moral of the *Hadith* was that women should be treated kindly. So kind of God to be merciful on her since he created her crooked and she was stuck being that way. But she had not been treated kindly, either.

She flipped through the book, quickly glancing at the pages, and the next *Hadith* her eyes rested on said, "Ali, there are three matters which should not be deferred: the Prayer when its time is due, the funeral as soon as it is ready, and the case of a woman without a husband, when there is a suitable spouse for her in her class." Huda read this one again, then moaned and rolled her eyes.

She turned the page and read another *Hadith* about woman's role as a wife: "When a woman observes the five times of prayer, fasts during Ramadan, preserves her chastity and obeys her husband, she may enter by any of the gates of Paradise she wishes." Then another: "Paradise lies at the feet of your mothers." Huda slammed the little paperback shut and tossed it onto her pillow.

Huda appreciated and admired Leila. Leila really believed these things but had never tried to force it on her, and such a friendship was worth gold. But Leila had not been challenged. She'd lived her innocent life, with a sweet college romance that might even result in a happy lifetime union. She could be the woman that these *Hadith* were talking about, and feel special to God. But Huda could see no place in this for a polluted woman like her in Islam.

Even so, she was a Muslim and she did love Islam. The *Hadith* were not the words of God; they were the words of the Prophet. The Prophet Muhammad was a great man who brought God's message to earth, but he was in the end only a prophet. She sat up and reached over to her shelf where a small pocket-sized Qur'an sat tucked next to a small *Injil* Bible, between some enormous law tomes. She paged through this little book and let her eyes float over the lovely Arabic script. This was truly a beautiful book.

She flipped to the middle and found Sura Mariam, one that she had always particularly liked. She started reading it in a low voice. Though she'd never learned proper Qur'anic recitation, she did sometimes listen to it on the radio. She enjoyed the poetry, regardless of the words, so she read for a bit without really paying attention to what she was reading. A little smile came to her lips when she thought how horrified dear Leila would be to find her sprawled on her bed, without a head covering or having washed up, reading the Qur'an the way it sounded best to her, not according to the rules.

Soon she got to the part of the Sura where the boy Jesus was born, her favorite part, but today it jumped out at her more clearly than ever. It was the story of a baby who had been miraculously conceived who, as soon as he was born, spoke comfort to his mother – a woman who surely was seen as a sinner by all those around her. Huda took those words as for herself. The fruit of the perceived sin, even if in Mariam's case it wasn't true, were her very source of comfort. Fate, *nasiib*, can lead to wonderful and beautiful things.

Huda closed the Qur'an and placed it, along with the Leila's booklet, on the table. She rolled over on her back and stared at the ceiling. Good would come from this. She had told Leila her secret. She didn't know why it had come out today, but Leila hadn't judged her. The booklet may not have comforted her, in fact it had done the opposite in condemning Huda, but the very act of love represented in Leila's offering was a beautiful gesture. And now, bolstered by the sound of Qur'anic verses echoing in her mind and the beautiful story of Mariam, Huda smiled at her ceiling and breathed a sigh of contentment for the first time in a very long time. She would graduate and she would find an internship and she would help her family, and out of this tragedy something good just had to flow. Something.

Later that evening, on her way to the toilet Huda ran across Roxy. Well, the girl had rushed back into her room so quickly that Huda didn't catch a good glimpse of her, but Roxy's long black waves were matchless. Maybe it wasn't her. Roxy would have said hi, even by the bathroom. The girl with amazing wavy black hair skirted quickly into Maha's room and the door lock clicked.

Huda went back to her studies in her room and managed to do some good memorization. At quarter to ten, two of her roommates returned and started preparations for dinner. Huda decided it was time for a bit of a break, and so went to ask Leila if she knew anything about Roxy being around.

She walked out to the hallway and knocked on Leila's door. Aisha answered, wishing Huda a good evening. "*Mesa al-kheir*."

"*Mesa' al-noor*," replied Huda.

Aisha smiled but held the door open only enough for her head to peek out.

So Huda asked if Leila was there.

"She was. She's been in and out all day. But she's not here now."

"Oh? You don't expect her back tonight?"

Aisha opened the door just a bit more and stared at Huda for a moment before answering, "I don't know. She didn't sleep here last night, but she's been around. Maybe."

"It's not like her to be out this late."

"No. It's almost 10:00, huh? Why don't you check across the hall? I thought I saw her heading over there earlier."

Aisha looked past Huda's shoulder in the direction of Maha's door.

Huda thanked Aisha, who quickly invited Huda in and finally opened the door wide. Huda thanked her again, Aisha insisted, offered to make some tea, and Huda smiled and wished Aisha a good night as she started walking to Maha's room. Aisha bid Huda a good night and quickly shut the door.

So Huda knocked on Maha's door.

A moment later came a muffled, "*Meen*?" Who's there?

"It's Huda, from across the hall... Maha's friend," she added in case they didn't remember her.

After a few seconds during which Huda thought she heard whispers, Leila opened the door and slipped out into the hall quick as lightning. In an unmistakably conspiratorial voice, she asked Huda what was the matter.

"Oh," said Huda, trying to sound innocent and not curious, "I was just taking a study break and thought I'd say hi. Your roommate said you might be over here."

"Yes, I am, but..." Leila looked around. "I'm sorry, it's that I'm a bit busy now."

"Busy? With what?"

"You know..." Leila looked at the floor.

Huda was more intrigued than ever, but it was clear Leila wanted her space. "That's fine. Hey, just one question. I thought I saw Roxy earlier. Has she been around? I haven't seen her for so long; it'd be nice to catch up."

"Oh," Leila said again. "Yes, she was here, but I'm not sure where she is now."

"Well if you see her, please greet her from me. Tell her I miss her and am thinking of her."

Leila smiled quickly, nodded, then disappeared back into the room. Huda wandered back to her own room and started picking out books to take to the study library downstairs. But before she'd finished packing, there was a knock on the door. It was Leila.

"You have a few minutes? Come here," she beckoned, leading Huda back to Maha's room.

One of the benefits to having Roxy around was her mobile phone. Leila loved using the mobile, but she still didn't have her own. But not only did Roxy have a phone, it was a nice one. So while Roxy and Huda chatted, Leila sat on a bed in another corner of the room pretending not to pay attention to their conversation, which was easy. She was only half-interested as she busily wrote text messages and fiddled with the games and other features on Roxy's camera phone.

It took her a while to figure out how the phone worked, so for a good ten minutes she fiddled with the settings, finding the ringtone, playing different ringtones to see what Roxy had available, and deciding she liked the current one, one of Tamer Husni's newest hits. She played around with the keypad and figured out how to switch between Arabic and English as the phone's primary language, and she found the camera and where to look at photos. Then she finally came across what she was really looking for, the text messaging system, and figured out how to type a message. She quickly ran back to her own room and got her phone book.

The first message she sent was to Ahmed. Surely that wasn't against his silly studying rules. "Ya Habibi. A-Salamu Aleikom. How are you? How's the studying? I miss you very very very much."

Send.

Oops, she forgot to say this was from Leila. He might think Roxy was after him, or maybe he just wouldn't know who it was from. She wrote another one. "This is Leila. I miss you!"

Then she decided to write Nisreen. "Ahlain, Habibti! A-

Salamu Aleikom. How is the studying? This is Leila. I want to see you. In-House Wednesday? Let me know, 1000 kisses."

Leila put the phone down after sending these two messages. She glanced over to where Roxy and Huda were whispering on the mattress on the floor. They seemed to be completely ignoring her, engrossed in their conversation about the kinds of things Leila assumed that girls-with-more-experience talk about.

She picked the phone back up and fiddled around a bit more. She looked through Roxy's photos. They were mostly of Roxy, and some of Bassel. And they all looked so beautiful. Glamor shots. Long black hair falling gracefully over one shoulder while Roxy blew a kiss at the camera. Roxy sitting on the armrest of the sofa in her living room, arm stretched out across the back of the sofa. She was smiling broadly in this one. Then there was a photo that apparently Roxy had taken of her and Bassel together in one of those Old City Arabic House Restaurants. They were both laughing. A series of photos of Roxy in a sleeveless peach-colored sequined evening dress, full-body shots with a variety of poses. Bassel standing with his hands behind his back in a suit, up against the door to their flat. From the photos Leila would never imagine anything was wrong. Actually, Roxy had been in the Medina for just over a day now, and if it weren't for the fading but still unmissable bruises on her face, Leila might have been tempted to think she dreamt the whole thing up. Roxy was smiling again and laughing again, listening to music on the radio. But, Roxy was not leaving the room. She seemed absolutely determined to avoid going out, and that was completely out of character.

Leila looked through the photos again, trying to find a hint, something that could explain how this happened. What she saw was a woman who was in control, who took the initiative to pose or take the pictures, who wasn't waiting to follow her man's lead. This, even though Roxy was half the age of her husband, and Leila knew Bassel to be an extroverted leader-type himself. She kept scrolling through the photos, enlarging Roxy's face, looking for any physical blemish or sign of emotion. There was lots of happiness, but no attempt to hide the fact that the happiness in and of itself was a pose. She blew up the full-body shots to their full size, which on this phone was a very close zoom. In every photo, Roxy's body was flawless. Perfect. Slim in all the right places and shapely in all the right places. Leila scrolled up to the face, the hair. All perfect. Like a doll, or the perfect Damascus socialite. Beautiful, flawless, festooned. Excessive, ostentatious, fake.

Leila looked up at the real Roxy, who was leaning toward Huda and seemed to be speaking earnestly. Leila searched her demeanor for a sign, something to show the real Roxy. She looked back at the close-up of Roxy's face in one of the evening gown photos. Then at the person across the room. She searched both faces, looking, searching.

Her thoughts were interrupted by the vibrating of the phone. Ahmed! Leila quickly pushed the back button half a dozen times. This got her to the main page, but she didn't see any button for reading messages, so she fumbled through the phone's interface until she found the messaging center, then the inbox.

"My dearest Leila, it is fabulous to hear from you. Whose phone? Yes, In-House sounds good. 3:00 Wednesday?"

Leila's heart sank. She told herself this was silly, that it had only been not more than fifteen minutes, but she was amazed at how quickly she had excited herself with anticipation of Ahmed's reply. Nonetheless, it was good to hear from Nisreen, so she quickly hit the "reply" button.

"Friend's phone, she's staying with me a few days, so you can call. I'll see you Wednesday. Much love. And give my greetings to..." Leila stopped as she got to this sentence. Should she send greetings to Ahmed, specifically, or would that be too obvious? Should she greet the family, even though she didn't know them? She opted for Ahmed and pressed the send button before she could change her mind.

Then she went back to exploring the phone. She found the games section, and chose a game where she had to match up colored squares. As she played, it occurred to her that if she was going to sit here, she really should be studying. Just one game. But she lost rather quickly, felt she could have done better, so started another game before she stopped to think about it. She got into the groove of the game this time, and as she played, she thought about the photos of Roxy. Something was gnawing at her: there was something about Roxy that had captured her imagination from the beginning, and today was mystifying her. But she couldn't figure quite what it was. When she finished the game, she looked up at the ceiling, feeling sad. Ahmed hadn't replied.

It had now been almost an hour that Roxy and Huda were talking about who-knows-what. Leila decided it was time to break in. "Can I make us some tea?" she asked as she stood up.

Both girls looked at her, with apparent surprise at the reminder that they weren't alone. Both nodded without saying anything, so Leila grabbed the teapot and went out to the kitchen to get some water.

When she came back in, she put the water on the electric burner, tossed off her slippers, and joined her friends on the mattress. In as cheerful a voice as she could work up, she asked, "So, what are you two plotting?"

Neither girl said anything at first, just looked at each other with half-smiles. Now that she was close-up, Leila could see that Huda's eyes were red and swollen.

Leila quickly put her hand on Huda's knee and asked,

"What's the matter? Did something happen?"

"No, no," replied Huda. "Nothing." She took Leila's hand in her own and patted it. "But what I told you this afternoon? Maybe I was wrong."

"Wrong?" asked Leila. She had no idea what Huda meant by that.

"Yes..." Huda faltered a bit, glancing at Roxy. "What do I--? How do I--?"

"What is it?" asked Leila, feeling that perhaps she sounded a bit more enthusiastic than she'd intended.

No one answered for a second, and Leila looked from one girl to the other then back again, feeling very confused.

Finally, Roxy spoke. "Well, what Huda thought happened to her wasn't exactly what happened. She wasn't, uhhh, raped. He just... well, ummm... oh you don't want to know the details. What matters is that Huda can get married. She's still a girl, still a virgin."

Leila wasn't fully following, but she somehow felt like shrinking. She inched over on the mattress, away a bit from her two friends and looked down. But if he didn't rape her, then what happened? Was she supposed to understand this? She was embarrassed to ask, but curiosity got the best of her. "I don't get it. Sorry. So what did he do?"

Roxy looked intently in Leila's face. There was no masquerade or veil in her eyes. She just asked, in a motherly tone, "Do you know what you're asking? Do you really want to know?"

"Of course!" replied Leila without hesitating. "Why not? I have to know these things someday, don't I?"

"Do you? Really?"

"Yes. I do." And with that statement, Leila felt the last vestiges of the village girl float out of the window. She didn't know what to expect, but Roxy's look told her... well, she didn't know what the look told her, except that this was where the line might be drawn between a girl and a woman.

Roxy glanced over at the teapot and saw the water starting to boil. "Okay, then. I'll explain it to you. Let's have some tea." Huda quickly jumped up and offered to make it.

Roxy moved over to the space where Huda had been sitting so she was now a few short inches from Leila. She looked down at her hands for a moment, then shifted in her position so she was facing Leila directly. "Look at me, 24 years old and I'm... Wow. Here's the thing. You know about the bleeding, right? On your wedding night you're supposed to bleed? In my village, actually, after the wedding, the couple goes back to the husband's house and the two families wait until the husband brings back a white sheet with blood on it."

"I've heard of that happening."

"Well, the idea is, I guess you probably know this: your blood is a sign of your innocence, of your purity. If your husband makes you bleed, it's because you're still a virgin."

"Yes, I'd heard that before. And if you don't bleed, he can send you back to your family."

"In my community," said Roxy, rolling her eyes. "In my community, girls are killed if they don't bleed."

"Really? I didn't think that happened anymore."

"Oh yes, it happens."

Leila was scared by the thought. She'd always been told to be careful with her body, so that she'd bleed on her wedding night. She knew she wasn't supposed to ride bikes, do too much exercise, or do much of anything with that part of her body, in case it made her bleed early. She knew that her future and her family's future depended on it. She didn't know that girls were killed for not bleeding.

Roxy continued, "Well, I can tell you that I did bleed on my wedding night, and it hurt. It hurt so much. It really wasn't much fun at all. Not at first, anyway."

"So, your point is that Huda didn't bleed?"

"Well, essentially, yes. But I have heard that some girls don't bleed - which of course is very dangerous if your future depends on bleeding. If a girl doesn't bleed and her husband is convinced she's a good girl, I don't know, I think I've heard that he can cut himself or her somewhere else, just to show the family. But anyway, it may be possible that Huda would have not bled, but she probably would have – or will when she gets married. See, she did not actually have sex. Do you know what sex is?"

Leila pursed her eyebrows and thought a second. "Well, it's what a man and a woman do when they're together."

"Well, yes, although of course a man and a woman do things other than sex."

"Like what?" asked Leila.

"That's not the point." said Roxy. "So look: In sex, the man's body enters her in, well, in a specific place. And when a girl has never had sex, then there's something in that part of her body that is untouched skin. When it's broken is when she bleeds.

Leila was beginning to feel queasy. She swallowed hard and kept her eyes on Roxy.

"Anything else isn't sex. Do you see what I mean?"

No, of course she didn't. "Yes."

"So, a man and a woman can touch. A man can touch a woman anywhere on her body, but if that specific act doesn't happen, then it's not sex. Well, Huda didn't experience that, do you see what I mean?"

"So, if not sex, then what is it?"

"It's all kinds of things. He could have touched her all over, and he did some awful things, but it's not for me to tell you what exactly happened in that room. He could have even touched her in that part of her body, but he never broke that seal, that protection of her virginity. The professor may be an evil son of a dog who doesn't mind shattering the dignity of who knows how many girls, but he was considerate enough to stop at the seal of her virginity."

"So..." said Leila.

"What?"

"Well, does that mean that when Ahmed has touched me, it's never been a problem?"

"Did you think it was?"

"Well, sometimes, I felt things..." Leila felt her face turning red. "Like a shiver."

"Where did he touch you?"

"Usually he just held my hand. But a few times he held my..." her voice trailed off. She didn't want to conjure up a reminder of the thrill, and the sense of dirtiness.

"Feel free," said Roxy. "This is between you and me, really."

"Well... my leg."

"Your leg?"

"Yes."

"Did he ever touch your skin, or just your clothes?"

"Oh, no! Never my skin! Well, except my hand. Is that awful?"

"No, it's perfectly natural," assured Roxy. "And if he touched your leg and never skin, I don't see anything at all the matter with that."

"Really?"

"Yes, really. It's perfectly normal to enjoy being with someone, and to feel a bit of a thrill when he touches you. It means you're in love. It doesn't mean you're giving up your innocence at all."

"Are you sure?"

Roxy didn't reply immediately. In fact, all of a sudden, she went quiet.

"Roxy?"

"Maybe I shouldn't talk more about this. I mean, look where I am. But I wouldn't worry that you've done anything wrong with Ahmed. You're fine, just like Huda is still fine and has her whole life before her."

Huda was now sitting on the carpet in front of Leila and Roxy, who hadn't really noticed her come over with the tea all prepared, cups and sugar laid out on the tray. She now caught their eye and, with the biggest smile Leila had seen in the years of their friendship, asked how many sugars her friends wanted.

Chapter Six

When Maha, with her two cousins in tow, got back to her room, Roxy had moved in. She'd been there for three days and was still unwilling to go anywhere except for the bathroom and kitchen on the same floor. She had washed her hair and used Maha's hairdryer and brush to style it. She'd helped herself to a change of clothes from the closet. Neither Roxy nor Leila knew who they belonged to, but from the style and size, Leila guessed they were not Maha's. The bruises were fading nicely. On Tuesday night, Roxy had actually tuned the radio into her favorite station and danced.

Bassel had called several times, and sometimes Roxy had answered, forcing herself to sound busy and concerned with studies. Most of the time she had pressed the "cancel" button as soon as heard the special ringtone she'd chosen just for him.

So on Wednesday, right about noon, Maha unlocked the door, toting a bag of clothing and another bag of food. She found Leila on the bed in the corner studying and Roxy plucking her eyebrows on the mattress under the window. There were kisses and hugs all around. Everyone was very tender and deferential to Roxy, who waved off their concerns as if nothing had happened.

Then they sat around and drank tea made by Leila and talked about exams, the upcoming Alissa concert, the hottest new stores in Bab Touma and at the Four Seasons hotel, and celebrity gossip. Maha asked if the girls had found everything they'd needed, the girls assured her that they had, and Maha told Roxy she was welcome to stay as long as she wanted.

Leila soon looked at her watch and jumped up, collecting

tea cups and placing them on a tray. "I have to go! I'm late!"

"Give them to me," offered the roommate whose clothes Roxy had apparently borrowed. "Rest a bit."

"No, no, it's fine. I'll clean them up."

But Maha's roommate took the tray from Leila's hands, so Leila grabbed her books off the table and told the girls to stay seated and enjoy their afternoon. Roxy came up to her and gave her a big hug. "Thank you, you're an angel," she whispered in Leila's ear. Then she gripped Leila's two upper arms and stared into Leila's eyes. She just stared, and Leila stared back. Leila waited for Roxy to say something, but Roxy just smiled and gave her another quick hug.

"I'll be back this evening," Leila announced to everyone. "Do you want anything from the city?"

"*Bidna salamtek*. We want your well-being," came the chorus of replies.

So Leila walked out of the room and pulled the door shut behind her. She was now standing all alone in the corridor. It was one of those lovely clear days where the breeze flowed in the windows at the end of the hall through to the stairs and up to the roof. She looked back at Maha's door, wondering if she'd forgotten something. But she soon remembered the time and her appointment, and rushed into her own room to get ready.

An hour later, Leila walked into the now-familiar setting of In-House. Nisreen wasn't there yet, so Leila took a seat at the same table as she and Nisreen and Ahmed had occupied a week ago. Had that truly been only a week? She pulled out some lecture notes she'd shoved into her purse at the last minute and started to memorize.

Nisreen was ten minutes late, but she did show up, looking classy as always. Today she was wearing a bright pink scarf with big bug-eye sunglasses tucked into the scarf on top of her head. She wore black jeans and a pink and white striped shirt with a little black vest. Leila took one glance at Nisreen, then looked down at her own jeans-fabric overcoat that had been her Ramadan gift last year, the most stylish piece of clothing she'd ever owned, and she had begged her mother for the whole month of Ramadan to get it. She adjusted her scarf and straightened her coat as she stood up to greet Nisreen.

They followed the now-familiar routine of kisses, pleasantries and argument over who would pay and for what, and Nisreen headed up to the counter. Leila sat down, once again, and people-watched. Today at this hour the cafe was almost empty. There were two women, two toddlers and two strollers near the counter, the mothers trying to enjoy each other's company while keeping track of their unruly children. They looked Syrian, but then again they didn't. At the far end, seated on one of the white sofas, there was a young man working on a computer, clearly a foreigner, probably an Arabic student or else maybe a journalist. Then there was a couple sitting and laughing intimately at something on a mobile phone. And then there was Leila.

She thought of Huda. Huda would fit in here, but she didn't come. Never. No one at the Medina could afford this. Even before, two years ago when they'd first met, it was rare for Huda to go out, and since then it had become even more rare. Leila tried to imagine what Huda had been living with for the past two years. What it would be like to have made the decision to give everything away to succeed, but then to have failed, to have thought her life was over before it began. Leila couldn't imagine and felt terrible for not being able to imagine. Maybe if she'd been there she would have helped her friend. Maybe if she'd been willing to listen just a little bit sooner. Yes, Huda had her family, but somehow she didn't. The most important people in her life had to be protected, so

Huda would never tell them her story. And yet God had granted Huda a friend at the university, or so Leila had thought, but Leila had not been a true friend. Somehow, even this seemed to revolve around Ahmed. The greatest thing to have happened in her life caused so much trouble.

Nisreen came back with two bright colored fruit smoothies. She put a mint-green one in front of Leila. "Kiwi-Lemon with cream."

"Thank you," replied Leila.

Nisreen took a seat next to Leila, so both girls had a view of the room. Her own drink was pale pink, and the two girls sipped in silence for a while, gazing up at the music videos flashing across the big flat-screen television.

After a bit, Leila pulled herself away from her thoughts and asked Nisreen about her studies.

"Everything is fine. I think I'm ready for my poetry class, and translation. Like you said, I've memorized all the lecture notes. Yesterday I was on the Internet and read that memorizing things is one of the least effective ways of learning. The website said that when you memorize you inhibit your ability to understand, and so it's much more work for the brain, and much more effective, to have to process something in a new way, to rearrange and discuss material, than it is to memorize it. So what we are learning at the university is not making us learn; it may even be doing the opposite."

Leila just nodded.

"What do you think? Don't you think we should have to analyze and write and discuss, not memorize all these stupid notes?"

"Oh, I don't know," shrugged Leila. "I've always learned by memorizing, haven't you?"

"Well, yes."

"So what else would you do?"

"I don't know. The website had lots of examples. But it's not up to me. It's the university. Don't you think that a university that claims to be the top Arabic university in the Middle East should use more modern techniques?"

"I guess. I don't know."

"Well, I do. But, like you said, I'm memorizing. We'll see if it works."

"I hope you do well."

"Me too!"

Leila didn't reply. Instead, she was slouching and tracing shapes in the condensation on her plastic cup. After a minute, Nisreen shifted in her seat and asked, "Is everything alright?"

"Yes, it's great! I mean, I haven't studied at all, but that's okay. I'll get there."

"You really aren't worried?"

"You know, I keep up. I've studied a bit. Malish, it's no big deal."

"So, then, what's with you?"

"What do you mean?"

"Something's on your mind."

"It's been an interesting week, that's all," replied Leila as casually as she could, slouching down further in her chair.

Nisreen put her cup down and shifted once again in her seat. "Come on, tell me. You know I love a good story."

Leila looked up at the TV screen and took a sip of her drink. She looked at Nisreen who was staring back at her. Then she sat up and said, "Alright. Now, I can't tell you who this is about, and don't try to figure it out. It's probably not who you think it is anyway. But I heard something this week."

"Heard something?"

"Well, someone told me about something that happened to... emm... her. I can't stop thinking about it."

"Tell me. I'll keep it just between you and me."

"Have you ever heard of girls having to... you know... with their professors?"

"You mean--"

"Yes! Like as their bribe to their professors!"

Nisreen leaned forward wide-eyed. "You mean, someone told you that that happened to her?" she asked incredulously.

"Well, umm, yes."

"I can't believe it!" Nisreen exclaimed.

"Shhh!" Leila waved her hands gently down towards the table. "This is so sensitive."

"Oh yes, of course," whispered Nisreen conspiratorially. Her eye twinkled. "Wow, I can't believe you actually met someone who told you that happened to her."

"It's crazy, huh?"

"No, I hear about it all the time! But I've never met anyone, or met anyone who knew anyone, who would talk about it. This is excellent!" Nisreen declared, failing to remember to whisper.

"Please," pleaded Leila.

"Sorry."

"But... why do you say it's excellent?"

"It's just that it's one thing to hear rumors, and even to believe those rumors, but it's another thing to confirm it. I mean, she - your friend - could come out and bring the whole thing into the open, make a formal accusation."

"Do you really think that would make a difference? Excuse me, but you're crazy."

Nisreen giggled and took another sip of her smoothie. Then she put on a much more serious face and said, "You're right, Leila. It's not something to joke about."

"You know, it could happen to you."

"Actually, that is what is wrong with this place. No, I really don't think it could. Because of who I am, who my father is."

Leila hadn't thought of that.

"Anyway, though," continued Nisreen. "You're probably right, that it wouldn't make any difference. What can your friend do, except tell a friend?"

"I know." Leila's heart sank further. "I don't think she told anyone at all, actually. I only just found out about it, but it happened a long time ago."

"May God comfort her, encourage her."

"Yes, I know. But you said you've heard of this before?"

"Oh yes, there are all types of rumors," stated Nisreen, all business now. "That marks are not based on passing, they're based on *wasta*, connections. And of course you can get that *wasta* from lots of places, not only from who your father is."

"So why do you study?"

"I want to learn and I want to pass. I don't want to go through life thinking I succeeded because my father, or my brother, made it happen. You of all people should understand that. I can't believe you hadn't heard of this before."

"No, of course I'd heard of it. Once I was chatting with some Kurdish girls in the building. One of them had just failed and swore it was because she was a Kurd. I didn't believe her, though. But Ahmed too has told me of friends who have given professors gifts to pass. But I'm not sure I ever believed it. Anyway, that's not the point. This is something completely different!"

"What do you mean?"

"A girl, giving herself... I mean he is taking her very identity from her, isn't he?"

"Well, yes, I guess."

"What do you mean, you guess?" exclaimed Leila. "Ever since I heard I have been trying to imagine for one brief second what it must be like to be her! How I could live with myself, every day, thinking my life was over."

Nisreen started to stay something but clamped her mouth shut. The two girls sat in silence for a bit.

Leila eventually said, "I don't know, I just can't... I mean, why did this have to happen? You wouldn't understand, lucky you."

"No," Nisreen replied. "I don't think I can imagine. I don't think you can imagine either, though, can you?"

So much for respecting the elder, thought Leila.

"I mean," continued Nisreen. "How did you escape? How have you passed your courses, year after year, without anything happening to you? Maybe it's all about luck. Maybe it's because you didn't draw attention, and because your people aren't hated, and because you worked hard enough you didn't need the... extra help. How will I escape? Maybe for the same reasons, maybe because of my family, I don't know. But we can't imagine. And the tragedy is that your friend can only be a very close friend indeed if she told you. Let's say I had a friend with the same story. The two couldn't meet each other and talk about it; they will never be with someone who understood. That's the tragedy, is that your friend will not - cannot - stand up and tell the world what happened to her. She can't even tell her own family. Am I right?"

"Yes, I suppose. But why should she have to talk to someone else who experienced it?"

"Because you can't imagine, so what do you have to offer her? That's why. Why did she even tell you, did you think about that?"

"I was actually more concerned with why she didn't tell me sooner. For years she didn't tell anyone."

Nisreen made a good point, but Leila was uncomfortable having her boyfriend's little sister explain the world to her. She wanted to change the subject, but something wouldn't let her. Maybe it was true that a girl just had to talk, needed to share. Leila wanted to imagine, even tried to force herself to imagine, what it was like to be in that room, to be Huda. In her imagination the evil professor looked a lot like... like... it was someone she could picture vividly, but she couldn't place. Maybe the guy who sold the bus tickets to go home? No, someone more educated than that. Maybe one of her own professors? She couldn't remember who. Anyway, she pictured him, tall, strong, just a little bit heavyset. A five o'clock shadow, but carefully tailored to look that way. Slightly graying hair. Bassel, Roxy's Bassel! That's who she was picturing. Her stomach turned, but she forced herself to continue, to imagine Huda in a room, with a man who looked like Bassel, him holding Huda in an awkward hug...

Leila shook her head and forced herself to listen to Nisreen.

"...and that's why I have been thinking about going abroad and studying psychology abroad. Counseling is something people here really need, and no one is offering it to them. People don't realize what women in our country have to deal with. We're expected to take things in and to live the challenges all alone."

"You would want to be a psychologist?"

"Not a psychologist. A counselor. Here people don't realize that the two things are actually very different. It's like treatment, helping people like your friend live a healthy life. Making it so that an event like that does not have to end their life."

Leila appreciated that Nisreen was careful not to press her on who it was, or on the details of the story. Though she was sure Nisreen was wrong about what she thought happened, she was trying very hard to protect Huda's confidence, so she just let Nisreen talk.

"So how's Ahmed?" she asked Nisreen all of a sudden.

"Ahmed?"

"You know, your brother."

"You're asking me?"

"Yes. I haven't talked to him all week."

"Ohhh," breathed Nisreen, raising her eyebrows. "Now I understand."

"What? What?" What was the matter?

"Oh, nothing. Just that he hasn't mentioned you for a while, and he used to always talk to me about you. The other day I asked him about why he's been so quiet and he stood up and walked out of the room."

"Where was that?"

"At home."

"Does that... Do you mean... Does your family know?"

"Oh, Lord, no!" Nisreen exclaimed. Then she stopped herself short. "Wait, actually, tell me what's going on between you two."

"What were you going to say?"

"Oh, nothing. I don't think I understand. Tell me, then maybe it will make sense."

So Leila found herself pouring her heart out to her dear future sister-in-law. She told her how Ahmed had asked for a month of distance, to study. How she thought at first that the request made sense, but then had a feeling something was wrong. How much she loved Ahmed. She told Nisreen what happened when she got to the village last week, and that she couldn't wait forever for him. She explained that Ahmed needed to move soon, because she loved Ahmed and couldn't imagine living without him, but there was the looming threat of her mother's own plans. She told Nisreen that she'd mentioned this to Ahmed in their last conversation. She reminded Nisreen that she couldn't live without him.

Nisreen said nothing, just took the final few sips of her smoothie. Leila did the same, all of a sudden desperate to return to the Medina, to the relative security of being the one giving comfort to Huda whose life had been rewritten for her several times in the past two years, and to Roxy who was living across the hall now, in hiding from her husband.

Leila casually glanced at her watch and exclaimed how late it was, and how she needed to get back to her studies, and that surely Nisreen needed to study as well. She jumped up and grabbed her purse and took Nisreen's hand as she kissed her on each cheek. Nisreen stood up slowly and, as she kissed Leila back, asked, "Is that phone still with you?"

"You can write me on it. I'll get the message."

"Don't worry about it, it will be fine. I'll invite you over for dinner, maybe Friday?"

"Really? Oh, thank you. Yes, Friday would be great!" Leila gave Nisreen another quick hug and floated out of Damascus's hippest coffee shop. In two days, she would see Ahmed!

The next morning, Leila awoke to a knock at her door. She rolled over and opened her eyes half-way. She saw one of her roommates eating breakfast on the other side of the room and closed her eyes again, groaning ever so slightly and hugging her pillow. She heard the girl's steps headed towards the door and drifted back to sleep.

But she was soon awakened again by none other than Roxy, nudging her relentlessly. "Good morning! Come on, get up! It's breakfast time!"

Leila groaned again and hugged her pillow a bit tighter.

"*Yalla*, get up!" hissed Roxy as she shook Leila's shoulder.

Leila opened her eyes now and looked up at her friend, as beautiful as she had ever been. She rolled over and lay on her back. "What time is it?"

"It's 9:30 already! Come on, I made a great breakfast. We're all waiting for you!"

"All?"

"Yes, I made breakfast for us. Maha, the girls. I just called Huda, too. She should be over in a second. She was awake already. You're late."

"It's still early," protested Leila.

"*Yalla*. We're waiting," said Roxy and quickly walked back out of the room.

Leila sat up and rubbed her eyes. Her roommate had quickly settled back into her own breakfast and, other than her, Leila was alone. She slowly put her feet down and felt around for her slippers. Then she stood up and stumbled out to the toilets. She went to the kitchen and washed up carefully, pulled out her prayer rug and did morning prayers, then made her bed. Within ten minutes she was knocking on Maha's door.

Sure enough, the girls were all there, but not waiting. They'd already dug into a lovely breakfast of labne, scrambled eggs, cut up vegetables, cheese, butter and jam. Each girl had a little cup of tea, and there was an empty spot with a full cup of tea waiting for Leila on the rug.

"Good morning," she said to the group, and they replied in unison.

From the far side of the group, Roxy lifted her arm and waved. "*Tfadali*! Help yourself!"

Leila slid into the spot saved for her, with one knee up and the other leg tucked under, and took the piece of bread handed to her.

The girls ate eagerly, enjoying this specially-prepared breakfast. They felt the love and the energy that had flowed into each dish by Roxy's hands. There was a sense that this wasn't just any Thursday; it was a special day. They felt like first-years, experiencing the Medina again for the first time. The world just waiting to be discovered.

"I hear Jabal a-Sheikh is beautiful this time of year. We should go one day."

"Yes! I've only been there in winter. It must be beautiful in the summer. That dry cool breeze."

"Huda, how far is your village from Nahr al-Bared, that Cold River that people go to just to sit in when the weather's hot? I heard it's near Latakia, is that near your house?"

"Actually, Nahr al-Bared is near Hama."

"Oh. Do we know anyone in Hama?"

"There was a girl down the hall who invited me to visit her village there, but that was three years ago. I don't think that would work anymore. I haven't talked to her since."

"Oh. Well, maybe Jabal a-Sheikh is just as nice."

"It's very nice. I've never heard of Nahr al-Bared. But people come from all over the world to go to Jabal al-Sheikh."

"People go to Nahr al-Bared from the Gulf."

"They do? Is it nice?"

"Well, I've never been there."

"Neither have I."

"Neither have I."

"Anyway, girls, Jabal a-Sheikh is only an hour from here. There are *service* that go straight there. That'd be a great outing."

"Yes, we could do a picnic!"

"We could make salads and buy fatayer, and my mom sent some sweets the last time we were in the village."

"What a great idea! That'd be beautiful! We could invite the guys: they might want to come and play ball. Then we could hire a whole *service* van just for ourselves."

"How beautiful. I haven't actually been there at all yet."

"So when should we go? Tomorrow's Friday. Is everyone around?"

"Oh, I need to study."

"I'm going to my uncle's house."

"How about Saturday?"

"I don't know. Let's see."

"Hey, I know! Let's have a picnic here, in the Medina. This week. Jabal a-Sheikh will have to wait until after exams, perhaps."

"Yes, after exams, before we all go home for the summer."

"Forever."

"Oh, don't remind me. Let's plan a picnic, right here at the Medina."

"We can take our gas burners downstairs, and I have an arguile that I hide in my closet. I know the director of the building, so no one says anything."

"Yes, let's! Tomorrow! I'll make the tabouli."

"I'll bring some fatayer."

"I'll bring my gas burner, and make tea, and those sweets."

"I'll... I'll... I'll cook something special!"

The conversation continued, around and around and around. Leila didn't know whether there would actually be a picnic the next day. She knew that she hoped not, because tomorrow was Friday, and of course nothing would stop her from an invitation to see Ahmed again, and to finally meet his family. She shivered slightly and turned back to the conversation. The plotting and scheming continued, with new ideas being thrown out, and it was so fun to dream the Medina adventure again.

Breakfast was over sooner than it had started. The window was wide open, there was a breeze, and the sound of people milling about downstairs was floating up to the room. This was a day when anything was possible, which was just one of the reasons why Leila was stunned out of her slippers by what Roxy had to say after all the other girls had left.

Maha's two roommates had gone to visit friends in Building 11. Huda had quickly run back to studying. Maha had offered to clean up, but Roxy had insisted on cleaning up herself and had encouraged Maha to take a shower while there was hot water in the building, even though there was no need to plan around the water schedule in June when the tanks on the roof produced naturally sun-heated water on a daily basis. Nonetheless, Maha trekked off to the shower and Roxy quickly moved the dishes into a tray.

But she didn't wash them. Instead, she sat down on the mattress beside Leila and immediately started talking. "I realized this morning that I've been here for five days now. I woke up early and couldn't go back to sleep. So I went up to your favorite place on the roof and watched the sunrise. It was my first time outside since I got here, you know. And when you came this weekend, I had hardly been out for a week. What a beautiful sunrise! You and I should go together to watch the sunrise tomorrow.

"Leila, *habibti*, you've been wonderful. You have been a true friend to me when I didn't know who to turn to. It was definitely God who made me think to stop by your room. I'm not even sure if I believe in God, but your friendship has been something of God to me. Thank you so much for coming when you did. I don't know what I would have done without you."

Leila started to reply, saying it was nothing, no more than what anyone would have done, but Roxy kept talking.

"Which is why I need to ask you for help again. I know it's a bother, but I don't have anyone else to go to. Mary and Ghalia can never know about this, do you promise?"

Leila nodded.

"I mean it. They can't know." Roxy continued, "I think I've known this for a very long time, but I only just now realized that I knew it. I need to leave Bassel. It's been fun, these three years, but it's over. I always thought I'd have to find a way to explain him to my family, or, you know, leave them. But deep down inside I knew that it was my family I wouldn't leave. And now it's over. I don't want to believe it, but it's true. It's not fun anymore, and he never meant for me to be around forever. Both of us have known for a while that it was over, and maybe that's why this happened, because we started to pretend. I don't know.

"But what I'm saying is, I need your help. Leila, I can never see him again. Never. It's impossible. You need to help me with this."

Leila quickly asked, "But how will you do that?"

"I've been thinking about it, and that's why I need your help. See, there are two things. The first one is leaving him. And the second thing is going back to my family. This is just between me and you. Please don't tell anyone! Ever." She was holding Leila's arms tightly. "Now, to leave him, I need to ask you to go back to the flat and get my things. We need to figure out a way to find a time when he won't be there. We can go back together--"

"No, Roxy. You can't do that. I'll go."

"But if he finds you there?"

"Can I take someone with me? Maybe Maha or Huda?"

"We'll talk about that. First I need to figure out a way to get him out, to know he's out. I need to make a list of things you need to get. And I'll need to figure out how to return certain things to him, like my phone. Will you help me with this?"

"Of course."

"Great. I'll make a plan. But here's the real thing, here's what I need you to do for me, and only you, no one else in the whole world, can help you, see you, even know you're doing something!" Roxy glanced at the door, where there were footsteps passing through the hall. Once they had definitely passed, she continued in a whisper, with her face about three inches from Leila's. "I have heard that there are doctors here in Sham who can do a surgery, a surgery to make me a girl again. I need to find a doctor, but it has to be someone safe for my health, and, most important, someone who will do this secretly. You need to find that doctor for me."

Leila stared at Roxy. She didn't know what that meant, but at that moment the door opened, and a wet Maha walked in. "*Naieman*," she called out, congratulating Maha on her new cleanliness. Maha thanked her and quickly stepped into the alcove with the closets.

Roxy pulled Leila close and gripped her hand. She said, "Please, find this for me. I will give you anything, do anything for you. But please, you're the only one who can do this. I need you. And don't tell anyone." When she let go, Leila realized that Roxy had pressed something into her hand.

She quickly shoved it into her pocket, excused herself, and stepped out into the fresh breeze of the hallway.

The roof today was hot, but the wind was still refreshing as long as Leila stood out of the sun. Avoiding both the sun and the sewage fumes left Leila with a very small corner of space in which to stand, right next to the door leading back downstairs. She hovered in that small space, leaning against the wall and staring out at the roofs of the other Medina buildings. It was too hot to be studying outdoors, and there wasn't another human soul in sight. Leila took a deep breath of the warm breeze with the scent of the desert out east, then she reached into her pocket and pulled out the little package Roxy had slipped into her hand. She unrolled three 1000 lira bills, more money than Leila spent in a month. There was nothing else, no explanation, no note, just the money.

Thoughts and confusion swirled around in her head. Roxy... surgery? What terrors had that girl seen? Then there was Huda and her tragedy, which wasn't so tragic but still was devastating. Meeting Ahmed's family, tomorrow!

Graduation looming. Studying! For a few days now, a nagging impulse to study had been growing in Leila's gut. Since classes ended two weeks ago, she'd barely caught more than an hour or two in short spurts. Exams started in three days, and while Leila had not been worried about taking a bit of extra time away to visit Roxy or to have coffee with Nisreen, this was getting to be too much. Failure had not seriously crossed her mind until yesterday as she was heading back to the Medina after seeing Nisreen. But now a kernel of fear had sprouted in her belly, and she felt her gut tightening as it dawned on her that it was not inconceivable that she would, for the first time, fail, on her very last set of exams.

Leila closed her eyes and saw the cover of *The Lord of the Flies*, then the cover of *Pride and Prejudice*, then an anthology of poems she'd read but would surely have to read again, and then she pictured the massive pile of lecture notes that sat scattered on her shelf and under her bed. The wad of lecture notes still shoved into her purse, that she had dutifully carried around with her everywhere she'd been for the past week, with the hope of taking advantage of every free moment to study. She'd done so, which had rendered all of one translation lecture memorized. And at the moment, she couldn't even remember what that lecture was about, much less the content!

She longed to sit with her books, to spend time buried in piles of paper, to transport herself to the imaginary world of a novel, or the metaphorical way of seeing the world that she'd discovered in her poetry lectures. She longed to spend a day, just one day, doing absolutely nothing but memorizing. She actually found that she wanted to mull over obscure rules of English grammar, rather than think through her failure as a friend to Huda. She wanted to think about the problems of her favorite book characters like Oliver Twist, or Lizzy

Bennett, or even Atticus Finch, rather than work out how she would spend this month away from Ahmed, and at the same time devise a way to have him approach her family. She would certainly prefer to memorize, not poems, but the professor's analysis of his favorite poems, than find a doctor to do Roxy's surgery.

Leila was honored that Roxy trusted her above all people, and thrilled that she had been given responsibility for Roxy's return to family life. A gush of excitement rushed through her with the thought of conspiring to enter Roxy's flat when Bassel wouldn't know and to clear out Roxy's belongings for her. This was real adventure, the kind she had always longed for!

But surgery? What surgery? How could surgery possibly be what Roxy needed in order to get divorced? Leila had heard of women getting divorced before. It often ruined their lives, like that of her mother's sister Aunt Mariam, who had moved in with her brother twenty years ago. Aunt Mariam had two daughters, and for twenty years now had not seen them. They had been raised in the home of her ex-husband's family and then had both married out to local villages, but Mariam had not been invited to the weddings, much less had a say in her daughters' life decisions. For the past twenty years, Aunt Mariam had stayed at home, helping some with the housework, and learning Islam. She had memorized the whole Qur'an and taken *tajwid* classes to recite it perfectly. She now taught younger women the art of Qur'anic recitation, so her life was not empty. But everyone pitied Aunt Mariam. They talked about how she may have been a bad wife in more ways than one, but her failure to bear her husband a son had crowned her destiny. Aunt Mariam had friends from her Qur'an study groups but was not trusted among the women in her own family. When Leila's mother talked about her sister Mariam, it was with pity and the understanding that her life had ended the day her husband had said to her face, "I divorce you."

But no one had ever talked about Aunt Mariam having surgery. Nor any other divorced women. Of all Leila's years of overhearing gossip among her various aunts, cousins and other women in the village, Leila had never heard divorce and surgery mentioned in the same conversation. Surgery was for cancer, or for eye cataracts, not for marriage!

Leila thought of where she could go for help. Her first thought was Nisreen, who, though three years her junior, was a woman of the world and a wealth of knowledge. Nisreen knew about all kinds of things, and what she didn't know, she somehow found out. But Nisreen knew Roxy, and Roxy had been adamant that Leila not involve another person. This was one of those situations, though, where alone was not good. She longed to share with Huda or even with Maha Roxy's request, so that at least they could think of something together. But here Leila was alone. She had been given the charge to step forward, to face the world, alone. Another shiver passed up her spine, one of intense excitement at the thought of being truly independent, even if just for this one task. But the same shiver soon retraced its steps down her spine, as the fear of failure gripped her.

A million questions swarmed through Leila's head, each one drowning the other out. Leila found herself completely overwhelmed by the uncertainties, by the need to understand how the last week - what should have been one of the greatest weeks of her life, of joyful endings and beginnings - how this last week had reshaped itself so many times over. A tear welled up in Leila's right eye as she stared blankly ahead, toward the mountain without really seeing it. The tear threatened to blur her vision and her nose twitched, so Leila rubbed her eye, swallowed hard, and started wandering around the roof. She told herself that the various emotions of the past week were a gift from God, the opportunity to really live life, and to live for more than just passing, graduating and marrying. Wasn't life just one big test, an education, tailored for her by God? It was her lot in life, and it really wasn't all that awful a *nasiib* - especially considering that she'd just learned that two of her closest friends had been through so much.

The tears threatened to well up again as she tried to empathize with Huda and Roxy, but Leila once again managed to force them back. She picked up the speed of her walk around the roof and started to feel sweat accumulating on her back. Then she decided that she needed to make a plan and marched back to her shady corner. As the sun was reaching its highest point in the sky, the shade was quickly disappearing, but Leila planted herself in the deepest pocket of her corner and pulled out the three thousand lira. What was it for? Roxy had said not to involve any person, so maybe this was her way of compensating. Was it payment to Leila, or would she find she needed it?

Leila stood there pondering the cash until her shade was gone, and a plan was finally forming in her mind. First she would study. No, first she would spend some time reading the Qur'an, to regain her focus. Then she would spend the afternoon studying. For a few hours, she would study better than anyone had ever studied in the history of the university - well, except perhaps for Huda at this time two years ago; no one could study better than that. Then at five o'clock, she would make a doctor's appointment, with a doctor she didn't know, hopefully with a woman. She would go to somewhere near Bab Touma, a neighborhood far from here. She had heard there were lots of doctors over there. And she would use Roxy's money to buy information about the surgery.

At five o'clock, minus three minutes, Leila put the last of

her translation lecture notes down. She had managed to have a good study afternoon and her brain felt clear for the first time in days. She sat back and looked out the window at the courtyard, where the activity was just beginning to pick up as the afternoon heat died away. She enjoyed a sense of achievement, of focus. It was time to put the studies away and get to the task at hand.

She debated visiting Roxy to tell her what the plan was, but decided it'd be better to have something more to tell her than just a vague idea. All afternoon, Leila had been forcing herself to stop thinking about Ahmed and Nisreen and wondering if Nisreen had called yet. But she knew Roxy would take the message, and anyway, Leila could always call Nisreen later in the evening. So, though every nerve ending of her body wanted to go spend some quality time with Roxy's phone, Leila forced herself to go up to her own room, put the lecture notes on her shelf, shove a new set of notes into her purse, straighten her scarf and put on her overcoat, and head out into the nascent evening.

As she walked to the back of the Medina, Leila could almost feel Ahmed's hand holding hers. With every tall dark man she passed, she did a double-take, somehow expecting, or at least hoping, to run into him as she walked through their old stomping grounds. She imagined the conversation they'd be having right now: studies, plotting their future together, Ahmed's graduate school applications. She imagined telling him all about Roxy and her current quest, and decided it was a relief not to have to decide what of her friends' confidences to share, for she wanted to keep no secrets from her man.

Walking out the back gate of the Medina, where guards were checking carefully the student cards of every young man attempting to get in, Leila fingered the cash in her pocket. The cash gave her the freedom to flag a taxi that would take her directly to Baghdad Street, which she thought was the street housing many doctors' offices.

Sure enough, fifteen minutes and fifty lira later, she found herself standing on the side of a busy street, overwhelmed with the number of signs advertising doctors' offices in all the buildings around her. Dr. Mohamad Zatari, rhinologist, trained in France; Dr. Moussa Sader, expert in all inner organs, trained in Europe; Dra. Lina Malouf, dentist and dental surgeon, trained in Canada; Dr. Mahmoud Sheiban and Dra. Zeina Kheider, general practitioners with expertise in bone structure, muscle development, and pediatrics, trained in Germany and Hungary. The four-lane street was lined with buildings on each side as far as the eye could see in each direction, and each building seemed to have at least one doctor's office in it. Carefully reading each of these hundreds of doctors' signs, Leila walked up to one end of Baghdad Street, where it hit the main highway leading out of Damascus, and turned around. Then she walked to the other end of the street and reached a big traffic circle, overwhelmed by the selection. Time would not wait for her indecision, though, so she determined to stop at the first woman's doctor's office she found and hope for the best.

Thus five minutes later she found herself in the waiting room of the Madame Doctor Muna Maasoud, French-trained optician and eye surgeon, where she was told by a plump bored-looking receptionist no older than herself, that for five hundred lira she could see the doctor in fifteen minutes. Leila handed her the money and was asked to fill out a form with her name, address, phone number and birth date. She made up a name and phone number, left the address blank, and put her best guess at Roxy's birthday.

The receptionist, who was wearing bright pink lipstick and thick eyeliner and a plain white headscarf, went back to playing a game on her mobile phone, which had a tiny pink teddy bear ornament hanging from it. Leila tried to mentally rehearse what she'd say to the doctor.

Mercifully, the fifteen minutes passed quickly. A woman with her young bespectacled son came out of the doctor's office calling back greetings for the doctor's brother and mother and aunt. Dr. Muna, herself short and plump, came to the door and waved them off with a wide smile, then turned to the receptionist who handed her the yellow form that Leila had filled out. Leila slouched down in her seat, imagining herself sinking into the floor and reappearing somewhere nice, maybe In House with Ahmed sitting across from her.

"Ghada? Come in."

Leila hopped up and walked up with an external confidence, hopefully conveying that she was only here to confirm she still didn't need glasses. She shook Dr. Muna's hand and followed her into the office, noting that the doctor pulled the door shut behind her.

Dr. Muna sat down behind her desk and gestured for Leila to take the nearest chair. The room was full of eye doctor equipment: a big machine which looked like binoculars on steroids, an eye chart on the wall, sample eyeglasses, contact lens kits, and some fancy lighting. It was spacious but not luxurious, and Leila felt she had chosen well. This doctor seemed friendly and kind, and very practical.

"My eyes are fine," she blurted.

"Well, that's great! Then this will go quickly, we just need to confirm--"

"No, you don't understand. I'm not here for my eyes."

Dr. Muna picked up her pen and put it down again. She looked around her own office as if to discern whether she was offering some service she didn't know about.

"You see, I just needed some advice," said Leila, trying to

get to her point as quickly as possible, before she lost her focus and found herself learning that she did in fact need glasses for a stigmatism in her left eye, or cataract surgery at the tender age of 21. "I'm here about something different, you see. I know this is strange, but I need to ask a question. I read somewhere that doctors owe their patients confidentiality, that whatever I tell you is a secret between you and me. Is that true?"

"Well," Dr. Muna replied slowly, blinking at her new client. "Yes, it is. But I'm not sure I understand: Are you my patient?"

"Can I be?"

"You made an appointment, didn't you? But you don't want anything for your eyes?"

"No. Is that a problem?"

"Well, I am trained as a doctor--"

"Good," said Leila quickly. "So what I tell you and ask you, is just between you and me?"

After blinking a few more times and picking up her pen and fiddling with it for a moment, Dr. Muna put it down on the table in a definitive gesture and turned to face Leila head-on. "Absolutely."

"This isn't for me. This is for a friend. And I don't know anything about... well, anything. But my friend asked me to help her, and I don't know where to start. But this has to be completely confidential."

"Yes, I understand that," said Dr. Muna.

Leila decided to just get it all out. "My friend, you see, she's married. But her family doesn't know anything about it. They think she's still at university studying. Well, I went to her house on Saturday, and she looked terrible. Her face was bruised and swollen, she was walking with a limp, and she looked like she hadn't bathed or eaten, or done anything, really, for a very long time. She never told me what happened but, well, I guess it's pretty obvious. She doesn't have any children. We brought her back to the Medina - that's where I live, the university city - and she's been staying with us. I guess she has decided she needs to get out of the marriage and go back to her family. After seeing her the way she looked on Saturday, I think that's a good thing, right? It's not my decision, of course. She's the type of person who does what she does. But she said that to do that she needs a surgery." Leila stopped and took a deep breath, then sighed and waited.

Dr. Muna didn't say anything but seemed to expect Leila to keep talking, so she did.

"But I don't know what kind of surgery she means. Why does she need surgery to get divorced? But she has asked me to find a doctor who can do it, because she doesn't want anyone in her family, not even her cousins who are her best friends, to know. So I came here and found your office and want to be your patient, so that you can tell me, with all secrecy, how to find someone to perform the surgery, whatever the surgery is, for my friend."

Now Dr. Muna was nodding, and saying, "You came all the way across town and found an eye doctor to ask me what kind of surgery your friend needs and who can do it?"

"Yes."

"Very well. Do you really want to know the details of the surgery? Are you sure it's for your friend?" she asked with an eyebrow raised.

"What? Me? Oh, no! I don't even know what she's talking about!" She felt a flutter in her leg where she last remembered Ahmed touching her and sensed her face turning red.

"I believe you. If it were you, you probably would know what to ask for, wouldn't you?"

"I don't know."

"You would, believe me," Dr. Muna looked like she was on the verge of laughing, making Leila feel oddly disturbed and reassured at the same time. "Now, to tell you what kind of surgery, well, that means understanding what happens on the wedding night. Do you know about that?"

Leila shrugged.

"What's your name? It's not Ghada, is it?"

"Can I just be Ghada?"

"I suppose you can. So what's your friend's name?"

"Just call her my friend for now, can't you?"

"We'll come back to that, Ghada. Now, on the wedding night, traditionally that's the night of first sex, the night a girl loses her virginity. That happens when a man penetrates his wife, breaking something called the 'hymen' in the process. This is a thin flap of skin that protects the entrance to the vagina."

Leila nodded, having no idea what the doctor was talking about.

"Do you understand?"

Leila nodded again, a bit slower.

"I see. I guess the details aren't all that important. What is important is that when a woman has her first sex, she usually bleeds out. You may have heard of that."

"Yes," Leila now bobbed her head, remembering Roxy's lecture. "I know all about that. That's the sign of a woman's purity, of her family's honor. But a girl has to be careful not to break it before her wedding night, like riding horses or something like that."

"That's right. A broken hymen is not necessarily a sign of not being a virgin, but unfortunately, many people in our society still think it is. If your friend is married, though, then we can assume she is not a virgin. Therefore, no matter what, her hymen would already be broken."

"Which means she wouldn't bleed if she got married

again." said Leila slowly.

"Exactly. You said her family doesn't know she's married, right?"

"Right."

"So, I would assume that when she says she needs a surgery to get divorced, it's not to get divorced, but it's so she can go back to her family and marry someone that they approve of without them ever knowing about her first marriage."

"That makes sense."

"Good. So now, what else can I do for you?"

"Wait! That makes sense that the surgery has to do with her bleeding, but you still haven't told me what the surgery is!"

"Oh. Well, so there is an operation that can be done to sew the hymen back together, or else to replace it if it's ruined. The surgery even inserts a red liquid. That way, when she has relations with a man again, she will bleed just like one expects of a girl who has never been with a man."

Leila cringed and tried to push out of her mind the vague images, growing slightly clearer every moment, of Ahmed touching her in all the places he had seemed to want to touch her, and all the times she had brushed him off, driven by some internal force that told her it would be wrong. Then a picture of him standing next to a bed, and her sitting in a pool of blood.

"Yes, it is quite painful," continued Dr. Muna, misreading Leila's facial expression. "Although it's not as bad as the first time," she added with what sounded to Leila like a giggle. "But, truly, it is a gift for the girl who sees no other way. It could save her life. Unfortunately, it is completely unaccepted here in Syria, because, well, after all, it is a way of deceiving one's husband. Tell your friend that she needs to be completely and entirely sure before doing something like this. It is dangerous. She should certainly consider carefully her decision to leave her husband."

"Oh, she has to leave him!" exclaimed Leila. "But she will ask me if she can do it, not if she should do it!"

"If your friend is absolutely determined, she needs to understand the risks. Any surgery in that part of the body makes her vulnerable to all kinds of diseases. And there is, as in any situation, a risk that someone will find out she has been deceiving her family and her future husband. Additionally, this is not a surgery done openly in the city's top hospitals. But that's probably part of why she asked you to figure it out on your own without involving any friends or family. It's probably why you are here asking a woman eye doctor to help you with gynecological surgery. Strange though it is, it was probably smart, your luck, to come to me."

"Really?"

"Like you said, I am bound by doctor-patient confidentiality, so there is no danger of me reporting anything. But also, I can recommend you to a doctor who can perform the operation."

"Oh, that is wonderful! Thank you, Dr. Muna!"

Leila walked out of Dr. Muna's office gripping Dr. Muna's business card, and with a sheet of paper on which was written a name and phone number. She was amazed at how easy this had been. And at how far Roxy was willing - was needing - to go in order to return to the life that might have been hers all along.

As she approached Building 14, Leila quickened her step. By now, Nisreen would have most certainly called, and Leila would know what to look forward to the next day. Perhaps there was even a message from Ahmed himself! She was still feeling shaken by the doctor's matter-of-fact way of talking about relations between a man and a woman, and though she wanted nothing more than to spend an evening with Ahmed, there was a slightly disgusting taste that seemed to creep into her mouth whenever she thought of him. Nonetheless, she skipped into the foyer and almost ran up to Maha's room, where the door was slightly ajar. Leila barged in and saw Roxy and Maha and a girl she didn't know smoking cigarettes over almost-empty cups of coffee. They all looked up at her in a haze and a bit of a daze. "*Mesa Al-kheir*," greeted Leila, and Maha replied by inviting Leila to take a seat.

As Leila removed her shoes, Maha stood up to grab a coffee cup from the pile of dishes on the table. She brought it back and poured out a shot of the black bitterness. Leila could hardly contain herself long enough to take her seat, thank Maha for the coffee, and refuse the strange girl's offer of a cigarette.

"Did anyone call for me?" she asked, looking at Roxy.

"No. Why?"

"Well, I was expecting a call. Have you checked your phone recently?"

Roxy's eyebrows raised and she exchanged some kind of knowing look with Maha. "Really? Who?"

"A girlfriend."

"You sure? Anyone special?"

"Have you checked? Maybe it rang and you didn't hear it."

"It's been with me all day, my girl," said Roxy with a trace of pity. "Maybe she'll call later."

"Where is it?" and Leila grabbed the phone Roxy waved at her. She navigated the menu, checking the messages and missed-call lists, in the now-desperate hope that Nisreen had contacted her and Roxy had somehow missed it.

The new girl put out her cigarette in the ashtray and stood up to leave. She casually said goodbye to Leila and Roxy and went to the door. Maha followed her, and they chatted for a few brief seconds, just long enough for Leila to tell Roxy that she had made progress on their scheme.

Maha quickly closed the door, turning the key this time so it would stay closed, then turned around and questioned her friend. "So, Leila? What's going on?"

Leila all of a sudden felt shy. "Well, I..." Her hesitancy was enough to convince Roxy and Maha to keep nudging and teasing her, so she soon found herself explaining that she'd given Roxy's number to Nisreen, who had promised to call her to invite her to family dinner on Friday - tomorrow. As Leila spoke, her heart sunk, wondering what it meant that Nisreen had not called.

Roxy exclaimed, "That's marvelous, you finally get to meet his family!" She tapped Leila on the back.

Then Maha commented, "You don't look so happy, Leila. What's the matter? Shouldn't you be thrilled?"

Leila looked up at her and replied, "But she didn't call. What does that mean? And what do I do now?"

Maha lay a hand gently on Leila's knee and said, "Don't worry."

Roxy patted Leila on her back again, this time a bit softer. "It's still early. You'll see. She'll call." Then she busied herself piling coffee cups onto a little tray. As she stood up and headed to the door with the dishes, she said, "Tonight's a special night. Do you feel the beautiful breeze coming in through the window? At ten o'clock, let's have a party on the roof. Just the three of us. No, let's call Huda. She needs a roof party. We'll take up the tape player and dance the night away."

Leila watched Roxy head out the door and then turned to Maha, "She sure seems so much better. You didn't see her on Saturday. I hardly knew her. Thank you so much for all you've done."

"Don't mention it. We're all sisters, aren't we?"

"Yes, sisters... We are, aren't we?" Leila stood up and slipped her shoes on. "I think I'll go see if she needs help." She walked into the hallway and sidled up next to Roxy, who was splashing water all over the place as she rinsed the tiny ceramic cups. "Little by little, take it easy!" Leila laughed. "Have mercy on the poor cups! Here, let me help."

It was not hard to displace Roxy from her position in front of the sink. As Leila scrubbed and rinsed and handed the clean cups and pot to her friend, she said, "So, I got you a name and a phone number."

"A what?"

"A doctor. You know, who can..."

"Yes, yes."

"It was amazing, actually! I thought it was going to be impossible, but then I just walked into this woman eye doctor's office and she explained everything!"

"Thank you, dear."

"No, there's more. She said that it's very dangerous, and that you should be very, very sure before you try something like that. She was very nice. Maybe you should talk to her before calling this doctor. I don't know anything about him. I don't trust him, though."

"But you don't know anything about him yet. Call him and check into it for me, please?"

"Well, but the doctor said that this whole thing is very risky. She said that if there's any other way, you shouldn't do it."

"Oh, Leila!" pleaded Roxy, now in a very fervent half-whisper. "She doesn't know me. She doesn't know my situation. You should know better. You are the only person who really knows how much I need to leave! She cannot convince me to go back to Bassel."

"I didn't say that," rejoined Leila, now done with the dishes and patting her wet hands on her pajama legs. She led

Roxy, who held the tray of cups, to a corner of the hall by the window. "It's just that... I'm scared for you. Can't you be just a little bit scared?"

Roxy put the tray of cups down on the window ledge and placed her hands on Leila's shoulders. She gazed into Leila's eyes, and Leila felt like she was finally beginning to understand this woman before her. The confidence was real, but the fear was real, too. Roxy was full of life, but a deep type of life, the type of life that spoke thrill and enjoyment, because she knew, really understood, that it was not to be taken lightly. This spoke to Leila of something more profound than even an abusive marriage and the price of suffering in silence. It made her wonder what had happened to Roxy earlier in life that convinced her to face the world with such strength, with this energy that seemed to be borne out of a fear that if she didn't use it, she would lose it?

Roxy's silence spoke more than her words.

"I see," Leila finally said, after several minutes. "I'm with you."

"It's just," started Roxy. "It's not that I'm not scared, but, I just have to..."

"Malish. Don't worry about it. I'm with you."

Roxy released Leila's shoulders and turned to the window as she picked up the tray. When she turned back to Leila, the dazzling glimmer that said life was a dare had returned to her eyes. She nodded in the direction of her new room and commented, "Maha sure is great. Really great. I like your floor." She walked back in, placed the tray down and walked out again, this time to notify Huda of the ten o'clock roof dancefest. Leila watched for a minute, then walked back to her room to undress, put her books in order, and think about her longing to see Ahmed.

Chapter Seven

It occurred to Leila that she had been quite silly.

Quite silly indeed.

Nisreen had not called and, when Leila had finally caved to her desperation and tried to call her early Friday morning, she hadn't been able to get a response. The second time, Leila had let it ring until the phone service provider came on with a recorded message about trying back later. She also sent a text message, and it was all she could do not to send a second message. By mid-afternoon, Leila was a wreck, on the verge of tears and glued to Roxy and her phone as if her life depended on it. Roxy did her best to console Leila, but Leila did not particularly want to be consoled. She was mad and wanted to be miserable, after seeing her hopes raised and dashed, tossed to the ground like a bottle of cola dropped from the roof of her building into the courtyard below, spattering up nasty syrupy bits of foam and fizzing into nothingness.

Roxy spent those hours sitting next to her friend, distracting herself with nails, eyebrows, ironing clothing, picking fuzz up from off the carpet. She steadfastly refused to leave Leila's side. She quietly observed the progression from fiddling nervously with the phone, to pacing the meter and a half of carpet space, to flipping the pages of lecture notes with such zest that some of the pages ripped, to rocking back and forth embracing her legs tightly, to slumping her head over onto her arms, to dramatic sighs, to, finally, the release of quite frightening sobs.

Leila was fully aware that her friend was there by her side, attentively ignoring her. She was glad to not be alone but she felt like a silly fool. At this point it hadn't yet dawned on Leila that she'd been foolish to expect a call from Nisreen - no, her sobs were compounded by the sense that she was silly to be wailing in the presence of a friend who had borne such suffering so silently and stoically. A friend who did nothing silently and stoically, but who had demonstrated those virtues in her own moment of greatest need. And Leila just cried.

Roxy offered no input, no advice to Leila. She didn't tell Leila to stop crying, to get a grip. She didn't give Leila a hug. She just rubbed the cream into her hands more vigorously, and occasionally shoved the box of quickly-depleting tissues an inch further in her friend's direction. Leila was both touched and angered by her friend's aloof support, and her sense of embarrassment just made the sobs louder.

They sat this way for much of Friday afternoon, alone in the room. Maha had returned to her aunt's house for the day.

By early evening, Leila's tear ducts had shut down, and it seemed she could force herself to cry no more. She grabbed a tissue - it must be time to stop crying since there were only half a dozen left in the box - and wiped her eyes, nose and face clean. What a mess this crying business was! But she was already feeling better. She stood up and said she was going out for a few minutes. She ran up to the roof, where a cover of darkness masked her eyes, which felt swollen and surely looked even worse. The fresh air wafted across her face as she realized she felt strangely more relaxed than she'd felt all week. This crying business really was refreshing! It was this strange sensation of cleanliness, almost as if emptying out her soul through her eyes were the ultimate act of ablutions, cleansing her more deeply than any water on her hands or feet or even in her ears could hope to do. She felt her face, still raw from all the liquid, snot and tissues rubbed across it. It felt fresh like a baby's. For a few minutes, she stood staring out at the blinking lights sprouting all across the city as darkness took over.

Then she went back downstairs, where she spent the rest of the evening studying in Maha's room with Roxy, who might actually sit for her exams for once.

It was Saturday afternoon, when Nisreen finally called, that Leila realized just how silly she had been. If she had listened to Nisreen instead of just talking about her own woes on Wednesday, she would have known that Nisreen and Ahmed had accompanied their mother down to the village yesterday, where a cousin was getting married. Even without knowing this, Leila should have imagined that two days was not enough time to plan an invitation to family Friday dinner. It was a short, awkward conversation, which left Leila feeling like she was a very silly girl indeed.

"It's still early, you know," Nisreen had said. "Give me time. Ahmed says it is important for you to meet Mama and Baba, and so he likes the idea. See, you have nothing to worry about. Friday, *insha'allah. Shway Shway*, take it easy."

Silly Leila, putting so much weight on the words of a first-year.

But she pushed her feelings of silliness away and prepared for the task ahead. It was nearing five o'clock, when businesses opened back up for the evening, and she had put this off too long already. Roxy kept looking at her expectantly from across the room. Leila still had most of Roxy's money and had used some of it to purchase a phone card on Thursday, so she was without excuses.

At quarter after five, Leila queued up behind two other girls waiting to use the building telephone. She gripped the slip of paper that Dr. Muna had given her, so tightly that it quickly grew wrinkly and damp with sweat. She tapped her toe impatiently, then remembered that there were other girls around, so she leaned against the wall with her arms behind her back. That position quickly grew uncomfortable, so she crouched down for a few minutes, then stood back up and leaned against the wall again, this time with her arms folded, and tried to observe the comings and goings of other girls, to catch a glimpse of the young couples chatting outside in the courtyard.

Finally her turn came, and Leila's fingers trembled as she dialed the number on the paper.

"*Ahlain*," came a very gruff and groggy male voice.

"Is this Dr. Rami? Dr. Rami Obeyda?" asked Leila.

"Yes."

Leila was silent for a moment, trying to remember the words she'd rehearsed earlier today. "I... *yanni*, I mean... Well, I got your number from Dr. Muna, the eye doctor. She said you could help me with..." Leila looked around and saw a queue of four girls watching her, awaiting their turn. She leaned in close to the phone and held a hand up to shield her mouth from the girls' view. "With a sensitive surgery."

"Yes," he repeated, just as disinterestedly.

"So you are the right person?"

"Yes."

"So, can I make an appointment to come see you?"

"Yes."

"It's not for me."

Silence.

"It's for a friend."

"So what do you want?"

"I want an appointment."

"*Ahlan wa Sahlan.* You are welcome anytime."

"I, uhh, I don't know where you are."

Dr. Rami gave her an address, not too far from Dr. Muna's office, and hung up.

Leila held on loosely to the receiver, staring at the

address she'd scribbled on the paper and at the phone number. Should she call him back? She decided she had better do so. As she pulled the phone card out and quickly slipped it back into the slot, she could hear the next girl in line groan.

Three rings. "*Ahlain.*"

"It's me again. I think the line was cut."

"What do you want?"

"When should I come?"

"Just come."

"Tonight?"

"Why not?"

"Great! I'll be there in an hour."

"*Ahlan wa Sahlan.*" And he hung up again.

Leila quickly hung up and pulled out her phonecard. She attempted a small smile at the next girl in the queue, who was glaring at her as if she'd spent the last half hour chatting with her lover. Then she ran back up to her room to get ready to go.

Money was a wonderful thing. Once again, Leila traipsed out the back gate of the Medina and flagged a taxi, and within minutes she found herself at the Baghdad Street roundabout. Across the street was the comforting sight of Dr. Muna's office.

As she walked up the street looking for some sign marking the road where she was to turn, Leila realized that looking for strange places on her own was becoming almost familiar to her. It gave her a sense of maturity and individuality that kind of warmed her heart. So she confidently walked into a corner store and asked for "Mustafa Street." The shopkeepers chattered and waved and by the time they were done talking, she knew the number of trees on each side of Mustafa Street, but had little more than a vague idea that she had to keep walking towards the city center. So she did that and was able to follow street signs the rest of the way. She entered the building with the Binti Hairdressers sign. Dr. Rami had said that his was the ground-floor flat on the right.

On the right of the ground floor Leila found a plain, unmarked, heavy-looking wooden door with a knocker and a knob. A doorbell to the right was also unlabeled. She opted for the knocker and knocked twice, lightly. Hearing no response, she tried the doorbell, which echoed throughout the hallway. A middle-aged woman answered the door. She was shorter than Leila and quite a bit plumper, with frizzy golden-colored hair; she wore a gray skirt that came mid-calf and a button-down cream colored blouse, and she smelled of cigarette smoke.

She looked at Leila, down and then up.

When it became apparent that she was waiting for Leila to speak, Leila asked if this was Dr. Rami's office.

The woman wordlessly opened the door just far enough for Leila to slip in and then shut it quickly behind her. Leila entered and found not a doctor's office but a home. She was standing in someone's foyer, with a spacious lounge to the right and a hallway leading to the rest of the house straight ahead. She looked around as discreetly as she could, then looked at the woman who informed her after a few more moments, "The doctor is with a patient right now. Have a seat."

Leila followed the woman's arm motion into the lounge and sat on the first chair she came to. The woman walked away, leaving Leila to take in more of her surroundings. She was seated on a mustard yellow straight-backed armchair, one of about ten. There was a matching sofa, equally uncomfortable-looking, against the far wall. Above the sofa was a painting of the Virgin, in browns and greens, gazing down at the space below her. Above the chairs directly across from her were two black and white framed photographs of men in their forties. She tilted her head to see what decorated the wall above her and saw that there were large bay windows hidden by ornate, albeit musty, gold-colored drapes. She could hear muffled sounds of traffic outside.

Leila sat straight as a rod in a chair that was clearly made for appearances, not for sitting. She heard the clanging of dishes a few rooms over and could smell the faint scent of garlic and ghee wafting through the house. She was unspeakably glad that a woman had welcomed her in, because everything else about this place screamed to her that this was a place where she should not be.

A few moments later the woman returned bearing a tray with a single cup of coffee laid out on a saucer and a tall glass of water. Leila took the coffee with a quiet "thank you", and the woman placed the water on a small coffee table, which she pulled out from under a larger coffee table next to Leila's seat. Then she disappeared again. Leila took a sip of her sugarless coffee and placed it and the saucer down on the little table. She leaned back as best she could, resting her arms on the wooden armrests and closing her eyes, trying to calm herself. Ten seconds later, having failed miserably, she opened them again and got back to consuming her coffee.

It may have been an hour, or it may have been five minutes, but it was long enough for Leila to stand up several times and start walking to the door, only to force herself to sit down again and keep waiting. Finally, she heard a door opening at the end of the dark hallway and a man giving medical instructions about proper care and rest. Footsteps approached, and Leila was shocked to see a woman cloaked in all black, revealing no body contours at all, and nothing but her eyes peeking out from a thin strip. This was the attire of a woman from the Gulf, possibly the Emirates. The woman walked toward the door, half a step ahead of the man who was finishing up his medical instructions. She didn't so much as glance at Leila before slipping out into the night.

The man closed the door behind her and turned to Leila. He was wearing a brown suit jacket over black trousers and a white shirt with the top button undone. The doctor was not much taller than Leila and was quite stout, balding with an unshaven look and thick wire-rimmed glasses in the latest style. "*Ahlan wa Sahlan,*" he said and offered to shake Leila's hand, to which she replied by standing up and placing her right hand on her chest, refusing to look him in the eyes. His arm went limp and he shrugged. "Are you here to see me?"

"Are you Dr. Rami?" she responded.

"Yes, that is me. What can I do for you?"

"I called, an hour ago. I'm here about a friend."

"Yes, yes... the one with a friend..." he said with clear sarcasm. "We get many girls here who are inquiring about a friend, but you know... eventually I'll know. You don't have to tell me about how you got carried away with the boyfriend and how he broke your heart, but the body I know."

"No, really, it is about a friend, I promise!"

"Sure, that's fine. Anyway, come back to my office."

"If it's not too big of a problem, sir, I'd rather stay out here."

Dr. Rami looked straight at her, and Leila was not able to avert her gaze. She felt dirty and condemned. She wished the woman would come join them. In fact, Leila wished she'd never come. And she really wished Roxy would have let her bring a friend. But she wished most fervently that there were a way out. And she was terrified when it occurred to her that Dr. Rami could possibly do anything to his patients before he "fixed" them. She thought of Huda and how close she'd come to losing everything and, of course, just because Huda's body was intact, her heart was still probably permanently injured.

Leila started to tremble and resolutely sat down before the doctor could force her to follow him deeper into this house, to a room with a closed door, and before her body could force her to run out and escape.

"Very well, then," replied the doctor, and sat down in the chair immediately next to hers, leaning on the armrest such that his face was inches from hers.

Leila took her purse in her hands and repositioned it on the other side of her chair, to serve as a barrier between her and the doctor.

"So," breathed the doctor. "You're engaged?"

"Me? Wha-- No! I already said this is about my friend!"

"Sure, then, *she* is engaged?"

"Ah, no. She's married."

"Married? What's she coming to me for, then? *She* and *her* husband..." sneered Rami, whom Leila was not yet convinced was actually a doctor, "...should go to their regular gynecologist."

"I don't think they can do that."

"Why ever not?"

"Her husband doesn't know about this, and he can't know either. Not now, anyway."

"Go on, I'm listening."

"You see, she's been staying with me for the past-- Wait a second, do you really need to know the details?"

Rami was staring at Leila, with his arm leaning on the armrest that separated them. He just nodded and kept staring, but Leila must have looked horrified, because he soon sat up and put his hands in his lap. "What do you need, then?"

Leila sighed gratefully. "My friend needs to move back to her village without her family knowing that she was married. She needs to do surgery to do that. Can you help?"

The doctor stood up without saying anything. He waved

his hand at Leila with his thumb up against the other four fingers, signaling for her to wait where she was. She nodded, her eyes fixed on the floor, and he walked off.

Leila reached for the glass of water and took a quick sip. She heard light footsteps coming down the hall and was relieved to see the woman approaching. She entered the salon and sat down across from Leila. They smiled at each other quietly for a bit.

"You're not from Damascus, are you?" asked the older woman.

"Not originally, no. I live here now, though."

"Dera'a?"

"Yes, auntie."

Silence.

Leila worked up the courage and asked her, "So... is this a doctor's office or a house?"

"This is our home, but the clinic is in the back. He has another clinic, too, up on Baghdad Street."

"I see."

Silence.

After a bit, Leila asked, "Do you get a lot of patients here?"

"*Yanni*, sometimes."

Silence. When the doctor returned a minute later, the older woman stood up and exchanged a friendly glance with Leila. Leila nodded in response as the woman came over, picked up Leila's coffee cup and disappeared back down the dark hallway. Leila now turned her attention to the doctor, who remained standing this time. He handed her a few sheets of paper.

"There are a few things your..." He cleared his throat... "friend needs to know."

"Really. She is a friend."

"Yes, I know," he responded, a little less suspiciously,

perhaps. "Anyway. The first thing is that the surgery she wants is not permanent. It is recommended that she do the surgery 3 to 7 days before her wedding night - before her family checks, that is. It can be performed up to one month in advance, but any more than that and there is no guarantee that she will remain intact up until her devirgination. Are you understanding me?"

Leila nodded wordlessly, her eyes boring holes into the papers she now held.

"So I recommend that she come back when she is engaged and has a wedding date set. The second thing to know is that it is an outpatient surgery. The pain passes relatively quickly, but the first day can still be difficult. Therefore, it will be best if she can have a... a... friend with her." This statement was accompanied by a grunt, this time almost kind-sounding. "Third, there are three types of surgery which can do what she needs done. I won't trouble you with the description of each, because if you say this is for your friend, it is not relevant to you." He paused, perhaps waiting for Leila to change her story. "I find that a woman's condition determines the nature of the surgery appropriate for her. It depends on how damaged her hymen is, so I can only tell you what surgery she will need if I can examine her. As this operation is not for you," Another pause. "I need to see the patient before I can make a further recommendation or diagnosis. It is up to you - or her - to decide whether to come for a consultation now or when a date for the surgery is imminent."

The doctor now sounded like a doctor. He had taken a seat again, this time much more appropriately in a chair across from Leila. When he finished, she quickly skimmed the two sheets of writing, which seemed to be a more detailed explanation of what he had just told her. Then she asked him about cost.

"That will depend on the nature of the operation. For this conversation, I'll charge nothing, you're very welcome. The initial consultation generally costs 500 lira, and then there is the cost of the operation itself. Have your friend make an appointment, or just come in the evenings on Saturday, Monday or Tuesday, and we will plan from there."

Leila folded the papers and tried to think of any other questions Roxy would want answered. She asked him if the surgery would take place in this flat, and he confirmed that it would. She asked him if it was dangerous, and he went into a litany about his standards of hygiene and commitment to using the most modern of equipment and offered to give her a tour of the clinic in the back of the house. She brushed that suggestion of, but wanted to ask something about whether anyone might ever find out but didn't manage to formulate the question, so she stuffed the papers into her purse next to her lecture notes and stood up.

"Thank you very much, Dr. Rami, for your time. I will be in touch once I have talked with my friend. Hopefully we will be back soon." She nodded to the doctor, who bowed ever so slightly in response, and she shook hands with the woman who had drifted back from somewhere at the end of the hall when Leila stood to leave. Then Leila opened the big wooden door and fled.

Leila went by Maha's room when she got back, but the room was full of girls socializing over the bitter combination of cigarettes and cardamom coffee. Leila chatted a bit with Roxy and Maha and greeted the other girls, then she went down to the study room and memorized until the early hours of the morning. Finally she was getting somewhere, which was good, since her first exam was on Tuesday, followed by two on Wednesday and one on Thursday.

On Sunday, after waking, praying and eating, she went to

see Roxy again, eager to unload the weight of Dr. Rami onto the shoulders of the girl who needed him. But to Leila's surprise, Roxy was out, so she hit the books again. She all of a sudden found herself inspired to focus on her studies as she hadn't done for months. She did some pacing and memorizing, she did some reading, she copied out notes, and then she repeated the process. She found herself paying attention and discovering nuances to the poems that she hadn't noticed the first time she'd read them. She managed to memorize five translation lectures in three hours.

At about five o'clock, enjoying the emotional high of feeling like she'd become a well-oiled and effective studying machine, she reminded herself of her friends.

She actually regretted putting the books down, somewhat fearful that she might not be able to return to her current level of focus. And also maybe just a bit scared to think that memorization was a lot easier than talking to her hurting friend about a scary doctor. But she went and found Roxy peering into the trapezoidal fragment of a mirror that Maha kept on her shelf, applying mascara with the care a mother would give her baby. She was alone in the room.

"Roxy, I'm so glad you're finally alone!" burst out Leila.

"What is it?"

"I have to tell you about last night!"

"Oh, yes, that. We'll have to talk about it later. Maha's taking me to church tonight!"

"Church?" asked Leila trying to keep her surprise from showing.

"Yes, church. Isn't it a great idea? She said she was going and I just asked if I could go with her. She said *Ahlan wa Sahlan*, I was very welcome. I've never been to church. In all these years in Sham, this is something I've never done!"

"Well, yes! You're not a Christian."

"True. But why not?"

"As you wish. So--"

Maha burst into the room, almost banging Leila's back with the door as it swung all the way open. Leila looked at Maha as she grabbed a towel from the edge of a bed and patted her wet face dry. "Leila, *habibti*! Roxy's going to church with me. Do you want to go?"

"Me? Go to church?"

"Why not? It will be fun. My youth choir is singing tonight. I mean, I'm not singing, I've been too busy studying, but my friends are singing. *Yalla*, let's go!"

Leila hesitated, then asked, "Will you be back before ten o'clock?"

"Definitely. We might even have time for some ice cream. There's this great ice cream place on Qassa', just around the corner from the church!"

Overtaken by her friends' enthusiasm and her own natural high following such a productive day, Leila asked what time she should be ready and then went to put on her nicest overcoat and scarf.

Chapter Eight

Leila sat in between Roxy and Maha on the left side of the church, on a wooden bench covered with a thin maroon-colored mat. Even with the thin layer of foam, the seat was hard and uncomfortable. She knew there wasn't a soul in the room that hadn't taken note of her, that the scarf she wore with stripes in pastels might as well have flowers sprouting from it and fireworks setting off from the flowers. She knew that if ever there were a place where she would not fit in - where her headscarf would not fit in - this was that place. And what was the difference between herself and her scarf?

As she waited with her friends for the meeting to officially start, her eyes wandered from the bright whitewashed walls to the enormous red velvet curtain across the front of the room. She took in the big brown varnished wooden lectern in the middle of the stage, and the ornate wooden chairs behind. A large shiny black piano took up a large portion of the stage. And there was a cross prominently displayed above the stage. Leila shuddered as she studied it: tacked to the curtain above the chairs, it was simple and also made of dark wood, but it was completely unapologetic. That cross gave Leila the heeby-jeebies.

At the very top of the wall behind the stage, indeed above even that red curtain, she saw carved the words, "Come to me, all who are thirsty, and I will give you rest."

She read it again: "Come to me, all who are thirsty, and I will give you rest." She wondered what such a phrase meant, where it came from, and why it was written on the church wall. She liked it. She repeated it to herself a few times, and each time a tiny bit of peace rolled over her body and the room felt a tad less suffocating.

Roxy nudged her and pointed at the women in front of them. They were all unfolding pieces of lace and placing them on their heads. Leila looked at the row of women across from them, then turned to look behind her. She saw that most of the women either had lace on their heads or were in the process of putting some lace on their heads. Some women had black lace, but most wore either white or cream-colored lace.

Leila nudged Maha. "What's the lace?"

"Oh, those are head coverings. Many women cover their heads in church."

"Really? What do you mean? They're just pieces of lace."

"But the idea is that they are covering their heads in the presence of God."

Leila stared at her friend for a moment, then asked why they did it.

"Well," shrugged Maha. "I'm not completely sure. I think there's a verse somewhere that says that women should cover their heads in church. We just always do it."

"You do it too?"

In response, Maha opened up her purse and pulled out a cream-colored spot of lace. Then she dug around a bit and came up with a white one and offered it to Roxy. Roxy stared at it a moment and asked if it was required. When Maha assured her it wasn't, Roxy turned back to studying the rest of the room.

Leila watched, amazed. "There's a verse, in the Injil, the book of the Christians? Saying women should cover their heads?"

"Something like that."

Leila shook her head and blinked as she tried to get her mind around this. This demonstrated that the Injil and the Qur'an were in agreement, which of course she always knew, but she thought Christians had lost their true teachings. So why didn't Christians cover their hair every day if their holy book instructed them to? She also had trouble fathoming that they considered a triangular cut of lace to be the same thing as a head covering. She couldn't think of any way to ask any of these questions politely, though, so she just watched Maha unfold her handkerchief-sized piece of lace and lay it gently on her head. "Should I wear one?" she finally asked.

Maha smiled. "*Ya* my dear Leila. You're probably the most holy one in here: your head is completely covered!"

Leila nodded smugly and turned to face the front. So far church was nothing like she might have imagined. She also realized at that moment that they were surrounded by women, and that the men were all sitting to the far side of the room.

Finally there was some rustling on the stage, and when she looked up she saw two men in brown suits arranging some papers and seating themselves on the wooden chairs. Another man was settling in at the piano.

A moment later, one of the men got up from his wooden chair and came up to the wooden block. "Brothers and sisters, I welcome you here in the name of our Lord Jesus the Christ," he proclaimed into the microphone in a grand but quiet voice, speaking extremely formal and beautiful classical Arabic. He then quoted some verse from the Injil and explained something about the peace that they should all share amongst one another. Then he said a number, which was followed by rustling of pages throughout the room and a blast of music from the piano.

Leila looked to Maha, who handed Leila a book open to a page with the number the man had just said. Leila and Roxy read along as the entire room around them burst out in a song, the words of which were written on the page. She glanced over and saw that Maha was singing with particular enthusiasm and seemed to have the words memorized.

For the next hour and a half, Leila and Roxy followed the women around them in standing up and sitting down, in reading along, and sometimes trying to sing along. They exchanged glances when a basket was passed around: everyone was putting something in it but they didn't know what. Maha quickly grabbed it when it came to rest in Roxy's hand and put something in it herself before handing it to the woman behind her. As it passed her head, Leila heard a jingling sound like that of small change. They listened intently as the second man stood up and preached a sermon about healing and hearts. Then the youth choir, about a dozen people in their late teens, all wearing red t-shirts and jeans, got up to sing and dance. At this point, Maha pulled out a camera and stood up where she sat, snapping away throughout the song.

After just a few more words from the first man in a suit, the meeting was over. The women all folded up their lace hankies, and everyone stood and headed for the door. Several short and stout women came up to Maha, greeting her warmly with kisses on each cheek, and some of those shook hands politely with Leila and Roxy, but only a few. Leila and Roxy mostly just stood close to each other, chatting quietly about the unusual fashion choices around them. Roxy was quite taken with all the middle-aged women in shapeless skirts that just barely covered their knees, and the preponderance of blonde highlights, while Leila was most impressed by the floral designs on many girls' jeans and the bright colors of their blouses. Both Leila and Roxy agreed that the piano player was gorgeous.

As the room thinned out, Maha started to lead her friends to the exit, but just then a gaggle of teenage girls in red t-shirts ran up to Maha and threw themselves on her with kisses and giggles. "How'd we do? How'd we do? What did you think? Tell us, were we good?"

Maha smiled at her young friends and told them they had performed fantastically. They then begged to see the photos, so she pulled out her camera and held it up so everyone could see the pictures she'd captured on the tiny viewfinder.

Only after they'd paged through all the photos twice did one of the girls notice Maha's two friends. A petite girl with shoulder-length brown hair and a smile that seemed fixed in place turned to Roxy and Leila. "Excuse me; we were all so excited about our choir performance. You're friends of Maha's?"

Roxy offered the girl her hand and said, "Yes. I'm Roxy. Good to meet you."

"I'm Helen. Welcome to our church."

"Thank you. I definitely enjoyed your performance!"

Leila stood awkwardly for a moment, unsure of what to do, then Helen turned to her and reached out her hand. Leila introduced herself and shook Helen's hand.

The other girls all waved limply at Roxy and Leila, amidst a chorus of "Hi", "Welcome", and "It's good to meet you." But none of them introduced themselves or offered to shake hands with the new girls.

Helen made small talk with the two guests as the entire group of girls finally started wandering toward the exit, Helen leading Leila and Roxy in front. Helen was a first-year baccalaureate student, hoping to study English at the university and thrilled to learn that Leila was about to graduate with a degree in English literature. She asked Leila about the course, about the teachers, about the students. She seemed shocked to learn that Leila lived at the university, and that that was where Roxy and Maha and Leila had met. She asked if it was actually as dirty and as dangerous as everyone said. When Leila remarked that she loved living there, Helen seemed embarrassed. "I didn't mean anything by it; it's just that we hear these stories. But you both seem so... normal." Roxy chimed in, saying that she'd heard all the stories, too, and they were true. It was dirty and crowded and robbery was just one of the problems. She was glad she didn't live there herself, but she said it was a fun to be because she could make so many friends. The Medina was about people, not about the place.

Meanwhile, Maha chatted with all the other girls, who were insatiable for the compliments which their older friend handed out lavishly.

Leila and Roxy were just walking out the door when, behind them, they heard a man's voice with Maha and her girls. It was the piano player. All the other girls had taken a step back and seemed to be giggling as they watched him address Maha in a very friendly way.

Maha didn't introduce him to her friends. Instead, she spoke briefly with him, kissed him once on each cheek, then led the whole entourage of girls out the front gate of the church and past all the older men and women who were still milling around the foyer.

On the street, Roxy grabbed Maha's arm. "The piano player! Tell us... He's someone special, isn't he?"

Maha shook Roxy's arm off and tried hard to brush off the questions which Roxy kept asking, but finally she relented and agreed to tell them later. "The girls all want to go with us for ice cream. Shall we?"

Leila instinctively looked at her watch and saw it was half past eight o'clock. "It's 8:30 already," she said to Maha.

"Nonsense," interjected Roxy. "It's early. We'll be back in plenty of time!"

"I don't know. Is it far?"

Maha put her arm around Leila's shoulders and assured her, "Don't worry. We'll make it back by ten. I promise." Then she started walking, and all the younger girls followed.

Roxy and Leila took up the rear.

The ice cream lived up to Maha's praises, and the other girls warmed up a bit to the strange girls. They asked the innocent types of questions that Leila could remember asking and being asked when she first came to Damascus. Like whether her throat bothered her with that scarf wrapped around it all the time, and the brand and type of Roxy's eyeliner, and whether she had a problem with it running.

But Leila had a hard time enjoying herself as she kept looking at her watch and feeling the time drift by. When she it was half past nine, she nudged Maha and showed her the time. Maha nodded in agreement, but then went back to her conversation about other events the youth choir could plan.

A minute later, Leila nudged Maha again. "I'll go back alone with Roxy. You can spend the night at your aunt's. But we need to go!" Her whole body was tensing up now, and her hands were beginning to tremble.

"It's fine. We have plenty of time." assured Maha.

"They lock the door at ten, and we're on the other side of town. It's alright: you stay, but I have to go." Leila turned to Roxy and said that they had to go.

Roxy seemed completely unbothered, but Leila felt responsible for her friend who had been under the protection of a man for years. This was Roxy's first night out since coming to the Medina, so she didn't really know. Leila grabbed Roxy's purse off the table and waved at the door. "Malish, Leila, don't worry. We'll be there."

"Maybe, but we need to go," insisted Leila, and Roxy slowly started to stand up.

Maha finally stood up when she saw Leila and Roxy getting ready to leave. "Yes, I guess it's time to go. *Yalla.*" And she bade her farewells to her girls. Leila felt the tension mounting in her arms and legs and a headache coming on as Maha turned to each girl individually, exchanged a number of kisses, and had a brief chat with each. She forced herself to stop looking at her watch, to just leave herself in her friend's hands. She wished she'd never come.

Leila was in such a tizzy that she couldn't see straight or even barely stand up by the time Maha finished her farewells. Leila and Roxy quickly shook hands with each girl politely, and the three friends finally left the ice cream parlor. Then Maha switched moods: she rushed up to the street and flagged down a taxi, asking the driver to get them to the Medina, please, and quickly. The three girls jumped into the backseat and the driver zeroed the meter.

The taxi moved slowly through heavy traffic for the first few hundred meters, but they quickly found a side road shortcut and took the long way around town, where traffic was lighter. As soon as they were safely on their way, Roxy turned to Maha. "So, tell us!"

"Tell you what?" Maha asked with feigned innocence.

"The piano player."

"Oh, Samer?"

"Samer's his name?" Leila allowed herself to get in on the fun. "You're good friends, huh?"

"Well..."

"Ooooohie!" Roxy let out a whistle. "I knew it!"

"Knew what?" Maha was clearly enjoying the attention.

"You've got something going on."

Leila added, "He is very good-looking!"

"Samer and I have been friends for a few years now, and yes, I do suppose... well, nothing's official, but..."

"Don't worry," assured Roxy. "I saw the way he looked at you."

"You think so?" asked Maha hopefully.

"You go, girl!" exclaimed Roxy with all the zest and vigor of the girl Leila had met two years ago, back when hope and innocence had told them anything was possible. Roxy kept teasing Maha and started coming up with funny gestures and antics to go along with her jokes, and the three girls laughed the whole way to the Medina, where the taxi dropped them off with a full five minutes to spare.

Leila had been so good at studying and running around for and with Roxy, that she had managed to spend very little time missing Ahmed. But tonight as she walked back into Building 14, hearing the harsh clanging of keys on iron and watching happy couples as they were forced to say farewell, a pang of dejection hit her like a sledgehammer.

It had been more than a week since she'd talked to him, and he had never replied to the text message she'd sent on Roxy's phone. The only news she had of him was through Nisreen, but actually that was Nisreen's news, not his. What was the matter? Was he okay? Had something happened to him? Leila knew he'd said he needed time to study, but didn't he need breaks, too? Leila asked herself all these questions as they walked up the stairs, then she told herself she was being silly and that she might as well get back to focusing on Roxy's problems, on her studies, and on her friends. She had the rest of her life to worry about Ahmed.

But she began to feel a bit trembly and felt her vision blurring, so with a mumbled excuse when they reached the landing for their floor, she continued on up to the roof. Stepping out into the open, she turned a sharp right and leaned against the wall, closing her eyes and breathing deeply. The image of his face flashed across the cinema screen of her imagination. He was laughing, loudly and with abandon, with his head flipped back. His black hair brushed against his neck, and his mouth was wide open in a grin. This was how she most loved him: happy, almost recklessly happy.

That image flickered off and her mental screen went

black for a second before a new scene appeared in her mind. It was of the moment when he said goodbye at the Medina gates, ten days ago now. He didn't look happy, but his face... he was telling her something with his eyes and she had been unable to interpret his meaning. She stared at the image, refused to let it flicker off of her dark movie screen. The moment had lasted only a second, but the harder she stared at the image in her mind, the clearer he came back to her. His eyes betrayed neither happiness nor sadness, but there was something in them that she didn't like. It almost looked like boredom, but the rest of his demeanor had made it clear that this was an intense moment for him. She wondered if it was concern, a sense of bearing a burden. She peered into the eyes and had to admit that she didn't see devotion. In fact, as she looked at their slow but deep, droopy but furrowed shape, she decided it had to be regret. She saw regret in her man.

She wanted to ask the figure on the cinema screen what it was he regretted. Had he done something wrong, or failed to do something right? But the image did not reply. The Ahmed in her mind was nothing more than a picture that gave its message and then faded, leaving the screen black again.

Leila opened her eyes and found herself speaking out loud to her beloved. "Ahmed, speak to me! What is the matter? I can't bear your silence. Please, just speak to me!"

She knew he couldn't hear, so she walked over to the side of the wall facing the mountain. He lived in Muhajirin, the neighborhood between herself and Mount Qasioun, so she looked at the lights at the bottom of the mountain and stretched out her hand. "Speak to me," she whispered. "Speak to me."

Then she looked up at the sky and mouthed a prayer to God. She wasn't clean - in fact it was that time of the month, and she wasn't to be praying at all - but she had already gone to a church that evening, hadn't she? So without making a sound, she mouthed, "God, please, tell him I love him. Tell him I'm here, that I'm waiting for him. Please comfort him for whatever is bothering him and tell him that he has me, that he can share it with me. Please God, you are Lord of all the Worlds, and I beg you to hear me now."

Leila felt her whole body shivering even though it was a warm summer night. The emotion was overcoming her. She crouched down and cowered with her arms around her legs, and her overcoat bottom brushing on the sand and twigs gathered by the bottom of the wall. The shuddering continued and grew stronger. She felt like she was crying without tears and found herself continuing her strangely informal address to God. "Thank you, God, thank you that I have you. Thank you for the Medina. Thank you for allowing me to learn English and make different friends. All good things come from you, and I know that, and to you I owe all thanks. But, God, I don't think I can live without Ahmed. Please, don't let anything happen to him. Let this dinner on Friday happen - God, make it all work out. Make his family love me. Oh Lord of all the Worlds, praises to God, I need this. I need this like I need breath in my body. If something goes wrong... oh, no, there is no if, it just has to happen!"

She went on muttering like this under her breath for some minutes, crouched on the roof and shivering. She wanted to cry but found no tears would come. In a strange way, though, she was beginning to feel better but was also feeling a bit more anguished than she ever had before.

Roxy found Leila like this when she popped out of the staircase. She looked around the roof and, seeing no one else, ran over to Leila. "Leila, *habibti*! What's the matter?" She too bent down and put her arm on Leila's shoulder.

Leila looked up at her friend and saw an angel. A week ago she had found her friend despondent and damaged beyond her imagination. The physical evidence of suffering was clear all over her face, in her hair, in her clothes, in the air of her flat. And yet Roxy had welcomed Leila in and tried to show good hospitality. Now, here she was, trying to offer support to a friend who had nothing to complain about in life other than a boyfriend she hadn't spoken to in a little over a week.

Leila shook her head wildly to shake out the images and thoughts that had somehow overtaken her. Then she stood up, Roxy rising with her, her arm still on Leila's shoulders and a look of deep concern still in her eyes. "Is it Ahmed?" Roxy asked.

"It's nothing. Don't worry about it. I just needed a break from the stress of exams, I think."

"It's more than that, I know," Roxy insisted.

"*Malish*. Don't worry about it. I'm fine." And Leila really was beginning to feel fine. "Actually, I'm glad you're here. I've been wanting to talk with you." She rummaged in her purse, which was a bit dusty from falling on the ground during her panic attack, if that was what it was. She had to dig through a few weeks' worth of fiction and grammar notes, some loose bills, her room key, some tissues, an old tube of mascara, some empty and still-full gum wrappers, and a few other random pieces of trash, but soon enough she triumphantly held up two rumpled folded sheets of paper. She handed them to Roxy, who asked what they were. Leila told her the entire story of her visit to Dr. Rami, starting with the woman who opened the door, and ending with the message that Roxy could just drop in for a preliminary appointment any Saturday, Monday or Tuesday.

Roxy unfolded the papers and looked them over briefly, then looked up at Leila. "So you can't make the arrangements for me?"

"He said he needs to examine you to determine the

correct type of procedure. He really didn't believe that I wasn't there for myself..."

"May God give you good life for all you've done for me." This was the closest Roxy would ever come to apologizing for the hassle she was causing Leila, but Leila wouldn't begrudge her this. "So he said I can't do the surgery now?"

"Apparently, not unless you plan on getting married this month."

"At all?"

"I'm not the doctor, but it sounded like maybe you could, but it could break again before you're ready."

"Right. That's no good." Roxy looked over the pages again, then folded them back up and put them in her back jeans pocket. "Did you trust him?"

Leila hesitated. What to say? She hated him, but Roxy needed him.

When Leila didn't answer, Roxy sighed deeply and turned away. "I don't have a choice, do I?"

Now Leila put her arm on Roxy's shoulder. "You're the only one who really knows that, darling. In the end, you need to do what you know to be best and right, for you." She rubbed her hand up and down her friend's arm and then embraced her. The two were now looking up at the mountain together and stood there for a while in silence. Eventually, Leila added, "Dr. Rami was an interesting person as a person... but the place seemed clean and he seemed like an expert. And I'll be with you the whole time in case you need me for anything." That was the last thing she wanted, but did she have a choice?

Roxy pulled away and turned to face Leila. She smiled weakly then nodded and turned to wander off a little. Leila's eyes followed her, and she debated following her friend but decided it was time for her to go down and let Roxy enjoy the healing powers of the roof alone for a few moments.

Monday was another great study day for Leila. She woke up early - well, 9:30, but without any lectures or friend-duties that she knew of, she had a long stretch of time to do nothing but study and prepare for her exams, which would begin the next day. She sat up feeling fresh and confident, especially as a light breeze floated in from the window. The good beginning to the day heralded nearly eight hours of productive studying. She spent some time in the study room downstairs, some time pacing her hallway for a bit and the roof for a bit, and some time in her room, where a few roommates were doing the same, and conversation didn't go any further than offers to make a shared pot of tea and requests to open the window just a tad further.

Yes, it was finally time to focus on exams. This was not the season to be lovesick and she trusted her friends could now take care of themselves. Leila would give herself to the books for three more weeks. These were the last three weeks in her life when she'd be able to do this, and she would learn so much English in three weeks that the past four years would feel like nothing but a preparatory course for these three weeks. A few times throughout the day, she looked at her watch and was astounded at how much time had gone by, and she was still able to focus. Then she'd look at her diminishing pile of notes and feel assured that her focus was paying off.

But that all ended when Roxy knocked on her door at half past five, saying she'd decided to go to Dr. Rami's tonight, asking if Leila could go with her. How could Leila refuse? She asked for a few minutes to get dressed then headed off with her friend, leading her to a taxi, giving the taxi driver instructions, getting dropped off a few blocks early so as not to raise any suspicion, then guiding Roxy to the building and knocking on that enormous wooden door. The woman answered once again and greeted Leila like a long-lost friend. Leila's heart warmed to her, and she kissed the older woman back warmly. The woman looked surprised to see Roxy but welcomed her in, and the two girls sat down in the chairs that the doctor and his wife had occupied on Leila's last visit. The woman brought out coffee once again, but the girls barely had time to drink it before the doctor appeared. This time Leila knew they had to accept his gesture to follow them back to his private office, but not before she managed to triumphantly introduce her friend.

Leila took Roxy's hand in her own and the two girls followed the doctor back through the long dark hallway.

The examination was terrifying to witness. Leila stood by Roxy's head holding her hand while the doctor spread and bent her friend's and putting her feet in stirrups. He had some metal equipment, and his head disappeared below the sheet that covered her legs. Leila whispered to Roxy to let her know if he did anything wrong, and Roxy just squeezed her hand. Leila felt so defiled in this place and wondered how her friend must feel. Roxy was so strong, so energetic and courageous, but now Leila knew that she wasn't immune from the kinds of things girls worry about.

Try as she might, Leila couldn't keep thoughts of Ahmed at bay, this time with a sense of regret. She hadn't known what was right and what was wrong with him. True, they had never been more intimate than a touch on her fully-clothed leg, but what if his hand had wandered just a bit further up... how would she have known? What if she hadn't shaken free when they were walking hand-in-hand in the darkest tree-lined sections of the Medina? She knew he'd wanted to stay there with her alone, touching her, but all she'd known was fear. She hadn't known what to fear, just that she had to fear it. If she had overcome her fear, she might have been the one laying here on this doctor's table with her feet spread wide and a strange man, doctor though he was, digging around her insides with a metal utensil. Leila knew at that moment that she owed God gratitude for protecting her, but what she felt was an overwhelming remorse that it was her own weaknesses which had protected her. She wasn't strong enough to do the wrong thing, and she wasn't smart enough to know what was wrong, and so she had remained safe, but only by the power of her own failings.

Roxy remained silent and still throughout the ten-minute examination, but Leila saw her clenching her teeth and stopped herself from imagining what her friend might be feeling right now. As soon as it was over, the doctor released Roxy's legs and left the room, inviting the girls to join him in his office once Roxy was dressed. Leila stayed with Roxy but kept her head toward the wall to allow her friend at least one small fragment of remaining dignity.

The doctor's prognosis didn't make sense to either one of them, but they left with the information they needed. He could do it, and he seemed professional enough and his office clean enough to do it well. The price would be expensive, but not more than Roxy would be able to get Bassel to pay. It would have to be done one week before Roxy's marriage and should not be attempted a day earlier. So for now, all Roxy could do was get the money, keep Dr. Rami's phone number safe and hidden, move back to the village, and wait. And find an excuse to come to Damascus the week before her marriage, this time, *insha'allah*, to a respectable Druze man who didn't drink and who would care for her.

Chapter Nine

The old Huda would never have taken an entire Friday morning during exam season to run an errand like this with Leila. Leila liked the new Huda more. She made careful decisions and thought more about the needs of others. She seemed to see that Leila really needed her help and responded. The old Huda probably would have been too busy with something school or career related. But also, the new Huda was perpetually sad, there was no denying that. So while Leila liked her friend like this, she also felt like she was always trying to cheer up.

A clandestine ride out to Zabadani on a beautiful summer Friday morning seemed like the kind of thing that would bring cheer to Huda's day. After all, her friend was a morning person, and the only downside to this trip was that they had to leave at 8:30 a.m., really too early for a Friday. But as they walked out into the morning air, feeling the warmth of summer without the sun's brutality, even that seemed like a bonus.

The covert nature of their trip was what made the idea of this trip so fun to Leila, but Huda seemed more nervous than excited. The plan was for them to be in Zabadani before ten o'clock. Roxy had called Bassel and told him that she wanted to meet up with him at a cafe in the center of the city, at 10:30 that morning. That way they knew that he'd be out of the house during those hours. She had given Leila and Huda very detailed instructions as to where he parked his car and what it looked like, so they would be completely sure that he had left. Even so, since he'd never met Huda, she would knock first and ask for someone who lived in the next building over, someone that Roxy was quite sure Bassel didn't know, but who did in fact exist. That way, even if his suspicions were raised, he would find no incriminating information to confirm them.

Then, at around 10:45, when Roxy was pushing the limits of fashionably late, she would call Bassel in tears and tell him that it was too hard for her to face him. She'd practiced her crying voice for the girls last night and when they closed their eyes, they really believed she was pained and miserable. She would break the marriage off over the phone. He may have already been expecting it, which would make the conversation brief. Or he may be completely shocked, which would mean Roxy would have to tearfully convince him. She had her arguments all prepared: she couldn't break her parents' hearts, she missed her village and, really, they had both known deep down inside that it couldn't last forever. Only if necessary would she mention what he'd done to her. She didn't want to dwell on that, so she desperately hoped that he wouldn't make her. He would surely say they needed to discuss this in person, and she would have to refuse. Maha had agreed to sit with her to help her stay strong in her resolve.

With that most difficult part of the conversation ended, Roxy would then attempt to bring up logistics: return of the cell phone and jewelery and house keys, discussion of what things she could take (even though she had already made her choices and written them down on a list of about 15 items for Leila and Huda), negotiations for Bassel to pay for her restorative surgery.

Roxy had thought of everything. During a strategy meeting held the previous evening with the four girls poring over lists, phone numbers, and countless cups of Maha's famous bitter coffee, she'd provided Huda and Leila with a phone borrowed from Maha's aunt. Roxy's plan was to call them as soon as she hung up with Bassel and give them either the go-ahead to take Roxy's basic possessions, if in fact Bassel agreed to her terms, or else the order to attack, which would mean taking jewelery, her evening gowns, and certain silver items from the dining area bureau, which Roxy thought might render some cash. Roxy assured them that she would be listening carefully to the background noises on the phone to make sure that Bassel didn't get back into his car and drive home while chatting. If he did, that would mean the defensive strategy would swing into motion - Roxy would ask him where he was going, and if he said home or refused to answer, her tears would turn to wrath, and she would hang up. Then she'd call her friends with a 15-minute retreat warning. And so, she assured them, nothing could possibly go wrong.

Leila had hardly slept that night. She had carefully chosen her nicest outfit, most appropriate for a suburban Zabadani woman, carefully thinking back to any interactions she'd had with Bassel to make sure the scarf and purse she chose were not items he would recognize. Meanwhile, Huda had been fidgety, checking and reconfirming all the details ad nauseam until Maha, Roxy and Leila let out exasperated sighs and suggested they switch from battle planning to celebrating Roxy's new lease on life.

When Huda had met Leila in the hallway at 8:30, Leila could tell her friend was visibly stressed out. Leila had tried to point out that this was an adventure, and that the weather was beautiful, and that they'd be back well before noon. Huda's response was to ask Leila what would happen if they got caught, to which, of course, there was no good answer.

Now on the *service* van, the two girls sat on the row directly behind the driver. Leila reached over to slide the window open, so they'd feel the wind on their faces. "Isn't this just the perfect day?" she sighed with her eyes closed and her head tilted slightly back.

"It is very nice," replied Huda. "But I'll enjoy it more on the way back."

"Nonsense. On the way back the weather will have turned unbearably hot. We will be stuck to the seats and desperate for the wind, even though it will be hot on our faces."

"Thanks for that comforting thought." Huda replied with a chuckle.

"Just enjoy it. We're graduating, starting our lives this summer, we are young and free and--"

"Free?" Huda interjected with suspicion. "We? Are free?"

"Yes! Look at us, sneaking off to Zabadani, just the two of us. When else in life would we be able to do that?"

"Did you forget that this isn't what I wanted?"

Leila sobered up and looked at her friend, taking her hand. "Huda, you are my dearest friend. I know I've been a poor friend to you, but I do love you. I just don't know how to help you. All I know to do is say we should enjoy the good that we have. And a fresh summer morning and an adventure, well, that's as good as it gets." She slid the window closed so that only an inch or so remained open. "I guess the wind is a bit too much on the highway, though."

Huda looked down and, only after a few moments of silence asked, "You're nervous, aren't you?"

"About this adventure? A little bit, but it's going to work out fine, I'm sure. And you're with me, and together we're helping a friend."

"No, Leila. I meant... about this afternoon."

The smile disappeared from Leila's face in less time than it took Huda to utter those words. She turned and sat rigidly upright facing out the front window.

Huda sat next to her friend helplessly. She was smart enough not to mention that Ahmed hadn't called for more than two weeks, that Leila had had to remind Nisreen twice to make this appointment, and especially that Leila had not yet been in the home of any wealthy Shami family, much less the family of the man she hoped to marry.

Finally, Leila spoke. "No, that will work out alright. It has to. God wouldn't torture me or abandon me like that."

So Huda quickly changed subjects. "Speaking of, uhhh, God... You haven't told me about your trip to church last week yet!"

"No!" Leila brightened. "I have to tell you all about it!"

"Yes! What was it like? Did you like it?"

Leila started chattering about the church, the decorations, the types of things the leaders said, the songs sung, the women with their lace head things, the giggling teenage girls. She described every detail she could think of while skirting around the second question. Finally, she observed, "You know, I did like it. I was surprised how much I liked it. There was an air in there; I don't know exactly how to explain it. It just felt so... so sweet. Yes, sweet."

"Sweet?"

"Yes, nice, pretty. I don't know how else to describe it."

"Like an atmosphere of niceness, or something like that?" clarified Huda.

"Yes. Something like that." Leila nodded.

"I know what you mean. I felt it, too, when I visited a church."

"Oh yes," said Leila. "I'd forgotten you visited a church. But your church sounded more typical. This one didn't have any of the statues or the *bakhour* or anything."

"No? The one I visited had all that. How strange."

"Anyway, just between you and me, why did I feel such a nice atmosphere in a church?" Leila burst out. "I love Islam, don't take me wrong, but when the *sheikh* comes to speak, or when I listen to or read the Qur'an, it's not the same feeling. I love it, it's beautiful and inspiring. I can be completely captivated by a good Qur'anic recitation. But I don't think I've ever been anywhere where I just felt so pleasant!"

Huda asked, "Does that bother you?"

"It does."

"Why? Why should it bother you? Isn't God the God of all the People? Didn't he send Moses and David and Jesus and Muhammad?"

"Yes, of course he did! But the Christians have it wrong - they've rejected the last and greatest of the prophets!"

"Is that what the Qur'an says?" asked Huda honestly.

"The Qur'an? What does the Qur'an have to do with it?"

"It's your - our - book, isn't it?"

"Of course."

"So, does the Qur'an say that Muhammad is the last and the greatest? I know I've heard that before, but no one has ever explained to me why. When God's other religions are so beautiful, why is Islam supposed to be even better? Please, explain that to me."

Leila breathed out a very exasperated sigh. She thought through all of her religion courses, through the *sheikh's* lectures, and all of a sudden realized that she didn't understand. She knew but she didn't understand. She knew Muhammad was the greatest and last of the prophets, but she didn't know what that meant or why she was supposed to believe that. She knew that the Qur'an was the breathed word of God, spoken in the most perfect and beautiful Arabic that ever was or ever would be, but she didn't know how anyone had been able to verify that. She knew that Islam was the straight way and there was nothing better, but she didn't understand why she couldn't feel good with Christians. "I can't explain it to you. You need an *Imam*, someone with lots of good religious training to explain it. I'm not well enough versed in Islam."

"You know much more than I do," Huda acknowledged

readily. "But I have to admit that I don't see anything wrong with enjoying a church meeting, or learning something from Christians. We are all God's people, after all."

Leila mumbled an agreement and desperately hoped that Huda would stop talking about this. Today, it seemed that she and Huda wouldn't understand each other at all. When her friend said nothing for a few minutes, Leila started to relax again. A moment later she pointed out the sign for the turn-off to Zabadani. "We're almost there! Are you getting excited?"

"Nervous."

"Everything's going to go perfectly!"

At five minutes before ten, the *service* pulled up to the same spot where Leila had alighted nearly two weeks earlier, and this time Leila led Huda with confidence to Roxy's building. They first went around the corner to check the spot where Roxy said Bassel usually parked his car. Nothing. So they entered the building and Leila went up two flights of stairs, leaving Huda on the first landing. Huda rang the doorbell. Nothing. She rang again and still nothing. Then she knocked as hard as she could. A moment later, Leila came back down the stairs and took Roxy's key out of her purse.

The house looked exactly as Leila and Roxy had left it two Sundays earlier. Dark, messy and stuffy-smelling. There was a slight odor of something rotting in the kitchen and Leila regretted not cleaning up better, but she then quickly reminded herself just how stunned they'd both been, Roxy from what she'd lived through, and Leila because of the shock of seeing her powerhouse of a friend in such a state.

They shut the door gently behind them, hoping none of the neighbors would notice movement in this flat which had apparently been empty for several days. Then Leila reached into her purse and pulled out the list Roxy had written:

Makeup from dresser and bathroom sink. She'd told the

girls there was a makeup case on the dresser that would hold everything. *Jeans with sequined flowers. All blouses from top drawer. All underwear from drawer by the bed.* These items were easily found and placed in the suitcase, which was the fifth item on the list. *Curling iron. Hair dryer. Rounded brush.* All these were under the sink in the bathroom. *Painting of dog.* Roxy had said this should be in the lounge, but neither Leila nor Huda could find it on the wall. They had to rummage in drawers and under the sofa cushions, and they even went through the kitchen cabinets before Huda discovered it collecting dust on top of the entertainment center. *All schoolbooks and papers from the left side of the bureau in dining area.* This was a surprisingly large collection of books and lecture notes that were already starting to yellow on the edges, and stuffing them into the suitcase was a laborious task which, considering the likelihood that they'd actually be put to use, seemed pointless. There was one item of jewelery on the list that Roxy told the girls to take no matter the outcome of her conversation with Bassel. It was a small pink brooch which she said was a gift from her mother when she came to university. This was the end of the "required" items. The suitcase was bulging, and if they had to bring the supplemental items, they'd need to find another bag to put those in.

Huda and Leila rolled the suitcase into the foyer and looked together at the list again. Confirming they'd covered it, they then looked at the time: ten forty-five. Roxy would only now be calling Bassel. They'd been told not to make any calls if possible, as Maha's aunt's account would be charged, so they debated whether they should wait inside the flat or outside. This was a very hard decision, and neither girl had an opinion. If they waited inside, the chances Bassel would find them were greater. If they waited outside the chances anyone else would find them were greater. They opted for the most clandestine of all options: letting themselves onto the balcony and sitting quietly there with the suitcase.

Once they were seated on the balcony, Huda whispered to Leila, "I'm going to quickly go through the house one more time and make sure we left it in order and didn't forget anything. And see if there are any bags we can use if we have to take the other things."

While Huda was gone, Leila looked out at the trees behind the building. Fortunately, this building was remote, and no one could see her there on the balcony. She gripped the cell phone tightly and confirmed it had a signal. Huda returned a minute later with some shopping bags from designer clothing stores in Sham. She gave Leila a bag to set on the chair in order to protect her clothes from soiling, put a bag on the other chair, and sat down.

The two girls sat like this in silence for half an hour, occasionally whispering to each other, but then quickly going silent and peering down to the garden below them to make sure no one was there who could hear them. Leila kept peering at the phone, and Huda occasionally reached over to take a look at it herself.

When the phone finally did ring at 11:20, both girls jumped. Leila quickly carried it into the silent coolness inside and pressed the green button. "Aloh?"

"It's me. It's done."

"Well, did everything go alright?"

"Yes, he agreed. He knew it was coming. He begged me to come see him one last time. But Maha and I stayed strong." Leila heard an almost-giggle in Roxy's voice. "But he started driving home a little bit ago, so you don't have much time. He's not going to give me all the money for the surgery, but he will give me a little bit. So take the jewelery and the dresses. And get out of there! You probably have fifteen minutes if he comes straight home."

Leila's heart was beating hard now. "Is there anything else?"

"No, just don't get caught, okay?"

And without saying goodbye, Roxy hung up. Leila rushed back out to the balcony and saw Huda standing ready with the suitcase by her side and shopping bags in hand. "She said to take the dresses and the jewelery but we only have fifteen minutes!"

The girls rushed back to the bedroom and were much less careful than they'd been before, grabbing dresses and stuffing them into the shopping bags and then taking the jewelery from its box and stuffing it into their purses, like common burglars. Then Huda rushed around the house one last time, making sure the balcony door was closed as they'd found it and everything else was safe and in place. The two girls ran out of the house, Leila dragging the suitcase and Huda toting two enormous shopping bags. Leila locked the door and Huda helped her get the suitcase down onto the street. Then the girls walked as quickly as they could, trying to avoid drawing attention but worrying that that would now be impossible, and when they got to the end of Roxy's cul de sac, Leila suggested they go uphill and catch a taxi there, instead of heading back down to the main square. They walked two blocks uphill and were panting when they came to another street with some activity on it. It took five minutes to flag a cab, but when it stopped, they shoved the suitcase into the front seat and jumped into the back with the shopping bags on their laps, before the driver had a chance to get out and help or even say anything.

"Damascus. Medina Jama'eya," Leila panted.

And they sped back to the city, even hotter and stickier than Leila had predicted.

There were no words to express the terrific disaster that dinner with Um Ahmed and Abu Ahmed turned out to be. In a nutshell, it could hardly have gone worse. In fact, if it had gone worse that might have made it better. "The might have actually liked me," Leila explained to Roxy, Maha and Huda that night over flower tea, "if they hadn't found out who my family is. Um Ahmed's family hates my family! Something about a land feud between our grandfathers: I don't know, but when she learned my full name, I thought she was going to force me to leave at once."

Nisreen had introduced Leila to her parents as a friend from the English literature faculty who was helping her study. When Nisreen had met her at the shawarma shop down the street from her house, she'd explained that her parents did not know that this involved her brother. She and Ahmed had talked about it and agreed that they would only give Leila a fair chance if they met her without any false preconceptions. Leila's heart had been beating and she'd hung onto her friend's arm as she followed Nisreen up the hill to the house. She was sure her hands would have shaken too hard if it weren't for her friend's strong grip, so she muttered under her breath a blessing for such a wonderful friendship with her beloved's sister.

"I thought I was nervous to meet his parents, but when I found out he wasn't there, I felt this pain go through my body. I was so disappointed that I think that, all along, I had been mostly nervous to see him. When I walked in and was introduced to his parents, I could barely hold my arm steady enough to greet his mother. Nisreen had to guide me with her arm. Then he didn't come out. And as soon as his parents were looking elsewhere, I asked Nisreen, and she said, 'He's not here yet.' I was so depressed when she said that, but then after a minute to catch my breath, I could actually relax quite a bit more." The parents had given Nisreen and Leila quite a bit of space to chat on their own, Abu Ahmed watching a film on MBC Action and Um Ahmed puttering around in the kitchen. Nisreen had left Leila for a few minutes to go help her mother in the kitchen but had quickly returned with three glasses of juice on a tray.

Abu Ahmed had hardly spoken to Leila after initially nodding when she first came in. "He seemed like a nice mellow man, though," she explained to her friends. "He laughed and looked over occasionally to encourage me not to be shy and to drink my juice. I actually liked him quite a lot, and felt like such a man would be a generous and thoughtful father-in-law."

His wife, however, was not so disarming. "By God, I tell you, she rules that house like the most terrifying of mothers-in-law!" Leila actually wondered whether marrying Ahmed would be worth living with this woman. She clearly cooked very well and had a great sense of humor. When she had finally sat down to chat with the two girls once the food was almost ready, she'd blabbered on about English students and her frustrations with the way prices were rising. She had joked about the little frustrations she'd recently had while on an errand or with the person who came to fix the chimney.

Leila explained to her friends that the house was very nice, but it wasn't so wealthy that she felt it was inaccessible. It was a garden flat, just one block off the *sikke*, the main street running through Muhajarin, with nice tiled floors in the kitchen and smooth mosaic marble floors in the main room. The furniture was classic Damascene, detailed mosaic carpentry with little nuggets of mother-of-pearl, with bright green cushions accented with a gold pattern. The television was flat-screen, something Leila hadn't yet seen anywhere but in shop windows, and there was a DVD player, a VCD player, a Satellite receiver and a VCR recorder below it. She hadn't been invited in to see the rest of the house, but everything was clean and new and well-kept. The flat was small, though: Abu Ahmed was watching his film in the same room as the family ate their dinner, and the kitchen was only a short distance down a narrow hallway from the lounge.

"It sounds so quaint and wonderful!" exclaimed Roxy after hearing this description.

"Quaint and wonderful, perhaps," chided Huda. "But would you want to live with your in-laws in that kind of a place?"

"Yeah," remarked Maha. "Especially if she's as mean as you say."

"Well, I don't know if she's really mean. But she was mean to me!" Leila continued to explain that Um Ahmed had actually been quite friendly and yes, it seemed like she was one of those strong women who ruled everything around her, but maybe she wasn't that bad.

"Don't doubt a mother-in-law's power," warned Maha. "Or so I hear! My parents never lived with my grandparents, but my mother always says how glad she is that she didn't do that."

Huda and Roxy also didn't know from experience, but they'd heard.

"Well, my mother lived with my grandmother until just after I was born," declared Leila. "Then my grandmother lived in the same building with us when I was growing up. It wasn't bad, actually. Yes, they had their little arguments, but everyone living together seemed to make life a little easier for everyone else. My mother cooked one day and took half the food downstairs to my grandmother, and then the next day was my grandmother's turn. My sisters and I often cleaned my grandmother's house, but then she'd take us shopping or give us money to buy candies."

"So you would live with your mother-in-law?" asked an incredulous Huda.

"Why not?"

"I thought you said she hated you," Maha reminded Leila of the story she was telling.

Leila soberly continued her tale. Um Ahmed had been very kind at first, even if she came across as a strong woman who might be scary as a mother-in-law. She had chatted a bit and left the girls to themselves a lot, thinking they'd want to spend time together. She hadn't been interfering except to bring out the food, and later the tea, then fruit, then nuts, then coffee.

"In fact," Leila commented, "I was surprised at how she avoided personal questions. Usually a Dera'awi person hears me speak and immediately asks me about my village, family, you know, the normal things. She didn't ask me anything more personal than what year at university I'm studying."

The other girls all agreed that was odd.

But Leila had assumed she was just being polite. Or maybe just disinterested since apparently Um Ahmed had no way of knowing that this visit was about more than just Leila visiting her English tutee. (As if Nisreen needed Leila to help her learn English!) Or maybe she was pacing herself, since things had not continued so peacefully after the delicious meal. Um Ahmed had made frike, a barley-type green colored grain, with chicken, and yogurt and cucumber salad with mint and garlic, and fattoush salad. Her skill as a cook was exceptional - Nisreen had whispered to Leila that she never cooked herself because her mother loved doing it so much - and the combination of Dera'awi and Shami spices had sat perfectly on Leila's pallet. Abu Ahmed had given Leila her privacy and allowed the three women to sit on the floor around the tray of food, eating his own meal by the television out of a bowl his wife had dished for him.

After the meal, Nisreen had poured out the strong black tea prepared by her mother, placing one heaping teaspoon of sugar in the bottom of each small cup. Meanwhile, her mother had piled the dishes high onto the tray and carried them into the kitchen. While she was gone, Leila had asked Nisreen where her brother was. "I don't know, but he'll be here soon," she'd said. Um Ahmed had returned to the lounge soon enough and, sipping her tea, had finally asked Leila where in Dera'a she was from. Leila had answered, and Um Ahmed had commented, "I'm originally from Dera'a, too."

"What village?" Leila had asked politely.

"The city."

Leila had tried to sound impressed but wondered why this woman was so ashamed of her village background that she felt she had to lie about it. Ahmed had told her all about his mother's village, where it was, and his summer visits to the old house where they still grew olive and apple trees. Wealthy and cosmopolitan it may not have been, but Ahmed's stories had always made it sound idyllic.

"What's your family name?" Um Ahmed had asked the kiss-of-death question so casually!

As soon as Leila had answered, she'd immediately sensed that something was wrong. But she hadn't been able to figure out what, and Um Ahmed had simply finished her tea silently then gone to attend to washing the dishes in the kitchen. She had placed a tray of fruit on the table by the kitchen, catching Nisreen's eye to come over and pick it up. Nisreen had done so, giving Leila an apple and a banana off the tray along with a knife and a plate. Leila had slowly eaten the apple, while she and Nisreen joined Abu Ahmed in watching the film. "I think Nisreen felt even worse than I did," Leila pondered. "After all, she knew how much I was wanting to see Ahmed, and she knew how important this visit was... and I think she was embarrassed at her mother's unfriendliness. She's so lovely, you know, and her mother was all of a sudden acting like a monster, ignoring her guest so obviously."

"What else did their mother do?" asked Roxy.

"Well, not much. She disappeared. After the fruit, some plates of nuts appeared on the table by the kitchen, and Nisreen took the fruit tray and plates back and replaced them with the nuts. Between you and me, I just wanted to leave at this point! But I couldn't, you know... I was still hoping Ahmed would come and it would be rude to leave before the meal was over. And, I just really wanted to see him again..." All three girls sighed with their friend.

"So we sat silently through the fruit, then we sat silently through the nuts, and a bit later... Oh it was so awkward!" Leila didn't know how, nor was she sure she wanted, to explain to her friends the way that Nisreen had excused herself to do something, probably to talk to her mother and get the coffee started, since it was clear Leila wasn't having fun. Leila was left sitting awkwardly across the room from Abu Ahmed. This was a discomfort felt by both, so they stared intently at the television screen without talking. That was when the front door opened and Ahmed walked in.

Leila's heart had stopped beating for a few seconds then resumed in quadruple time. She had looked left and right and up and down and had caught a good glimpse of him each time out of the corner of her eye. He had looked, well, shocked.

"Shocked?" exclaimed Maha. "How could he have been shocked? Didn't he know you were going to be there?"

"Well, I think he knew..." stammered Leila. "I mean, Nisreen made it sound like he was involved in planning the whole thing. Maybe it was that I was sitting there alone with his father while the women in his family were elsewhere. I don't know. But even though I hadn't seen him for two weeks, I know him well enough to know he was shocked." In fact, he had for all intents and purposes ignored Leila, removing his shoes and coming into the lounge and asking his father where his mother was. "Ahmed's father was such a sweet man. He seemed completely innocent. He said, 'She's in the other room. There's dinner waiting for you in the kitchen. Oh, this is Nisreen's friend from university.' And Ahmed looked me straight in the face and... yes, believe it, girls!... he smiled that gorgeous smile in the same formality as on the day we first met and said 'Fursa Saida', a very formal introduction indeed. Then he disappeared into the kitchen, returning with his food and sitting next to his father, all three of us now watching the film. It was as if he'd forgotten the past two years entirely!"

Nisreen had reappeared as soon as the most awkward moment had passed, checking in on Leila while the water heated for coffee. Leila had looked at her friend's eyes for reassurance, but finding none, had fiddled with her hands in her lap, wondering if she could possibly just get up and leave now. Why didn't Ahmed talk to her? She figured it was because he didn't want to make stupid small talk with his girlfriend as a pretense, nor could he have a real conversation with her in front of his father. And sweet, kind Abu Ahmed would never compromise the innocence of this young woman, who he had welcomed into his home, by leaving her alone with his son! The girls all nodded at Leila's suggested explanation, agreeing that it was completely impracticable that Ahmed talk to her, though etiquette may have required otherwise.

"Well, that's it, basically. I drank coffee and left, oh except--"

"Yes, why do you say she hated you?" asked Huda.

Roxy and Maha chimed in, asking for more details.

Leila explained, "As I was about to leave, Nisreen walked with me to the door. She whispered that her mother apologized for not saying her farewells, but she hadn't known when she invited me that I was from my family. Nisreen didn't say much, just that there was a family feud between our grandparents, and her mother had been surprised to have someone from my family in her house. Nisreen said it in a very nice way, but it was obvious it was a big problem."

"You need to find out more!" exclaimed Maha.

"Yes!" added Roxy. "We need to find out whether that will be a problem, whether Abu Ahmed can set his wife straight, all that kind of thing. Leila, we'll work this out!"

Huda commented, "But I can't believe that Ahmed just... just avoided you. That's terrible. How could he have done that?"

"That's the part I didn't tell you about yet!" Leila's eyes brightened as she explained that the affair had not ended entirely in disaster. "Just as I was walking down the hill back to the *sikke* to catch a *service* back, I tell you I was so tense and so nervous and so angry and, well, he came out. He caught me right at the end of the street."

"Ooooh," all three girls sighed in affirmation. Romance lived on.

Leila sighed and smiled herself. "He said he was sorry for his family, and thanked me for coming, and said he'll call me."

"That's it?" asked Maha.

"Yes. Why?"

"He didn't hug you, or tell you how much he loves you, or that he will fight for you?"

"You're kidding!" laughed Leila. "On the street, in his neighborhood? Of course not. But he said he'll call. And there was a promise in his eyes. I know his eyes, and it wasn't like last time. Last time I was scared, but this time he made me a promise, I just know it."

"Sure," said Roxy firmly. "You need to have faith. He'll come through. He will work it all out. You'll see. You'll have to deal with that witch of a mother-in-law before you want to!"

The other girls all smiled and nodded and confirmed that Leila had done the right thing in going and that Ahmed had shown his love by coming after her, and that they all wanted to come to her wedding. Leila continued to shove down the little ball of doubt that kept coming up her throat and chose to be encouraged by her dearest friends.

Chapter Ten

Exams were now in full-swing, and there was hardly a spot in the Medina that one could go for a bit of personal time anymore. The rooms were almost at capacity with all the girls and guys who had come to town in order to spew back information that they'd memorized from purchased lecture notes, providing a near-verbatim record of a full year's worth of courses that they'd never attended. Many departments and professors were seeking to address the problem of rampant absenteeism by providing sign-in sheets in lecture halls and threatening students who didn't sign in with repercussions. But so far, nothing had changed. Some students found friends who would sign two names when entering the hall. Other students took a gamble that the threats were empty, and so far were winning that gamble. And still other students fell upon their *wasta* of distant relations or friends to smooth over any problems caused by their absence. But everyone showed up for exams. Students from Damascus had to leave their homes early to find spots on the mini-buses headed toward the Literature and Medicine campus in Mezze. Local families with university-aged relatives from the villages welcomed those bright-eyed youths into their homes for a few weeks in June. Students living in the Medina had to share their rooms and, in many cases, share beds that were hardly the size of individual prison beds. In fact, it was assumed by many at the Medina that the Syrian government stocked the dorms with the same beds as it provided to military barracks. These conveniently piled into bunk beds, and students zealous about their space might even attempt to stack them three high, but there were still on average six beds per room and on average ten students officially registered to each room, not to mention friends and cousins of residents. It seemed few rooms actually ever had ten students residing in them - even during exams season - but there still weren't enough beds to go around, much less mattresses, pillows, sheets or blankets.

Maha's room was a haven of luxury in the midst of this frenzy of studying, marked by students pacing with books in hand and muttering under their breath, and by a spirit of tense urgency that marked all interactions between students in the hallway, between students and shopkeepers, between young idealistic couples who hoped their love still stood a chance while they bickered to release the stress. Few more than half the students enrolled at the university passed each year, and everyone knew it. Whenever Leila peered down from the roof to the courtyard, she saw these irritable and irritated couples and, for a brief second, actually found herself grateful for Ahmed's absence from her life during this season. As soon as she looked away, though, she found herself only remembering the good companionship and friendship of a handsome man, and the pain returned.

Nonetheless, she and Huda had confided in each other that they were finding this month, their final season of exams at the University of Damascus, to be not only bearable, but fun and memorable, because of Maha's room. Maha had never explained to her friends the details, but they knew that she had an uncle or other such relation who was highly ranked in the Medina administration, and that was how she had a room that she shared with only two other girls who just so happened to be her cousins and closest friends. And they had an extra two mattresses, one that they used as their sofa under the window, and another that they pulled out if they had guests, such as this past week when Roxy was still living there and all three of the room's official residents were present and another girl from the family was staying with them. In fact, yet another girl from Sednaya, Maha's home village, had stayed in the room for a few nights, and this was when they had put the two spare mattresses up against each other on the floor and the three cousins had cuddled up together on the mattresses for the night. To their three guests, each of whom slept in her own bed that night, they insisted that this was a fun bonding moment for them, that they'd slept together since they were babies, and that not only was it fun, but it was comforting during exams season. Everyone had known that the girls were exaggerating and that the weather was too way hot at night for them to enjoy a good cuddle. And that the girls were making a true sacrifice, especially considering that roaches had been spotted on the floor of the room in the past few weeks.

But Huda, who usually had her room to herself and a couple of other girls she hardly knew, now found herself having to share her own bed with someone she had known in high school who had been assigned to her room but not provided with bed, mattress, bedding or even a key. Leila still had her bed to herself, but the Islamic Law students with whom she shared the space had bunched their beds up together and were piled on each other like magdus, the pickled eggplants that will only stay fresh if they are so tightly packed that no air, water or oil can sneak in between them. So, though they would have liked to have shared the burden, neither Leila nor Huda could realistically offer to give Roxy another bed so Maha and friends could have their room back. Actually, Huda and Leila had been chatting lately about what to do with Roxy. They were concerned that Roxy was overstaying her welcome, even though none of her hosts had ever let on that she was an inconvenience. The fact that she had hardly opened her schoolbooks, but instead spent most of her time cleaning and cooking for her new roommates, as well as for Leila and Huda, certainly helped. And anyway, Leila and Huda were enjoying Roxy's presence on the floor way too much to want her to leave, and it meant they had a standing invitation to visit Maha's chique room.

Every day during exams, Huda would awake early and go to the big unisex library as she had done almost every day of the past four years. Leila would awake late in the morning and pull out her books in her own bedroom, or else in the small girls-only library on the ground floor of Building 14. They studied from waking to ten o'clock each night, taking breaks only to actually write their exams. But the promise of their 10:00 respite made the pain of exam days lighter and kept the days moving quickly. The fun they had after ten each night ensured a good night's sleep for Huda and a good attitude for Leila, when she headed back down to the library for a few more hours of good memorization before sleeping each night.

The routine had been developed by Roxy and was driven every night by Roxy, thanks largely to Roxy's generosity with her time and her money. Roxy cooked a fabulous meal each evening, showing what marvels could be done with no more than a gas burner, an electric burner, two aluminum pots, one wooden spoon and one butter knife. She then had snacks and fruit and tea on the ready, but she never left much time for consuming those before hiking up the volume on the radio and starting her own little dance party with her friends. By midnight each night, the girls were all full, exhausted and refreshed. They finished off with some coffee or flower tea while chatting about everything under the sun except exams. Roxy had plenty of time to plan these parties, as her only adventure each day was a shopping trip to pick up the food she needed for the day and any other supplies for the room. On one very daring and frightening occasion, as she described it to the girls when it was all over (and all the girls protested, asking why she hadn't asked them to accompany her, all four of them knowing full well that they wouldn't have been able to go considering their current burden of studying and exam-writing), she had journeyed downtown to sell off half of her gold and leave a package with the manager of Nabil Nafisi Sweets shop for her now ex-husband to pick up at his leisure. The seller of biscuits and candies was an acquaintance of Bassel's but not a good friend. The package contained her cell phone, her house keys and nothing else. The dresses and the other half of the jewelry stayed with Roxy to pay for her surgery when the day for that came, but she hadn't yet devised a plan for storing them somewhere safe in the meantime. But other than that one foray into the city center, Roxy never left the gates of the Medina.

Leila asked Huda if it wasn't strange that Roxy, who before had never stayed two nights by herself or without going out on the town, all of a sudden was always at home. Shouldn't she be better by now? Huda had just nodded when Leila asked her this but didn't seem too concerned. "It takes time, you know," she found herself saying to Leila almost every day at some point.

"The other thing I'm worried about is how long it is taking her to get back to her village," continued Leila. "If she's not studying and not taking exams now, surely she never will. She has to go back home. She still hasn't talked to Mary and Ghalia, and she used to see them a couple of times a week! They must be worried sick about her, and she's in the same building as them every night. She really needs to go talk to them and tell them it's over, and then she needs to go home. I don't see how we're helping her anymore, now that she's divorced, has the money she needs, you know, now that she's made her decision. Do you think I should say something? Do you think I need to be the one to go talk to her cousins?"

"It takes time, you know," replied Huda, and Leila found that infuriating.

"Actually," Leila went on, hardly missing a beat. "I haven't talked to Mary and Ghalia for a month! And I used to see them all the time. I wonder if they're worried. I wonder why they haven't been by the room, come to think of it. Well, it was always me who visited them. Maybe I should... No, I could never keep a secret. Oh, why won't Roxy take the next step? Maybe I should talk to her."

Huda merely listened, and at another break in Leila's tirade, gently reminded Leila that she'd never been through this kind of trauma before and that it really didn't resolve itself overnight. Leila, of all people, should know that feelings aren't just about doing things and changing things, but that they take time and a process of resolving themselves. Leila had replied a bit bitterly that, while that was true, it wasn't normal to have the luxury of allowing emotions a chance to reign over someone's life.

So to both of them it came as a relief and a bit of a surprise when, in the last week of exams, just as they were settling onto the rug in Maha's room for a meal of mujadera, with lentils and bulghur wheat and caramelized onions and yogurt and tomato salad, that there was a knock on the door. Leila and Huda looked at the floor nervously, knowing that they were guests but not really wanting to share that status with half the floor, who so far seemed to be oblivious to the parties happening every night just a few meters away from their own frenzied studies. Maha glanced at Roxy with a question mark in her eyes, and Roxy nodded emphatically, trying hard to keep the enormous smile off her face. "Who is it?" Leila whispered to Roxy when she saw that Roxy was expecting someone. Roxy just smiled more broadly.

So Maha stood up and opened the door, and there were Roxy's two cousins. Roxy sprung up from the pan she was tending on the electric burner and gave each of her kin a powerful hug and a couple dozen kisses. "*Ahlan, Ahlan.* I'm so happy to see you!"

It seemed to Maha, to Leila, to Huda, and to Maha's three cousins that, at least for Roxy, this was a reunion that had been years in the making, not merely a month.

Once everyone else had greeted the two sisters and all were seated, and once Huda had run across the hall to collect some more plates, since Maha's stock of both plates and bowls was already stretched to the limit, Roxy addressed her cousins. "I'm so glad you came tonight. And I'm so sorry I didn't call you before."

"Actually," offered Ghalia, "We were back in the village. It's a coincidence we found your note today, since we had only come back today to spend a few days packing our things and saying goodbye."

"In the village?" asked an indignant Roxy. "What about exams?"

"Oh, you know," replied Mary. "We've each already failed a year once, and when we got to these exams, it just didn't seem like we'd be able to make it. And, well..."

"Mary has met someone and will probably get married in a few months!" exclaimed Ghalia.

"Really? Many, many Congratulations! Mabrouk!" said Roxy with enthusiasm, although her friends saw the sad look in her eyes, loneliness perhaps. "But what about you, *habibti*?" Roxy now turned to Ghalia. "Why don't you stay and finish?"

"Oh, I don't know. You know, I think English literature, a university degree, just isn't for me. And I want to be back near my family."

"But Ghalia, you're so smart, and so responsible!" objected Leila.

"If she wants to be at home with the family, then that's a

very noble thing." Huda interjected.

"Yes, I know, but--"

At this point, Roxy blurted out her own tale. "I'm divorced."

Dead silence in the room. Mary and Ghalia just stared at their cousin. Maha started dishing out the mujadera on the plates and passing them around the room.

Finally, Mary spoke. "How long? How long have you been here and we didn't know?"

"I'm sorry, *haiati*, my life." Roxy blinked hard.

"But why? What happened? Why didn't we know?" asked Ghalia.

"It's too hard. It's just over. I'm sorry; I just couldn't explain it to you. It's still so hard. But it's over." It seemed to Leila that all the emotion and frustration that she'd seen in her friend that Saturday afternoon when she had come face to face with the physical scars of Roxy's suffering were now returning full-force as she confronted her family with the truth. If it was this hard to tell her cousins, who were always there for her, who were used to participating in their cousin's adventures, then what would it be like to confront her family, who didn't know anything and who couldn't know anything if Roxy wanted to escape with her life? Leila glanced at Huda, whose hand was now holding Roxy's. Leila now saw that it really does take time. For the last several weeks, the old Roxy had been with them, making life into a daily treat for her and her friends, but that had just been a cocoon to hide the development of a new Roxy who was now beginning to crack her way out. Perhaps Roxy had been trying to deny that she was in fact no longer the same and never would be.

Mary and Ghalia just sat there and said no more. All nine girls were sitting in a big circle. Roxy didn't touch her food, and neither did her cousins, but the other girls all ate slowly and silently, not daring to look up. After a few minutes, Roxy got up and left the room without a word to anyone.

"What happened?" asked Ghalia as soon as her cousin had left. "What's going on?"

Maha took over the conversation. "Roxy didn't tell you for a reason. It's nothing you did, though, you can be sure. She loves you so much, and don't doubt that. But it's not my place to tell you her story. She really needs your support right now. You need to help her, even if you don't know why. She didn't do anything wrong."

"I knew that she was messing with the devil when she married that man!" spewed out Mary.

"It's not that simple," continued Maha, although in some ways it really was that simple - but Roxy had not once talked about Bassel in such terms. "Just, can you be there for her? Go with her back to the village? She needs to move home, you know."

"But what about..." Ghalia's voice trailed off. What about when her parents find out?

Leila now spoke. "Don't worry about it. I know you're her closest friends and she loves you so much. We may never see her again, but here in the Medina, we're all sisters. We've looked out for her, and everything is going to be taken care of."

The sisters looked at Leila and then at each other, and Leila felt a pang of compassion for them. They had been Roxy's closest friends but were now being told that, because of their intimacy, they couldn't be a part of this. But such were the things of life, and Leila also felt a small wave of pride.

"Please, eat." Maha gestured to the sisters' untouched plates of food.

The girls reluctantly complied, and soon enough Maha and her cousins were into a discussion of the new season of Star Academy, the hit Lebanese television reality show for would-be performers. As Huda was clearing up the plates and getting ready to carry them to the kitchen with Maha's cousin, who was also just visiting - for several weeks - Roxy came back in. She went straight to her cousins and took one hand from each girl into her own hands. "Please know I love you. You are my sisters and always will be. Can I go back to the village with you?"

Without hesitating, both girls nodded and Ghalia declared, "Of course, sister. Your parents will be so happy. They ask about you all the time! But they will be disappointed that you're not graduating, too. Maybe it's a good thing we're not graduating either. That way we will all go back together!"

Mary added, "We were going to leave day after tomorrow. Does that work for you?"

Roxy nodded, and just like that, she was back in the care of her family, no longer Leila's, nor Huda's, nor Maha's, responsibility to help.

Except for one thing. The next morning, Roxy knocked on Leila's door at the ungodly hour of 10:00 a.m. One of Leila's new roommates answered the door, and Roxy barged in and started shaking her friend. The other girl just watched from the door and then wandered back to her spot on a bed near the window where her books were spread out around her. "*Yalla, habibti*! Let's go! We need to finish this!"

"What do you mean?" asked Leila as soon as she had rubbed her eyes open and sat up in bed.

"There's one more thing I need to do, you know?"

"But you can't do the--" Leila glanced over and saw half a dozen girls studying throughout the room, then continued in a whisper. "You can't do it until you're about to get married."

"I know, I know," replied Roxy impatiently. "I'll worry about that when it's time. But I can't take the dresses back home. I need to sell them and store the money somewhere."

"What will you do with the money?"

"I was thinking about it, and I spoke with Maha this morning. You know how her aunt sounds more like a cousin or a friend than an aunt. I think she'll keep it for me."

"Wow!" Leila was wide awake now. "You're going to sell your dresses and gold--"

"Not the gold. I'll give that to Maha's aunt as gold. It's easy to store."

"So you're going to give money from the dresses, plus a bag of jewelery to a stranger to store for you?"

"She's not a stranger," protested Roxy. "She's Maha's aunt! Anyway, do you have a better idea?"

Leila shook her head, partially in denial and partially to shake the cobwebs out of her head. "Alright, then. Let's go." she declared, and got up to get dressed.

As they neared the back gate of the Medina, Leila asked Roxy if she knew where she would go to sell the dresses. Roxy said her plan was to go to the main *souq* downtown and find a dressmaker. They would either be interested or they would point her in the right direction. So the two friends flagged a taxi and asked to go to Bab al-Hamidiyeh, at the entrance to the old city. They rode in silence, which gave Leila too much time with her own thoughts. As the taxi passed the Faculty of Commerce, she saw a tall man with wavy black hair and had to look twice to be sure it wasn't Ahmed. Her thoughts quickly spiraled. First, she was possessed by a desire to see him, then she reminded herself that there were only three days of exams remaining. Then she realized that his last exam may have already happened and if not was soon to happen. This led to the realization that in one week's time she would have to leave the Medina and Sham and return to the village, which was followed by guilt for having avoided contact with her family during the past month, due largely to fear of marriage proposals being mentioned. Then she started wondering how she would get the message to Ahmed that time was of the essence, then she panicked that she was running out of time, then panicked even more when she considered that he hadn't talked to her since that day at his parents' house when she'd been so intimidated and then so sure that he still loved her.

She barely noticed as Roxy told the taxi driver to pull over and paid the fare, then dragged her out of the taxi. "Come on! We need to get this done before there's any chance of running into him. I'm sure he's absolutely furious with me already!"

Leila followed, stumbling behind Roxy, who was tightly gripping Leila's wrist. Leila tried to focus and get herself to stop thinking about her own dismay. Roxy needed her this one last time. "Have you talked to him since that day?" Leila asked.

"Me? Oh, no. But I'm sure he went home and saw what you took for me. Imagine if he were to see me today, of all days! Carrying these dresses he bought for me! But it's his fault for not giving me what I needed." Roxy shuddered and walked even faster, dragging Leila behind her.

Both girls were panting when they got to the first dressmaker who, after hearing Roxy's query, pointed them to a shop a bit down the street. The man there told them to go to Hamra, the other nice shopping district.

"I can't go there. That's where I got these dresses, and anyone could recognize me. And Bassel goes there all the time. You have to go for me!" Roxy's eyes were shining, and she was staring at Leila like a madwoman.

Leila didn't want to do that for a number of reasons, including fear of getting caught herself without any friends to fall back on, laziness, and a suspicion that this dressmaker didn't know what he was talking about. She persuaded Roxy to try another place, then another, then another. They finally found someone who would buy the dresses for not as much as Roxy had hoped, but for what could still be considered a reasonable price. Leila encouraged Roxy to make the quick deal rather than tarry around increasing the chances they'd be seen or worse.

Safely on the taxi back to the Medina, Roxy relaxed. "I'm going to miss you, darling. You have been such a wonderful friend to me."

"I'm going to miss you, too," said Leila.

"We'll need to keep in touch, you know. Meet up every couple of months. You come to my wedding and I'll go to yours. On weekends you can come visit me, and on other weekends I'll visit you. We live so close together."

"I don't know that--" Leila was going to say that she didn't know that her family would like the idea of having this crazy Druze girl in their home, but she decided that this was not the moment to be concerned with such details. "Yes, you're right. We need to keep each other's numbers and call each other and visit. I will definitely come to your wedding if you come to mine."

"When will that be?" asked Roxy, with the familiar tease back in her voice.

Leila sighed and looked at her hands. "Roxy, I'm scared." There. She had said it.

Roxy understood and, for once, didn't just say the obvious thing to comfort her. She put her arm around Leila's shoulder and pulled her close. "You are an amazing wonderful girl. Any man will be so lucky to have you. You are funny, intelligent, romantic, beautiful... never forget that. Never underestimate yourself."

"But I only want one thing."

"I know. And I hope you get it. You deserve it. But don't ever let him intimidate you with his big house and his bossy momma and his fancy career. He will never be good enough for you, and he should treat you with respect."

Leila rested her head on Roxy's shoulder and stared out the front window of the taxi. "Thank you." And as an afterthought, added, "I will never forget you."

Leila had only one more exam. She forced herself to study, even though it was Roxy's last day. She knew Maha was also studying today, as well as her cousins, since otherwise they would probably have left already. They liked being in Bab Touma more than the Medina, and this wasn't their last year, so they weren't feeling as nostalgic as Leila and Huda and Roxy were.

Apparently everything for Roxy was complete once the question of the money had been settled. Leila worried about how Roxy would get her surgery, knowing it was unlikely she would be able to come to help her friend once she was back in the village - unless Roxy got married after her, in which case she'd be back in the city with Ahmed and have her freedom. Hopefully. No, of course Ahmed would give her freedom, she told herself. But she couldn't offer to help right now, and she knew Roxy would cross that bridge when she came to it.

Meanwhile, Roxy had prepared a maqloube for their last meal together. This was an amazing feat considering the limited supplies she had in the Medina, and it was a huge treat for all the girls. The rice and chicken dish with fried cauliflower and eggplant, all boiled together and then flipped to make a huge mountain of food, was a meal their mothers had made for special occasions. The room had a feel of anticipation when Huda, then Leila, then Mary and Ghalia walked in around 10:00. Roxy was just putting the finishing touches on the cucumber and yogurt salad while the pot of maqloube finished cooking on the gas burner.

Everyone noticed that Huda had an enormous smile on

her face, but when pressed for an explanation, she kept saying, "Later... Later," and grinned even more giddily.

Everyone was there that night: Maha and her roommates, Ghalia, Mary, Huda, Leila and Roxy. They all watched as Roxy took the lid off the maqloube pot and replaced it with an upside-down aluminum tray, the same tray they usually used to serve the tea. Maha then grabbed a towel and lifted the pot off the burner, while Roxy held the tray steadily in place. Then, on Roxy's "one, two, three!" Maha pushed the pot against the tray as Roxy quickly flipped the tray over, bringing it to land right in the middle of the rug. All the girls sat down and watched as the cook did the honors of making sure the food had fallen out of the pot by banging the spoon on the base and hearing its hollow echo. She then slowly lifted the pot to reveal a perfect mound of food: a thick layer of rice, then thin layers of onions, cauliflower and eggplant, topped off with a bounty of chicken chunks. Maha handed Roxy the other pan, which held browned nuts, and Roxy sprinkled the nuts over the top of the food.

The music was already on, and Maha put the teapot to boil on the gas burner while Roxy started dishing out the food amidst flattery from all her friends and companions. They then passed the yogurt sauce around, and each girl dribbled a bit on her plate. They all assured her that it was the most delicious meal they'd eaten since they first set foot in the Medina, and she just smiled and ate more herself.

"I have good news," Huda announced, once everyone was seated and eating.

"Tell us!" commanded Roxy, with food in her mouth, and she was echoed by many other muffled encouragements.

Huda's face was beaming but her voice was calm as she told the group, "I got a job."

"Oh, wow! That's excellent!" Roxy's enthusiasm was ten times Huda's own. She put her plate down and stood up, grabbing Huda's hands and pulling her up, then hugging her while jumping up and down. "Congratulations!"

Leila and Maha also stood up and gave Huda hugs and congratulated her. Then Roxy grabbed all three girls into a bear hug and declared, "I knew things would work out. This is a sign from God that we should all trust things will work out! Isn't that wonderful?"

"What's the matter?" Huda all of a sudden broke out of the hug and turned to face Leila.

Leila stared back at Huda for a second, not understanding why her friend was asking this, but then she realized that her face was wet. Tears were streaming full-force down her face, and her nose was beginning to stop up. She reached up and wiped her cheeks with the back of her hands and mumbled, "I don't know. I don't think anything - I'm so happy for you!" She said this with such sincerity that Huda smiled and gave her another hug, whispering into Leila's ear, "Your dreams are going to come true, I just know it."

And Leila felt the tears come even stronger as she hugged her friend back.

Once they had gotten all the jumping and screaming and giddiness out of their systems, the four girls sat back down to their meal, and Maha asked Huda for details about the job. "It's an internship, really, but it's paid! Isn't that amazing? I can hardly believe it." This internship was in finance and business, which wasn't the specialty Huda had hoped for, but it had the rare potential among legal fields of leading to a very lucrative job. And it was in Latakia, which was only half an hour by van ride from her house, so she would be able to move back in with her family and help them. And even though it was just an internship, she had earned this position entirely on the basis of her own merit, with no evil professors or doting uncles affecting the decision one way or another.

Once she started working, she could prove herself and make her own *wasta*, and anyway, this particular firm was famous for giving its interns full-time jobs after one year. Her dreams may not all be coming true, but wasn't this as close as she could have hoped for?

The fun went until almost three in the morning that night. Leila was aware that she had an exam the next day, but she wouldn't give up her last night with the girls for anything. At around 2:00 she was able to convince Roxy, Maha and Huda to end the night up on the roof. They stood there for an hour, reliving memories and encouraging each other about their prospects. They teased Maha about her boyfriend and asked if he would go with her on the church summer camp she was planning for the coming months. Maha still had a year of school to go, but the girls joked that as she enjoyed Samer's company this summer, she may forget about university and be the first one of all of them married. Then they turned to Leila and repeated all the clichés of encouragement, that things would work out between her and Ahmed, and anyway, she was now the best English speaker in the university and could do anything she wanted. They told her they were going to miss her novels and with her gone, they might even read a novel or two themselves. Then Huda commented about her fear of no longer having friends around with whom she could have a real conversation, and Leila reminded her to always look to Islam for her comfort, Maha reminded her to always pray, because God was listening even if no one was around. Roxy predicted a hunk would be working in the same office with Huda and would fall madly in love with her, and she would be making intelligent baby Hudas. They together would be a most high-achieving family, Roxy swore. And then they all encouraged Roxy to keep her heart open, that there was someone good out there for her, but reminded her that she didn't have to be in a rush. They told her that she had brightened their lives and they would miss her so very much.

As they walked back to their respective rooms that night, this time Roxy heading over to Mary and Ghalia's room so they could make an early departure in the morning, they hugged one last time and kissed and confirmed that they had each other's home addresses and phone numbers and promised to keep in touch. Their spirits were high as they thought of their own and each other's bright futures.

Exams were over. Roxy was gone. Huda was leaving today, and Maha had already gone back to staying with her aunt, even though she promised to be back again before Leila moved out. In the two days since her last exam, Leila had grown increasingly tense, and in fact had only slept one hour the night before. She had been down to the phone late last night to call Nisreen and hadn't gotten an answer. Then she'd gone back upstairs and thumbed through the English Bible on her shelf a bit before going back downstairs. The queues were still there, but very short now, as the building was now down to its last couple hundred residents. In four days, the gates to the building would be locked at 10:00 and not open again until after the summer. Leila's shelf and her bed would belong to someone else, and the roof would no longer be hers.

When she had arrived in the foyer to try calling again, this time daring to try Ahmed's own number, she'd seen just one girl talking on the phone and no queue. She had glanced at her watch and seen it was midnight. She'd debated and decided she couldn't call him this late, nor could she phone Nisreen. Surely they were still awake on a summer night celebrating the end of exams, but still, she shouldn't do it. So she had gone back to the roof and spent a restless two hours pacing aimlessly before going back to her room, where she was completely alone after having shared it with eight others only one week earlier.

It was pointless trying to sleep, so she'd picked up the Bible again and opened it to the center, where she'd discovered a huge section of poems, which were much more familiar in style to her than the prose stories she'd seen in the rest of the book. She'd opened it randomly, and come to the following words: "My God, my God, why have you forsaken me? Why are you so far from saving me, from the words of my groaning? O my God, I cry by day, but you do not answer, and by night, but I find no rest. Yet you are holy, enthroned on the praises of Israel. In you our fathers trusted; they trusted, and you delivered them. To you they cried and were rescued; in you they trusted and were not put to shame. But I am a worm and not a man, scorned by mankind and despised by the people. All who see me mock me; they make mouths at me; they wag their heads..."

Leila had read this over again, then again. The reference to Israel aside, she felt somehow connected to the writer. She was astonished and touched by the brute honesty expressed, the idea of someone complaining to God. This was exactly how she felt, but she felt guilty for feeling that way. After all, if her life was truly submitted to God, then she was fully submitted, right? She should only say good things to God. But here was a holy text expressing misery and loneliness and rejection. Leila had found this slightly comforting, so she had read to the end of the poem, looking for the happy ending. The poem ended with more appropriate praises of God: "All the ends of the earth shall remember and turn to the Lord, and all the families of the nations shall worship before you. For kingship belongs to the Lord, and he rules over the nations. All the prosperous of the earth eat and worship; before him shall bow all who go down to the dust, even the one who could not keep himself alive. Posterity shall serve him; it shall be told of the Lord to the coming generation; they shall come and proclaim his righteousness to a people yet unborn, that he has done it." Done what? Though she didn't understand their meaning at all, she also found these words deeply comforting.

So Leila had finally drifted off to a restless sleep. Even with the small comfort the verses offered, her heart was still full of fear and despair. She knew her friends couldn't stay at the Medina to be with her when their families were expecting them, but she couldn't leave until she heard from Ahmed. That would be impossible! But who would be there for her if he didn't call, if it didn't work out?

She'd awakened at the crack of dawn unable to return to sleep. It was a perfect summer morning, and she had pulled her blanket off her bed and dragged it onto the roof with her. With a scarf on her head and a blanket wrapped around the rest of her, looking just off over near the mountain she had witnessed the most glorious sunrise of her life. All of Damascus was the color of a sepia photograph, brownish-golden. As the sun rose, it cast its rays on different buildings, making different sets of windows glisten in a dance showing off the beauty of this ancient city that was full of both life and death, joy and misery, frivolity and pain. Convinced no one else would be out on any of the other roofs at this hour, Leila had dropped the blanket and danced around like one of the nymphs in the fairy tales she'd read, forcing herself to soak in every last bit of the moment's beauty.

The image of the sunrise still reflected in her eyes, and she could still feel the afterglow of the sun's rays on her face, when she went to Huda's room late in the morning. Leila had promised to help carry her bags down to the back gate of the Medina, where Huda would catch a mini-bus to the Harasta station to catch her bus to Latakia.

Huda had one duffel bag of clothing and two large purses

filled with her books and random bits and pieces she'd accumulated over the years. Four years summarized in three small bags. Ignoring Huda's protests, Leila shouldered the one with the books and took one handle of the duffel bag. Huda took the lighter of the two purses and the other handle of the duffel bag. They walked clumsily down the staircase, and Leila waited in the main entrance area while Huda stopped by the director's office to sign out and return her key.

A moment later, the two girls were walking for the last time together to the back gate. This may be Huda's last walk ever on these paths. Side by side with the duffel bag between them, there was little to say. Each girl was wrapped up in memories sparked by the landmarks they passed. The little convenience shop near their building's courtyard, the little river that ran through the Medina, the entrance to the largest men's building, the little row of shops that had sprung up in a previously grassy area during their third year, the "library" and the huge cafe that sat facing each other, the statue of the late president (God have mercy on his soul), the row of pay phones, and the men at the gate that even now as the university city was emptying out, insisted on checking men's identity cards before allowing them entry. The two girls embraced and once again promised to keep in touch. Then Huda flagged a minibus, Leila helped her put the bag on the floor, and just like that, Huda was gone.

Leila wandered slowly back to her room. What was there to do? Should she go shopping? There was nothing she needed, especially considering she was already packing up to go home. Should she go for a walk up to her favorite juice shop? While the idea was appealing, she wasn't particularly hungry, and she wanted to be nearby in case Ahmed called. Oh, what if he didn't? The next three days would be torture as she sat around, the lone girl loyal to the Medina - or unable to break free - with no studying to be done, all novels read and packed away into her own oversized purse, and no crazy dancing man or hopeful couples left to be observed from the roof. Yes, there were the foreign girls two floors down who wouldn't be moving out until the end. She could befriend them. There was also the building's director who had always been nice. She could find new friends, but she was saying farewell to the Medina, not moving in. The season for creating adventures for herself had passed.

No, now all that was left for her was Ahmed. She stayed for him and for him alone. He was worth waiting for, she told herself, even as that nagging voice told her for the thousandth time since exams had ended that a man who didn't come find her the moment he left his last exam was not worth her love. She insisted on giving him the benefit of the doubt, considering that he might have come by when she wasn't in the room, or he may have faced a family emergency. How would she live with herself for the next three days, waiting?

And as she approached Building 14 once again, she resolved that if he didn't call today, she would have to go find him tomorrow and explain her need to return to the village, try to make him understand the urgency of the situation and the need to resolve family problems and propose yesterday, not tomorrow.

Leila prepared herself a very simple lunch of bread and za'atar spice with olive oil, accompanied by strong sweet black tea. Then, with the hot summer wafting over her and her belly somewhat satisfied, she finally drifted off to a solid, sweet sleep.

At four o'clock, she bolted upright, suddenly awake but unsure why. Then she heard it again. It was the bell, ringing in her room! She ran to the hallway window and saw the sight that she had longed for more than anything she had ever longed for in her life. He had come for her.

HIKMA: UNDERSTANDING

The roof was mostly unchanged. The sewage still wafted out of a pipe on the west side, and dirt and clutter still accumulated in the corners. The concrete blocks stood where they had always stood, unperturbed except for another layer of filth at their base. But it wasn't quite the same, either. There was now a bed with a mattress by the ledge, and someone seemed to be drying her clothes on a line drawn across the bedposts. Leila also noticed that the door to a lower roof had been opened, and some girls were sitting there studying.

As so many times before, she was completely alone up here, and the feeling of beauty and freedom that came over her every time she emerged from the dark stairwell hit her once again, powerful as always.

Leila walked slowly around the roof, gently brushing her hand on every inch of the ledge as she went. She didn't want to miss anything on this opportunity to return to this place where she had lived the happiest years of her life. When she finished walking around, she went to her favorite of the two concrete blocks and leaned against it. Her belly was bulging too much for her to attempt jumping on, so she just stood by it, resting her body against the block as she gazed up at the mountain. She closed her eyes and then opened them again, not wanting to miss a thing. Hamoudi was downstairs with Nuha, who now lived in this same building, room 90, and he would be calling for Mama soon enough.

It was a miracle, really. Security had cracked down at the Medina and non-residents were almost never allowed entry anymore. But when Hassoun came to town today, she'd begged him to let her come along to visit her sister, who she hardly ever had a chance to see. He'd happily agreed, making sure Leila had a phone with enough units to call him if anything happened, and calling Nuha to make sure that she'd be available to receive her sister at the Medina gates. So much had changed in the short three years since she was last on this roof, Leila mused: she now had her own phone - which worked in both Syria and Kuwait - and her sister was living here with a phone of her own. That was a rarity in Leila's day!

So Nuha had met her, and taken Leila's handbag while Leila held little Hamoudi by the hand and led him into the Medina. The guards had probably been too shocked by the appearance of an obviously pregnant woman to say anything, too ashamed to confront her, and too certain that she couldn't possibly intend any harm. So Nuha had led Leila and Hamoudi straight through the front gate and to Building 14. Leila was panting as she'd climbed the stairs, and had to stop on every other landing, muttering curses at the elevators that still never worked when she needed them. Nuha had commented that the elevators hadn't actually worked at all since she'd moved in two years ago. So now everyone had phones, Leila had chuckled, but no elevators. Interesting trade-off.

But when they'd arrived at Nuha's floor, an exhausted Leila had insisted on continuing up the stairs. Nuha had protested, saying that her sister needed rest and that the last thing she wanted was for her brother-in-law to be mad at her for wearing Leila out, but Leila had insisted, using all the authority of a big sister. She'd handed her son over to Nuha and slowly walked the three remaining flights of stairs up to her roof, thanking God for this gift, this chance to relive the happy moments and, perhaps, to put the painful moments to rest once and for all.

Leila made herself leave the support of the concrete block and walked over to the ledge overlooking the courtyard. She really was tired, and knew she should go rest with Nuha, but she didn't want to let this moment end. She sat up against the ledge and breathed a sigh of relief as her legs were able to relax a bit. Then she peered slowly down to the courtyard and looked at the few groups of students and a handful of couples that were sitting there, even though the weather wasn't gorgeous on this particular autumn day. She let her mind drift back to her final day in the Medina.

That last conversation with Ahmed had been so much more awkward than Leila ever could have imagined. As they'd talked, she'd seen so many things in his eyes: pain, regret, resolution. It was the resolution that had convinced Leila to give up the fight, to believe what he was saying. He had been courteous and kind as always, apologizing for his absence, for the time it had taken him to call her. He had assured her that he really hadn't stopped thinking about her. But he had said these kind words in a much more formal tone than ever before, and he had most certainly been keeping his hands to himself during this conversation. Leila now stared hard at the spot at the far end of the courtyard where that fateful encounter had taken place.

After Ahmed had finished apologizing and speaking his soothing words in an unusually formal tone, Leila had forgiven him everything and made sure he knew it by the adoring look in her eyes. But then he'd said he owed her an explanation. He'd told Leila what his mother had said after their meeting. After Leila had left the house that day, his mother had gone into a tirade about Leila and her family and what Leila's grandfather had done to her own grandfather. "But you don't hold a grudge from generations past, do you?" Leila had exclaimed.

"I don't." She remembered as clearly as if it had been yesterday what he'd said then. "But my family will never forget. And I cannot go against their wishes."

Leila had been furious. She'd been risking everything for this man, for two years, and now he was saying that he would not fight for her. She'd asked him if he had said anything to his mother in her defense, and he'd explained that Nisreen had tried to defend Leila, but to no avail. Leila had asked again what he had said, and he didn't answer.

"You never told them, did you?" she'd finally concluded.

Ahmed had refused to look her in the eyes again for the duration of their conversation. Leila couldn't understand how she had still known, with a certainty that couldn't just be chalked up to vain hope, that he'd still felt something for her. But he had not been willing to tell his family about her. He had nothing to lose, but he wouldn't even gamble nothing for her. Had he never really loved her? The look in his eyes that she'd interpreted as love, had it just been amusement? Lust?

Leila still didn't know, and realized that she would never know what Ahmed had wanted with her. Now, with the clarity of time on her side, she doubted he'd ever intended to marry her, but she still thought his affection for her was real, that she had been more than just a toy to play with. He probably to this day didn't know what he had wanted, and maybe wasn't even sure that what he had now was what he wanted. Perhaps he had never been as enlightened as he'd feigned to be, and deep in his heart, he would never be able to see a girlfriend as a potential wife. Over time, she had actually come to pity him.

After returning home, Leila had started to pay attention to the older women a bit more and had heard her family's side of Um Ahmed's feud. To her it had made no sense at all, and she still didn't care about that one way or the other. In fact, she'd come to thank Um Ahmed's stupidity for saving her for something so much better. So now, through the same village gossipers she knew that Ahmed had obtained a prestigious business internship in Canada and was working there. He may never return to Syria, since he was engaged to marry a Canadian girl of Syrian Shami descent.

Leila whispered, "Good luck, *habibi*. I will always remember you," and felt that maybe that ghost would finally find rest in her heart. She did not regret knowing Ahmed or her relationship with him. She still got a bit nervous when she thought about how close he could have come to taking advantage of her physically, but she was overall grateful for his friendship, for having had the opportunity to experience love and passion during her Medina years, for the sense of adventure her affair had contributed to her university experience.

No, she did not regret it at all. Her only regret was how she had spent her last day in the Medina. After it had become clear that Ahmed was going to be spineless and noncommittal - he never actually broke it off with her, he left that dirty work to her - the conversation had become quite awkward until Leila finally had her chance to shout at her guy in the courtyard and stomp off into the building where he couldn't follow her. And he hadn't even tried to protest when she'd told him how ashamed she was to know him, that he was the son of a dog, and that he deserved to die a thousand painful deaths for the way he treated her. She'd stomped halfway into the building, then turned around and stated, "But I still love Nisreen. Tell her goodbye and good luck, and she is welcome to call me." Then she'd continued in and when she was safely out of reach and a dirty window stood between her and Ahmed, she had looked back to see him one last time. Adding to her rage, he had simply stood up and walked away, looking sad but not shattered.

As the hard ledge became more uncomfortable, Leila shifted positions and decided to check out the mattress on that new bed. Sure enough, it was soft and dry, and she seated herself down in a spot where she could stay for a while. She remembered her final preparations as she'd packed up her room. It had been too late to catch a bus to Dera'a that night, and her family wouldn't have been waiting for her anyway. So she'd stayed one last night packing, folding sheets and blankets, and giving the room one last sweep for good measure. She had not left the building at all, and hadn't even wanted to go up to the roof. She'd just puttered around her room, except for one trip down to the phone to inform her family she'd be back mid-day the next day. She'd fought back tears when she heard Nuha announce so cheerfully to everyone that Leila would be moving home tomorrow.

At ten o'clock, she had heard movement in the hallway and seen that Maha had come back to her room. It had been a precious last night, and for Leila it meant the world that she'd been able to talk with a friend about what had happened with Ahmed. She fingered the mattress under her tired bottom as she thought about the mattress under the window in Maha's room. That mattress had been a safe haven, a place where she could be herself, where she and Huda and Roxy had all shared their deepest thoughts and fears and dreams, encouraged each other, cried together and played together.

She prayed a quick blessing for Maha, who came from privilege but who had been willing to share that privilege with her neighbors. Actually, Leila had just spoken with Maha last week. They still exchanged text messages from time to time, Leila from her Kuwaiti phone and Maha from her Lebanese phone. Maha had recently married Samer and moved with him to Lebanon, where he was studying to be a pastor. Her story reminded Leila that some people's dreams did come true, at least if you came from a certain type of family.

Leila hadn't spoken to Huda since that tearful farewell,

but Maha still sent Huda a text message every so often, so had been able to keep Leila up to date. Huda was still unmarried and working as a lawyer for an import/export business. Maha worried that she was unhappy. It seemed Huda was very lonely living in the village and working long hours at a boring job. But when Leila thought of how close Huda had come to throwing her life away entirely, and then how Huda had thought for two years that someone else had ruined her life, she resolved to remind Maha next time they talked, that they should thank God that Huda was alive and healthy and able to help her family at all.

And Roxy... Leila still got a call from Roxy twice a year, almost without fail. It was not planned or scheduled, and it was always a one- or two-minute conversation, as Roxy rushed through her news and then asked Leila for news. It had taken a while for Roxy to get re-married. For the first year she'd sat around the house doing very little but spend time with cousins and neighbors. After a year, though, her mother had introduced her to a young man from Sweida city, and he was reasonably handsome, but also sweet and gentle. Roxy had explained this to Leila in about 10 seconds, and Leila had understood that this was exactly what Roxy wanted, to live the quiet life of the wife of a gentle man. They'd been married a little over a year now, and Roxy had probably just had her first child last month. Leila didn't know who went with her to get the surgery - she hadn't seen Roxy in person at all - but all reports from Sweida were good.

Ah, marriage... Yes, Leila thanked God that Ahmed had been her university boyfriend but that Hassoun was her husband. In the end, the system worked for her, she thought as she leaned back with her arms behind her on the mattress. Hassoun was indeed the man she'd always dreamed of, perhaps not as dynamic and exciting as Ahmed, but he respected her and her opinions. He worked in Kuwait and had taken Leila and their son and soon-to-be child to live with him. Whenever he returned to Syria, he brought her to see her family. And before Hamoudi was born, she had accompanied him on other business trips. She had been to Jordan, Saudi, and Turkey. What else could she hope for?

She met Hassoun the traditional way, through an introduction of her mother to his mother. He was from Dera'a, but a village far from hers. He was a doctor, and had many interesting doctor friends who Leila got to entertain. Some of them were European and American, so she spoke English regularly. Hassoun was a good man who asked for her opinions about things. He encouraged Leila to work, whenever the children didn't keep her from it, so before Hamoudi was born, she had worked as an interpreter at the same hospital as Hassoun worked, and since then she worked from home as a translator. She loved working, but she loved her family even more.

Speaking of family, she realized the sun was actually already beginning to set. She had hardly spent any time with her sister, which was her pretense for coming. And her sister deserved her attention, not just that of her beautiful son. Leila stood up slowly and felt the baby shifting in her belly. As she wandered to the stairs, she walked as slowly as she could, deeply breathing in the Damascene dusk air. She missed this city, and hoped that someday, once they'd saved up enough money, she and her family could move here and Hassoun set up a private practice. She had talked with him about it, and she knew that he was considering the idea. Her life may not look quite how she'd pictured it, but when this happened, all her dreams really would have come true. And even if it didn't happen, things were going well, and maybe whatever was to come would be even better.

Lingering by the door, she leaned against the wall one last time, with her back to the stairs and her front to the mountain. She closed her eyes and pictured Roxy dancing on the rooftop with absolute abandon and Maha coming up to join her. Huda then took their hands and they made a circle together. They all gestured to her to join them and she pointed to her enormous belly. Roxy shouted out, "*Malish.* It's fine!" and continued to beckon, but Leila continued to protest. So all three came over and stretched their arms out to her. Leila froze that picture in her mind and opened her eyes, taking in the lights on the mountain that were just beginning to flicker. Then she turned around and slowly walked down the stairs to the waiting arms of her son and to the tea prepared by her sister.

Appendix: Basic Vocabulary for survival in Damascus (unless otherwise noted, the feminine variations are listed)

note to reader: All spellings of phrases are my best attempt at a simple, readable transliteration. Words should be read as they are written. Here are some descriptions of some of the more different sounds:

- *"**kh**" is pronounced like a spitting sound, or a very guttural "h".*
- *What is depicted as an apostrophe "'" is indicative of the Arabic letter "'ein", for which there is no English equivalent. It sounds kind of like a hiccup, but much more suave. Its uniqueness has led the Arabic language to be nicknamed by some as "the language of the 'ein."*
- *A "**q**" would not be pronounced in the Damascus vernacular, rather it would be replaced with a guttural stop. But most people from the Druze mountains, including Roxy and her cousins, as well as many people from the Alawite region, including Huda, would pronounce this as a "k" coming from very deep down in their throat.*

Greetings
Sabah al-Kheir (reply: **Sabah al-Nour**): Good morning
Masa al-Kheir (reply: **Masa' al-Nour**): Good evening
Tusbahi 'ala al-Kheir (reply: **Wa anti bi alf Kheir**): Good night
Marhaba: Hello
Ahlan or **Ahlan wa Sahlan** or **Ahlain**: General greeting best translated as meaning "welcome"
Kifek or **Shloanek**: How are you?
Shukran or **Islamu**: Thank you

Expressions

Habibi (for a man) or **Habibti** (for a woman): My dear

Tfadali: Be honored, make yourself at home

Haram: Wrong/forbidden

Mamnu': Against the rules

Aieb: Shame (as in, Shame on you!)

Lissa: Not yet

Ya: Oh, (as in, Ya Leila = Oh, Leila!)

Ya rait: I wish, or I hope

Yalla or **Ya Allah**: literally, Oh God, but in usage it may mean a variety of things, most frequently "let's go!"

Naieman (reply: **Allah yenaeimu aleiki**): literally, "grace", but it is what one says to someone who just had a bath or haircut

Nasiib: fate, lot in life

Shway Shway: Little by Little, or Have patience

Yanni: literally, "it means", but in usage most frequently used to say "sort of"

Insha'allah: If God wills it

Hamdulillah or **Alhamdulillah**: Thank God

Frequently used nouns:

Wasta: connections, i.e. people that one might know that will help her get ahead in life

Hijab: woman's islamic headcovering

Hadith: the sayings and writings of the Prophet Muhammad, second most important religious text in Islam, after the Qur'an

Souq: market, shopping area

Abaya: a type of long cloak worn by women for modesty

Arguile: also known as shisha, hookah, narjila, water pipe, and probably various other names. They are water pipes with flavored tobacco which may be smoked over the course of several hours. In Arabic, one "drinks" an arguile (it would not be correct to say one "smokes" an arguile).

Shebab: youth, or young guys

Service: (pronounced "serveece") 12-15 passenger vans which are the primary mode of public transportation in Damascus

Mezze: dips and appetizers typically included in Middle Eastern meals, especially served at restaurants

Sheikh: community leader

Imam: religious leader

29426619R00224

Made in the USA
Lexington, KY
25 January 2014